THE FAR ARENA

Richard Ben Sapir

SEAVIEW BOOKS

New York

Manufactured in the United States of America.

FIRST EDITION

Trade distribution by Simon and Schuster
A Division of Gulf + Western Corporation
New York, New York 10020

Designed by Tere LoPrete

Library of Congress Cataloging in Publication Data

Sapir, Richard.
The far arena.

I. Title.
PZ4.S242Far [PS3569.A59] 813'.5'4 78-8270
ISBN 0-87223-506-8

For Betsy John, who is courageous and beautiful. With many thanks for sharing so much.

Acknowledgments

This book had the help of many people—researchers and critics. Some of them were paid. Some of them weren't. I mention them all with thanks: Judith Netzer, Fred Fogel, W. B. Murphy, Ward Damio, Marolyn Sawyer, Betsy John, Carol Ettinghouse; and Steve McGee, who helped me to climb into the gladiator's arena in Pompeii through the back way so I saw it from the outside of the town.

GLOSSARY

aedile	a Roman magistrate, not a major political position.
atrium	the front parlor in a house, used by wealthy men to conduct business and receive retainers.
aureus	a gold coin. The abbreviation for the element gold, "Au," comes from this coin.
bestiarii	gladiators specializing in guiding and killing animals. Some would kill using their teeth to break the necks of dogs or foxes.
bones	the forerunner of dice. Bones were thrown for combinations of smooth and rough.
centurion	a military commander of one hundred men.
cohort	a fighting unit of the legions.
dominus	"master" or "lord."
lanista	a trainer, and often owner, of gladiators.
latifundia (sing., latifundium)	giant farms of the Roman Empire, their like not seen again for nineteen hundred years until the modern agricultural corporation of industrialized society.
peristilium	the private part of a house, used only for family and friends.

praetor	Roman governor of a province. A highly lucrative position. It was said the Roman had to make three fortunes when a praetor: one to repay bribes; a second to repay himself for the cost of the games; and a third for himself. Pontius Pilate, mentioned in the Gospels, was a praetor.
secutor	a gladiator using sword, shield, and helmet, most often matched against retiarii, who used tridens (spear) and net.
sella	a chair with a back. Roman chairs ordinarily lacked back supports.
sesterce	a coin.
stola	a Roman woman's formal gown.
stylus	a pen. Romans used quills from geese.
tonsor	a slave trained as a barber. The modern phrase "tonsorial parlor" comes from this Latin word.
tribune	a high politico-military post.
vigilis	a combination of police and firemen.
vilicus	an overseer on a latifundium.
wooden sword	as a symbol for a gladiator being allowed to leave the arena free, a wooden sword was given at the games.

THE FAR ARENA

CHAPTER

I

Lucius Aurelius Eugenianus,

son of Gnaeus, Roman,
and Phaedra, Greek;
adopted son of the great Lucius
Aurelius Cotta;
husband of Miriamne, freed Hebrew;
father of Petronius, Roman;
offender of the gods of Rome;
and, therefore, enemy of the
Senate and People of Rome,

did not feel the core bit of the Houghton rig neatly take a piece of his gracilis muscle from the right thigh, 8.2 meters beneath the glacial ice north of the Queen Victoria Sea.

The body was quiet as an unborn thought in a dark universe, stopped on the bare side of life, stilled on its way to death by the cold. Even the hair did not grow, nor did the enzymes and acids eat away at the cells. More still than death it was, stone perfect still.

The retinas of the eyes were solid. The ligaments were solid. The blood that had stopped suddenly in the veins and arteries could be chipped with a knife. Each hard corpuscle was where it had been when the body rolled nude, bouncing along ice, as stiff as wicker, into what was then called the German Sea, far south and centuries before.

At that time, being lighter than water, it floated north and joined with other ice, and, being lighter than ice, it moved within the ice northward, an inch, sometimes a foot a year, sometimes many feet. While some ice broke off and moved south or east to warmer places only to become water again, then mist, then rain, and sometimes ice again, this form remained in its unbroken water and moved north.

Life stopped.

No part touched oxygen until the core bit, on its way toward a deeper part of the earth, went through a small piece of thigh and brought it up through a barrel core to a dark, chill night at the top of the world.

It was the long night of winter, and the men who worked here covered their faces and hands with layers of leather and fur and nylon and all the insulation that living skin needed not to freeze into pale death. Timers, worn under the layers of arctic shields, buzzed when the men had been out more than their allotted number of work hours.

Three white domes, technological wombs in a frigid world, supported the life serving the drilling rig. Exterior tunnels, like rigid veins, stretched from the domes to the rig and between each other.

There were no roads up here, and the nearest warm life was an air base two hours away by snow machine.

Up from the ice came core samples, perfectly round pieces of ice. Arctic mittens guided the core tube coming up from this outer layer of the world, this external skin at the earth's cold top, and at one-meter intervals sawed off a section. Then the mittens cradled each section and carried it through a tunnel that felt warm, even though it was below freezing, because it merely protected against the sharp wind. The derrick man brought the sample into the laboratory dome and laid it in a rack above a long white sink.

He took off his arctic mask and felt the mouth part crack in his mittens. His breath had frozen to ice.

The rockhound, the geologist for exploration, sat on a high chair over the sink. He was a big man and wore checkered long johns under a bright red shirt and worn blue jeans. He signaled for the derrick man to push the sample down from the holding rack to the sink.

The derrick man wanted to talk. Dr. Lewellyn McCardle did not want to talk back. But if the man took off his mask, it meant he was going to stay. He would find something to start a conversation, which might begin with the weather or the new equipment or the food, but it would end up with how badly the superintendent in charge of the crew was doing things and whose side was the rockhound on.

McCardle, a big man of much flesh and bone and muscle, had to take the extra care that large hands needed with precision instruments. He shaved off an end of the core sample.

"Ice, huh?" said the derrick man.

"Yes," said McCardle.

"You check everything, don't you?"

"Yes," said McCardle.

His round face was red, and the tufts of remaining hair mingled strawberry blond with white, and it would have been a very cute face if he were not six foot three inches tall and closer to three hundred pounds than two hundred. He was bigger than most men of the small crew, even the roughnecks and roustabouts who were known for their size. He sometimes suffered a locked knee from an old football injury. He had a Ph.D. from the University of Chicago, but the men always called him Lew.

He felt the rotary drill, which had restarted, send its vibrations up through the floor, a new synthetic compound which a vice-president of Houghton, back in Houston, Texas, promised would use air as insulation so effectively, everyone could "walk around in his bare feet up there, and never need anything more than slippers inside at most."

Lew hadn't even bothered to pack slippers and wore boots indoors. Those who had brought slippers, like the young superintendent, kept them in their duffles. The superintendent had told Lew McCardle that to pack slippers showed faith in Houghton, in Houghton engineering, in Houghton management, in Houghton integrity.

Lew McCardle had worked for Houghton for twenty-five years. He was going to retire after this last exploration. He had faith that his employer would pay his retirement. He had twenty-five years of faith. He also knew cold-weather explorations. He didn't pack slippers. He had more faith in the ice than in the new Thermal-Floor-Pack.

He brought two books instead. His size helped with that. Oil men did not particularly like people who read books, nor did they trust them. Somehow Lew's size, and his origins in a backwater Texas town, compensated for his reading. He even read poetry. This they overlooked because, while he was "funny," he was also nice.

The derrick man finally found something to talk about. It was good enough to unzip his arctic jacket.

"Lew," he said, "what's that?" He pointed to a pale discoloration in the tube of ice, like a whitish banana skin, smaller than a jagged fifty-cent piece. Lew swung an overhead fluorescent bulb circled in a jeweler's magnifying lens over the discoloration. It always happened in these cold-weather domes that you began to even smell your own body. It was like living in a sock.

"Are you staying or going?" he said to the derrick man, without looking up. "If you stay, take off that outer layer before you start sweating up. Your body has got to breathe. Or go now."

The piece had streaks of pink. Lew put his left forefinger and thumb around the discoloration. He could see the ridges in his fingers under the lighted magnifying glass. He pressed the finger ridges against the discoloration. It gave, but there was no crunch of crystals cracking.

McCardle suddenly looked at his hands. Then back at the discoloration.

"You cut yourself?" he asked.

"No," said the derrick man.

"You can cut yourself and not feel it," he said.

"No. I'd feel it. I'm warm. I'm all right."

"OK," said Lew. "Then nothing. Thanks. Good-bye."

The derrick man peeled off his outer coat down to a light windbreaker covering a layer of sweaters. He scraped the melting ice from his arctic mask.

"What's the nothing?"

"Nothing is nothing," said McCardle.

"C'mon, Lew. Shoot. Yer not gonna be like the jerk running this. C'mon. What is it?"

"It is a piece of flesh."

"Yeah?" said the derrick man, amazed. He bent over the sample in the sink. The choppy surface was now glistening smooth along the tube, water reflecting the ice. It was melting. The derrick man bent low over the discoloration. He sniffed.

"It smells funny," he said.

"That's you," said Lew.

"Maybe," said the derrick man. "What kind of flesh?"

"I would say human."

"There's a person down there?"

"No. That's eight point two meters."

"A body?"

"Maybe."

"Where does human flesh come from but a body?"

"Maybe it's a piece of an arm."

"Do you think we're on top of a graveyard?"

"No," said Lew. "It's ice for a good way down. We've got ice for some time. I don't know of any peoples who bury in ice."

"Then what's a body doing down there?"

"I don't know. And please don't be making the crew more nervous than they have to be. We've got enough to deal with with the cold."

"Sure, Lew, but what would a person be doing this far up? Do you think there are other oilmen?"

"That ice we're going through is very old, thousands of years. I don't know how old. But more than several centuries. We've been using fossil fuels for only a single century."

"What about the Europeans?"

"By we, I mean man. Mankind. This happens sometimes near the surface. It won't do anyone any good if you mention this. Please."

"I swear to God, Lew, no one'll know shit from these lips. Like they're sewed closed. Swear to God."

"Thanks," said Lew.

Forty-five minutes later the tool pusher, driller, and second-shift driller were in the lab dome, taking off their outer layers of clothing, asking to see the hand.

"No hand here," said Lew. He was working on the possibility

of electric logging the bore hole if there should be a sufficient heat increase at lower depths. It was a possible backup measure to core sampling.

"What we picked up at eight meters," said the tool pusher. "You know what we're talking about, Lew."

McCardle went to the sink. The ice had melted away into a small retainer drain, leaving an odd cookie-thick wedge of glistening material. It looked like gun wadding for an old-fashioned musket. It curled.

"That's it?" said the tool pusher.

"That's all," said Lew.

"Not much," said the tool pusher. "It's from a person?"

"Probably," said Lew. The rotary drill had to be working short crew with all the men in the lab. Perhaps the superintendent was out there. He was young and didn't trust anyone anyway, McCardle knew. He also knew that if the superintendent weren't so new and anxious to succeed beyond expectations, the drilling crew wouldn't be in the dome looking for reasons to help him fail. It happened this way on explorations that were cut off from civilization, as much because of distance as for Houghton's not wanting people to know where they explored, if possible. The superintendent of the crew had to be good and seasoned to prevent the sort of flareup that was coming.

"Are we drilling through bodies nowadays?" said the tool pusher, who three times in Lew's presence had felt forced to tell the crew superintendent how many sites he had worked on and how many came in before the superintendent was born.

"We didn't go through a body. We went alongside. That flesh is not big enough to be through," said Lew.

"It's wounded. Look, pus," said the tool pusher.

"That's not pus."

"What's that pinkish, yellowish straw kind of stuff?"

"Probably blood."

"Blood's red. I never heard of no blood that weren't red."

"There are things in the blood that make it red," said Lew, and he forgot whom he was talking to, because then he went on. "Red blood cells have to combine with the oxygen in the air to be red. In your body, the blood is pale. But now you take something or someone who's been at low temperatures for a while, the red cells get destroyed and the white cells increase. So what you get is pinkish, and sometimes it could be yellowish. Like straw."

"What about red-blooded? Ah never heard of pink-blooded. Or yellow-blooded Americans?" said the tool pusher, his flat Texas twang ringing like nasty prairie dust in Lew's face, looking for a fight.

"Red and blood are also symbolic. Red's always been a symbolic color. In ancient Rome it was called purple, and today we call it royal purple. Although we aren't sure what they meant by purple. It could be grape purple or blood red. You see, words—"

"Blood's always red," said the pusher.

"When it's got red blood cells. But when red blood cells have been driven out, it is straw-colored."

"Looks like pus," said the tool pusher.

"All right," said Lew. "It's pus."

"How do you know it's blood?" said the tool pusher.

"I've read. I've also seen some work done in low temperatures. In Oslo there's a Russian doctor doing work in thermal reduction. We've used him for emergencies."

"What's thermal reduction?" said the tool pusher.

"Really, now," said Lew.

"You could have said cold," said the tool pusher. "The skin's gray. Was he black, white, yellow?"

"I don't know. I am not sure it's a he. I'm not even sure it's human. Wherever that is, it's been there a long, long time."

The tool pusher accused Lew of being a suck for the superintendent, and Lew only had to stand up from the stool he had perched his backside on and the men put on their outer gear.

They almost bumped into the crew superintendent entering the lab, ripping off his cold-weather mask. They pushed by him moodily. He stared angrily at Lew, veins throbbing in his forehead.

"Where is it?" he demanded. Lew pointed to the sink.

"Well?" said the superintendent.

"That little grayish thing in the yellowish stuff," said McCardle with flat respect.

"That's nothing," yelled the superintendent, a ferret of a man, his temper always near the surface and now bursting out in the lab.

"That's what I said," said McCardle.

"Then why do I hear we've drilled through someone? Why are you telling that to the crew?"

"You're not listening to me," Lew told the superintendent.

"That's a piece of an elk or a whatever down there. That's not human."

"It probably is human flesh," said Lew. His voice was even and he was remembering every word he said. It might be needed if this young man tried to blame Lew for whatever happened, if something happened.

Suddenly there was a cave quiet in the dome. Nothing whirred around them. The silence came like doom-trumpets in a nightmare. The drill had stopped.

"Jesus Christ," said the crew superintendent.

"Your machinery can't afford down time at these temperatures," said Lew.

"My machinery, right? Not ours, huh? I'll remember that, McCardle."

He snapped his mask back on and ran skidding out of the lab dome.

Lew shrugged. He would keep his tongue, because if he could keep his tongue for twenty-five years, he could keep it for one more project that would mean his retirement. Whether they drilled in, striking oil, or whether it was a dry hole, he would collect his pension from Houghton . . . if he couldn't be blamed for trouble.

But it was as inevitable as it was unwanted that he became involved as mediator between the crew and the superintendent. They chose his lab to fight.

"You've got two minutes before that down machinery needs blowtorches to start it again, and that means you may not get it to start again," Lew shouted into noise. They turned to him.

Now they could hear the wind, like a giant sucking maw, reminding them that the machinery had given up its pitiful temporary life in the long, cold night. If nothing else, Lew wanted to hear the grinding drill move so as not to hear the wind.

The superintendent was appointing blame for the stopped machinery when Lew interrupted to announce it was one minute and thirty seconds.

"What would satisfy you?" Lew asked the tool pusher.

"Respect," said the tool pusher, adding, "for the dead."

"We'll say prayers over that elk down there, if that will make you happy," said the superintendent.

"Do you want it dug up?" asked Lew.

"It might be a good idea—find out what we've got down there and do proper things," said the tool pusher.

"Never," said the superintendent.

"All right," said Lew, standing and using his massive body as a calming influence. "I just wanted to find out where everyone stood while the machinery froze and your bonuses went. Just wanted to know."

"All right, on your say-so, we will use a crew and possibly damage the rig to dig up some fossil. But I want you to sign a paper for it," said the superintendent.

His dark eyes twitched, and his head bobbed. He had just taken a vote in his mind and was announcing the election results that Lew should sign a paper taking responsibility.

"No," said Lew. "I am just trying to keep the facts in front of us all." He nodded to the crew, a glum, hostile group, packed together in their arctic wear like a cramped sports warehouse. Lew noticed one man perspiring now. It could be dangerous outside. Sweat became ice.

"I never heard of a crew digging up a fossil. We're looking for oil, not archeology," said the superintendent. He was smaller than the crew, and he glowered as though he had to make up for it. "Go ahead. But I don't want to stand around and watch something this stupid. I'm going back to the rig and I want help now. Whoever wants to dig in the ice, go ahead on your own time."

The driller and two roughnecks went with the superintendent through the passage while Lew plotted out where the piece of flesh was, and where, if there was a person, it might be. He took the exact point where the discoloration in the ice core had occurred and drew a theoretical ball around it, seven feet in every direction.

He made a mock-up of the rig. The center of the ball was in the drill shaft. The tool pusher said they could drive casing down around the hole and keep on drilling.

"It's going to be a job," said Lew.

"We've got jackhammers. We've got a John Deere. We've got everything. They didn't want us running out of parts," said the pusher.

"I know," said Lew.

And what he did not tell the tool pusher was that whatever they found would only have to be buried again, if it were a person. But the tool pusher wouldn't have been interested. There was a fight going on, and whatever was down there was only an issue to fight over. The fight was really between men.

Lew sketched in a rough diagram. The tool pusher asked Lew if he wanted to join the digging, and Lew refused. The superintendent, who had obviously been waiting until the rebellious tool pusher left, came into the lab to talk. The talk was out of Management 304, Harvard Business School. It was problem solving. It was goal-oriented.

Lew McCardle passed gas and went back to the electronic log. They were going to need it now for sure.

"All right, Lew, what have I done wrong?"

"In this sort of exploration in this part of the world, it takes sort of a subtle hand to get the crew calmly working."

Lew felt banging jabs on the soles of his feet as little cracking coughs came from outside. The jackhammers were going through the ice. They were going after the body.

"What do you mean by that?"

"I mean you're ambitious."

"I don't want to end up like you, Lew. I don't want to end up a geologist after twenty-five years."

"All right."

"I don't mean to be insulting, but you had everything, McCardle, from a doctorate to being from the same town as the Houghtons and the Lauries, to playing football for that cow college the company supports."

"That's what you want. I have what I want."

"You could have been a president of this company."

"What do you want?" asked Lew McCardle. His voice was soft, somewhat weak, as though something had been punched out of it.

"For me?" asked the superintendent.

"No. From me," said Lew.

"Support."

"I'm a geologist. I make less than you. I'm thirty years older than you, and I take orders from you."

"Then support me."

Lew was quiet. He had been quiet twenty-five years, and he only had to be quiet for the rest of this project. He was good at being quiet. A person got good at anything he practiced.

Four days later, after much repacking of the upper borehole, the John Deere—as the men called the multipurpose cold-weather tractor vehicle—groaned, hauling up something. The whirring of the drill stopped.

McCardle timed it. After forty-five seconds, he felt the whir of the rotary drill come through the thermal-pack floor again and up the soles of his feet. The men had done their digging and hauling in good time. And, more importantly, they had continued drilling while they had gotten down to where they wanted to go with the jackhammers and picks. The jackhammers had stopped a full day and a half before the drill stopped, which meant they had gone into the final work by hand power.

"Blechhh," said the tool pusher entering, about half a coffeepot of drinking after the drill had stopped two hours earlier in the day. "It's awful. We put it in one of the unheated domes, the windbreaker. I don't want that thing melting. It's weird. Did you see it?"

"What you dug up?"

"Yeah. Blech," said the tool pusher, shaking his head and making sounds as though he were clearing a taste from his mouth.

"No," said Lew. "I didn't see it, and I don't want to see it. There are two things I want, tool pusher. I don't want to have anything to do with what you dug up. That's immediate. Long-range, like five weeks maximum, I want to retire with my pension money."

"It was a body, Lew. It was a man . . ." said the pusher. And then pausing, "Once."

McCardle withheld his answer. "You don't want to know about it, right?" asked the tool pusher. Lew knew he wanted some comment, some explanation, for the body that had been found and whatever condition it was found in. Just a body did not cause that sort of revulsion in a tool pusher, least of all an experienced one who had been around oil fields.

"That's right," said Lew McCardle.

"OK," said the tool pusher.

The body, as Lew found out, was small. A little fellow. Just about five feet tall. But what had unnerved the crew, according to the derrick man and a couple of roustabouts, was that the little guy was nude.

"Bare as a babe in afterbirth," said one.

"The core tube took out a piece just under his ass. From the thigh," said another.

The body was christened Charlie and remained in the windbreaker dome for a week, as the drill bit went into the first layers of earth. A duplex pump had to be winched out of the windbreaker dome, and a variation of a bull-nosed reamer bit, for rotary, had to be installed. But two roughnecks dropped the pipe string, which shattered in a cold that made metal as brittle as porcelain. And that was another delay. The drilling was not going well.

"We snaked it out with a catline," the tool pusher told McCardle later, referring to how the shattered pipe string was removed from the hole.

Lew nodded.

"We got a boll weevil," said the pusher, referring to the newness of the superintendent. "I've never seen one this green at an isolated site."

"This kind of weather is not good for that kind of talk," said Lew finally. "This kind of weather doesn't tolerate much."

"Well, rockhound, what do you say?"

"I say it's pretty sloppy, dropping a dead line anchor. You know everything becomes more brittle at these temperatures."

" 'Ceptin' Charlie in the shed. You know he didn't grow no beard."

"I'm not his barber," said Lew.

"Well, dead men's beards grow. Charlie's didn't."

"They grow because the hair follicles are alive after the body is dead. But this body was eight point two meters down in ice."

"But hair can grow through ice."

"Low temperatures reduce and sometimes stop physical action. That's why you found him with his skin on."

"You think so?"

"If we hit Charlie somewhere in an Indonesian jungle, you wouldn't have even found the bone."

"But how did he get here without clothes on?"

"I don't know."

"We're two hours by snowmobile to an air base. How did he

walk here nude? And don't tell me he strolled there in the summer, 'cause this shit is permanent up here."

"Nothing is permanent," said Lew.

"How did it get here, rockhound?"

"Tool pusher, ice moves."

"All the way up here?"

"It's been there a long time."

"We shouldn't have dug it up."

"You didn't ask me then."

"Yeah. Well. We should have let Charlie stay."

"You've got jackhammers. You can put him back."

"We can't do that now. You wouldn't say that if you saw him. I've seen bodies, Lew. They're meat. This one is just—just—. We can't put Charlie back. None of us would go for that."

Lew's cot was in the laboratory. At one of the inner chambers of the laboratory dome at the side was the downhole tester he had put together himself. It measured the pressure of existing conditions. It was very important. As Lew lay down at the prescribed time for sleeping—you had to sleep by the clock when you didn't have the sunrise and sunset—he noticed part of the downhole tester was under his cot, and he hadn't put it there.

When the superintendent came in later for his twice-daily geological discussion, Lew mentioned this.

"You're lucky. These bimbos have gone through tools lately like Cracker Jacks. You've got yours. Charlie has cursed this site. He has, Lew. I don't believe in ghosts or anything, but Charlie's spirit is ruining this. Charlie is ruining my career."

Two nights later, Lew woke up in terror and he didn't know what had terrified him. He looked around the lab, and everything seemed to be all right. The lab smelled somewhat ripe, of course, and undoubtedly it would be even worse if he had gotten some fresh air and entered it new. But that was normal. Something was incredibly wrong. He didn't know what it was, but it was wrong. His feet sweated in his sleeping socks and his stomach curdled and tightened, and then he realized the drill had stopped.

And he was awake. The sound had been the constant background humming; the drone coming up through the floor had started as annoying and had become necessary as his body had adjusted to normal feelings. Now it was stopped. The silence had wakened him.

Two A.M. And it was stopped. Lew got an interdome line working and finally reached someone. There had been an accident, a serious one.

Somehow the drill got working two minutes and forty-three seconds later, but the superintendent, his ferret face strained with deep, dark circles under his eyes, came to Lew and said they had to get Charlie out of the site.

"Nobody's sending in a plane here," said Lew. "You've got that John Deere up here with the plow in the windbreaker to push the ice and snow back over everything if we drill in. They don't want some pilot getting locations over the air. That's why we drove this stuff in, everything."

"Lew. You're just a geologist. Stay that way. You're not getting paid enough to worry about that."

"I agree," said Lew McCardle.

"Can you get the body out of here?"

"You want your geologist to leave? You want your rockhound off site?"

"Yes."

"We've got roughnecks. We've got roustabouts. That's what they're for. They should get rid of it."

"They won't go, Lew. Maybe you'd better not look at the body either."

"Do you want me to take this body away from the project and bury it somewhere?"

"No. Totally away. Go to the air base. Snowmobile it away at noon. There's the best light then. Take it to the air base."

"I can't show up at an air base with a body unexplained," said Lew.

"Keep it in its tarp. The crew says you know some doctor who can use parts and stuff, frozen."

"You're talking to the crew again. Well, that's good. But I want a signed document ordering me to leave the base. I need it. This is my retirement. I've put in a lot of consecutive years without vacations to get this. I can't walk off my last site without a signed and witnessed document."

"You got it, McCardle."

And so shortly before noon, Lew dressed for the cold. He put the document, signed and witnessed, against his chest under the long johns, and nylon socks under wool socks, and a sweater over the long johns, and pants over the long johns, and nylon outer pants over the pants, and the arctic boots over the socks, and two layers of gloves, and a head mask, and wool head pullover, and a jacket with a head covering over all of that. Then he left the lab and made his way with the tool pusher, driller, and others following.

Inside the windbreak dome they pointed to Charlie. It was a tarpaulin-covered mound resting on an Akron-fresh rubber tire, with cleats so sharp and new they looked as though they could cut paper. Above the reddish brown tarpaulin, white frost had formed on a strut. Many had breathed there recently, Lew observed. Their breath had made the frost. There had been a lot of looking.

A floodlight with an unmerciful glare made Lew feel he was entering some strange precivilized temple of a hostile god—its incense, heavy motor oil; its altar, the tire; its object resting on top. The tool pusher flipped open the tarpaulin, and Lew saw what had upset them so much.

In a mound of blue gray ice, a body on its side was running. He could see the black hair and large clear sections of white skin. Its left arm in front, its right arm in back, left leg forward, right leg in back, it appeared to be running. It was running. It was running, thought Lew. It was running and someone had stopped it. Like a movie frame it had been stopped.

Its right rear thigh had the smooth even borehole through the outer flesh. It was the only smooth cut on the dark blue mass before Lew's eyes. He circled to the front of the body.

Its eyes were closed. Its mouth open. There was the tongue. Dead tongue in a dead mouth, yet so clearly seen. It appeared to be praying. The left arm in front appeared to be asking for something. It was nude all over. Bare as a baby. Yet muscular. And little.

The little fellow was so small Lew's arms could stretch from head to toe.

"What do you think, Lew?" asked the tool pusher.

"I think Charlie isn't Jewish," said Lew.

There was a short, brave laugh at this witticism about the penis not being circumcised. Of course, it also meant that Charlie was probably not born in an industrialized society where circumcision was now practiced for sanitary reasons.

"You wonder where he was running to when he was froze like

that," said the tool pusher. "Like he was headed somewhere and he was stopped. Is that what you're thinking?"

"The ice will make him too heavy for the back seat," said Lew. "We'll have to sled him behind my machine."

He wanted to start right away, while he had that brief hole of light. He was fairly certain he would reach the air base with no trouble if he took precautions. But this was not an American interstate road. If he made mistakes, if he got careless now or panicked driving off in some desperate direction, there could be two solid corpses up here.

"Good-bye, Charlie," said the tool pusher as they strapped the tarpaulin cover to a sled hitched to the snowmobile. Lew patted his chest, feeling the paper against his breast. This was his last site in twenty-five years. He didn't say good-bye to the men.

CHAPTER

II

Dr. Semyon Fyodor Petrovitch had been nauseated all morning, and he was not sure if it was something he ate, something he drank, or possibly the nurse he had slept with the night before. Medically, he knew there was no disease he could contract from sexual intercourse whose symptoms of nausea would appear the following day.

Morally, however, he felt he was being justly punished for not even liking the woman, but rather taking her because he was there, she was there, and both were willing. Somehow, it went better with roses and soft words. And perhaps that was why he had drunk too much and eaten too much, to make up for the lack of romance. He was not eighteen anymore. He should have had higher standards, he felt.

Unfortunately, this late afternoon at the university hospital complex, he was paying for it, and he could not return to the apartment his embassy had provided him here in Oslo because he had promised to meet an American scientist today who was bringing a specimen.

It might be a good one.

A whole body? Dr. Petrovitch had asked. What sort of decomposition was there? None that the American could see? In glacial ice? What sort of ice? Where?

"Do you want this, Dr. Petrovitch?"

"Possibly. And you are?"

"Dr. Lewellyn McCardle. We met at the conference in Stockholm last year."

"There are many conferences, doctor. I am part of a Scandinavian–Soviet Friendship Pact, so I do make many appearances."

"Sort of a mundane thing. It was on cryogenic applications to medical problems. Frostbite, if you will. You were gearing it somewhat for a lay audience. We were more interested only in how we could immediately save lives."

"Saving lives is never only, doctor. I don't seem to place your name."

"I'm sort of tall. Geologist."

"The Texan!"

"Uh, yeah."

And then Dr. Petrovitch remembered; he remembered the Texan, because that was what the big American had seemed to be reluctant to divulge last year. When asked where he came from in America, the American had said, "All over." He had studied in Chicago and California; "all over," he said. But where was he born?

"Oh, just a little place in Texas," he had said, and Dr. Petrovitch until that time had never known there were any negative feelings about people coming from certain parts of America, least of all Texas. The Texans he had met always seemed rather proud of it. Cowboys and all that.

So, feeling somewhat embarrassed by accidentally stressing the one point he had assumed the American had felt somewhat uneasy about, Dr. Petrovitch had said he would certainly be happy to take the specimen. But he had not mentioned what part of the university complex he would meet him at.

There was his office on the third floor of one building, and the laboratory he shared in the basement of that building, and the hospital itself, which was another building. Now, which entrance in which building? Where did one deliver a frozen cadaver?

When confronted by this dilemma, Dr. Petrovitch tried to remember which air base the American had phoned from, so that he could send more specific directions, instead of the University at

Oslo hospital complex. Failing to remember, Dr. Petrovitch prepared to receive a cadaver somewhere.

There were many ways it could be received. A good specimen whose sustained low temperatures had retarded body action could go directly into one of the cryogenic cylinders in the lab to be examined later.

A decomposing corpse, however, was just that, a corpse. That was not his area. The normal body process at normal temperature was to take apart the body and put it back into the life cycle of the earth. A decomposing cadaver would have to be taken to the emergency room of the hospital. There it would be pronounced dead, and proper papers filled out. Dr. Petrovitch expected it would not be a decomposing corpse. The American was a scientist, and he should understand the limitations of cryogenics.

Therefore, thought Dr. Petrovitch, the body would have to be a specimen.

Probably.

He decided, after pushing three different buttons in an elevator between the ground floor that led to the emergency room of the hospital and the basement which led to the laboratory that he shared, to wait in neither place, but in his office, justly suffering the physical pangs of a too late evening the night before.

One of the more attractive nurses suggested that he should not smoke in the elevator, and he apologized, saying that he had not thought about it. For three floors they politely discussed smoking while he was trying not to stare at the delicate and lightly freckled breast cleavage appearing between the white lapels of her uniform. He wanted to be gallant, but he found himself turning his gaze forcibly, time and time again, from her chest. He imagined her breasts bare. They were perfect. Breasts always were, in his imagination. He noticed the glimmering of opportunity, when somehow and not too smoothly she let him know she would be alone that evening.

He tried to decline the evening without declining the person. It came out that he preferred a frozen corpse to her.

When he reached his small office, the phone was ringing. It was the emergency room. An American was there with a specimen. Did Dr. Petrovitch want it brought to the laboratory?

"I don't know. No. Tell him to wait there. What does it look like?" he asked in Norwegian. He was fluent in four foreign languages: Norwegian, Swedish, German, and English. He preferred to work in two, however—Norwegian and English. Norwegian because he had worked here for the last four years and English because of American scientific journals.

"What does the specimen look like?" he asked again.

"I don't know, Dr. Petrovitch. It's outside in a truck, and the man who brought it said you wanted it. He didn't say where."

"Tell him . . . tell him . . ."

"Yes?"

"Stay there. I will be down to look at it," said Dr. Petrovitch, deciding on the sure course. Not only was he nauseated from the night before, but now the annoying little tension of trying to make sure he met someone at the right place in the sprawling university hospital complex made his stomach contract in little pains.

He ignored this and rapidly straightened up in front of a small mirror he whisked from a desk drawer. He was in his early forties, and his fleshy face hovered dangerously close to fat. His dark lips and dark eyes created a sense of unhappiness that if not dispelled by a definite smile gave the impression he was constantly dissatisfied with his surroundings. But when he smiled it was a leap into total joy.

He dressed well, he knew—today, in British tweed jacket and gray flannel slacks, with a white Italian shirt and a severe British regimental tie. He was not one who believed in denying himself the pleasures of life, and in no way did this detract from his commitment to his work.

He thought about this as he left his office on his way to the other side of the university complex. He had sought work as part of this exchange program just because of his commitment. Not that Moscow would deny him any equipment or space. Indeed, the space was better back home. But back home the cold war was still being fought, this competition with the West.

It had led to dramatizing those scientific achievements which most captured the imagination—creating a two-headed dog through grafting techniques; parapsychology; and of course the freezing of the cat's brain for two months and returning it to certain functions, that is, getting it to transmit waves which could be recorded.

The important work here was not so much with the brain but with the blood, which at normal temperature provided life and which at low temperatures became crystallized, causing massive destruction of cells. It was not that the brain had been revived but that extensive work had been done with blood elements. Unfortunately, red blood cell counts and white blood cell counts, osmotic fragility, and hemolysis hardly trumpeted the triumph of socialism among the masses.

Therefore, significant work was subordinated to the imagination of some propagandist. It was natural, humanly natural, to drift into what would gain the most fame.

But Semyon Fyodor wanted more. He wanted more for his country and for the people whose labors had paid for his education. He wanted more for all those scientists who had preceded him and on whose work he built. What Dr. Semyon Petrovitch wanted was to add another solid brick to the body of knowledge for others to build on. He was not in competition with the West. He was partners with them, from the ancient Egyptians to the latest brain surgeons in New York City.

This made him no less a Russian, no less a believer in his form of government. It made him want to work outside of Russia and escape the competitive nature of Soviet science.

These things he thought about, going down in the elevator toward the main floor. He suddenly noticed the nurse with the cleavage had taken the elevator down with him and he had ignored her. He was also aware that his headache was gone and his stomach contractions had ceased.

He left the elevator stepping briskly. The big problem with cryonics, low-temperature medicine, was that too many people around the world had treated it as some form of medical miracle, like resurrection.

Even today, especially in America, rich people with good bank accounts and a fear of death were arranging for their dead bodies to be incarcerated in capsules, temperatures rapidly lowered with liquid nitrogen and sustained in that state by technology supported by the interest of those good bank accounts.

They froze the dead. And then expected some future scientist to resurrect the dead body. As Dr. Petrovitch had told one person at one of those awful embassy parties, "You don't need a scientist, you need a Christian minister. They believe in resurrection, I don't. It is possible as an article of faith, sir, not as a fact of science."

The embassy had also prevailed upon him to speak at one of those cryonics societies that had sprung up around the world, many of whose members entertained some fancy of having a double life, one natural and the other through freezing.

"Yes, we might have a chance of suspending animation through cryonics. First, we need a volunteer. He, or she, has to have a good heart, be in perfect physical condition, and ideally be in the late twenties. Then we drain his blood, rapidly replacing it with a substance, probably glycerol, which also has a very good chance of killing him at normal temperatures, and we lower his temperature fast enough during this process—a very chancy combination of blood transfer and temperature reduction. Do I have any volunteers?"

There was a hush in the hotel room, rented for that meeting.

"That may work if we had a volunteer," Dr. Petrovitch went on. "Let me tell you what will not work: terminal cancer patients, already weak from the ravages of the disease; old people whose bodies have given out and have little chance of surviving now, let alone against the massive assault upon the body a freezing process entails; and, most of all, those people who have just died. If their bodies are not capable of sustaining life at ninety-eight point six degrees Fahrenheit, how are they going to do it at below zero degrees Celsius?"

And then came that persistent rationale for the most unscientific of expectations. A hand had been raised and that old statement made. Dr. Petrovitch kept reminding himself not to be cruel as he heard it.

"Sir, I am not a scientist or a doctor. But I do know this. If we bury someone, put them into the ground to decompose, there is a zero chance of recovery. There is no chance. But if we freeze someone, on the chance that a later age will have cures for the disease, that person has a better than zero chance of recovery. Isn't that so?"

And Semyon, stifling his rage, his voice lower than normal, each word precise, had answered:

"Yes, better than zero. You are correct. It is as good as this lucky krone I have in my pocket, which I will sell you for everything you own. Put this krone in your mouth and you will never die. It is magic. Now, the odds are certain you will die. We have precedent for that assumption.

"So, you are certain of dying. But perhaps the psychic belief that holding this krone in your mouth will give you eternal life, will keep you from dying. That, too, is a better than zero possibility. And just as good. If you want resurrection, may I recommend some excellent Lutheran churches in this country."

The meeting had broken up. There had been a protest to the embassy that if Dr. Petrovitch was an example of the Soviet–Scandinavian Friendship Pact, he was certainly not doing the Soviet Union any good, and that the writer had been previously well disposed toward communism before Dr. Petrovitch's appearance at their meeting and now felt otherwise.

The real tragedy of the meeting came with a beautiful, pale blonde woman in her early twenties. There was an offer of seduction, and Semyon had taken it. In the second week of the affair, Semyon, glowing from every active corpuscle in his forty-two-year-old body, was asked to look at the girl's father. Perhaps Semyon could do something with low-level temperatures to help the father. What diseases did the father have, Semyon had asked; heart failure had been the answer.

"I would suggest a heart specialist."

"But they failed, Semyon darling. That's what killed him."

The woman had wanted him to get her father dug up after eleven months of burial.

After that, Semyon Petrovitch refused even to consider any prospect concerning his field that did not come from a reputable scientist.

Early spring was coming to Norway, and Dr. Petrovitch breathed gusts of moisture as he trotted through the courtyard between building and hospital. He tried to remember what the American scientist looked like, but all he could remember was Texas and that the man was somewhat tall.

At the emergency room, he saw someone who had to be Dr. McCardle, but he didn't remember him that tall. The man was dressed like an Eskimo. A giant in fur.

"Dr. McCardle?"

"Yes. Dr. Petrovitch?"

"Yes. Where is the specimen you have for me? A whole body, yes?"

"Yes," said the American.

He stuffed a big glove in his parka. He explained he had been traveling since the day before and had just flown in and had kept the body wrapped in a tarpaulin. He was tired. He was sweating. And he was glad to be here.

Dr. Petrovitch reached for a piece of paper that the American was taking out from his shirt, but the American yanked it back and apologized. It was company business, and the body was outside.

"Fine," said Dr. Petrovitch. "How did it die?"

"I don't know. I'm a geologist. We found it. Like the mastodon found in permafrost in your country."

"It is a human body, isn't it?" asked Dr. Petrovitch. Suddenly he was experiencing severe doubts about what this man had brought him. A small rented van was parked, blocking access for ambulances.

"Yes, it's in there."

"How bad is the decomposition?"

"I didn't look at it long. I didn't see any."

"Uhhum," said Dr. Petrovitch, registering this fact and waiting for the rear door of the van to open. The big American swung the door open easily, and water broke out of the van. Dr. Petrovitch saw a brownish tarpaulin. The lights from the hospital glistened off the dark water at the bed of the truck, as though the water had broken out of the tarpaulin itself.

The big American reached inside and, with an effort to get the closed tarpaulin off, ripped a strand of cord with his massive hands. He pulled back an edge to the wall of the truck, and Dr. Petrovitch saw dark hair through a smooth covering of ice.

Obviously, the melting process had begun in the truck itself but had not reached the body. With grunts, the American climbed into the back of the truck, and both he and Dr. Petrovitch eased the tarpaulin away. The American had amazing strength, and Dr. Petrovitch cautioned him not to drop the water-slick ice with the specimen inside.

A small light in the back of the van showed flashes of skin, with very little discoloration.

It was a muscular young man. There was a wound, Dr. Petrovitch found, in the right thigh. It should not have been the cause of death.

"That was from a core tube. Went through it," said the American.

Dr. Petrovitch pressed his forefinger into the cylindrical wound. He tried to feel the crack of crystals between thumb and forefinger. It was rubbery. He tried to find a vein, but there was not room enough to do this by eyesight since he was wedged against the side of the van, and the frozen specimen was right against him. If there was a vein at his fingers, it too had yet to be crystallized.

"My God," gasped Dr. Petrovitch, who did not believe in God. "He's beautiful. Thank you. Thank you. Thank you."

CHAPTER III

In the back of the truck, his knees wet from incredibly cold water that had seeped down his open jacket underneath his pants, and trying desperately to protect the piece of paper authorizing him to leave the drill site far up north, Lew McCardle heard massively confusing comments from the Russian doctor.

"Why not?" said the Russian. His dark eyes were wide, his face just across the slick ice mound between them, and he was grinning as though Lew was supposed to understand "why not?"

"Can I let it down?"

"Certainly. Do you have sinus trouble?"

"No."

"Then why not?"

"What, why not?" asked McCardle.

"Let it down carefully. Carefully. Carefully."

Lew eased the block down to the cold, wet floor. His fingers were numb. He blew on them. Petrovitch yelled out for a nurse. He yelled out for orderlies. He wanted an assistant. He wanted the hyperbaric chamber. A nurse came with a light sweater over her starched uniform. She wanted to see the patient. Petrovitch said it was none of her business.

Petrovitch said it was an emergency because he said it was an emergency. McCardle squeezed out of the truck. Petrovitch grabbed McCardle. The nurse grabbed McCardle. Lew McCardle asked what was going on.

"Don't ask nurses questions. Give them orders," said Petrovitch.

"You're accepting the body?"

"We have. It's mine. Come. We'll get a reasonable nurse. Don't worry, you're part of it."

"I'm not worried," said McCardle. He said it to Petrovitch. But Petrovitch was out of the truck and back inside the hospital. McCardle said it to the nurse.

The nurse didn't speak English well. She was not Petrovitch's nurse. Lew tried to brush the water down off the outside of his pants. It didn't help. It was inside. The body rested on the bottom of the dark, wet truck. Now the driver wanted to go. He had to get back to the airport. He had been hired when Lew had landed from the air base. He was an Oslo driver. He had agreed because the American had said it was rush. Well, where was the rush?

Orderlies came out wheeling a raised chrome platform about waist high. They slid a thin piece of white plastic underneath the block of ice, between it and the truck. Someone ordered the driver not to rock the truck. The driver said he had been rocking the truck since the airport and no one minded then. The nurse told him to stop rocking the truck. She had forms for McCardle to sign.

McCardle wasn't signing any forms. He told that to the nurse. She said someone had to sign forms. One didn't go delivering cadavers hither and yon, with no one caring. This was not Brooklyn, America, and gangster people, said the nurse.

McCardle told the nurse it wasn't his body. It was Dr. Petrovitch's now.

Dr. Petrovitch had his own problems, the nurse said. She wanted McCardle inside the office immediately to fill out forms. She said she wanted no part of madness.

The block of ice, slick and smooth now, glistening as the driveway lights from the emergency room hit it, came out of the back of the truck on the plastic sheet, ever so evenly, ever so carefully, onto the chrome table.

The orderlies pulled up the sides of the white plastic sheet, and McCardle noticed the plastic was opaque. It covered the ice mound with the body in it. Orderlies folded it closed, but it dripped, water flowing down the chromium legs of the wheeled table. The orderlies quite smoothly and steadily pushed the mound up the small gradual incline that had received so many wheeled stretchers and guided the high table, each keeping a hand on the plastic-covered mound, through the doors and into the hospital.

On the black driveway the water drippings had become hard. It was ice again.

McCardle was left with the truckdriver, whom he paid, and the nurse with the sweater, whom he followed, and the question why was it important if he had trouble with his sinuses.

"Because you can't go into a hyperbaric chamber if you suffer sinus trouble."

There were no further explanations. He would first protect the piece of paper authorizing his departure from the drilling site. Second, get in touch with Houghton Oil Corporation representatives here to make sure he was doing the right thing. Third, he would cautiously answer any questions they might have. Geologists at exploratory sites were not supposed to discuss their work.

McCardle decided to say nothing until he had authorization from his company. Another nurse, with an operating mask and green cap and a green gown, intercepted McCardle.

"You're the American," she said.

"Yes."

"Come with me. Get undressed. Come. Come."

McCardle followed her to a small well-lit room with three chairs on narrow white metal legs. The seats appeared to screw on. Her hands pulled at his jacket. It was a reach for her.

McCardle pulled away.

"What's happening?"

"Dr. Petrovitch wants you to be a part of this. He is grateful for the specimen. Come. You've got to get scrubbed."

"How am I going to infect a cadaver?"

"We're saying it's not. That's how Dr. Petrovitch can claim the hyperbaric chamber immediately."

"It's not going to get more alive by going in now," said McCardle.

"Doctor, you don't know its temperature exactly. We don't know exactly its interior temperatures. The exterior was obviously melting. So why not now?"

"Because it's dead. I know it's dead. I found it dead."

"Of course it's dead. We know that," said the nurse. "Get undressed and scrubbed. I'll explain."

The explanation was shocking to Lew McCardle, partly because he had not been aware of the extent of advances in low-temperature medicine. He had attended that lecture run by Dr. Petrovitch in Sweden the year before, but he was not aware so many plans had become actuality.

"If we treat the patient as a totally rehabilitable patient, we find we are always more successful. We assume all the functions of the body can be induced to proper functioning. We make the body prove to us we are helpless. We don't know what will respond to treatment, especially with a total case such as you have brought in.

"But if we make the assumption we will try to save everything, just as we would try to save all the functions of a frostbitten arm, then who knows? Perhaps a kidney will survive. We are sure we are capable of reviving skin tissue. It was a perfect specimen from appearances, Dr. Petrovitch was saying."

"I don't know," said Lew McCardle. His jacket was off, his pants were off, and he was stepping out of his arctic boots. He needed a shave, and, from the wincing eyes over the nurse's mask, he realized he was ripe.

"The wet's from the ice," he said about his dark, wet long johns. He felt very tired and old, and in need of washing and rest. He tried to sit, but the nurse wouldn't let him rest.

"Our technique is like that with any part of the body suffering frostbite. It is alive until it proves it does not respond to everything we can give it. Dr. Petrovitch heads a small staff, without lavish funding or quarters, but we are all proud of him and what we can do. We are proud of the limbs that work today because we did not accept their loss when others did."

"Nurse, that body is dead."

"In ten, twenty, thirty minutes we will accept it. But not now. And why not? Why not see what we can save, yes?"

Lew McCardle pushed his document through the sleeve of a fresh green operating gown. He didn't have time to transfer it to the other hand that was getting into a sleeve also.

"I guess," said Lew.

His hands were scrubbed at a sink in a room down the hall

while he held the document in his mouth. The nurse gave him a plastic bag for it when he said he was taking it with him. They covered his face with a mask, his head with a hat, and the nurse, with great discipline, washed his feet and pulled on fresh new socks.

"I'm not too clear," said Lew. "Do you do research or treat people? Usually they're separate, aren't they?"

"We do what we can do. Dr. Petrovitch is a great man. Most other men with his achievements would have been popularly famous. Popularly."

"Let me make one phone call first. I think I had better reach one of our offices," said Lew.

"Too late," said the nurse. "You're in the entry lock."

"But this is a storage room," said Lew, pointing to the stacked cartons against a light green wall and three chest-high machines with burnished steel exteriors, waiting, their plugs pinioned to their sides by plastic clasps.

"Yes. Once we begin, we have to have everything here we might need. We can't open the doors to bring in extra machinery until it's all over. It's all here."

"And when you declare it dead, do you open the doors and let everyone out?"

"No. Then you go into a decompression chamber. This is why we asked you about the sinuses. We're all going under compression."

"I just delivered the body. I didn't sire it," said Lew.

The door to the main chamber was open slightly, and a rubber-gloved hand signaled for them to enter quickly.

"If the patient is declared dead, then you may go immediately to decompression. We have a phone link from there. You can call your office."

"I've heard of Catholic saints being made saints vox populi, never people dying that way."

"Vox populi?" said the nurse.

"Voice of the people," said McCardle. "It's Latin. When the Catholic Church makes a saint, or declares one, sometimes it is the people themselves who demand that a person—"

"Please, please, doctor . . . we're in a hurry," said the nurse, and Lew bent down to enter through the lock and to wait until he was told everyone had now agreed what he had found was dead.

Dr. Petrovitch, in operating gown and hat, nodded as Lew entered.

"Thank you," he said to Lew, whose head had to be kept bent as he maneuvered for a place to stand. The nurse guided him.

"I will explain everything. Don't speak to Dr. Petrovitch, speak to me," whispered the nurse. The chamber was a giant tube. Twelve feet wide and about twenty feet long, Lew estimated. There were five women and two men. One woman—a nurse—standing by a dark hole in the far side of the chamber, received instruments through the hole and was stacking them.

"I thought nothing entered," said Lew to his nurse.

"Nothing big. We can get small instruments, but large amounts of plasma and machinery have to come in from the entry lock."

"And we leave that way?"

"No. Through the rear lock," said the nurse.

Lew felt a heaviness about his head. Oxygen, the nurse told him, was now being pressurized into his system and into the systems of everyone else in the chamber, not of course for their benefit but for the patient's. The problem with frostbite, just as with gangrene, was that the blood no longer carried sufficient oxygen to the tissues.

The chamber pressurizing oxygen into the patient made up for the failure of the body. And there was no way to do it without treating the doctors as well as the patient.

Lew bent over sideways to hear her. He felt perspiration collect in his rubber gloves and remembered his nails had not been clipped. He felt them squishing at the tip of his gloves. He had a sudden strange desire to clip his nails.

He felt a push at his head, guiding his sight toward the back of a green apron.

The specimen was on its back in the shiny, drippy block. Someone had chiseled out a section to the groin. A tubular metal drill pointed just beneath the scrotum. It whirred, spitting back pieces of ice that clung on gowns and then quickly became water spots. Other drills were working. At the head, one technician was drilling holes into the open mouth, another was making two passages to the cranium.

Lew tried to follow the explanations. The foil tabs were for any possible brain waves to be elicited. They were going to pump out all of its blood and replace it, since immediate tests had shown that the red cells were all but driven out completely from the blood, and that the normal enzymes and salts in the protoplasm of cells was so concentrated now because of the low temperatures that its own blood would kill it at normal body temperatures.

"The blood itself cannot possibly carry oxygen in its current form," she whispered. "Its three-dimensional molecular structure has been broken down. It can't carry oxygen without it."

"Could you simplify?" said Lew.

"We're going first to elevate the temperature rapidly by pumping warm water into its digestive tract, while we simultaneously exert oxygenated heat on its external surfaces. That's the most crucial time, those first moments of normal temperature. At those first moments we pump out its old blood and put in new. We establish a cardiopulmonary bypass and provide renal dialysis. It gets an artificial bloodstream, heart system, and kidney system. All of this has to be done within one minute when it hits the critical normal temperatures."

The little figure was still running in its glistening cell of ice, but this time toward the ceiling. One leg was forward, the other back, one hand reached to the ceiling, and the open mouth now had a big plastic tube in it. Wires and tubes stretched down to the chest and head. Tubes burrowed their way in through the remnant of covering glacial ice to each limb. It was as though every advance of modern technology was now by wire and tube hooked into that stopped body hauled up from the crust at the top of the world.

A nurse read things from a list on a clipboard to Dr. Petrovitch. He nodded and grunted at each sentence. Once he shook his head. A nurse checked the chest cavity. It looked like a convention of wires leading toward a terminal in the ice. The terminal was the chest.

The nurse put the board down in front of her stomach. She looked to Dr. Petrovitch. Petrovitch inhaled. He looked into the eyes of everyone in the room.

Lew felt embarrassed by the intensity of those black eyes, as deep as the holes of space, Lew thought. Breathing should have been easier. The air was almost doing it for him. Lew felt his own heart beat, heavy and solid. There was quiet in the chamber. No one moved. It was as though they all stood at the opening of something so subtle and so deep it went on forever.

Then it all happened quickly. Petrovitch nodded and machines were operating. Heavy, glistening shiny yellow pads went over the top of the mound. A nurse called out seconds.

Lew saw a clear bag of clear liquid go down a few centimeters in a sudden drop. The top of the yellow pads lowered in a simultaneous jerk.

Dr. Petrovitch put his hand on top and pressed steadily down. That was where the leading foot had been. Foul, putrid water gushed out of the end of the table into white plastic buckets on the floor. They had no handles and Lew saw the water getting darker.

The front foot was down, and the whole mass of ice was down, as though the yellow pads had exhaled bulk. The ice had given up something and was now water in sealed plastic buckets set against the far wall, away from the body it had held.

Hands removed the shiny yellow pads. One of the pads hit Lew's socked foot. It was hot.

The head was free of ice, Lew saw, the hair slick and wet like a just-born infant. The pale, smelly blood collected through tubes in plastic bags. The new, dark red blood coursed into the body. Lew suddenly realized there were no bottles in the chamber, only bags.

He asked why, and the nurse, so engrossed, did not answer him. He reasoned it out for himself. In oxygen under pressure, dangerous gases could be created by air pockets in bottles.

A nurse removed the yellow pad at his foot and stored it too.

It was a muscular little body with a burn scar at its side and a white healed wound on its left shoulder and several on its right forearm. The right thigh pumped blood. What was once a smooth core hole was now an ugly, bloody wound.

The mouth closed on a large tube. Suddenly, the body jerked as though its stomach was being sucked out. It jerked again, then tremors shot through its shiny fingertips. Forty-two seconds were called out, and Dr. Petrovitch roughly pushed away scalpels paused at the chest cavity. The chest moved. It expanded up, contracted down. Expanded up. Contracted down.

"Is it breathing?" Lew asked.

"No," said the nurse. "Machines. It's at normal temperature."

"What's he doing now?"

"He's seeing what's working. He's going to shock the heart now."

"How do you know?"

"Look."

"What?"

"There."

Lew saw only another machine. A nurse turned a dial, then turned it back. She was blocked by another doctor moving around Petrovitch.

The body jerked again, and a foul putrescence, dark and bitter, vomited out of the sides of the mouth. White pads wiped it away until Petrovitch said something sharply. Big red welts on the cheeks showed where the pads had wiped. They had also taken away an outer layer of skin.

The pads were stored with whitish smears set gray against their pure white gauze.

The nurse no longer counted seconds.

"The heart is working."

"My God. By itself?" asked Lew.

"No. No. In consonance with the machine. It's the machine's energy. But the muscles appear to be responding."

"What does that mean?"

"It means that a muscle with machine help is functioning."

"That's amazing. Is this the first time?"

"No. It's been done with the pancreas and other organs. And the pancreas has functioned alone without machine stimulus."

"So what's happening?"

"It's not dead yet," said the nurse.

"Shhh," said Dr. Petrovitch. The nurse had talked too loud.

If it wasn't the hyperbaric chamber pressurizing oxygen into all of them, it had to be the tension. Eyes watered and did not blink. Sentences were cut short. Instruments came and went on the slightest nod or sound. People hung on expectant orders.

"What?" whispered Lew.

"Shhh," said the nurse assigned to explain things to him. She poked him sharply. She wanted him to get out of the way. Lew moved to his right, two steps. His neck hurt from bending over. He found himself holding his breath. He had been standing in front of some form of oscilloscope. It had a round face with a white grid and a smooth-flowing green sine curve, keeping its pace with time like restful moving green hills.

Lines taped to the floor ran to the edge of the table, to the head. Lew felt dizzy. His own breathing was heavy. Even with that body now being electronically goaded to function in one organ or the other, to see it work like the living drained Lew, taking away feelings of stability. He felt alarmed. Ironically his old football injury caused him no pain whatsoever. He glanced at the oscilloscope connected to the body's brain.

A sharp spear of a line interrupted the smooth hill flow of the sine curve, and then there was smoothness again. Lew noticed electrodes on the chest wall of the body. Petrovitch looked back over his shoulder. He motioned Lew to move. The finger contracted. Lew stepped farther to the side.

Petrovitch said something hoarsely in Norwegian. Lew made out "much work, challenge, extremely dangerous now."

There was a hush.

A nurse called out the number of minutes in Norwegian.

"Time since normal temperature," said Lew's nurse.

"I heard."

Suddenly, the nurse dropped her head in her hands and began sobbing. She no longer talked in English and Lew couldn't get an answer.

Dr. Semyon Petrovitch himself had to explain. He pointed to the oscilloscope Lew stood near. The lines were jagged and harsh, like jarring interruptions of a honking horn during a peaceful symphony.

"You're shooting waves into the brain, right?" said Lew McCardle, trying to fathom what had caused the emotional outburst. Petrovitch's eyes, too, held tears, filling up the lower rim.

"No. Not going in. Coming out. We are receiving brain waves. Those may be thoughts," he said. And then with great strength, forcing the words out again, overcome by his own wonder, he said, his voice hoarse as though he had been yelling, possibly within his own mind, screaming out prayers that only a doctor might scream to a god he did not believe in, Semyon Petrovitch said:

"I think it thinks."

Lew McCardle felt his body very weak, and he waited for the sine curves to reappear in a smooth, easy, gentle hill pattern. Jagged peaks continued. The body was not yet dead. It now had one more death coming to it.

At this time, at this place, for now, it lived. And maybe thought. A doctor clamped the thigh wound.

I am dead. But if I know I am dead, then I am not dead. Yet I will soon be dead. I am in the snows and the cold of the barbaric North, and I do not hear the legionnaire who has brought me here, nor see those who have stripped me of garments and left me defenseless against an invincible cold that even fells men swathed in animal skin. I feel warm. But I have heard barbarians and other Germans of the north country say the final grip of the snow death is feelings of warmth and goodness. They call it the blanket of the snow god. Romans laugh at these German gods, although some legions on the Danube border in Gaul honor them. The Roman will honor any god, I suspect, because he believes in none of them. Nor do I.

We passed the last Roman camp months ago. It does not matter. It could have been years ago. Why am I not dead yet? I have accepted it. Yet my throat feels the strong hard beak of a bird tear at it, and my stomach burns like molten bronze. This cannot be death. I feel pain, a familiar companion, and the certain proof of life.

I hear dog-bark grunts of a barbaric tongue at many leagues and now very close, as though yelling my ears from my head. My limbs are there but do not move. My eyes are sandy pools, and I suspect light but do not see it. I taste the sewers of death in my mouth. Taste? Am I living?

There is no taste. I am warm again and my body has gone off to its gentle sleep, and I think. Is that death? No. Dreams are of a different stuff, and I can put my mind where I wish it.

Some say Dis greets all in the underworld, that the spirit escapes through the mouth. But I have seen men with their mouths mashed solid into their throats. Where does the spirit go then? Others say, mostly slaves, there is a final beautiful place of eternal joy for those who live a certain way. But this hope is too much a hope for a cunning mind. No, I have seen too much death not to know it is but a last sleep, leaving nothing. It is neither fearful nor wonderful, only eventual. It is the one kept promise of birth. And I am forced to await it with an active mind. So this is the way snow kills. Perhaps it is worse than the sword.

The sword does not make you dwell on what a fool you are.

CHAPTER

IV

First Day — Petrovitch Report

Patient poor. Pulmonary bypass unit disconnected, 9:22 P.M. Systolic pressure 120 mm. Diastolic 80 mm. Circulation, therefore, good, but patient experiencing apparent paroxysmal ventricular tachycardia, variable and occasional rapid heartbeats. This caused by ventricular node unable to send clear signals to the heart. State of shock feared imminent.

Electroencephalograph records unusually intense brain-wave activity as though experiencing severe dream or nightmare.

Why am I not dead? Where is my death? I know death. It is a proud and free thing in a quiet place. Disembowel the dead, it is free of needing its stomach. Cut off an arm, it does not care. It has triumphed over the shouts of the mobs themselves. No emperor can harm it further.

That is death. I know death. In death I will not think about why I was marched to the German Sea. In death, I will not remember, nor stand as my chief accuser. Where is my death? That one and only debt owed by life waits. But it does not tarry for those who fear it.

I will not think.

Second Day — Petrovitch Report

Condition poor. Elevated SGP-T level due to some liver damage, but 1 mg./100 ml. creatinine indicates kidney functioning. Also, blood urea nitrogen remains under 20 mg./100 ml., which also supports belief that kidney functions, perhaps perfectly. Paroxysmal ventricular tachycardia experienced by patient at 2 A.M. and 4:55 A.M. Danger of shock remains high.

EEG (electroencephalogram) reports continued intense brain-wave activity for long periods of time. Vocal activity reported at 8:17 A.M.; instruments thereupon set up to record. Apparently it dreams, but the words are barely audible. Language unidentified.

I burn. The sun comes and goes quickly like torches with sudden flames. It is dark, then light, suddenly, as though I have slept a moment and the day has come.

I am on my back. My skin singes. Little bugs in my blood eat their way out of my pores with their hot, sharp little teeth. Pain I know. There are limits and then there is no more.

The pain of the body has a line over which it will give up its senses. The mind, I suspect, is limitless, its pain only shoveled silent with the grave.

I smell rotting flesh. I breathe it. I taste it. I am it.

I hear German talk, grunting barking sounds. If they are the far-north Germans and have followed us to the sea, why don't they take this helpless flesh and end my pain?

It is not the death but the dying that claims the price. And not the body but the mind that tolerates so many never-ending taxes.

I deserved what happened to me. But my loyal slaves did not. My family did not.

If I could die without thinking, without remembering, without saying to myself, "if here," "if there," "if only." I am not dying. This must be life. Death is a quiet thing. My mind bangs like so much clattering armor in the arena tunnels, and not one soft pillow for rest.

This must be life, for no death could give such freedom to the mind for self-torture.

My divinity, my emperor, my Domitian would love to witness this game where I fight myself. But this one he is denied.

He may think he has a right to my pain, and in truth, if there is such a right, this emperor did have it. For he trusted me to pursue my own self-interest. And he did not know that within me was a lunatic waiting for the worst possible time to take charge of my life. If not a lunatic, then myself, hidden so well from Rome, the mobs, and the emperor, that ultimately it hid from me.

None knew the real Lucius Aurelius Eugenianus when all thought they did. What they knew were their own fancies and what my retainers fed to the city in darkest rumors, so flagrant only the well-fertilized Roman mind would root in it.

They said many things about me when everyone thought they knew Eugeni. They knew so much about me. They said I fought in the arena because I would die naturally without the cheers of the mobs. They said an Eastern god gave me the power of eternal victory when I was a baby. They said I had a powerful hex on all my opponents. They said I refused to hear the names of my enemies. They said I only fought gladiators who had cursed the name of the people and the senate of Rome. They said I fought rarely because I felt the gladiators of today lacked the skill of yesterday. They said I fought rarely because I had become afraid. That I had become too slow. Too old. Too rich. Too thin. Too fat.

They said I slept with lionesses. With the empress. With our divine Domitian himself. With both. With no one.

They said I fought for whole provinces and reveled in my wealth. They said I gave my money in donatives to the legions facing the barbarians in the North for every yellow head that rolled, in vengeance for my father who was an officer most brutally tortured by the barbarian, priest of Apollo most brutally tortured by the barbarian, a scholar most brutally tortured by the barbarian, a patrician who had fled his seat in the senate to join the legion and was tortured by the barbarians.

Or Gauls.

Or Jews.

Or Parthians.

Or Scythians.

Or Dacians.

But most liked Germans. They thought them the wildest. And success in the arena was not so much what went on in the sands but in the minds of the crowds.

Just to see death was nothing. One could wait near the aged for that. But to see one's fears or hates performed in blood, that was the arena. And it was in the mind.

The disaster started, like most truly thorough cataclysms, with a promise of benefit. And it was my mind that was to blame. Perhaps if the negotiations for the match had not taken place on the latifundia themselves, I would have been more suspicious about the sponsors of the games.

But knowing that I trusted no one but myself for the final examination of who would be matched with me, they placed the young man in the middle of the latifundia, so that I had to see these vast farmlands they were willing to trade for my appearance.

I had latifundia. I hate the smell and sweat of the thousands of slaves who labor in these fields without even knowing where they are, only that if they work, they eat. They are the lowest slaves, not even having names on bills of sale, but going with the latifundia, one hundred more or less. And by that, meaning they are not even important enough to be numbered exactly: twenty-eight hundred field workers, one hundred more or less.

All the way through these lands south of the city, near Brundisium, I had kept curtains drawn on my litter. If I could have trusted another to tell whether an opponent was fast enough or trained enough for a good performance, I would not have gone myself.

I did not care that the family sponsoring the games had sold off its armorers and tanners and carpenters from these latifundia and replaced them with field slaves beside cold forges and stilled saws. That was the affair of my chief slave of accounts, Demosthenes, who had used my wealth to make a fortune so vast, numbers could not describe it accurately.

My responsibility to emperor and self was that what happened on the arena sand did not turn a crowd into a mob. So the opponent had to be good enough, but not so good that I would pay with my blood.

An aedile, wishing to be named praetor, in which office he would have a whole province to tax, wanted to sponsor games with my appearance to win political favor of the mobs.

The young aedile met me formally at a newly built replica of a wooden arena, placed in the middle of the lands his family wanted to trade. His purple patrician piping was loud and so wide on his toga, it almost made sounds.

He ignored my slave, Demosthenes, in gray-stained tunic with ink-blackened fingers and hair so untonsored it looked as though it had never suffered comb or oil.

Ironically, it was Demosthenes who determined any financial aspect of the match and Demosthenes who, while still a slave, was rich enough many times over to buy all the patrician family's holdings.

Yet it was on me, in my white toga with thin equestrian-rank piping, that the concern was focused. Equestrian rank required only wealth. Patrician required bloodlines, granted only to those with the brilliance to select the right womb to be born from. Still, freedmen were becoming equestrians nowadays, as I had become, and their sons could marry into the right blood and rise to the rights of the oldest of Roman families. I dismissed conversation about the land and went right into this small arena. The wood smelled of fresh sap—probably built by the carpenters just before they were sold off. His mother, her gray hair piled like a pyramid above her head, her face an old pedestal with heavy cosmetics to distinguish the triumph of time over flesh, sat with her jeweled hands resting on her formal white stola. Behind her was the lanista, a trainer of gladiators. He hoped that his secutor would be acceptable to me. For then he would be paid many times over the cost of the training and purchase.

There were many formal greetings from the son, the mother, and the lanista. "Greetings, Lucius Aurelius Eugenianus, most Roman of them all."

"Most Roman of them all," I said to the people, without mentioning their names or looking at them. Down there in the sand beneath me was my proposed match.

He was a beautiful young boy with sharp muscles and clean features. Yet back in Rome, features would be meaningless, especially since this was a secutor who would wear a helmet. I never liked large arenas because one is never fully in control of so large a mob, and only the most gross movements are noticeable. A really fine match that would be appreciated in Pompeii would bore the Roman mob, and a bored mob could threaten the city. Many a riot had given courage to an assassin's hand, and every emperor knew this. I had Domitian's valued trust, and I was not about to squander it for three latifundia.

"With water rights," said the mother of the aedile, who was directing his career as she had directed his father's. My slaves dismissed this as a relatively minor addition to the contract, although they knew quite well it was crucial. They had not become wealthy making me poor. I pretended to heed their comments.

"He looks very agile and skilled," I said, pointing to the young secutor who was showing his moves to us in the aedile's small private arena. A thrust here, a parry here. At first basic strokes, then becoming more elaborate with thrusts off blocks and double blocks and thrusts. His feet skipped lightly over the sand. His body was not oiled, and I saw no sweat. He could go a long time. I mentioned this also.

"Should he but break skin, I would personally have him strangled," said the lanistra, like most, always in need of money.

"There will be much blood and elephants before your match. I have already paid for this. The mob will have a surfeit of blood," said the aedile's mother.

"It is my secutor who should fear for the mob, for if they are not satisfied, it is his life the mob will demand. The mob loves you, Lucius Aurelius Eugenianus," said the lanista.

"Assuming my blade at his chest and his back on the sand," I said.

"You are Lucius Aurelius Eugenianus," said the mother with real amazement in her voice. "This is a sapling."

"I am past thirty years," I said.

"You have my oath on my life that he will provide a performance and a performance only," said the lanista.

"I give you my Roman word," said the aedile, looking to his mother. "And I give it before this lanista and this secutor that should in the heat of the arena any damage come to your person, they shall not live to reap rewards from such a victory. Thus, my word is given."

"There will be elephants?" I said.

"A score in combat. And lions," said the aedile.

"Everyone has lions," I said. "Romans have seen so many lions they are as common as street dogs."

"Lions with women," said the mother, grinning.

"It won't work," I said.

"That is our problem," said the mother.

"It becomes my problem when a mob wants more blood. And while I believe your Roman word, and the lanista believes your Roman word, it is another thing for this secutor to give his life freely for that Roman word."

"It is not his life to give or to save," said the lanista, who should have known better. But looking at the sand, I knew I did not need his assurance, and I was right.

"I guess there have been many pairs here this day," I said.

"No," said the lanista. "The secutor has been alone."

It was all but done. I did not trust my life to a Roman word, of course, but rather to what I saw: deep heel marks in the sand. The lanista need not have added that the secutor had worked only against wooden and fabric dummies. I knew that, just as surely as I knew the secutor had one set of strokes to show me and another he killed with.

Many lanistae, seeking to save expense, work their gladiators against dummies too much. The gladiators develop unnecessarily heavy thrusts this way because it is more satisfying to drive a spear or sword deep into lifeless objects.

It also makes them look more powerful to untrained eyes. But when they do this, they must plant their driving foot deeply into the sand. And while practicing, this is barely noticed. In the arena, it begs death because they announce their blows as though praetorian horns led the way. First the foot, and then the thrust. It is only a small moment, but to a seasoned gladiator it is a gift of the man's life. A far greater guarantee than a Roman word. The secutor was all right for me.

I looked to Demosthenes lest he have any final word on the value of the property. He had stayed quiet behind me all this time.

"Plus three million sesterces," he added. "We must buy ships to import carpenters, tanners, ironsmiths, potters, and armorers. There are none here. I don't know how these latifundia managed without them, but we need them. They will cost."

Caught in their own chicanery, the patricians stammered their way through denials, through accusations, through everything, saying that the skilled slaves they had sold had brought in only a fifth at most of what Demosthenes had estimated they would cost.

I did not wish to go against Demosthenes, so I feigned concern. Domitian had requested the family to provide me, so they too had a goad behind them for this match. Also, if the games were successful, and with me they should have been, the aedile would become a Roman praetor, who while governing a land would make back three times what he invested in the games. A praetor could tax the eyes out of a beetle.

The family agreed to make a payment of two million after they had gotten the praetorship. Demosthenes advised me loudly against it.

"Dominus," he said, "we will need the skilled slaves immediately."

The mother sighed. "It is a shame to Rome when a gladiator can extort a Roman when she seeks only the rightful position for her son. 'Extort' is the word, too. And by whom—a gladiator?—when most gladiators are matched in the tens of pairs. A gladiator negotiating freely," she said. She lowered her eyes. "Done," she added.

Now came the question of which arena would be best. Sponsors often did not understand, and it was my responsibility to help them, if they could be helped.

"I would suggest the Flavian amphitheater," I said. It sets off a single match much better. . . . The arena at the Vatican is too large. It's better for animals. Races even. It does not make a gladiator look good."

"It makes the sponsor look very good," said the woman sharply. The son, who had been watching his political career hang on his mother's nods, agreed.

"The Vatican," he demanded.

Each arena had its points. The Flavian was smaller, had awnings, and was better for a single match, but it lacked a direct escape route for the emperor should the mobs become uncontrollable. The Vatican had a tunnel to the palace.

And the Vatican did not remind Domitian, a Flavian, how the family's generosity had been wasted. They had paid for and built the amphitheater at the square of the Colossus of Nero, a statue of the Claudian.

But instead of calling the Flavian amphitheater the Flavian amphitheater, they kept the familiar name of the Colossus, calling it the Colosseum, and Domitian resented that.

"I would recommend, once again, against the Vatican," I said.

"Gladiator, to your swords, if you please," said the mother.

I should have known. Perhaps it was negotiating at a latifundium, which I hate, which let me become careless. Demosthenes had done what he was supposed to do. I should have done what I was supposed to do. We should never have taken so much money from them before the match. If I had known we had broken them, I would have loaned them money or even returned it for the financing of the game.

But on the day of the festivities, it was too late. And it was a hot day. And the Vatican arena had no awnings.

The promised lions mounting prostitutes turned out quite naturally to be a farce. They failed to couple with the women, who had been heavily drugged. Women could do it with bulls and asses, but no conscious one would ever think of surviving a lion, much less induce it to mate. The prostitutes stumbled and the lions yawned, and then the master of the games, undoubtedly under the orders of the patrician aedile who was drinking his way through his day of glory just as undoubtedly with unwatered wine, ordered bestiarii into the arena. And this might have saved the day if they had killed the lions, but the aedile was saving money, and they slaughtered the drugged prostitutes and merely goaded the lions back toward their pens. Laughter turned quickly to anger, and there were no elephants. The patricians had spent their wealth, assuming I would save their games. They were broke.

There were convicted criminals in armor. When things go bad, they go bad without end. This crew must have violated some laws of commerce, for weapons seemed strange in their hands. They quickly reached some form of mutual truce, whereby sword met shield and shield met sword and a harmless clanging ensued, which further aggravated the crowd. And worst of all and most unforgivable of all was the slowness with which events followed one another, so what might have served as reason for mirth now became that ominous rumbling of one hundred and fifty thousand people, larger than most cities and some nations.

This was the sort of danger that only three well-equipped and seasoned legions might thwart. But by law as ancient as the kings before the Roman Republic, no emperor except Sulla dared bring a full armored legion inside the city walls. Available were only the praetorians who protected the emperor; three urban cohorts, who were supposed to defend the city in emergencies but actually protected the emperor like the praetorians; and the vigiles, who were supposed to subdue armed gangs and fires but only subdued their own swords and staffs for the hand that offered coin.

If the mob got its head, there was nothing in Rome to stop it.

Two men in plebeian seats started their own exhibition with fists, and the crowd cheered them until eight of the urban cohorts assigned to the arena without weapons got between them. The cheering was an especially dangerous sign. It showed the crowd had lost interest in what was happening on the sand.

"They're fighting, and he's still there," said Plutarch. He was a big round man and stood on a firm table in my cubicle looking out of a small vertical hole which was at the level of the sand. From there he could see the emperor's seats. When he said "they're fighting," he meant the crowds. When he said "he's still there," he meant the emporor.

There was no further explanation necessary. In this cubicle his word was supreme. He was a slave, and yet none of my patrician guests were allowed to interrupt him. He could tell by sounds what crowds were thinking. He knew my weapons, what they should be kept in, when they should be given, who should give them, who should rub my muscles, when the oils were ready.

He had been trained as a gladiator, and I had bought him as that, but his real talent was servicing my arena needs and understanding that the most crucial element was timing. The empire consumed thousands of gladiators each year, most of them better than Plutarch had been.

None was better at servicing a gladiator, yet at times Plutarch would mention how he wished he could have taken to the sand to win his freedom and wealth. And yet at other times, he mentioned he was glad he had not killed, which might have been because of some strange Eastern cult he had joined.

"These games are gone," he said.

"Nothing?" I asked.

"Nothing they can do."

"And he's still there?"

"Waiting for you, dominus."

Plutarch's large frame alighted clumsily on the floor. I rose from the small couch where I was being oiled. Everyone looked to me.

Plutarch shook his head slowly. The games were doomed. I looked to a solid patrician friend who understood a bit of politics.

"He should know better," I said to Marcus Quintus Varro, a former officer in the thirteenth Gemina and an owner of land near Herculaneum. I asked that he go quickly through the arena tunnels to the emperor's seats and tell Domitian to leave. Nothing was going to save these games, and he should not be associated with them.

"He would know himself, would he not?" said Varro.

"He should," I said; and he knew it was of great import because I never spoke to my companions before a match.

"I'll go," said Vergilius Flavius Publius, a young patrician of such catholic earnestness that a refusal of anything to him became an affront to his dignity. Publius was delicate, with a soft face, and a voice that squeaked when he got angry, which was often, and I could see him ignored or halted by some arena slave, happy to safely affront a patrician toga. Arena slaves have great authority over things like gates and locks and little passages, and they exercise it wantonly at these times.

"I can do it," said Publius, forgetting no one is allowed to speak to me first.

"Publius," called Varro, but Publius was through the body slaves and armored slaves at the entrance before Varro could stop him, and I was in my own thoughts where I meticulously strip all distractions before an event. I only realized Varro had not gone when I heard the mob begin the low, rolling chant of my name. "Eugeni, Eugeni, Eugeni."

Plutarch climbed on the table again.

"He's still there," said Plutarch. I should have been in the tunnel before the portal to the arena sand, but my slaves had not led me there.

"What?"

"Domitian remains," said Plutarch. "We're keeping you here so that he will know to leave."

"Do they riot? Only riot would stop Varro."

"I'm here," said Varro.

"Oh," I said.

"Domitian has not been informed," said Plutarch. "He will know to leave when you do not appear. We keep the master of the games outside. When Domitian leaves, you go."

All was well. I have good slaves, and everyone crucial to my survival knows that freedom and wealth follow jobs well done. In a few moments I felt the touch on my shoulder and followed my men to the portal.

I could feel the stamping of feet on seats outside in the very stones near my head. There is a sweet smell of mountain air in the fetid tunnel, where I feel I am young and can run all day. There is no darkness or sun, and every sound is clear.

"Blade's sharpened," said a slave into my ear, which meant the secutor had added recent sharpness to his weapon, which would have been unnecessary if he intended just a display.

We walked into the sun on the sand. As the light came full to me, my slaves stripped off my unfastened robe and put a spatha, a long sword with a point more like a spear than a sword, into my right hand and a shield into my left hand. The shield is soft wood, the size of a child's bowl, reinforced with steel that can block, parry, and punch.

The secutor wore a yellow helmet of solid gold, carried a short sword and a shield, and was girdled with gold and bronze. His sword arm had leather wrapping. Domitian was not in his box, and the secutor, not thinking, went to the empty seat for the formal obeisance. I went to the aedile, whose mother's face boiled red. The aedile, too drunk to realize he had financed a farce, smiled at me. I made great comic motions to the crowd, and the mother yelled down at me that she would litigate over a breach of contract, meaning that I was not fulfilling my obligations to the games by making mockery before them. It was not the worst of all possible threats, since not only did I already have the property, but several magistrates in the patricians' seats were smiling with me. I did not circle the arena to let the people examine my body as usual. I gave a cursory salute to the aedile, who waved in return, until his mother slapped down his arm forcefully. She knew the danger of the riot and, were she not a patrician, undoubtedly would have fled discreetly from this seething crowd. But patricians tend to throw their lives after fortunes and consider the fear of death some inferior instinct to be suppressed. While I, raised as a slave, know better and only disguise my fear.

So I pretended boredom there under the hot sun, and careful I was to make my gestures gross, because subtlety is invisible to one hundred and fifty thousand pairs of eyes.

The secutor finally offered a longer formal salute to the aedile, and the mother graciously accepted it. The crowd hooted and made gestures. And I, very casual in appearance, got a large stain of blood between me and the oncoming secutor, who also tried to salute me. I did not return it, and the crowd applauded and chanted, "Eugeni, Eugeni, Eugeni," which sounds like Scythian drums when it picks up rhythm. It appeared as though I were leading the crowd in contempt of the games.

Even on the sand, blood can be slippery, although not as slippery as on earth or rock or wood. There, blood is like oil, which is why sand is so necessary for the games. The secutor, trying to avoid the stain, appeared unwilling to close on me, and I, in my casual, circling shuffle, appeared bored and above it all. Yet any discerning eye would have noticed that the spatha, hanging limply from my right hand, never touched the sand, and the small punching shield, while seeming to casually dangle at the end of a relaxed arm, always stayed waist high and facing the secutor. Just as he set to show that it was really I who ran, I turned my back on him. If he had allowed this act to continue and had then engaged me in a performance of some duration, whereby we could seduce the attention of the crowd, a small possibility would have remained that we might save some glory of the games that day. Although I could not see such a dissatisfied arena allowing a loser to live.

I turned. He closed and gave me that planted foot, and my spatha was in and out of his throat like the snapping of a catapult before he got his ponderous shoulder and full body into his sword. His thrust came anyhow, weaker and slower for having been mortally struck, and I slapped it away with my shield and wrested off his gold helmet as his head went by.

To the stands it looked as though I had just touched him gently with the tip of my weapon to keep him away and that removing the gold helmet was the greater labor. He struggled around on his hands and knees like a cow waiting to be mated, and I trotted with the helmet against my chest towards the "Portal of Life" as though nothing were wrong.

I did not wait for a signal of death from either the crowds or the vestal virgins, whose official responsibility it was to judge these matters, but who always followed the will of the crowd. They would pass their decision on to the emperor, who by tradition gave the final decision on life or death.

Domitian was not in his seats. No gaudy praetorian helmets with ornate plumes or brightly worked chest plates dotted the seething crowd where Domitian normally would sit. He had escaped through his tunnel, and the lack of praetorians there meant his retreat had been neat and successful.

Already, the first to his seats to get his fruits and wines and any stranded goblets were having the life crushed out of them by those who followed for the pillage. There were no barriers to the crowds, because an emperor's appearance at the games showed he was part of the people of Rome and, while a god, he was made of the same stuff as they.

Three large men fell into the arena dragging a vestal virgin. Smiling broadly, I trotted waving from the arena, as though this were the grandest day of the empire.

The mob shouted my name, but in moments they would tear at me to get an eyebrow for a souvenir or some other part they thought worth collecting. Mobs do not have leaders, even if they yell their names in praise. They only have objects in front of them, which they will either follow or destroy, depending on some mindless whim.

This mob was larger than many city-states the empire had conquered. With a roar, the seats flooded out onto the sand, like a spring gusher down a dry riverbed. It was off, and I was through the Portal of Life just in time, where Plutarch had my armored slaves ready and protective. They formed a wedge around me and moved me off down the arena tunnel, banging, pushing, and cutting.

We passed the master of the games, screaming full lung that Rome, the sponsors, and he were being abandoned. If he survived this riot, he would be crucified at least. Officially, it was his responsibility to ensure that the games were successful and orderly. But he had undoubtedly accepted bribes not to complain.

The patrician family had just as obviously reasoned that if a bribe cost them 2 and the elephants cost 200, therefore they would save 198. That is, if they had the other 198 to begin with.

They had undoubtedly depended on the young secutor to kill me, thus making the games a success very cheaply. Like many brilliant, logical plans, it was more easily and swiftly put together unobstructed by the unreasonable block of what really happens in these situations. It was not hard to imagine them saying among themselves, "Why hasn't anyone thought of this before, the fools?"

The master of the games should have known better but undoubtedly had succumbed to their logic and money.

At my cubicle my slaves were already heaving vats of water at the heavy wooden door. They were wetting it down. Plutarch ordered the door shut behind us, saying if someone hadn't gotten here by now, it was too bad.

"No," I said. "We'll wait."

We heard the mobs from the slit behind us where Plutarch had earlier looked for the imperial presence. The armored slaves looked nervously to Plutarch. They understood how much safer they would be with the door shut. Plutarch, his massive, fleshy head unmoving, stared them down.

Screams came from the tunnel outside, and we knew the mobs were near. Suddenly a slave, laughing, tumbled into our cubicle.

"That's him," said Plutarch.

"Lock it," I said. And with their bodies, three slaves heaved at once, and the door shut with a solid crack.

"More water," ordered Plutarch, and slaves splashed the dry inside portion with its reinforced iron latticework. Three stiff iron bolts went into place, as the slaves lashing them into place got wet from the slaves watering the doors.

A slave had been saved, and his joy caught on. There was grinning. There was confidence. We had saved a life from the mob. We might save all.

A watered-down door would not stop a determined fire. But, it would delay the success of flames and stop initial attempts. The mob, having very little patience, would most likely pass on to a more quickly gratifying object. I ordered wine for the slaves, told a little joke, and felt a hand on my shoulder. It was Publius. He was demanding a slave be crucified. Not only did he not know the name of the slave, but he did not know the owner. Only that this slave had stopped him from reaching Domitian and—Publius had witnesses to this—had laid a hand on Publius' person.

Now Publius was not necessarily for crucifixion, he said, and were it up to him he would have it outlawed. Yet, since there was crucifixion, this slave most assuredly deserved it if anyone ever deserved it. We all agreed that Publius was right and told him to take another cup of wine.

"Of course, I was right," said Publius.

"My gold helmet," said someone in a corner. During the panic, none of us had smelled him. But the lanista, who had so cloyingly assured me his secutor would only offer a performance, had apparently wedged himself in with me and my armored slaves. It was a smart move. Perhaps his first.

"If we could open that door safely, I would throw you out."

"That's all I have left after you killed my secutor."

"You lost. The helmet is mine," I said, realizing I was still holding it. My hands were sticky. There was blood on the helmet. Not mine.

"We had an agreement," said the lanista. He wore a new toga, this one apparently quite fine. The family must have paid him first. "We had an agreement."

"Which you and your secutor had no intention of keeping," I said. "What great fortune would have been on both of you had he slain me. You would have owned the greatest gladiator in the world, and he would have seen not only his freedom but great wealth in the future. You lost."

"Greekling," he said, the worst thing a Roman can call another. He knew my mother was Greek.

"How dare you, barely a knight, call the great Lucius Aurelius Eugenianus a 'Greekling,' " said Publius.

"The helmet is mine," I said.

"Would you make a loan of it to me?" said the lanista.

"These new families that dare to use the word 'Greekling' are an abomination," said Publius. "And how laughable that it should be used on one adopted into the Aurelii by Lucius Aurelius himself, by whom Eugeni was personally given his names. Yes, Eugenianus is a Greek name, but Eugeni is the most Roman of them all," said Publius.

"I can repay it in your service," said the lanista.

"Your service is worthless, the proof of which lies outside on the sand, unless of course it has been torn apart."

The thundering mob had been launched in a single roar, and now the sounds were scattered into shrieks and moans as it turned on itself. For some reason, mobs raped, and one could hear the screams of the women which excited the assaulters more.

"We, the Flavia," said Publius, "do not even allow the word 'Greekling' to be used by our slaves."

"I am ruined," said the lanista.

"How can one as low as you be ruined?" asked Publius.

The lanista took a cup of wine, I had water, and we all waited for the mob to dissipate itself. Even now Publius wore a smile.

Why did I like Publius? In most things, he was nothing I admired. In an age when it was said people had almost forgotten how to speak for fear of Domitian's spies, Publius' mind was at his tongue. He had only to think something to feel free to express it.

He believed in everything. No god came to Rome without Publius' worship or rejection first. At one time he even said there were no gods. If it was new, Publius had done it, worn it, or eaten it. He was even celibate for an afternoon and attempted to get everyone to join him, until he had a cup of wine and saw an attractive breast bob. By morning he had written four scrolls proving with finality that long-term celibacy caused lunacy and was a danger to the empire.

He had been an officer of the Third Cyrene legion fighting in Judea. Others saw blood, baking heat, and fanatics' daggers, living with the fear of fighting those who do not value their lives. Publius discovered a new wine.

He was on the tribune's staff but begged to bloody his sword instead of his stylus. It was said, but Publius denied it as a vicious rumor, that, unauthorized, he had led a wedged formation against an empty cave. Insulted by the tribune, Publius left Judea and returned to Rome without permission—a breach of discipline that normally would bring death. His family, far relatives of the Flavia who ruled Rome, interceded. It cost them half their estates to save his life. He stopped talking to his father because of the complaints over the size of the enormous bribe.

He married into a fortune, slept one night with his wife, who conceived, and found domestic life did not suit him. After a week he compared it to endless slavery and wrote an ode likening it to eternally rolling a rock up a hill. This, after he had written an ode to the married life as the strongest stone in the empire's walls.

Why did I like Publius?

Perhaps he could live with a freedom I could not survive. Perhaps it was his innocence of the hardness of the world. Perhaps it was his enthusiasm for everything. Sometimes, even after his life brought me ruin, I still smiled when I thought of him.

We were quiet in the cubicle, not because at this point the mob could hear us in its own screams, but because men waiting to fight for life do not have much to say. Except Publius.

"Better to wait," he said.

"Of course, none of us could get out now," said Varro.

"I mean later for the feast. Everyone in my family, all my friends are coming, except my cheap father. I didn't invite him."

A body suddenly blocked the slit to the arena. I ordered the lamps put out, for now the cubicle would become stuffy if they remained lit. We stood in darkness.

"They will be so disappointed that you are late for the feast," said Publius. He was talking to me.

"Shhh, Publius," I whispered. "There is a riot. If any of your guests are foolish enough to attend, I am not one of them."

"That is the lunacy of the mob. They do not realize how important your feast is," said Publius.

It was dark, and the dark made the quiet seem more necessary, as though all ears became stronger when the eyes were not in use.

"Eugeni . . . ," said Publius.

"Shhh. I want to go home, Publius. To my wife. To my son. I want to protect them. Shhh."

"Now, Eugeni," he whispered. "Everyone knows mobs always attack only what is immediately in front of them. And we know they always veer towards the Capitoline. Everyone knows that. This is not a time to lose our heads, correct?"

"Correct, Publius. Shhh."

"No. Just a moment for reason to overcome mindless panic. Now you, above all, have a house designed for protection against mobs. The streets leading to it are narrow, your walls well fortified and manned by slaves trained by you personally. Personally by you. There is no better training in the world. Correct?"

"Shhh. Yes."

"The safest place in Rome is your house, yes?"

"Yes. Shhh."

"Then gracious Miriamne and bright and sturdy Petronius are safer than any of us, yes?"

"Shhh."

"Against that certain safety lingers my life, but it rests secured on your word. Because I know you, least of all, will never surrender to panic and illogical action." This Publius was sure of and he had no worry, he said firmly.

"Publius, how was your life staked on an evening of drinking and eating?" I asked.

That was not the point. The point was my word. And he had no doubt that I would lay down my life for my word, just as any real patrician would. Varro laughed, and the ruined lanista ignored us. The slaves concealed their mirth, knowing that to laugh at Publius was to risk a blow.

"The problem today is that some families are very new," said Publius, the remark being intended for Varro, who thought this more amusing.

"Publius, this may shatter your perception of me, but I have been known to lie. The arena is the greatest lie of all. How many times have I refused the wooden sword, saying I would rather die gloriously before my beloved Romans than accept the serenity of a retired life? Do you believe that?"

"That's for the mob. Every sane Roman coddles the mob, although I think a stiff dose of Roman steel would be better. Yet that is another thing. A Roman's word to a Roman is what I talk about."

"You want to hear a Roman's word to a Roman, Publius?"

"Yes," he said.

"No," I said.

"That's incredibly Greek," said Publius.

We heard yelling close outside in the passageway. Several hard raps came at the door. No thud of a ram. The men sat in a semicircle around the door. Should it be rammed successfully, we did not wish to be thrown into chaos by our own men being hurled backwards into the rest of us. We could use this semicircle as a barrier and a successful one at that. For this, I wore a light chest of armor. Varro stood to my left, and Publius, with a short sword, wedged his way to the right side of the door, where he assumed there would be the most action.

"I will show you how a Roman dies," said Publius.

"You have already shown us how a Roman eats, gossips, and drinks," said Varro.

"Quiet, Varro," I said.

Through the stone an occasional cry could be heard. There were many calls for mothers, a thing common to dying people of any age. Someone poured liquid into a goblet.

"Water or wine?" I asked.

"Wine," came the voice of Publius.

"No more wine for anyone," I said. I heard no more pouring. Publius was drinking unwatered wine.

"Can I leave?" asked the lanista.

"No. The bodies will be there later," I said, meaning that I understood he wanted to get to the possessions of the dead before the gangs.

The body pressed against the slit muffled the sounds.

"See if you can move that body up there, Plutarch," I asked. We heard the sound of a spear against stone looking for a hole, then dull, small thuds, and a grunt from a man putting weight behind the spear.

"Dead," said Plutarch. "Won't move."

Because of the blockage of the slit, we did not know when it would become dark, so I forced a longer wait.

Finally, I told the slaves to open the door. This they did with the help of swords used as pries. The stench of flesh where it had been burned by pitch started someone wretching behind me.

"Body," said Plutarch.

Apparently, someone using pitch against the door had been pushed into his own flames and death. I felt the door. It was charred and sticky. A piece of skin came off on my fingers. I rubbed it back into the door. The water had been a good precaution.

We had survived. We proceeded with the armored slaves ahead of us and behind us. Publius complained of the slow pace, although he knew as well as anyone that should we move quickly we would attract as much attention as if someone yelled. And attention meant people, and people meant the mob.

In the arena, where the mob had milled, we saw the empty movement of the wounded. The groans came like the winds. The sand smelled of urine and retching fear. Publius stepped on a small child and wanted to take it until Varro pressed Publius' hand to the child's belly. It was cold.

It is the children who suffer most in these incidents, most often trampled to death when trying to hold on to their mothers. Publius threw it away, as though stained. In a short while it would be stiff. The bodies would be removed, and the arena cleaned with fresh sand, and whatever was burning would be quenched, and whatever was burned would be rebuilt. Thus was Rome, queen of cities, center of the world, invincible. Eternal, because it was always born again.

Within days the emperor and senate would offer up some object for hate, and blame that on the riot, so that emperor and senate would not have to face the citizenry. I was sure that the aedile was dead. He could not have escaped. When we left the tunnel and walked onto the sand, I saw that no one around him had escaped, including those who were first to attack him. I could tell this by the piles of bodies mounted around his seats.

We moved to an exit out of the plebeian seats, and when a slave reported the mobs were off beyond the Capitoline, all of us moved quietly, surrounded by my armored slaves, off towards the Colossus of Nero near the Flavian amphitheater, beyond which is my house with the high walls and large arbor and warren of small, protected streets to delay the easy speed of a mob.

"My house is that way," said Publius, pointing beyond the gates of the city.

"Yes," I said.

"They are waiting for all of us. I have promised, on your promise. My brother comes from Hippo by sea, just for the sight of you and your fame. I told them you were my friend."

"Publius, even if we would not have to hack our way through a mob to reach your house, dear Publius, friend Publius, I wish to go to my home, not yours."

"You promised," said Publius.

"Quiet," said Varro.

"To the dung of Mars's ass, I will not quench the fire of my tongue," said Publius, and his voice boomed above the groans of the streets of Rome. "You're coming because you promised, and I do not fear some goat rabble of a mob. I am Roman."

"Publius, shh. Still your mouth. I am not going. Now get back with us. You stay with me until a new day," I said.

"Is that your last word?" said Publius.

"Last," I said.

"Greekling," he yelled, and I found myself cuffing him across the face, perhaps because the word offended me, but mostly because it was loud, and in this sort of a city one attracted attention as one would the threat of crucifixion.

To most men, a slap would be cause for anger. To Publius, it seemed like an offense against the gods. He threw his short sword at me, and it bounced off a slave. He demanded an apology. He demanded my life. He damned the life of every Greek ever born of a she-goat. Which, of course, was every Greek, yes, including Alexander who probably was not Greek in the first place but a Scythian or a German. Otherwise, why would he have had yellow barbaric hair?

"Get back with us, Publius," I said.

He began a speech about living life as a Roman, and, since the slaves in front had already started a healthy pace into the streets, I could not stay to reason with him. Varro whispered that young Publius had been drinking unwatered wine as he waited for the mob to pass earlier in the afternoon.

I thought I had heard him yell apologies. But it would not matter. I was sure he would engage some other drunk that night and spill his blood in some useless fight over who had the right of way in an alley both would vacate shortly, or who had looked at whom first. He did not. In his drunken anger, heated from the first insult by a slave, to our last words, and constantly fueled by wine, Publius preserved his life long enough to ruin both of ours ultimately.

It would have been expected that Publius would waste his own life, it being a race between the inordinately good fortune that had kept him alive so far and his incredible lack of moderation as to which would triumph first. But I, Lucius Aurelius Eugenianus? Friend of Domitian? Seducer of the mobs? Owner of latifundia and slaves the size of nations? I, who stood beneath the protection of the influence of the Aurelii? I, who myself had become a powerful patron of many?

I, Lucius Aurelius Eugenianus, chest to chest in the same arena with Publius? Piddling Publius? Scented, squeaky-voiced, intemperate Publius?

CHAPTER

V

At the Dominican convent in Ringerike, a suburb of Oslo, a small package from Dr. Semyon Petrovitch of the great University at Oslo waited in the office of the mother superior.

Strangely, it was stamped confidential; and if it were like the other mail for Sister Olav, the mother superior would have opened it. This would not have been an invasion of privacy because there was no privacy to invade—privacy being one of the distractions on the grand journey to one's Maker if one chose the way of the contemplative life. But "confidential" it was stamped. And this made it like almost everything else in Sister Olav's religious life—different.

But like everything else with Sister Olav, there seemed to be some complication. The order had paid a great deal for her studies at Oxford, and then she had requested to be a contemplative, which meant no use of that education through teaching. The mother superior was not sure how Sister Olav had managed this, but even in becoming a contemplative, decreed by the metropolitan of Oslo, there had been a further complication. She would teach one year in preuniversity courses at local schools while living at the convent and then teach no more and become like the rest of the sisters under the mother superior. If a woman who had declined a doctorate from a great British university could ever be like women from these Scandinavian countries, who had no university training, many coming to the convent in their teens, like the mother superior, who had come so long ago and who had suggested that Sister Olav might be more suited for another calling. At least another convent. She was also twenty-one, older than other novitiates. And when she would take the fifth and final vow of the order, she would be twenty-nine, older still.

The mother superior and the package waited for Sister Olav in the barren office with white walls and the somber, black crucifix riveted into the stone of the building like a parapet from which one did not retreat.

"I'm sorry, Mother Superior," said Sister Olav, "for being late. And I will be late again for my class."

Sister Olav was pale, paler than most of this Nordic people, with skin so light it looked like clear white porcelain, setting off the lips as pink, although there was, of course, no lipstick. Yet it looked as though she wore it, and the mother superior caught herself staring at Sister Olav's lips when she first arrived, stopping herself from saying there was no need for makeup in a convent. The eyebrows were pale to whiteness, two almost invisible strokes above light blue eyes that somehow had to carry an intensity unnatural for their coolness. If it were not for the total involvement in almost every word she uttered, Sister Olav would have been an incredible beauty. But the force of the woman overpowered features, even those as elegant as Sister Olav's, set like a jewel in stark black habit.

"I have a package that is marked confidential. Is there any reason you know of that I should not open it?"

"No, Mother Superior."

The older woman nodded. Sister Olav was almost Swedish in her accent, which was quieter than the normal Norwegian pronunciation of words. Although a Norwegian girl, it was rumored Sister Olav's family had moved to Sweden to get a better early education.

The package appeared overly wrapped and required scissors. The mother superior snipped down into a letter covering another box.

"You have no objections to my reading this, then?"

"I have no private life and do not want one."

"Good," said the mother superior. "This is from the University in Oslo. I see it is from the hospital attached to it. Dr. Semyon Petrovitch, which is a Russian name. A department of cryonics medicine, and it begins, 'My Dear Dr. Marit Vik, Your name has been given me by a professor of the Romance languages as a possible authority on the language being spoken in the enclosed tape recordings. It is believed that the language might contain some Latin root, and you are recommended most highly.

" 'I have two apologies. One for the tape recordings themselves. They are bad because the person is mumbling, possibly incoherently. Secondly, my apologies for asking that you treat this in strict confidence, as I am working on a scientific experiment which could be compromised by commercialism and publicity. If you can identify any word, we would be most appreciative.

" 'I am yours truthfully, Dr. Semyon Petrovitch.' "

The mother superior concluded the letter and then inquired who the professor was who both knew and recommended Sister Olav.

"I did not know you had a Ph.D.," added the mother superior.

"I don't. It was probably a student I knew who assumed I had accepted my doctorate and now is undoubtedly a professor near here. I am not sure who."

"One meets so many people when one travels so much," said the mother superior. "Do you think you should listen to the tape recordings? I am sure we can get a player somewhere."

"I don't know."

"Why don't you know?"

"Because I am late for my class."

"Then do not let me detain you longer," said the mother superior.

Sister Olav rushed to the classroom. She had not mentioned why she was late. It would have embarrassed her. Today, and for the rest of the semester, the class would read and translate the *Aeneid*. She especially loved the poet Vergil, and loved best the *Aeneid*, and when she had begun to read, preparing for today's class, she had not stopped reading until, while pondering one passage about time, she had realized she had forgotten the time and looked at her wristwatch. Other than the mother superior, she was the only sister with one.

"Oh," she had said. And was stopped on her way to class to answer questions about a package. When she arrived at the room, there was a substitute civil teacher, who was overly polite in assuring Sister Olav her tardiness was no great thing. Like other Scandinavian countries, Norway was overwhelmingly Protestant, and, the religious wars having ended centuries before, the residual contempt had been composted into an overripe courtesy, nourishing massive blossoms of delicate human concern. One could not walk through quickly without damaging, if one were in a rush. Like now. For this class. "Thank you. Thank you. Thank you," said Sister Olav, as quickly as she could and as respectfully as she could and as firmly as she could. She turned to the class.

"My apologies for being late, especially today. I suspect some of you are wondering why we ran headlong into Vergil and into his *Aeneid,* instead of discussing the poet first. I had my reasons," said Sister Olav and gave the substitute civil teacher a very thankful nod as that woman finally shut the door behind her.

"When I first read this poet, it was like discovering sunlight. I find in Vergil the beauty of the discipline of Latin, the economy and genius of this language which gave a civilization and an organization to a world of warring tribes. In much of Europe, the Middle East, and the north of Africa, we see working remnants, like roads and aqueducts, of that civilization of almost two thousand years ago. Can any of you imagine a house built today lasting two thousand years, or a road? Vergil gives voice to their feelings of destiny and duty. How many of you felt this way about Vergil?"

Sister Olav looked around the class at the twelve teen-age students. This was a special class for advanced learners, the average student in this school not taking any Latin at all.

There were no hands.

"I am sorry," she said. And she was, for them. She began the famous lines of the great poem about the founding of Rome, "Arma virumque cano."

This poem she did not have to mentally translate into Norwegian. She knew the words and the meter and the meaning as one.

As she orated, she did not look at the slim, red-bound volume but recited from something deeper than memory.

She closed her eyes and drifted with the meter, almost like a child hearing a beloved aunt tell a familiar story, each word an old friend to be greeted again in proper order with other old familiar friends. But with this poem, like mature works, there always seemed to be a new dimension, a new reality from which to experience one's being.

Sister Olav knew she could most happily, in fact deliriously, live a life as a Latin scholar. And this was the problem.

The most threatening problem. It was the reason, too, why the metropolitan of Oslo allowed her, after so many thousands of pounds invested in her education, to abandon it as a danger to her soul. Her argument was quite simple.

She found herself uncontrollably thinking poetry during the Mass and more and more considered her religious duties an interference.

The metropolitan had asked her if she did not think that perhaps her calling was not the Dominican order but scholarship.

"I would lose my soul, Father," she had said. She did not call him by his more formal title. It was a powerful argument.

To be sure it was not a whim, she was told she would teach for a year while living in the Dominican convent at Ringerike. If at the end of one year she still felt the same, she would forgo her scholarship and become a contemplative, taking final vows for the order. Granted, this was rare, but so was the situation.

"A pity such a fine education cannot be used in this world without such a danger, Sister Olav," the metropolitan had said.

But it was a danger, as her tardiness this day had shown, and danger again as she realized she had taken the time of twelve students, sailing off into her own reverie on the magnificent winds for the *Aeneid*.

"Per," she said pointing to the first pair of eyes she met. "Please. The translation beginning with the first book."

"My apologies, Sister Olav, I did not prepare my translation. My father was ill last night, and we had problems at home with the plumbing, and my mother was ill, too. I am sorry."

"He is sorry he watched the television movie," said a girl viciously. The boy spun around briefly with a nasty look.

There was an explanation, he said. He did watch a movie, he said.

"But it was because it was about Rome, and I thought there

might be something I would miss, whereas with the wonderful poem of the *Aeneid,* and my favorite Roman poet who was born in 70 B.C. and died in 19 B.C. after writing . . ."

"The movie was about gladiators and killing and sex," said the girl.

"Whereas the *Aeneid,*" said the boy, "will be with us, forever and eternal, because Vergil is the greatest poet, like sunlight. Which I feel also. And the movie was so bad I am sure we will never see it again." He waited, wondering whether this surprisingly neat bit of dodging would work.

"It was an American movie," said the girl. "I turned it off, to do my studies. I am prepared, Sister Olav."

She had done him in again, thought the boy.

"Thank you," said Sister Olav. "But there is something more important going on here."

She pressed her hands over the slim volume. The room was warm on this chill day in the early spring. She spoke directly to the young man, Per, and she spoke slowly.

"You watched the movie because it was entertaining, and this unfortunately was not. Unfortunately for you, because I think this is better fare," she said tapping the book. "But since you watched a movie about gladiators, I think you should know most gladiators were slaves, and, more often than not, they were to the best of my knowledge often not the main attraction at the Roman games."

"This gladiator married the Christian and gave up killing," said the young man in defense of his misspent evening.

"Most of them did not have the right to give up anything. Most were slaves, and it was such a difficult life, free men would rarely stay in the arena when they had a choice. It was not like soccer or boxing."

"My father says the games were used as an opiate for the masses," said the girl, "to keep their minds off the class struggle."

"That is a Marxist interpretation, and while it has some validity, the games to the Romans meant different things at different times. At first they were religious, in honor of the dead, and they evolved into politics. But that's for historians. We are learning a language."

"She is anti-Christian, Sister," said Per, seeing a good way to retaliate against his tormenting classmate.

Sister Olav slapped her right hand forcefully on the book. "We have a choice here. Do we concentrate on the good things of

Rome, or do we waste this good morning on one of the more shameful aspects of Roman life, which I am not altogether well equipped to deal with? In other words, do we deal with the philosophies and legends of what many believe may have been the greatest civilization man has known, or do we deal with its garbage? That is the question. Glory or garbage. What do you want?"

Not a moment passed before the girl proclaimed she was not anti-Christian. "The gladiators and the lions and the tortures were all part of an oppressive slave society," she said.

"Gladiators were the best fighters in the world. They were real men. That's what you hate," said the boy.

"There were prostitutes under the seats, too," offered another boy.

"And animals that were trained like you wouldn't believe," said another young man, who had ponies on his father's farm.

In the back of the room, one girl, who tended to stare out the window in a dreamy state quite often, jumped in with facts about which races went into the arenas and how, when her father had taken her to France, there was still an arena left, but she didn't know if it was a fighting arena or a theater.

The period ended and no one translated the first sentence of the classic poem.

At the convent another package had arrived and the mother superior suggested that since Sister Olav did have the knowledge to possibly help the university, she should do it. Dr. Petrovitch, said the mother superior, was almost certain the language had some form of Latin base.

"There are many forms of Latin. It was the world's main language at one time," said Sister Olav.

"The university has also kindly sent us a machine to listen to the tape recording," said the mother superior, in a manner indicating that if the university people were nice enough to do one thing, then the convent should respond.

Sister Olav noticed that a tape was already in the recorder on the mother superior's desk. It was also a very cheap tape recorder, not like the ones linguists used.

The first tape was a mumble with a possible Latin word which was similar enough to any Romance language—French, Spanish, and the like—to make the pronunciation uncertain even with a good machine. The speaker, a man, said he was cold.

But on the second, a few words were clearer. Sister Olav's face reddened, and she cleared her throat. She inhaled the stale air deeply and felt a flush warm her from her toes to her forehead.

"Yes?" asked the mother superior, concerned.

"Where did this come from?" asked Sister Olav, her voice now demanding and not obedient.

"The university."

"May I see the postage mark?"

"It was Oslo. Why do you ask?"

This time the mother superior was stern.

"I have a class. And today we discussed the Roman games, and on this tape, as you may be aware, the Latin is first person, generally, and while the person is mumbling, it is clear the person considers himself a gladiator, or someone close to a gladiator, who is bargaining for his services. Moreover there is a reference to an emperor in the familiar."

"I didn't hear that. I am not totally ignorant of the language of the Church," said the mother superior. "Even though it is not classical Latin."

Sister Olav turned the plastic dial on the handle of the little tape recorder and replayed one word three times.

"He is praying to God," said the mother superior.

Sister Olav shook her head. "After the emperor Augustus, Roman emperors were considered divine, gods on earth. But do not look shocked. I think this is the work of one of my students and not a product of the university."

"How can you tell?"

"In the more coherent tape, there are five grammatical mistakes. Those youngsters have left their sloppy little fingerprints."

CHAPTER VI

Third Day — Petrovitch Report

Condition improved. Now critical. No paroxysmal ventricular tachycardia in last twenty-four hours. Tests for motor-nerve conduction velocity today. Astounding. Basic reflexes abnormally good. SGP-T level down. Liver function improving. EEG of brain activity, still inordinately intense. Important questions remain to be answered by American.

Some men are sentenced to the arenas, others are sold into it. Vergilius Flavius Publius talked his way in. Like a trireme adrift in a shifting sea, young Publius navigated his besotted way through a night that felled many an armored and cautious man.

Morning finding him alive and vocal, he attempted to share some master stroke for governing the empire with the senate of Rome. The senate, grappling with a city aflame, lacked its usual tolerance for wild schemes of drunken patricians and ejected him. Publius thereupon attempted to lecture slaves near the forum on the degeneracy of Roman virtue, this degeneracy being especially prevalent in the senate. He proclaimed the patrician class as being unworthy of the name Roman. He said the empire was being run by Greeklings. He said the greatest man in the empire was half-Greek and more Roman than all the senators set end to end. He praised my name. He cried. He cursed my name. The slaves, having duties, failed to pay Publius what he considered proper heed. He dismissed them as slaves. Slaves should act like slaves. It was when senators acted similarly that the empire was in trouble. Slaves and senators being unworthy of the beneficence of his genius, he stumbled his way through the smoldering city to the Circus Maximus where Domitian, who loves the races, was examining new horses. This was not a race day.

The praetorians, sensing a gift of a solution to a troubled city, allowed Publius entrance. Standing before the emperor, awash in wine and untethered confidence, Publius cautioned the divine Domitian to show more respect for the patrician class, lest he make a Caligula of himself. He noted Domitian's virtues and faults from weaning to administration, then passed out in his own vomit.

He recovered shortly, according to my informants, and was given more wine by a slave. A sober man would have taken good counsel of fear when he saw Domitian smile. Everyone of the arena knows he takes great pleasure in blood.

Nor did Publius wonder why an emperor would pay such respect to his words, thinking it a proper response in the natural order of things. Domitian said he always had a great respect for the Flavians, of whom Publius was one and thus a distant relative of Domitian himself. And, therefore, the emperor would not hold Publius to his word, especially one given in wine.

Publius answered that his word was the word of a Roman. A praetorian officer interrupted his divine emperor, and even this did not loosen some little stream of doubt in Publius' dam of confidence. The officer said the emperor should not hold a man so young to his word, a man who obviously had many years to go to reach his mature strength and skill.

And if this were not enough, yet did Domitian play his game out further. He argued with the praetorian, and there stood unsuspecting Publius, witnessing an emperor justifying himself to a bodyguard.

"Publius is a Roman," said Domitian. "A real Roman is born

with sharpened steel in his blood and a taste for combat in his liver. This is a Roman you worry about. If we had but a thousand Publiuses, no border would ever suffer trespass, nor barbarian muse some thought of confronting the eagles of Rome."

Publius weaved and was held steady by slaves. He said he had one regret and that was that there were no barbarians within his grasp. He would like to see the entire arena filled with Germans, yellow-haired and horrifying.

The emperor said this might be arranged after Publius fulfilled his promise, which the emperor would be willing to forget, since Publius was a patrician and perhaps did not wish to appear before multitudes in combat with only a Greek.

To this Publius answered, "Roman steel is Roman steel and cuts everywhere." While this was distinctly unclear to logical minds, Domitian interpreted it as Publius' being unwilling to desecrate a promise.

"You are matched individually with that Greek, Eugeni," said Domitian and then turned loudly upon his praetorian. "You see what a Roman promise is. It is greater than his life, greater even than Publius' friendship for that gladiator. This is a Roman you look upon. Look well, there are not too many surviving in the city today."

And Domitian called in many from outside to look upon a real Roman. He had senators witness this also as well as those of the equestrian class and, of course, the praetorians.

My informants and retainers had this news to me even while Publius stood before the gathering crowd. As each new citizen of importance heard this, an informant ran from the circus to my abode. This took some time because my city home was a well-fortified network. On the outer fringes were the tall buildings with living units stacked one upon another, a peculiarity of Rome, where space is so important that people would live vertically. Behind this square were what appeared to be wide avenues, but they all narrowed and turned into the one at the right of the square, so that, should a raging mob burst the outer perimeter, it would be fed like rivers into the wide avenues and then pressed rightward, which is the natural direction of people in hysteria. This would bring them into conflict with others of the mob also pressing rightward. One does not stop a strong force like a mob, one delays it and teases it elsewhere. The real entrances to my home were narrow passageways off these turning streets that led to the walls of my home which enclosed my gardens and sleeping cubicles and kitchens. From several cubicles there were also underground passageways that led outside the farthest tall buildings. When one depends on the mob for one's fame, one takes the proper precautions against its flittering affections.

Since there had been a night of riot, my informants were delayed at each perimeter, lest a disguised madman seek to enter. When you are part of so many people's thoughts and fancies, as am I, you have many strangers thinking themselves passionate friends or enemies without your slightest real collaboration. In any case, I was too late to stop what had begun.

My questions were brief. Who witnessed the promise? Which senator? Which equestrian? Which faction? Were there those who ridiculed the promise? Where did the patricians stand? Had this information become public knowledge yet? No matter, it would soon be so. When the sun was directly above us, I knew the fate of Publius was inevitable. I would have to kill him in the arena. I could not keep him out. I could not substitute some other combat or even provide games myself or help his family provide games.

Domitian had found in Vergilius Flavius Publius his distraction for a smoldering city: the arrogant patrician who would meet the mob's dear Eugeni. Eugeni, who had twice refused the wooden sword, who had proclaimed his greatest ambition was to please the people of Rome, who had often said publicly he had one fear and that was that his life should be wasted at the hands of invincible time instead of ending in the glory of the arena.

Of this absurdity and others like it was my fame made, and Domitian knew it well. Freedman Eugeni, who loved Rome with his life, would face individually an arrogant young patrician who disdained the people of Rome. The city would accept nothing less than his blood.

By the time Domitian's emissary arrived, I was prepared.

The emissary outlined Domitian's thinking: "By sponsoring the games himself, Domitian shows his love of the mobs; and since you will be matched with Vergilius Flavius Publius, our divinity puts further distance between himself and that distant relative."

"Domitian doesn't need distance. What greater love of the mobs than giving one's own because he has violated the sanctity of Rome?" I said.

The emissary quickly shook his head lest that idea linger in the air one moment too long. "One cannot get enough distance from that lad. Domitian will follow your match with bears, and—this is a good one—will hunt the bears himself from a platform. He will end the games with Jews, Germans, and criminals. The games will be in ten days. What do you think?"

"Ten days? Mars's ass. Ten days."

"Yes? No? What do you say?"

"It will need blood."

"We have it. There is a crime wave we are ending within days. There will be enough convicted criminals."

"You have the bears?" I asked.

"We have the bears."

"Bears, how?"

"We have them."

"How?"

"We had them. A transaction. The family that sponsored the disaster couldn't meet the price."

"The family that sponsored the disaster that started the riots wanted to add bears, and you held out for more money? You paid with a city instead."

"They didn't have money," he said.

"Yes, we all know that now," I said.

"Well? Ten days. What do you think?"

Kitchen slaves brought us fruit and wine and cheese. I drank water. Domitian's emissary commented on the quality of the wine and on the fact that I never drank even the gentlest of wines. He said Domitian believed I had stronger reasons than just my cautions for the arena, since a little wine fortified the liver. I raised my hand signifying I wanted to think.

Domitian's scheme showed a sound knowledge of the arena. My match with Publius would be talked about, discussed, and argued about and would become the major point of interest before the games. The match itself would be, of course, nothing, especially for a large arena where my skill and Publius' lack of it would barely show. But if it were followed quickly by Domitian hunting bears, to sustain interest, and then much blood at the end, the crowds would in all probability leave feeling well satisfied with the day.

Merely an unbalanced match between Publius and myself would

leave the crowd without the great discharge that comes from spectacle and blood. Domitian had arranged it all: interest, spectacle, and blood. And for his political purposes, he once again directed the mob's hostility towards the patrician class, his only real rival for power. Publius represented the patricians; I, the crowds.

"Good," I finally said.

"Domitian thinks you should add some extra device."

"What?" I said.

"He does not know."

"I will fight without wrappings around my loins," I said.

"That is only done in small arenas," he said.

"It will be good," I said. "It will signify that I came to Rome without even clothes, and the people gave me everything I have."

"Brilliant," he said. "Domitian's retainers will spread this word throughout the city."

"No. My retainers will. Your retainers will say Domitian will not allow this, and this will further heighten interest."

"Domitian will appreciate your risking your body."

"It is not great risk, and Domitian knows this. It is only in the mind that nudity is more dangerous than having light cloth."

"But might it not dangle in the way?"

"I am a man, not a horse. At the end of the match, Domitian will offer me the wooden sword again."

"And you will refuse again."

"No. This time I accept. Domitian will say he does not want the virtue of Eugeni desecrated by an inferior opponent as was witnessed here today, and he offers me the sword so that the purity of my glory will now belong to the gods and the people of Rome eternal. He asks the mob if they agree, and I succumb to their will. I say no twice, the mob screams yes, and Domitian himself descends to the arena to hand me the wooden sword personally. He presses my left hand around it, and, in confusion and despair, I begin to fall on my real sword. Domitian gets in between me and my sword. I kiss his feet. He raises me, I weep profusely. He walks me around the arena, his arm over my shoulder, and we both ascend to his seat—emperor and his devoted gladiator. There he makes me a senator by his decree and the voice of the people. During the captives or criminals, I attempt to return to the arena but Domitian stops me. He must stop me. This is important because with barbarians one doesn't know what pointed weapon goes flying around."

"You're accepting the wooden sword? You are finished with the arena?"

"Yes," I said.

"But you arrange your own matches. You are leaving fortunes lying fallow."

"It is not that profitable. My wealth is more rumor than real. You and Domitian should know how worthless is free information."

"But you received great latifundia for your brief efforts yesterday," he said. "We know because we are seizing the late sponsor's property, and you left nothing."

"The latifundia's value is that they are contiguous to other lands I have."

"They came with slaves and water rights."

"Oh, did they?" I said surprised. "That is Greek business, and I do not follow it that well. I am so poor at figures, I do not ask gold or any other wealth from Domitian for the match he has arranged."

"You ask for the wooden sword."

"Which Domitian, before the people, gives as the instrument of their will. He wins greater favor from the mob for this."

"Domitian will not like losing you."

"He will love the gesture of saving me from taking my own life, I, so despairing of leaving the arena and the people I love."

"Why do you want to leave now?"

"I am old. I should have left before. Any fool can ride the chariots of victory. It takes judgment to get off at the right time."

"You were old yesterday, Eugeni," said the emissary shrewdly. "And you will be only ten days older when you mount to the right hand of the emperor and your senate seat. It is not you who have changed."

I denied this, but he was right, of course. It was not my thirty-three years. The crowds had changed and had been changing for years, and one day just for the pique of it they would call lions or elephants to be loosed on me. When I had begun, crowds threatened to become a mob if things went wrong. Now they entered the arena as a mob. When I had begun my journey with the sword, owned by the Aurelii, a quick accidental kill, even in the great arena, would cause a few groans, maybe even applause for the speed of it. But today it was all spectacle and farce, and a sponsor without elephants was lost.

It was time I had gone.

On the second day, my retainers picked up the first stories of Publius' family's attempting to offer me a fortune not to appear in the arena with Publius. This was even discussed privately in the senate, I found out from two senators in my debt. If they were not in the senate, they would publicly be called my retainers. They asked if I had any special action I wished them to take in the senate, any stories to be confided to others. I said no.

On the third day, Publius secretly examined armor: Greek, hoplite, secutor, and Roman legionnaire—the last never seen in the arena because of its bulkiness. In that afternoon, he stored away the hoplite and secutor armor. I was asked by one of my people if I wished the armor cunningly damaged in any special spot and covered with colored wax. I said no. I was also asked if I wanted his water drugged at the arena. I said no. Nor did I want some beam accidentally to fall on his sword arm.

"It will be hard enough getting him to move properly," I said.

On the fourth day Publius was well into training. He took not even heavily watered wine. The family had hired an old veteran of the Twenty-second Prim. Genia, which had been stationed facing the barbarians in Germany, under the theory that any lanista would be in the reach of my influence. The centurion, who had campaigned with one of the lesser Flavian generals, could not be bribed to discuss his methods. But he drank much and talked freely. He told many that Vergilius Flavius Publius might have a little surprise for that breast sucker and his old muscles.

On the fifth day, Domitian's emissary returned to tell me that Domitian's sources had just found out Publius would appear in legionnaire armor.

"Oh," I said.

"I hear that the young man has surprising strength," said the emissary. "And speed. Accidents can happen, Eugeni."

"Not in my arena," I said.

"Perhaps, some drugging at the last moment?"

"No!" I said angrily. "He will be wearing regulation legionnaire armor. My problems will be getting him to move in it, not slowing him down. Domitian knows I am a prudent man and a cautious one. Yet, even if I were weaponless, I could not fall before Publius. And this is not a boast. I am not boastful, as Domitian knows."

The emissary apologized for his foolishness, and I said that foolishness discussed openly ceases to be foolishness. I asked him why Domitian had spread rumors of a great family bribe.

"To ensure that you will be there to kill little Publius."

"My life and fortune are not enough," I said laughing.

"Publius is a friend of your wife and son, we hear."

"He was, yes."

"Then forgive us, because when it comes to your wife, no one advances past your atrium for business, into your peristilium," he said, pointing behind my shoulder where farther back the living quarters of my house were.

"I don't understand," I said.

"We do not know of anyone but Publius who has seen your wife."

"Our slaves see her every day."

"In proper society."

"We rarely participate."

"Strange, yes?" said the emissary.

"She is a wife," I said and made sure to smile. "My family is my family. My son goes to proper tutors and returns home. I live here, my son lives here, my wife lives here. The arena can see all of me it wants. This is my home."

"It is that valuable?" asked the emissary. Domitian and his servants always look for that weak area they think of as love, especially in people they need.

"It is a home," I said with a touch of drudgery in my voice. "Where the proper things are done in private. My son's first beard is to be shaved, and we will have proper ceremonies. It is a family."

"Domitian respects the family. It is a building block of the empire, as important in its quiet ways as the games. This match is important to Domitian. Strange things happen when gladiators make friends of gladiators."

I showed a bit of anger. "This is the arena. If I loved Publius to my very bones, it would not matter. The arena is the arena.

The greatest lie of all is that gladiators do not make friends of gladiators. It is no more true than that every match is a man fighting for his life. The mobs wants Publius' life. If Domitian himself warily serves the mob, who am I to oppose it?"

"You do love Publius?" said the emissary.

"Yes, and I tell you this openly so that Domitian will cease to suspect me and cease spreading lunatic rumors that he thinks protect him."

"Is that what you wish me to tell him?" said the emissary.

"Absolutely and do not get a word wrong."

When he heard this accusation, Domitian laughed, I found out later. He told a praetor from Gaul that I would have made an excellent emperor, if not born to the arena, and himself an excellent gladiator, if not born to Vespasian and the princeps, which is another word for emperor.

I received reports of this over three days in varying shades, the most accurate being from a slave who earned his peculium from one of Demosthenes' financial units. (The peculium is that fund by which a slave may buy his freedom.) With Demosthenes, this fund was quite naturally one of the larger fortunes of the city and yet still not enough to equal his worth or the price he himself had set.

It was clear. I was leaving the arena. This was the good opportunity and something that required other things to be ended also. Demosthenes had earned his freedom, not in what he could buy, but in what he had given.

And so with great formality I went to his main countinghouse, which on the outside appeared like one of the finer buildings, marble not brick, but on the inside was a poorly lit, confusing hive of busy clerks. Demosthenes trusted no one, and while some slaves appeared to be loitering, they really were watching other slaves. In turn, these too were watched.

The building smelled like an overworked armpit. It was hard to breathe. In deference to my own slaves, I kept them outside. Where the peristilium should have been open to the sky and where sunlight should have bathed fresh green plants, there were darkness and vertical wooden boxes.

Demosthenes had been told I was coming, and he greeted me in his own room, sealed off by a door as though it were facing a street, or sealing off a tunnel for defense.

"Demosthenes, I come here today to honor you. I come here today to thank you and do homage to you and your gods, for truly you are a glory unto your manhood and your people and your friends."

"Yes? What is it?"

The room was lit with foul-smelling lamps using the cheapest oils. His eyes glanced at scrolls piled at his side on a broad wooden table with pegs that held the scrolls secure. How a man could read so much in a lifetime, I did not know.

"Get the disk that came around your neck when I purchased you. I will break it with my own hands. We will do this before a magistrate. You are free. Your peculium is yours for your wealth. You have given me more than wealth, you have given me loyalty and your great cunning."

"There's nothing more than wealth," said Demosthenes. "As for the disk, it is somewhere, and we'll have a magistrate do the proper notations later. Now, is there anything else?"

"I am freeing you in honor also of my son's first beard. You will in freedom, I hope, serve him when the time comes as well as you have served me."

"Good. Is there anything else?"

"I am freeing you, Demosthenes. You might show a bit of joy, at least at the fortune you have saved yourself."

"It is logical that you free me, and I expected it, Eugeni. I have served you well, and I am just about the only man in the empire who could do what I do. This is so. And I do it free or slave, because as your slave I am really free."

"That moves me deeply, Demosthenes."

"Because you are half-Roman and therefore half-idiot," he said. "You have given me what I want. I am princeps of this fortune."

"You might want to indulge yourself with some of it."

"A waste. Here I am conqueror of the world, not the Roman. But I accept your offer; send me that woman slave in your house."

I did not understand. There were many women in my house. "Which?"

"The one who followed you into the vestibule once. Barbaric eyes."

"Green blue?"

"Yes," said Demosthenes.

A trumpeting laugh filled me. "That is my wife."

Even in the lamplight a blush shone obvious on his face. He became even more interested in the table before him and between us.

"I'm sorry. I'm sorry, dominus," he said, giving me fórmal title of owning him.

"Dominus, no longer," I said.

"I am sorry, Eugeni."

"Never apologize for good taste." It was hard to breathe, and yet there was more we had to discuss. The coming match was my last, and there would be some necessary financial arrangements. Demosthenes saw this right away.

"He won't settle for a performance," said Demosthenes, as we walked out into a small passageway, open to the sky but for a small iron grate. Standing underneath that grate, as raw sewage splashed out between our feet, I realized again what was so obvious. Men often enslave themselves in conditions far more difficult than another master might inflict.

"Domitian's emissary has not asked for extras, yet," I said.

"Ten million sesterces for that wooden sword. Ten million. Not a copper, not a grain less, not a handful of soil less. Ten million."

"Five at the most. At the most. Maybe six if I lose my wits," I said and guided him back to his stuffy room.

"No. No. Domitian moved on that sponsor's family's land immediately and found out we had it before the games. Our divinity has been seizing estates furiously. I say he sees assassination plots against him so he can seize the estates. He needs money," said Demosthenes.

"Too many rich men are still rich. The poor are sentenced to the arena or the cross along with the rich. Many of the plots are real. Ask Tullius."

"I don't trust Tullius. He likes too many little boys too often. He is a loyal freedman, but he is not one of us." By that he meant Tullius was Roman without Greek ties.

"You sound Roman in your virtue."

"Everything is money. Domitian will move on your estates."

"He can't find them all. He will not kill the cow that freely gives him milk," I said.

"And so freely. Ten million. I should have it bagged already."

"Do you ever smile, Demosthenes?"

"What for?"

His voluminous accounts were so neatly rolled on this large table between us. I could not resist suddenly reaching over and scattering them. They were for my service, of course, but I just had to do it. Any other man on his day of freedom would be drunk.

"Laugh, Demosthenes. The world is funny."

He screamed at me, ordering me out.

"I will do it because you are a freedman," I said with a great smile.

"You will do it because I demand it."

"No. Because you are free. It is an important thing." I threatened another fastidious pile of round scrolls, and Demosthenes succumbed.

"All right. Because I am free," he said.

"Good day, freedman. Always free in my heart, always with respect in my heart."

"Get out."

I demolished another pile of accounts. He threw a sella at me, very clumsily.

"Should have been a stylus, Demosthenes. You never miss with an account."

"You may just have misplaced twice Domitian's fee by your insanity," he said, pointing to a corner of the table now empty.

"Quiet or I'll burn them."

"I'll burn you and your muscles," answered Demosthenes.

"Money does not burn."

"Money does everything, Eugeni. Get out. Go play with your swords and your politics. A man of thirty-three. Shameful."

"Thirty-one," I said.

"Thirty-three and every day of it."

He says thirty-three, but he says it from corners of the room. The room smells. But smells differently. It is not the smells of ink and must and scrolls and human sweat never aired.

It is a strange smell. Demosthenes, poor Demosthenes is not there. He could not be there. What I did to poor Demosthenes. It serves me right to hear him call after me that I am thirty-three. But how would he have known? I did not know with certainty how old I was, only approximately.

It is just punishment that I lie here in pain. Can I see? Is that a figure talking. Yellow hair. No, it cannot be. She wears pure white. And her hair is light yellow and her skin pale as death. And yet in white like any ranking toga.

Perhaps not death, but madness.

CHAPTER VII

"Publes, Publi?" Lew McCardle was confused. "No. There was no one I knew by that name. No. No one at the site, I think. I didn't know all the names, but I would have remembered that one."

Dr. Petrovitch appeared deeply concerned. His hand rested on the tape recorder that had played that name. It had come from what Dr. Petrovitch had described as "a constant conversation, almost a reliving of something."

He played the tape again. He smoked. Lew could sense Dr. Petrovitch was examining him as much as listening to the tape. They were in Dr. Petrovitch's small office—Dr. Petrovitch behind his desk, Lew in a chair, fidgeting. He had purchased a pair of bluish slacks and a gray sports jacket that almost went with the slacks three days before, when the home office told him to wait at his hotel for further instructions.

"Before returning to the site?" he had asked.

"Wait," he was told. That was two days ago, and he considered buying another jacket, one that might go with the pants, if he had to wait another day. It was hard finding big men's clothes, even in Norway.

Petrovitch's office was a collection of official plaques of recognition, Western comfort technology such as quartz lighters, digital clocks, and an electrically powered plastic statue of a little boy about to relieve himself. The boy shot whisky from his organ when you pressed his red cap. McCardle had seen one once in the duffle bag of a rigger. He didn't know bad taste could be that well exported.

Petrovitch played the tape. It was a man mumbling. "Yes?" said McCardle, confused by the strange mumbling sounds. Why should it be played for him?

"Do you recognize that voice?"

"No."

"When did he injure himself?"

"I don't know, Dr. Petrovitch."

"You didn't hear him call out, Pubbly, Pubbles, Pubble?"

"I heard."

"Was that the man who killed him? Or who you thought killed him or—let us be realistic—tried to kill him? Eh?"

"Eh, what?"

"Eh, attempted to kill?"

"No."

"How do you know?" asked Petrovitch.

"I don't know," said McCardle.

"What if I said you had a wounded worker, perhaps frostbitten, perhaps with serious exposure, and you did not want for one reason or another to risk an investigation. Maybe you even thought the body was dead. How to get rid of it? Well, why not science?"

"Do you think that, Dr. Petrovitch?"

"I think we have a very peculiar body, speaking a language we are just beginning to identify. I think you owe me explanations now."

"I discovered it at eight point two meters, guaranteed in glacial ice. Guaranteed."

"This was not the first attempt to kill John Carter."

"His name is John Carter?" asked McCardle.

Dr. Petrovitch shook his head. "I have named him tentatively. I want you to look at it. I want to show you a peculiar body."

They had to take an elevator downstairs and go across a park in the cold weather to reach the hospital, where a doctor grabbed his arm to shake his hand and congratulate him.

"Don't believe wild rumors," Dr. Petrovitch said. "Give me time. Just time. Thank you." He dismissed the man by not waiting for an answer but plowing on through the corridors with McCardle at his side.

"I hope to get my office into the hospital," said Petrovitch, "or get hospital facilities into my office building. They have me stretched out here. But the hospital facilities are good. Excellent."

John Carter, as he was listed as a patient in the hospital, had a private room at the end of a hall, with special equipment from the intensive-care unit.

"I am exercising a bit of discretion," confided Petrovitch. "Secrecy if you will. Why not give him an American name, eh?" The name on the door was listed as "Carter, John," and his doctor, "Petrovitch, Semyon." The disease was, innocently enough, "frostbite."

When Petrovitch opened the door, a person stumbled backwards out into the hall like a pea from a too-tight plastic bag. The room was packed.

White-coated medical personnel, a few secretaries, and a young, very blond man—whom Dr. Petrovitch identified to Lew McCardle as someone who should know better—filled the room like a clandestine party.

Petrovitch, in faltering Norwegian—faltering because it had to bear rivers of anguish—explained to everyone that they were being unscientific, that they were ruining chances of a scientific approach to anything, and that they did not understand what had happened; their very presence was both harmful to the process and to the patient.

"That's the man who found him," said someone in English, pointing to Lew.

McCardle couldn't see the patient through the upright bodies, but he did see the top of a plastic tent.

"You should be ashamed, all of you," said Petrovitch. "All of you."

"Why are you hiding your achievement, Dr. Petrovitch?" asked another nurse.

"Because we don't know what exactly we have achieved. Now, please. You will all know everything, when we know."

"I am sorry," said the young, very blond doctor. "We have been unprofessional. The excitement got to us, so to speak."

"That is when you need to be a professional," said Dr. Petrovitch. He squeezed the arm of the doctor, and winked. And to the little crowd in the room: "We really don't know what we have. Please, give us time."

"Was he frozen, really, in ice?" asked a young secretary, but the cold disapproving stares of her colleagues quieted her, and a flush filled her cheeks so suddenly they could have made noise. "Sorry," she said with a squeak and put her hand over her mouth.

Dr. Petrovitch waited for the room to empty.

The little fellow breathed with a faint wheeze in a clear plastic oxygen tent. His cheeks appeared raw where the nurse had wiped away vomit in the hyperbaric chamber two days ago. Clear plastic tubes ran up his nostrils. Lew got his first good look at the man. He had high cheekbones and now had the beginnings of a stubble of a beard. He was quite muscular, and now Lew saw a healed welt on his right side. The scars on his right forearm and left shoulder appeared raised, like pale ribbons. A small microphone hung from the top of the oxygen tent down above the mouth. It was attached to a running tape recorder.

"The problem with anything to do with cryonics is the mystery attached to it. They think miracles. There is no such thing as a miracle," said Petrovitch. "Yet here they are like children, looking at a body in intensive care, when we have a whole hospital of them. But this one, they said, was dead, so we have a miracle. Not so, Dr. McCardle. Not so. Now what really happened?"

"What I told you, Dr. Petrovitch."

Petrovitch looked deep inside, into the inner space that has no dimension. It was a thought poised in time.

"Nude, eight point two meters, eh?"

"Yes."

"Some other mysteries, we have, Dr. McCardle. The man has scars."

"I see. I've been looking at them. They seem raised, Dr. Petrovitch."

"Because those wounds have not been sewn but have been cauterized. It is an ugly way to heal a wound, by burning oil or some substance. It is a painful way. I do not know of anyone who does it that way today. Do you know how it got those wounds?"

"No. I said I found it, Dr. Petrovitch."

"Yes, that is what you said, and I had hoped you would help clear this up now and get it out of the way. Nevertheless, you have enough to do."

Petrovitch reached into the cabinet under the tape recorder. Inside was a box with about forty cassettes. Lew saw labels of time. Apparently, the people here had been recording every minute of the little fellow's mumbling.

"I want your word as a scientist that you do not know this man and really did discover him in the ice you delivered him in. I need that now. I need your word, Dr. McCardle."

"Well, yes, you have it. I gave it. It's so."

"All right, I accept it. We will proceed under that assumption. We have other questions that just need answering desperately, such as why the knuckle on the right hand was not set correctly? And it has the strangest set of calluses I have ever seen, on the inside of the right hand and the back of the left hand. I have never seen calluses on the back of the hand like that.

"And it's got two burn welts just beneath its ribs on its right side. I don't know what put them there."

Lew McCardle shrugged. He wasn't following the conversation. He had thought Dr. Petrovitch was suspicious about something, then he felt he was part of Dr. Petrovitch's project, and now he got the tapes pushed into his hands.

"He has been talking a mile a minute. He is reliving something. It tortures him. The language is not Italian, nor is it Spanish but close to both of them."

"Why are you giving me these?" asked Lew, looking at the tapes in his hand.

"To help with the translation."

"I'm leaving today, Dr. Petrovitch."

Petrovitch looked puzzled. "I am sorry. Then my embassy must be wrong. They said you would be working with me handling the nonmedical, nonscientific sort of things."

McCardle put the tapes back in the Russian's hands.

"Sorry," he said.

"I must know where you found him then. I must know before you leave."

"I can't tell you that for a while. All my information is owned by my company."

"And therefore," said Dr. Petrovitch, rising to the attack, "I must assume you had an injured man and, not wanting the publicity or notoriety, quietly pretended he was frozen."

"That is ridiculous, doctor."

"Then why are you reluctant to tell me where?"

"Because it's company policy."

"Well, that leaves me high and dry, Dr. McCardle. I need your supportive data, and I cannot fathom why you would deny them to me unless there is some unpleasant explanation."

"I see your point, doctor," said McCardle. "I am retiring very soon. I will have plenty of time to give supporting data then. Write to me, Houghton Oil, Houston, Texas, U.S.A., and I will give you all the supporting data you need. And more than that, Houghton will probably give you some funds because we do like to be known as the committed company." McCardle spoke softly and slowly, trying to give reassurance from his voice.

Dr. Petrovitch squinted his face suspiciously, then shook hands.

"Thank you anyhow. And thank you. Thank you for the specimen."

The body jerked and with a voice distant in its own belly called out what sounded like "Meramney, Meramney, Meramney," and then it was quiet. Dr. Petrovitch observed secretions from the corner of the eyes of the body, as though it were crying. Petrovitch noted that, mentioning that certain glands now worked, on a chart on a table beside the bed. He looked at his watch and also wrote down the time and the date.

"The language, again, escapes us," said Dr. Petrovitch. "But never mind. That is our problem. Do you have cars at your home?"

"Yes, two."

"Do they drive well?"

"I don't know. My wife and daughters use them."

"Do they have tape recorders and radios in them?"

"I don't know, but probably. I haven't been home for a while."

"And bars with whiskey."

"I doubt it," said Lew.

"I may be able to visit some day. That would be nice."

"If you do, come on down, as we say."

Back at the Hotel Haakon, Lew found his room had been changed to a suite, and he tried to explain to the concierge that he couldn't afford a suite, had not ordered one, and was moving out, probably this evening.

The concierge said if he wished he could check out whenever he wished, but that he was now in the main suite. It was paid for, and they were most happy to have him.

In the living room of the suite, Lew McCardle found out why. It was one of the major shocks of his life.

"Oh," he said, when he saw the elderly man rise to greet him with a wide-open, friendly grin and an outstretched hand.

"Oh," said Lew, standing confused in the doorway and not knowing whether to enter without an invitation. "I have permission, instructions rather, in writing saying I was supposed to leave the site. It's in writing from the superintendent, sir."

And as soon as Lew had said that, he realized how silly it was. And he was further put off by the friendliness. James Houghton Laurie III, chairman of the board of Houghton Oil himself, was inviting Lew into the suite.

"Lew, you ol' Maky, where'd yew get thet gawdawful jacket, boy? Take it off before anyone finds out you're working for us. They'll think we've gone dust-bowl broke down at Houghton," said Laurie, getting up out of a soft chair to shake the hand of Lew McCardle and suggesting they put some good sour-mash whiskey into the boy's stomach before they talked of the problems of the world and of Houghton and of Lew McCardle. Just two old Makys —Maky being the nickname of Texas Mechanical and Christian College, known for its sometimes very good football teams, its relatively good petroleum engineers, and the fact that until the 1960s every student had to attend Sunday services, drunk or sober, sick or well. Houghton Oil underwrote Texas Mechanical and Christian.

"These fancy, spiffed-up foreign hotels drain my blood. C'mon in, Lew, and let's put some good whiskey in our bellies before they dry up from the piss these damned Norwegians try to pass off as booze."

"Yes, sir," said Lew. And he wondered whether he should have brought his discharge paper from the site up with him from the hotel safe, or whether he should mention it all again.

"Good to see a Maky face," said Laurie. "Especially when there's trouble."

While both he and Laurie could call themselves Makys, Lew had attended that school, while Laurie, who had gone to Harvard, sat on the board of directors with other Lauries and other Houghtons. In 1907 a Houghton did actually attend Texas Mechanical and Christian for a semester.

It remained a school where Houghtons and Lauries got employees, not their educations.

Yet, they had boasting rights to the old campus. And when they wanted to be down-home, so to speak, they were Makys.

"With or without water, Lew?" asked James Houghton Laurie. He had his hand on a crystal tumbler, and he half-filled it with dark Tennessee sipping whiskey. The room had gilt-edged furniture with several small marble-topped tables and delicate painted chairs, the sort Lew McCardle sat on gently, testing whether it was really made for sitting.

Mr. Laurie could talk Texas or he could talk Wall Street. He looked like a sweet old man with a gentle tan and age spots and a smile like a red old crease going across his face. He wore a soft white shirt with a blue polka-dot tie, gray, soft trousers, and casual black shoes. His jacket was thrown over a chair.

If Lew were that rich and had gone to Harvard also, he thought, he would talk down-home Texas, too. He could afford to.

"Lew, we're on the three-yard line ready to score in the Cotton Bowl, and time is running out, and we're going in over your hole. What I'm asking for now, what we're all asking for, is some of that old blow-'em-out Lew McCardle blocking."

Mr. Laurie motioned McCardle to sit on a thin-spoked chair with delicate flowers painted on the legs. Lew sat. The chair held.

"Do you remember the Arkansas game? You must have knocked that defensive lineman ten yards back. I have never seen such a hole you gave to our running back."

"Did we play Arkansas?" said Lew, trying to remember. He took a good, solid drink of the whiskey. Lew would meet a Houghton or a Laurie every few years at some formal dinner. James Houghton Laurie was the one who took Texas M and C football most seriously. Lew had spoken to him more when he was an undergraduate at the school playing tackle than he did later, after his advanced degrees, when he went to work for the company.

"Damned right we played Arkansas. Beat 'em in the last two

minutes. You blew your man out of his hole like he was made of straw. It was the greatest block I have ever seen."

"I'm sorry. I don't remember. I remember Michigan, though."

"What happened at Michigan?"

Lew McCardle tapped his left knee. "Torn ligaments."

"Ended your career."

"No. I played the next year."

"Something ended your career."

"No. You're thinking of my not going to the pros."

Mr. Laurie snapped his fingers. "That's right. You could have been something in the pros."

"I did all right considering. I'm happy with Houghton and what I've got. I've got the early retirement. I've got a good house. I've got two cars. I've got vacations, and I can pay for my wife and daughters."

"You didn't do all right, Lew, considering." The dusty twang was gone now. The words were chosen and sharp and quite specific. There was no grin on the tight, tanned face of James Houghton Laurie III of Houghton Oil. "Considering your degrees and your skill and your intelligence, you did not do well, considering."

"Considering where I came from and what I could have been, I did very well."

"We both came from North Springs, Texas, Lew."

"We did not come from the same place, sir. We came from the same town."

"You have a chance now, Lew, to make up for all your missed opportunities. To make that doctorate from the University of Chicago pay off. Lew, I am talking about a vice-presidency for you. For your wife, Kathy, for your children. I am talking about my country club. I am talking shares, shares in Houghton, not that employee-option thing, real shares at good prices in a company whose worth you might help increase."

"I'd be happy to, sir. Houghton has been good to me. I never would have left the site unless I was ordered to."

"Lew. I know that. I trust you. You can't buy trust. You can't rent it. But you've got it."

"I am ready to go back to the site now. I'll go now."

"No," said Laurie. He raised a hand. "There's another rock-hound. We sent him up a couple of days ago. We need something more. We need trust here. It was not a wise decision to send that thing down from the site. And I know it wasn't your decision. And believe me, you don't have to show me some piece of paper saying you were told to leave that site. You've given me your word. And you're a Maky."

"Thank you," said Lew.

"Why, you may ask, was it a bad decision?" said Mr. Laurie, stopping Lew from answering the question which Laurie was about to answer himself. "Because it was unlucky. It was also stupid. But worse, unlucky."

Mr. Laurie sighed. He rose from his seat like a man weary with the world. He went to the bed on which his jacket lay. From an inside pocket he took a thin black box. He held it aloft briefly as though it were evidence.

"A treacherous world," he said. "I have bodyguards in the two rooms next to this. I don't go anywhere without them. I don't use the phone for anything more than ordering a hamburger. A treacherous world."

"You mean terrorist kidnappings of business executives?" asked Lew.

Laurie turned a dial on the box and it sounded like a radio with heavy interference. He put it on the small, gray marble coffee table between them.

"No. Those kids don't mean piss. I'm talking about Gulf, Standard Oil, Royal Dutch Shell, Norway, Kuwait. I'm talking oil, Lew, a treacherous world and a needed commodity."

"I know there's competition," said Lew, and got such a baleful look from Laurie that he added: "More than competition."

"That's just about right. More than competition. This isn't a radio playing. It cuts bugging of our conversation. I don't know how it works. It's the latest today, and tomorrow it won't be worth a piss in a rainstorm, because there'll be a new one you've got to have. We use it, they use it, everybody uses it. Everybody just keeps getting better at listening in on others and stopping others listening in. Never ends. That's competition."

"I see how difficult your job is," said Lew.

"Thank you," said Laurie. "If this were the best of all possible worlds, we would be proud of what that Russian doctor is doing. We would say to the world we found it here, here on our exploratory site and here and here. Do you follow?"

Lew nodded. He finished his drink. Laurie poured another. Lew noticed creases in the tanned neck and freckles above Mr. Laurie's color.

"We are about to make major bids on exploratory alien rights," said Laurie. "We don't want it known that we are exploring before we buy the rights for it. We don't like doing business like this, but everybody does it, and if we don't, we go out of business. It's like that black doo-hickey buzzing away. You've got to have it. All right, we have it."

"I don't know too much about bidding, Mr. Laurie."

"You know enough to just realize what I'm talking about. If we know for sure what we're bidding on, we've got the right atmosphere. I'm talking bidding atmosphere, and I don't want it spoiled. Now, if that thing the Russian is working with becomes known worldwide as some kind of miracle, there are going to be more reporters and other kinds of newspeople than you've ever seen. And what we want quiet is going to be found out and is going to be noisy as hell. It'll ruin the atmosphere. Everybody is going to know who and where and what is going on up there. Now, this is a fluid situation. That cadaver could get up and walk and say he's Louis XIV of France, and then forget it. It's carnival time above the seventieth parallel."

"I was aware of what kind of site we were drilling."

"Good. I imagine the men do tend to know what they're working on and some of the broader ramifications. But I'm not just talking about international publicity. I'm talking about such harmless little questions as how far did you haul it? What did you bring with you? How deep down? Glacial ice? Permafrost? What? Those sorts of things."

"They already know the depth of discovery of the . . . thing."

"All right. We'll live with it. What we're looking for, Lew, is someone to block for us. And by that I mean I don't expect you to go demolishing some opponent somewhere, but sort of like brush blocking. And by that I mean delaying any sort of great publicity and sort of specific answers about where you found it and how. That's what I mean."

"I won't say anything to anyone. I'll go home now. I've put in a lot of consecutive time and I'm close to retirement. I haven't given information other than the depth of the ice to anyone. And I'm sorry about that. You can trust me to keep my mouth shut, Mr. Laurie."

"We need more than that, Lew."

"Sir?"

"I am the goodwill ambassador of Houghton. I go from country to country promoting our commitment to the benefit of mankind. We are a committed company. Houghton Oil is committed to the energy of man and the welfare of man. Because we are committed, we are assigning one of our vice-presidents—a learned man with a doctorate—to assist the project of Dr. Semyon Petrovitch, in cooperation with the Scandinavian–Soviet Friendship Pact. This vice-president will allocate funds from Houghton to support this project. This vice-president will make sure that for at least a month, maybe two months, answers to certain questions are delayed, no matter whether the patient lives, which would attract publicity eventually, or dies, which would require some answers for Norwegian health authorities or whatever. It is a fluid situation, Lew. We need someone sensitive to our interests. You must use your judgment."

McCardle was about to tell Mr. Laurie that he was not a vice-president. But now he knew he was, just as Semyon Petrovitch had known he would be working on the project. Lew seemed to be the last to know these things. He listened to who would do things for him back at Houghton, different ways to get funds—there were donations to the university which came from Houghton Public Affairs, there was dead, solid cash which came from a Crédit Suisse account, and then there was his personal account here in Oslo.

There was more money looking back at Lew McCardle now than he had ever made cumulatively.

"We don't expect you to hide the damned body in some ditch, but we do expect judgment."

"I don't know if I'm fit for this, Mr. Laurie. I'm a geologist. I've chosen this area. It's been good to me."

"We're going to be better."

"I don't want better."

"Why not?"

"Because this is good enough. This is really good for me. Considering everything, I feel quite lucky I've got what I've got and gotten where I've gotten."

"'Lew McCardle, you can't do this to us. We need you."

"There must be better people."

"Maybe there are. But the Russians have cleared you, we trust you, and you have been accepted to take your sabbatical leave from us with this university here."

James Houghton Laurie turned off the thin little black box on the elegant coffee table between them.

"My name's Jim, Lew," he said. And poured another drink.

"All right, Jim," said Lew McCardle.

"Lew, whatever happened to your pro career? If I remember, everyone said you could have been another Luke Sikes. He was all pro with the Chicago Bears, wasn't he?"

"He died two years ago."

"I know. I read the alumni news. Had two pages. He was something. He was the best to come out of M and C."

"He was a day laborer in Sante Fe."

"I thought he was a policeman?"

"He was for a while."

"The alumni news didn't say he had stopped."

"No. They didn't."

"You know, Lew, Luke Sikes is in the Football Hall of Fame in Canton, Ohio."

"I know," said Lew McCardle, who had contributed to a fund-raising appeal for a sustained monument to Luke Sikes, which also took care of the family's funeral bills. Sikes had died owing almost two thousand dollars on an annual income twice that. And he owned nothing. And Sikes had been arrested twice for breaking and entering in petty crime. "I know," said Lew McCardle. But what he knew was that he could have been another Luke Sikes, and he wasn't.

Lew and Jim, two old Makys, had a final drink, and old Jim boy said he didn't expect to hear from ol' Lew for a while.

Vice-president McCardle finished the bottle of Tennessee sippin' whiskey. He drank from the crystal glass. He phoned Houston, Texas. He phoned home. A housekeeper answered.

"Lew who?" she asked.

"Lew McCardle. Mrs. McCardle's husband. Tell her Lew is on the phone. I'll hold." He cupped a bit of the whiskey in the cradle of his tongue and breathed in its aroma.

"Yes, Lew. Is that you?"

"Yeah, honey. How are you?"

"I am fine. More than fine. Do you know that they are investigating us for the club? Not any club. But the one with Lauries and Houghtons?"

"I'm a vice-president."

"Fantastic. What a surprise," she said. The voice still had the clipped Connecticut sounds. She had never lost her accent. And she had always sounded like money, and, once, she said money didn't matter. But that was when they were young, and he was a graduate student at the University of Chicago, and money didn't seem to mean any more than how much you had instead of who you were. Which is what it was back in Houston.

"I'm in Oslo, Norway. Why don't you and the girls come on out and visit? I'll be here a while."

"What about Paris?"

"I'm in Oslo."

"You said that. Can you get to Paris?"

"Not right away."

"When can you, Lew?"

"I don't know."

"When you can, let us know, and all of us will fly out to meet you. That's wonderful about your vice-presidency. Fantastic, Lew, I didn't think you had it in you. When did you say you'd be in Paris?"

"I didn't, honey."

"Oh," she said.

"Give my love to the girls."

"They'd go to Paris. I know."

"Yes. Well. When I can," said Lew McCardle wearily and ordered up whatever kind of whiskey they had in the hotel. They brought up a bottle of scotch. He drank it from the bottle. In his whole career as a geologist, the most important thing in it was keeping a hubbub away from that little fellow he found in the ice. He wondered what the men back at the site were doing, and he could bet they weren't drinking scotch whiskey in a fancy hotel suite.

He tried to remember the Arkansas game that had so impressed James Houghton Laurie. The old man used to come into the lockers and stuff twenty-dollar bills into your hands, and a Ulysses Grant fifty-dollar bill if you put someone out. He used to talk of Maky guts.

In McCardle's first game, one of his teammates rubbed some

blood from his jersey onto McCardle's as they were coming off the field.

"That's for Mr. Laurie. You'll see."

In the locker room, there was Laurie wearing a cowboy shirt tucked into what McCardle would find out later were British-tailored pants, which were tucked into five-hundred-dollar cowboy boots, so everyone on the team said.

As young McCardle passed by the older man, he felt a handshake and something crisply folded in it.

"That's hittin', boy. Makys hit. We're hitters."

It was his first payoff from James Houghton Laurie III. "He loves to see blood," said the teammate. "What he give you?"

Young Lew McCardle had opened his hand to find a ten-dollar bill. The teammate looked at it unimpressed. He had twenty dollars.

"Wait until you put someone out. If you do, jump around a lot and don't go back to the huddle right away so he'll see your number and remember it."

There was a hundred-dollar game once. Was that the Arkansas game? Lew McCardle couldn't remember. He tried to remember other things, good things. He tried to remember when the love was good with Kathy, and it was so long ago, and he had spent so much time trying to get back what the marriage had promised in the beginning, that he had never really made note of when was the last time the lovemaking was good.

It was not bad, he knew. But it was not good. It was just there. And he had often felt that it could have been better. But then again, it could have been worse, too.

He had done all right, considering.

CHAPTER VIII

Fourth Day—Petrovitch Report

Condition critical. Plasma volume totally restored. White blood count remains high, 1200 mm., yet hemolysis appears to be diminishing, and red blood count increasing. EEG activity enormous. A state of semiconsciousness. Repetition of one word 114 times over a six-hour period. Word: "Meramme." Language as yet unidentified. Shock still remains severest danger.

It was too silly for a comment, so she got an embrace.

"Eugeni, be serious," said Miriamne, laughing. She could in her good way scold like a song and laugh like an admonition, never hurting but enlightening. We were in our peristilium, open to the good summer sky, surrounded on the sides by fresh and growing things with water bubbling from a small fountain into a long, curving marble pool that caught the reflection of each white fluff of cloud above.

Outside, through corridors, was the atrium where my personal business was done, the retainers and emissaries met and formalities were dispensed with. Outside that was the vestibule where people waited to be allowed into the atrium, and outside that were the streets of Rome, with walls surrounding my house of such plain and unadorned countenance that none who did not know I lived here would take a second glance.

"Miriamne, how can I be serious when you tell me that not only is there an all-powerful god, but that he takes specific interest in everything on earth, and that if I let him, he will lift my worries also."

"It is true."

"Then enjoy your truth privately."

"I want to help you," she said.

"You may worship privately in any manner that you wish, and this has always been so. . . . Even according to your legends, he didn't help his own only son who was executed like a criminal. In disgrace. I do have something on my mind which I must tell you, and it makes me sad."

"You don't understand, Eugeni."

"Shhh, woman. I must tell you something unpleasant."

"Then quiet. I have something pleasant, and you yourself said that this place, our place, for you and Petronius and me, was only for good things. I have a good thing to tell you."

"You have an interesting defense when cornered—to hurl our son at me."

"You are cornered. Now listen," she said, and her finger pointed right into my nose.

"If you promise not to strike me," I said in mock horror.

"I make no promises," she said and pushed me back on the soft pillows where we sat. There were couches but we both preferred the pillows. "Now listen. The pain was not a punishment. It was God's gift to take away the sins of the world."

"Then he is not all-powerful because he could do it by decree if he wanted."

"He wanted to show his love by his suffering."

"Don't you ever show your love for me that way. I get no pleasure from someone else's pain, least of all someone I love. Enough of that talk. It is sweet nonsense. Thank you, but please, listen. I have something I must tell you. It is about Publius, your friend, and our son Petronius' friend. It is a sad thing."

"The only sadness, Eugeni, is not to hope."

"There are other sadnesses in this world."

"They are but the seed dying so that the flower may bring new life. You do not know the plan of the one God who gave his one son for us."

"Very pretty, Miriamne, and you are often eloquent, but please, this is about life and death."

"I talk of that, too."

"No, you don't. I do not interfere with your private things that you have kept private. But this has to do with the world."

"And you are foolishly sad," she said. She put a finger to my nose and pushed me back on our pillows. "And it was you who said nothing sad should be talked of here in our special place."

"I had hoped this would be so."

"Could you imagine that God has made this whole world, all the empire and beyond, his own sweet garden if we but used it right."

"No," I said. Except for this Jewish cult of hers, which many slaves fancied, she was ordinarily most reasonable. This was not a time for her religion. There were serious and real things to be discussed. She could believe those good things because this peristilium in all Rome was perhaps the most protected place in the empire, well hidden and well fortified with armored slaves. Protected by informers and retainers and, as the last barrier, myself.

Through all this, Publius had brought the blood and screams of the arena and the heavy smell of urine and vomit and death, as though he had dumped them all from baggage carts into the clear waters of our peristilium pool.

"I am wiser of the outside world than you think, Eugeni," said Miriamne.

"Perhaps," I said.

"But if I am not, then how do you know your trust in me is true? How do you know my love is true? For that which is not tested is still unknown."

"That which is not tested is not broken," I said. "There is nothing that cannot be broken at the right time against the right things."

The pool fluttered with circular rings. Perhaps a pebble had fallen from the roof, or a passing bird had dropped something. The water calmed, and nothing was visible on the bottom of the gold and silver design. The water was clear and sweet-scented.

Miriamne waited for me to talk. It was hard. How did Publius wreck things so easily? Even my house was cunningly arranged into defenses and ruses just to keep things like this out. There was a public and private life that were supposed to be separate. Even the house was organized publicly and privately. The public area—the atrium—was where I did business. I had built a large vestibule with statues and wall paintings and some ornate sellae—chairs with arms. In this vestibule did my retainers wait in the morning for me to receive them. The vestibule led to the atrium, which was a large room surrounded by cubicles for slaves whose specialties were associated with my businesses. In the center was a luxurious three-legged table of rare citrus wood with inlaid gold and ivory. Like the statues, it was to show that here was wealth and power. Yet the atrium was sparse, to show that it was not an easy wealth. There was one sella for visitors. Thus, a group must show its leader by who sat. There was a sella for myself and one for whichever slave I needed for the visitor. There I had met Domitian's emissary.

Behind the atrium, through a long corridor where muscular armed slaves were posted, were the peristilium and the sweetness of my life. In the center, it was open to the sky above and a rich, gentle arbor below with a clean water pool of marble and gold tile.

Here were my sleeping cubicles, behind which were the kitchens with their cooks and undercooks and cleaners. Here too were the rooms of the tonsores, for shaving and cutting hair, and unctores, whose fingers worked soft oils skillfully into the body. Here was the room for eating. Here was the room for my son Petronius' scrolls. Here was the room for my wife Miriamne's worship of her peculiar god without statues. Here was the room of our household god, Mars, and, since slaves had been known to talk freely, here was the room with the bust of Domitian, giving him more hair than nature thought fit. Here, too, were the entrances to my baths.

My armored slaves did not allow anyone to breach their guard to my peristilium. Only the most loyal and wisest slaves kept guard here—the best of the thousands that I owned. And so Domitian would not suspect how valuable this area was to me. Even the selection of these slaves was discreet. Discreet even from Demosthenes. Only on special occasions were people invited into my peristilium.

Then how did Vergilius Flavius Publius make his breach? How did I allow it?

"Eugeni," said Miriamne.

"In a moment. In a moment, dear. I am thinking how I will tell you what I must tell you."

"Whatever it is, it will be good."

"It is not good," I said angrily.

Of course, it was no mystery how Publius invaded my life. There was only one way. The only thing he had ever used with any effectiveness. His mouth. I remembered quite clearly. Ultimately, it was his mouth.

It had been three years before, and he was the least likely of candidates for my peristilium. It was a day I made public sacrifices at three temples followed by my less important retainers and slaves.

Demosthenes was not there, nor was Tullius—a former centurion who made gifts for me to the praetorians. Nor was Galbas, with his influence with the urban cohorts and the vigiles, nor Sempronius, whose retainers watched Galbas and Tullius. These were my public retainers, and they made a racket of such extraordinary noise one would think the emperor had arrived to make sacrifice. Naturally, there were fights which some wanted me to witness because they were defending my honor. If I were to believe this, my honor was always sullied by someone weaker than they, and aging slaves without recourse to the courts bore me all manner of ill.

At the temple of Juno it was a public day, and the priests made the proper tributes and prayers before the beautiful goddess, one of the most beautiful in Rome because she was made by one of the more famous Greek sculptors—originally the Greeks called her Hera.

Some used Juno privately as protector of women and marriages, but publicly she was mistress of Rome, and publicly my presence acknowledged her as my goddess mother, an obeisance to the city of Rome.

"Just another rock," came a squeaky voice from the crowd, which was larger that day because it was known throughout the city of my sacrifice and gifts to the temple.

"Shhh," came another voice. "This is a temple. A feast day."

"Stupidity is stupidity no matter where," came the squeaky voice.

In other lands, such sacrilege might have earned a beating to death. But Romans are reluctant to shed blood in temples because that would ruin the formalities of religion—one of the important things in the solidity of the state.

"Publius, shhhh," came the second voice. They were behind me and the priests. And it was the first time I heard his name.

"Would you pray to a jar of garum?" asked Publius, referring to the common sauce made of fermented fish which cooks use on almost everything.

"Shhh, Publius," said the friend.

"This is no different from an open field just because someone smothered the grass with marble brought from another field," said Publius.

"Shh, Publius."

"Would I keep quiet in an open field?"

"Pub-li-us!"

"All right. If you're frightened. The gladiator wouldn't hurt you. He wouldn't make a copper on it."

"PUBLIUS!"

"All right. All right."

I saw him again the next day when he burst through my vestibule and waiting retainers and was stopped only in the atrium by large armored slaves to whom he threatened death. On my orders a slave held his throat easily with one hand. Publius held a package wrapped in sheepskin.

I was talking to one of the equestrians before he set out on a mission to Egypt for Demosthenes. In foreign travel it is always best to use citizens born Roman, for they have uncontested citizenship.

When Publius quieted himself, I signaled for the slave to release him. Publius did this as though breaking free by his own strength. The equestrian laughed. Even the slave smiled. Without asking what business he was interrupting, he placed the package on the table and unwound the sheepskin. It was a small clay statue of Juno.

"I accept your apologies, Vergilius Flavius Publius."

"Ah, you know of me."

"Some things," I said. "You were an officer with the Third Cyrene when it moved down from Syria."

Actually, the first thing I had been told about was his wedge attack against an empty cave, then about the big family bribe, then his family affiliation and his marriage.

"Yes. The whole campaign was run by lunatics, but then that was in the tradition of all the praetors in Judea. I could have maintained peace with a cohort. Those governing idiots have lost more than a legion and a half, not to mention those stationed there."

"And what would you have done?" asked the equestrian, the muscles in his jaw tightening. He had had experience in that region, which was why we were sending him to Egypt to most of our granaries just before the excellent crop cheapened wheat here in Rome. The equestrian must have been highly angered, for he would not ordinarily interrupt a conversation meant for me even though his had been interrupted.

"First, I would have made peace with the priests. It's cheaper to buy a priest than a legion."

"Which priests?" asked the equestrian. His neck now tightened. "The Pharisee, the Sanhedrin, the Christian, the Cohen, the Levi, the Essene, which?"

"The priests. A Hebrew priest is a Hebrew priest," said Publius and abandoned this point as though never trained in logic. He proceeded into a description of one of their sacred days celebrating their release from slavery in Egypt. To understand this was to understand the Hebrews.

"How?" said the equestrian.

And Publius spun a little web about Hebrew conflict with the Egyptians and how, if the praetors had not acted like Egyptians but like real Romans, there would have been no trouble.

"Then why do more Hebrews live in Alexandria than in Jerusalem?" said the equestrian. "The Passover feast celebrates the release from Egypt which happened more than a thousand years ago, Vergilius Flavius Publius ignoramus."

Publius said he was not about to trade insults with equestrians, ignoring the thin equestrian border on my toga.

"Your apology is accepted, thank you. Good-bye," I said to him.

But he was not leaving. He grabbed the statue I had thought he brought as an apology to both Juno and myself and smashed it against the expensive table which was inlaid with ivory and gold. This fine table had cost me two hundred times more than Demosthenes. It cracked, spitting ivory chips like teeth.

"There. That is my gift to you," he said.

"You may add seven hundred thousand sesterces," I said. "That is the cost of the table. My lawyers will collect the money, or my vilicus will collect your body." And by that I meant he would pay me money or himself in slavery, probably in the fields.

This did not bother him. "See, I have given you a greater gift."

"I see nothing."

"That is the greater gift. If that statue were anything but clay, I would be harmed. I have not been harmed. Watch. Look. Do my arms shrivel? Do my eyes grow cloudy with blindness? See my cheeks? Do they suddenly lack color?"

From far off in the back of the house, I heard Miriamne singing softly into this sudden silence. There is usually a working buzz here that never ceases. The equestrian looked at me confused. The slave's face became stone, waiting to see what I would order. Suddenly, Publius began singing, not in Greek or Latin, but in a foreign tongue. We all looked confused. Miriamne, who never came to the atrium, appeared and answered in verse. She stood there in long white stola, her face clean of cosmetics, her hair modestly plaited, calling out in some strange-tongued voice.

"Hebrew," whispered my equestrian.

Miriamne beckoned the young insolent patrician to follow her without my permission. It was as shocking as if the god herself had talked. And the young patrician followed. And I looked. Still. Mouth open. Looking. And him going with my wife through my corridors into my peristilium with my armored slaves looking as useless and motionless as statues.

Someone shoved something into my hands. He was a clerk. He had given me a sack of coins. It was for the equestrian. I felt nudging. The coins were for the equestrian. I gave him the sack.

"Thank you," said the equestrian. "That one deserted his unit, if it's the Flavian lad, and I think it is."

"Thank you. I know," I said and left the atrium and walked through the long corridor with cubicles, back into the peristilium, where Miriamne had taken it upon herself to order wine and fruits and cheese for this intruder, as though she were the man or a modern Roman woman.

I motioned her to follow me to the other side of the arbor under the warm, sunny sky.

"Explain yourself," I said.

"He sang a prayer I remembered in my youth. I was not born a slave, you know."

"I know, but why did you come to the atrium without my permission and intrude upon business, like some wanton Roman?"

"I have been lonely. I do not know many women, and many years ago you sent all my friends from this house because they knew me as a slave. Now I own the only people I see daily, and other than Petronius, who is a son not a companion, there is you. And you are my husband. I have no one. When I heard the answers in the tongue of my childhood, I came to see who might offer the companionship I hunger for."

"But he is a man."

"Can you not see he is a lighthearted boy?"

"Not between his legs, I can assure you," I said.

"Are you afraid of him, or me, or you?"

It was a good question, asked without fear. But then Miriamne had never feared me or lied to me. She was my wife of eleven years then. I could have married a Roman which would have been a proper and logical move. But I had chosen her, a slave. I had slept with her, as with many, but with Miriamne it was good in a special, warm way, and more and more I slept less with others and then only with her. So that when Miriamne bore me a son and placed it at my feet, I accepted him as a son and her as a wife, freeing her legally and legally making a marriage.

She had given me much joy in just watching her, the way she reasoned with slaves instead of whipping them, the way she washed and ate, and smiled and sang her songs I did not know. So when she asked this favor of allowing Publius into our peristilium, I could not in justice say no.

So it was his mouth that had gone through my defenses without a block or a struggle. He had gone through singing.

And now, in my own peristilium, resting on my pillows with my legal wife, I had to announce I was to butcher a family friend like any bought and sold gladiator. It could not be put off. Better told before the fact and the wound made clean, than let things be found out and have an awkward festering gash.

"The problem is Publius," I said.

"Is that poor boy in trouble again?" she said. Miriamne smiled, waiting to laugh.

"Yes. He is in trouble. He is matched in the games," I said. I did not look in her eyes.

"You have influence there. Can you get him out?"

"No. These are Domitian's games. And it's been announced. He asked for this match. He wanted it."

"Why?"

"He was drunk."

"Many people say things they do not mean when they have had too much wine."

"He said it to an emperor."

"Surely an emperor would know most of all that it was the wine talking."

I was grateful that Publius, so free in tongue elsewhere, had carefully not mentioned the arena or politics in my house. This he somehow knew was proscribed.

"Can you help him?" Miriamne asked, and she was so honest in this question, like a child to a parent, that a great sobbing shame seized me. Even the floor could not hold my eyes. I looked up at the sky through the square roof, then to Domitian's statue, and Mars, both in their votive places. My hands needed rubbing. Miriamne's amber buckle, beneath, took my sight, and I could not lift it. My mouth opened, but there were no words.

"You cannot help him?" she asked.

"I am matched with him, and you do not understand the arena, and there is nothing I can do. I must kill him. Now you have it. Are you happy? I kill people."

"Of course I am not happy, Eugeni."

"It is the way the arena is. And that is it."

"I can accept that it is the way it is, but not that it is the way it should be."

"Why is it that those with the least influence have the grandest schemes for changing all mankind? Rome is what Rome is. The arena is what the arena is, and that is how I have found it, and that is how I will leave it."

She struggled with tears, her neck quivering with the strain. "You are a good man, Eugeni. Do not trouble your heart for things you cannot control."

"I am a man and, like everything living, I want to live."

"And I want you to live."

"Good, then let us talk of other things," I said.

"What have I said to make you angry?"

"Obviously something, so let us talk of other things."

She cradled my head in her large hands, too large for Roman beauty, but beautiful to me.

"You are a good man, Eugeni," she said, and I put my face in her breasts.

"Please. Do not say that," I begged, and she sang to me, as she had so often sung to our son Petronius, with words I did not know, but which had been sung to her by her mother and her mother's mother before her in the days before Rome had come to her land.

She knew what we shared. Petronius, our son, had yet to be told.

For the shame that was upon me and for my helplessness, I hated Publius. Some gladiators hate or prod themselves to it, but they are always suspect of their willingness to kill. Why heat a dish that already tastes good? And by that it is meant, if they are willing to kill, why should they need anger?

Vergilius Flavius Publius had all my anger, titled, acknowledged, and secured. Sculptors had cut his face into it, his name on it. I hated him because he had made me helpless. Because he already shamed me in myself before my Miriamne and, worse was to come, before my son Petronius, who loved me and respected me, and whom I, with my cunning and will, had kept away from the whoredom for almost fourteen years. His life.

Armored slaves clanked noisily coming through the atrium. Kitchen slaves yelled for wine and apples and sweets. A young voice bellowed an ode of a popular poet, noisily, as though to test the strength more of lung than meter. Petronius, my son, was home.

He marched in eating an apple, bouncing with the sap of an early afternoon and an appetite on the fly. He greeted Miriamne as though she were a visiting ambassador and he were a senator. He greeted me, like an honored guest to our house, all proper and impeccable. His grammarian was famous for teaching the proper and formal way of things, and not even the oldest family of the city could sway that man to compromise with newer fashions.

We could have bought a grammarian and tutored Petronius at home, but the better families did not do that, preferring that young Romans rub and butt against each other as part of the finest education. Of course, the grammarian owned the best Greeks.

Because my name excited so much emotion in the city, Petronius needed armored slaves who brought him from house to grammarian and back to house. The slaves were trained by a lanista, not only to use weapons, but never to discuss slave gossip and any other things that might have to do with the arena games. There was not an armored slave who did not fancy himself a gladiator, unless it was flogged out of him.

"I have something to tell you, Petronius," I said.

"Yes, father?" he said. He wore a light yellow tunic, of perfect color and stitch. He was large, already as big as Miriamne, a big woman, but with a touch of sharpness around his black eyes.

His beard was a few tentative hairs around his chin, carefully unshaven, for the first shave would be on the morrow for his fourteenth birthday. Then, formally, in front of the proper people, our family tonsor would cut his beard for the first time, and this beard would be burned as an offering to Mars, officially our household god, and my personal god publicly, even though Miriamne did not even believe Mars existed and had often told me so.

It was not that I believed in Mars, or that he had anything to do with any victory of mine, or that it made one spit of difference if one burned calves before Mars or urinated down his finely chiseled helmet over his finely chiseled head.

One did not worship the gods of Rome for the gods, but for Rome. Religion properly and publicly pursued was a showing of one's place with Rome, and while Publius with his patrician foundation could afford to mock the gods publicly, I could not. I had to prove my Romanness daily. Because of this, Petronius would have to prove it less, and his son not at all.

"Are you ready for the tonsor, tomorrow?" I asked. Miriamne hugged Petronius firmly, then released him with the admonition: "He is your father. Honor him." And she left.

"For fourteen years, my father, I have been ready for the tonsor."

"Good," I said. "Very good. Very, very good. That is good. It is good. Very."

"Beards grow, father."

"Yes, do they not? What is it the famous Greek poet Horace said about beards? He said something funny, if I remember."

"Horace is Roman, father, one of us. Homer is Greek. A great poet, father, but not Horace."

Petronius yelled for a slave to bring him honey and plums before he finished the apple. He was ungainly and sat falling into the pillows like so much furniture cracking at the joints. But he had a sharp wit.

"This is a family secret. I am going to be made a senator. It does not mean I will ever be a patrician, but we will get you a patrician wife, and you may someday wear the broad stripe on your toga."

"Is that what you want to tell me, father?" he asked.

"You do not seem pleased."

"Why are you pleased? You own half the senate anyhow."

"What makes you think so?"

"Everyone says so."

"And what do you say?"

"I say nothing. I am your son."

And with this he made a reference to what I had taught him on a birthday; for each birthday I gave him not only some toy or gift of immediate joy, but something I had learned in life. A whitish burn welt remained on my right side. Burns remain forever, although it was only seven years before. He grew so quickly, yet it seemed like too short a time for seven years. Seven years before, Petronius was seven, and on that birthday he received a carved wooden doll that spun when a cord was pulled.

On that day, he learned his first lesson of each birthday. That first lesson was on silence about the family. I could never forget. Slaves had heated an iron and were sent away so that Petronius could be alone with me.

"I want to show how important it is that you keep family business family," I had said.

"I am seven and big," he said.

"Very big. You are important, Petronius. Now you must know that some things hurt. Some things hurt very much. You are old enough."

"A spanking hurts. Pebbles in sandals hurt, oh, so much."

"Yes, they do, Petronius."

"Mother spanks me."

"Because she loves you."

"You love me."

"Yes, I do."

"You don't spank me."

"No. No. I don't. Petronius, you are a big boy. And you can hurt me. The most dangerous thing in the world is the human mouth. Not its teeth, but its tongue."

"I don't want to hurt you, father. You give me things."

"Lift the handle of that iron there," I said, pointing to a rod as red as the coals it rested on at one end. We had done this before Mars's statue. Some soot from the coals collected on the ceiling.

Petronius, straining, lifted the cold, black end of the rod, almost dropping the hot point to the floor when he had gotten the rod up and out of the coals.

I lifted my tunic, exposing my stomach.

"Press the rod here as I talk."

"No. It will hurt."

"Do it."

"No."

"I will hurt you, Petronius."

"No," he shouted, and I snatched the rod from him and made him look as I pressed it burning into my stomach.

"With your mouth you can hurt me more than this, Petronius. Look, Petronius. Look at how little it hurts. But your mouth can hurt much."

It did hurt, but gladiators are often trained with hot rods to force the muscles and mind to do things they might ordinarily shy from.

The rod sizzled when it went back into the coals.

"You can hurt me more by saying things that are said in the house. The burn does not hurt. You can hurt by saying what is said here to your friends or anyone. What is said at home stays at home."

"Promise it doesn't hurt," cried Petronius.

"It doesn't hurt, darling. It doesn't hurt at all."

The scar carried two pale welts like marble fingers across the right side of my stomach. Seven years later it had not diminished. But when Petronius said he was my son, I could trust that I could disclose things, knowing he would not carry them elsewhere. The public thing was, of course, Publius.

"I have something else to tell you, which you may have heard. It is, of course, all over the city."

"Publius?" he said, smiling.

"Yes," I said.

"You are going to have trouble with the big amphitheater."

"How do you know? Where do you hear these things about the arena?"

"I know. Everyone knows. Everyone goes to the games but me."

"Yes, and not all of them come back from the riots."

"The trouble with your match that started the riot was that it wasn't held in the Colosseum where people could see it. That was the trouble with those games."

"There were other things," I said, dismissing the subject with a short wave of my hand. "The arena is none of your business."

"I have not said anything to anyone. I am told nothing, and it is no small burden you have placed on me, your son, to be ignorant of the only important thing in Rome today." He gestured like a grown orator, his face grave with the weightiness of his little problem. The grammarian had taught him well.

"There are many important things in Rome; they just do not tease the Roman mind," I said.

"The grammarian had all the boys stand and brought me before them. He said I was the son of Roman virtue. He said it was possible with a little Roman blood to be more Roman than someone with a mother and father both Roman and Roman since the founding of the city."

"And it did not amuse you that Publius is suddenly less Roman than I, because he is a foolish, defenseless person?"

"It made me proud to be your son. When he said the Roman blood of your courageous father flowed in your body and now mine, and not a drop had been diluted, I wept with pride."

"Knowing this was the same man who taught you that gods copulated with geese and that my father died trying to retrieve the lost eagles in wildest Germany, when you know quite well I paid in coin you saw with your eyes, put in the palm of the poet taking my instructions on my ancestry, which I told you was a lie."

"Your father was Roman."

"Very," I said. "And in no way did he ever do anything of virtue in his entire life. Ever."

"Why are you angry?" asked Petronius.

"I am offended that your mother's blood and my mother's

blood is suddenly inadequate for you. Your mother is a great woman and so was your grandmother."

"My grandmother was so great that this is the second time you have mentioned her, the first being that you would tell me about her when I grew up. No. Roman is the best thing to be."

"It is a thing to use, not be. Like my sword. But I do not bring too much of it into our peristilium. I am glad your birthday is close, for there is a truth I have found in the arena that will be the gift I will give you."

"And the one I want?"

"That is a surprise," I said, and I felt good again. For I did not like arguing with Petronius, especially since I now did not have such a secure advantage. And being my son, he knew just which thrust hurt the most.

"I want to see your match with Publius. Isn't it so, that this will be the last time you will be in the arena? That is the rumor. Isn't it so?"

"I thought it was a secret."

"More than two people cannot hold a secret. You have told me that."

"You wish to see me?"

"Yes."

"Kill your friend Publius?" I do not know why I expected him to say no, but I hoped it.

"Yes, it will make it more interesting. Someone I know instead of some musclebound youth you import to butcher."

"They say that, too?" My anger burned, hidden.

"Some say it. I assumed it was true because you are so calculating in everything."

"You want seats?"

"Your special seats from which one can see everything with the finest view. The ones in your network of chambers where the women are, and dancers are, and where the golden flute is played."

"The 'chambers' in the large arena is one cubicle. There is a slip at sand level from which a slave, standing on a small iron table, can see the emperor's seats. Through it we hear the mood of the crowd. There are no women, just body slaves and armored slaves, the kind that escort you around the city. There is a heavy door and jugs of water in case of riots. There are no flutes."

"Then I will stay there."

"You can barely see anything from there but what I have told you. The slit has often been blocked by an animal's body."

"I want this more than anything, father. Please. Please. It tears at my liver to be the only one in the entire world who will be denied this."

"You want the arena. Here is the arena." And for the first time I used my hand to strike him. I slapped one side of his face and the other side. I slapped again, and his fuzzy cheeks with the little beard welted and became red. And what was worse, I gave him that stone smile I use for small arenas where my face could well be seen. He begged me to stop, and I told him I was giving him the arena. He raised one finger begging mercy, as obviously his schoolmates had taught him was done in the arena. I stopped.

"There are the vestal virgins," I said pointing to the god of the house, "and there the emperor," pointing to the atrium. "Do you think you have put up a good enough fight for them to let you live?"

"This is unfair," he said.

"Welcome to the arena," I said, raising my hand in a gross gesture. He cringed, and no sword has ever cut like that sight.

I spent a life keeping the arena and even business out of my peristilium, and I myself had brought it in with my own hands. How I longed for the pain of that burning rod against my belly when lessons were so easy.

On the day of his birthday, the tonsor cut Petronius' beard. I gave the tonsor a gold coin, which would bring his peculium almost to the point of his freedom. The welts were gone from Petronius' cheeks, for I had been careful not to break bone or skin but only sting. The tonsor gave me the beard in a silver bowl, and I gave the bowl to Lucius Aurelius Cotta, the silver-haired patriarch of the Aurelii who had honored my house for this ceremony. Miriamne did not attend, which I had allowed as her right. She disapproved of Roman gods, belonging to Christians who constantly called upon her to interfere in our family life, especially with Petronius. Varro was there. Publius of course was not.

Galbas and Tullius had met my son in the atrium early that morning as I received retainers. With Petronius at my side, they offered gifts of gold and silver and prophesied great activities for Petronius' loins. He delivered well his spoken gratitude, each sentence as though he were born patrician and already in the senate place he would have from me.

In the atrium, the emperor's emissary said that the divine Domitian would have come himself but for the great burdens of state. He delivered three gold swords to Petronius, who swore, in an excellent memorized speech, his loyalty to his emperor who was Rome, indivisible one from another, each but a word for the other. The emissary smiled, amazed that so young a child could be so proficient in oratory. And I was truly proud, even though Petronius had no smiles for me. But I had many for him.

The emissary had other words, quiet and private for me. Domitian was worried. These were his personal games, and now the Vatican arena seemed too large for a single combat even with the other shows.

"I told you to tell him that," I said.

Petronius had taken his gold swords back in the house to an accounts clerk who would store them for an occasion on which they might honor the emperor in return.

"I spoke to him of what you told me. We have had a good riot and we need the big arena. But this is too big," he said. His words were hushed, as were mine, but each word was shot like stones from ballistae.

"It was not I who lured Publius into that arena."

"Domitian is worried about what Publius will wear!"

"So am I."

"So you agree with Domitian?"

"Absolutely. We are going to have real problems getting a good fight out of him in that heavy officer's armor."

"Can you talk to him?"

"No. I thought Domitian would."

"I have. Publius insists upon dying his own way. He says he may not have lived well, but he's going to die well."

"Oh, gods, and he's not even drinking," I said, raising my hands in supplication to the ceiling.

"Can you help him die well? If he dies well, it can work."

"He won't stop being Publius to die."

"You might disembowel him."

"Through a breastplate? No one would see it."

"Can you dismember him?"

"Maybe, but my spatha is made for fighting, not butchering. It's a thrust, not a slash."

"Take a short sword."

"Why not a feather?"

"Take a short sword auxiliary."

"It bangs, and it's clumsy. It ruins my style."

"What are we going to do?"

"I will do something."

"What?"

"Whatever I can do, and whatever Publius will help me do."

"In passing. . . ." said the emissary.

"How much?" I asked.

"Ten million sesterces."

"Never."

"You're getting publicly freed from the arena. You are getting a senate seat, and not only were you not born an equestrian, you have been a slave. And, Eugeni, you have made an immense, immense fortune under the benign rule of our divine Domitian."

"He's getting this show free from me."

"He needs money to make sure this is a good show."

"Ten million would never reach the arena sands. Except with hundreds of pairs of gladiators and perhaps new animals, I rarely see more than five million."

"Not enough."

"I have not said five million. I am not as wealthy as the great imagination of Rome has me. You have seen my retainers, their great length, their big appetites, their loathing of a day's work. Yes, much money has come to me. I watch it go by. I am a conduit, not a container."

"Seven million."

"Five."

"Six."

"Done, and my love and loyalty to divine Domitian."

"He has the wooden sword."

"Much more costly than three gold ones," I said, and the emissary smiled and said he would relay what I had said, for Domitian had a good sense of humor besides a great sense of justice.

I personally gave the emissary gold worth fifteen thousand sesterces, but in the coin of aureus. This was to assure Domitian's laughing at my jokes for his benefit, the money being for the emissary's judicious thoughts and words.

Thus were the morning preparations before Petronius watched the first shavings of his face go up in flames before the bust of Mars.

We endured Lucius Aurelius Cotta's sonorous account of his great family, to which we belonged. His patrician stripe was so wide and so bright a purple I could not help eyeing it, until I caught Petronius' sullen stare. Cotta went through the names of the great Aurelii, mentioning the consul in the distant past, when the republic was more a republic and not as it was today. He knew no tongue was free with Domitian's spies so prevalent, but he implied he did not like the strength of the patrician class diminished by the growing, almost complete, rule of the emperor.

For me, of course, I felt the opposite. I never could have become an equestrian in the old days of the republic and even to dream of Petronius wearing a patrician stripe would then have been folly. It was a time before Rome was the empire of the world, before the great numbers of slaves and before even the games themselves, centuries and centuries before. And I wondered if my family would last centuries and what my descendants would feel to know they had the ages behind them.

Petronius stood like a patrician. Lucius Aurelius Cotta mentioned the two praetors who were Aurelii. I played a small part in making one when Cotta freed me at the behest of the crowds at games he sponsored. I was seventeen at the time, had killed twelve, and heard the same speech about his family. But, where I had stood dumbly and answered only in gratitude, Petronius took the speech of the patriarch, turned it neatly around in return praise of the Aurelii, adding that no little virtue came to the family through his father, me, who showed Romans their worth by his worth in the most trying circumstances. In that manner, said Petronius so proudly and evenly, were the Aurelii shown to be most Roman of them all.

I could have cried with joy, for he had told the patriarch that we gave more to the Aurelii than we received, but I could never do that without blunt crudeness. Petronius did it with nobility and oil. Showing complete respect, he demanded respect. Unfortunately, the patriarch was a bit drowsy in years and failed to realize his speech was turned back to him.

He even made the mistake of responding that Petronius was

now freed by his own hand, not realizing it was a ceremony of early manhood not a manumission. To this, with full smile Petronius answered that the mountain thanked the pebble for lightening its load by rolling down it. Ordinarily this would be an insult, but Petronius said it with such sweetness and such a good smile that all, including the patriarch, laughed. And the patriarch apologized to Petronius for his mistake. Petronius accepted it.

In three years, I would give Petronius his toga and take him to the forum in it for the first time, and he would be a man. These were my plans.

After the supper of flamingo tongues, stuffed pigs, asparagus cooked in honey, peacock, and large slabs of wild ass, I spoke with Petronius alone, as I had on each birthday since I had first explained to him the danger his own tongue was to him and the family.

I reviewed the things I had told him, such as all things really serve themselves, and masters of people and crops only turn this self-interest to themselves. A plant grows not to give us food, but for itself. The pear is but the seed for a new pear tree, which we steal for our stomachs. These were things he would not learn in school.

I saw that he was cold to me, so I said that this truth I gave I had learned in the arena.

"Men are more alike than they are different. Despite what you see, men are virtually identical. Man makes the difference. Man says one is slave and one is master. Man trains to be different. But we are all alike. The slaves we own and the emperor we serve are no different but for the way they think of themselves and each thinks of the other. Syrians are not naturally sneaky, Greeks born sycophants, Jews nursed beggars, Germans wild in blood, or Aetheops stupid, any more than Romans are weaned courageous. Armies wear different colors to tell themselves apart."

Petronius interrupted me. "Do you have the chamber pot?"

"What for? Are your needs that urgent?"

"No. Yours are. You're spreading it in the room," he said, and his eyes were cold as winter. They could not have been colder if they were barbaric blue.

"This is true what I tell you. What we pretend is true for others is not true."

"We do not pretend, father. The only thing to be is Roman. You would have married Roman if you could have conceived Roman. Greek and Jew blood is stigma. But never mind, I will do what you should have done. I will put more Roman blood into my offspring than you did into yours."

I tried explaining the weaknesses of the mobs, which were composed of lazy Romans on the corn dole, and how his mother was the best of women.

Even Publius, acknowledging her virtue above Roman women, said: "Mother cannot read or write. You keep her in this house because you are ashamed of her. And look who you use to certify her worth. A Roman patrician, who has a mind pebbles could bang in, whose entire fortune would not pay a day of your retainers' expenses. A man of such little consequence that he would be an amusement in any other land."

Petronius said this without an oration stance, each word delivered dully and thumping like the last. His eyes and my eyes locked. He was not a boy anymore. I lowered my eyes.

"This is not so. Your mother has far more virtue than Roman women, who sleep about and pretend they're men."

"You did not hear the patriarch mistakenly give me manumission?"

"He is old. His mind wanders. It was funny."

"You were the only one smiling, father. Like a Greekling when embarrassed by his Roman better. I took offense, because I have learned that every day I must prove myself Roman, and with each effort that makes me seem more Roman, I feel less Roman. Publius in chains is more Roman than you will be in the senate."

"He will be dead and you will wear the broad stripe."

"Which you will pay a fortune for, because we must buy what others have by right. And people will say, look at how the patricians have fallen because now even the son of a slave wears the stripe."

"Did I hurt you that much with my hands?"

"Eat your barley."

"I am sorry."

"It was not I who cried afterwards," said Petronius.

And by barley he meant gladiator's food. Barley without wheat is a punishment for the legions, but it is a gladiator's staple which I eat for fifteen days before an appearance. With the sudden games Publius had brought down upon himself following the secutor match, I had eaten barley steadily for more than a month. The good food had been for my guests and as always for Miriamne and Petronius, although meat eaten regularly poisons the blood.

Perhaps it was eating barley so long when I could afford a granary full of peacock tongues or miles of bread as white as milk. Perhaps it was Petronius, from whom I had kept the sad history of his ancestry. Perhaps it was Publius, the first man I ever hated in an arena.

But all my discipline and all my plans and all the caution I had used so long were about to blow away like a small cloud in a sudden great storm.

CHAPTER IX

Lew McCardle had spent all his working life avoiding manipulating people and was surprised that, after two days of being a vice-president on sabbatical leave to the university, his biggest remaining problem was not managerial, but academic.

He had taken sole responsibility for determining the language snatches mumbled by the patient. He thought at first it would be easy, because he was fairly certain it was French. But he didn't speak French. Someone who did said it sounded Spanish. The Spanish-speaking person said it sounded Italian, and he finally ended up with a professor of Romance languages who asked if this was the same language Dr. Petrovitch had asked him about several days before.

Lew said it was.

The professor said it was some form of Latin. Lew said it didn't sound like it to him. The professor said he had recommended to Dr. Petrovitch a woman whom he had known at Oxford and who was in this country now, at Ringerike.

The professor hadn't said she was a nun, and Lew had to get permission from the metropolitan's office in Oslo before he found himself in the back of a rented limousine driving through the wet and gloomy afternoon of early Norwegian spring, looking for a convent of Dominican sisters in Ringerike. He wore a dark pin-striped suit with vest, white shirt, and subdued dark blue tie. If he dressed like a vice-president, he thought, he might feel like a vice-president. At least people would not as readily discern how strange the job was to him.

He could see how these winters could depress people if they didn't have intense things to keep them occupied. He missed the surety of his work, knowing his skills were needed, and being certain of his worth. He did not like this job, but he had done it well, discovering from the staff itself just the right deceptions and putting most people like pegs in proper holes.

Dr. Petrovitch himself shunned publicity like a disease and was overjoyed when Lew, through the Houghton grant to the university, got him an intensive-care unit built into the floor where his office was, cleared out the entire floor by funding new and larger quarters for other professors, and filled a technological shopping list for the Russian, sufficient for anything short of a small-scale war. The entire Petrovitch operation had become sealed.

The talkative staff was dispersed to other discreet jobs. The doctor who had worked with Petrovitch had always wanted to work in Russia where cryonics received, as he called it, "more respect and public notice." Even Petrovitch was amazed at how quickly the man was cleared for entry.

Houghton Oil suddenly had incredibly lucrative nursing jobs open in Indonesia for four-month periods.

Only one person proved not to have a price. It was the nurse who had explained to him what was going on in the hyperbaric chamber, the one who had cried at the first brain wave. There was nothing she wanted outside of Oslo. She wanted to continue working with Dr. Petrovitch. She was proud of what she did.

"I don't know what you want from me, Dr. McCardle, but I have given my word to Dr. Petrovitch that I would not discuss this current patient. You cannot buy my word."

"I'm sorry," said Lew. And he was deeply embarrassed by her integrity, and later he resented it.

One very buxom nurse, with massive shoulders and fat thighs, said she knew what was happening. There was too much money and secrecy for Dr. McCardle to be on the up and up. She knew what they were trying to hide.

"Really," Lew had said, thinking that any moment there would be a swarm of reporters and television cameramen coming to see the man resurrected from ice, back from the dead, miracle in Oslo. And of course the dreaded question: "Dr. McCardle, where did you find this miracle?"

"Yes," the nurse had said in workable but not perfect English. "He got frostbite by playing hanky-panky nude without his clothes on. He was one of your people doing dirty business. This is not Sweden or Denmark. This is Norway, and he got caught frozen doing dirty business."

"Please don't tell. I beg of you," said Lew.

"I don't talk. These things are not so unusual for Americans, who think because they leave home they can do anything here."

Lew begged three more people not to mention a word about a Houghton employee who got frostbite during a sexual excess, and within one day the body, John Carter, had become just another little dirty American story, to go along with dirty German stories, dirty Swede and Danish stories.

Coming up to Ringerike before the weak, pale sun had gone, Lew had watched the snow melt condensing that unmistakable layer of grime he had seen around New York City and London and other industrialized areas. Carbon, he thought, the waste of what was burned to make the world run. Perhaps that was what an education gave a man—the knowledge that you were looking at carbon and not just dirt.

The spring had begun, and by summer the sun would be almost constant with a short, brief night, as winter had a short, brief day.

The convent was an imposing stone structure that reminded McCardle of the stone strata of the region. This was a Protestant country, in that respect like Texas, yet here in Norway the Catholic families were usually the intellectuals. One would have to be an intellectual to take the name of Sister Olav, thought McCardle. He told the driver to wait. He entered the convent and was received by the mother superior, who had spoken with the metropolitan's office. She was in her late fifties and seemed quite effective, even in a white bonnet and black robe. She wore a large onyx crucifix on a beaded belt.

Why, she wanted to know, did Dr. McCardle of the university not use the university? She was not forbidding an audience with Sister Olav, but she had to know certain facts. He explained about delays and that all he wanted to do was verify a language on a tape he had. He didn't want a lengthy position paper from a whole department. He smiled. It was not returned.

Why didn't he go to Saint Sabina's, a teaching hospital in Oslo? He would have, he said, but he was given the name of Sister Olav at this convent.

Sister Olav had left Oxford before she had completed her language program, said the mother superior. Did Dr. McCardle know that?

No, he didn't, he said, but that wouldn't matter if she were competent.

Competence, said the mother superior, was not one of Sister Olav's problems.

But that was neither here not there, she said. She would see, if Dr. McCardle would be so kind as to wait, if the office of the metropolitan had given clearance. She would ask Sister Olav if she would give an audience to Dr. McCardle. Although this was supposed to be a cloistered convent, but one would not know it, would one?

Lew McCardle, standing there in the office with his gray gloves like a loose handkerchief in his large hands, feeling very awkward despite the cashmere coat and the five-hundred-dollar suit and the Italian shoes and the British tie and shirt, slipped into down-home talk and a surprising stutter.

"Well, uh, n-no, ma'am. I guess I wouldn't guess I don't know fer sure . . ."

"That's all right, wait," said the mother superior. "If you have permission from the metropolitan, and since your doctor has sent us a machine for these tapes, we will see what we can do. Although I cannot vouch for Sister Olav. She thinks people play games with her. And for that, the order has paid for her to go to Oxford. You do not play games with people, do you?"

"N-no, ma'am. Not at all, all," said Lew.

"I did not think so."

The ten-minute wait felt like a day. And Lew heard Sister Olav before he saw her. She was apparently reciting a prayer, yet it had too much rhythm. It had meter. She was reciting some form of what appeared to be Italian poetry. The mother superior escorted her into the room in which Lew waited on an uncomfortable straight-backed chair.

Sister Olav with a start stopped her recitation and looked to the mother superior, who motioned that she too should sit.

"Good afternoon," she said. She was tall, with perfectly symmetrical features and skin as soft as fresh-powdered snow. The lips were light pink and fine enough to be etched by a draftsman. She was apparently blonde because her eyebrows were pale yellow, almost white.

"Good afternoon," said McCardle.

"I was talking to myself," she said, and her smile came like a glory of marble from the fondest dreams of Michelangelo. She was beautiful but too intense to be attractive, he thought.

"I heard," said McCardle.

"It was more like reciting," she said, and her singsong English was softer than most Norwegians'. "It is a habit I hope to break."

"I do it often," McCardle lied.

"You wished our assistance with a language problem you have. Greek? Latin?"

"No. It's some form of Latin, or a language closely allied with it. I had some Latin, so I recognized a few words. I would like you to identify this if possible." Lew took a pocket tape recorder from his coat.

"Someone spoke that recently? In conversation?"

"Not exactly. He was just sort of rambling on."

"Vulgate," said Sister Olav. "It is undoubtedly vulgate, because that is the Latin of the church and that is the only Latin spoken today. That is, if it is Latin."

"We'll see," said McCardle.

He ran the machine and there was the rambling voice, slurring words, repeating the word "Pebbles" or "Poubles," sometimes angrily.

"That's very interesting," she said. "Would you play it again?" She listened with her hands clasped over each other, and, when the tape was done, asked that it be played again. After the third short playthrough, she shook her head.

"I am sorry, I cannot recognize what it came from. I have never read an ode or a play or even an edict that reminds me of that."

"Well, maybe it's not from something written down," said McCardle.

"That's very unlikely. Highly unlikely."

"Maybe the person is a priest talking."

"That certainly is impossible."

"Why?"

"This is not the Latin used by the church. Vulgate Latin used by the church is a deteriorated form of Latin, and by that I do not mean inferior, rather one that requires more pronouns. It is not quite as pure. Like street languages in the provinces that develop over a period of time."

"Down-home," said McCardle.

"If that is what you call provincialism. What you have on your tape recording is what we call classical Latin, which schoolchildren learn. It was the language of the Roman Empire or the civilized world, if you will."

"The ancient Roman Empire?" asked McCardle. He felt a heat in the room, like a blowtorch at his face. He was telling himself not to panic at this moment, while at the same time forcing a smile and telling the mother superior and Sister Olav everything was all right.

"Are you sure?" asked Sister Olav.

McCardle nodded.

"Well, there was only one Roman Empire, and technically it's not considered ancient. Egypt and the pharaohs are considered ancient. The Roman Empire lasted until about sixteen hundred years ago. But I can't place the play or the book of history. No. I don't think it is a history. Although they had so many. And the words, some of them are mispronounced. The grammar would never be allowed in a history. Never. Is this the same voice as on previous tapes sent by Dr. Petrovitch?" asked Sister Olav.

"Yes," said McCardle.

"Someone is playing a trick on you. I have never heard Latin pronounced like that."

"How should Latin be pronounced, if not that way?"

Sister Olav raised her shoulders in a shrug. The polite reserved hand upon hand resting on her lap had begun, moment by moment as she talked, stirring with sudden gestures. Now she shrugged under her black gown. The face, no longer composed, grimaced.

"No one knows with certainty. We've never heard a Roman speak Latin."

"Just about when would they have?" asked McCardle. "The one on the tape?"

"At least sixteen hundred years ago. Two to three thousand years ago."

"Jesus Christ," said Lew, forgetting where he was.

"That is the period, yes," said Sister Olav. "But I cannot place the work. They just wouldn't do that."

"Do what?"

"Use a Hebrew in a play of history like that. Miriam is a Jewish name, and while there were many Jews in Rome itself for great periods, they were not prominent in Roman entertainment. What you have in the second tape there is a love story. The man professes his love for this woman. The world which knows him, or thinks it knows him, will never know him. Will never know how he loves and protects from the world his Miriam, or as he says, his 'Miriamne,' the Latinized pronunciation. I am trying to think of where I have heard this, and I have never heard this."

"Sister, I had Latin, and I don't recognize it."

Sister Olav smiled. "Good. You would be correct because what you get in your schools is the stilted pronunciation. Without the words eliding, they run into each other. In poetry they elide, vowels join. This is an imitation of Latin speech, properly with vowels running into each other. Although the grammar is a bit faulty here and there. And there are only snatches, which would throw off even most scholars."

"Are you sure?"

"Please run your machine back. Here, let me," said Sister Olav taking the machine. The mother superior watched her, with lips becoming thin, like taut twine on a package restrained from bursting. There had been touching.

She played back the tape and then got what she wanted.

"Merahmo," came the husky voice.

Sister Olav smiled broadly. "Now, what you have," she said, her hands flailing, "is the Latinized Miriamne—in the accusative case with the first person of 'I love,' amo. In everyday speech these things run together, and you have, in proper Latin, Miriam, I love you, or Miriamne, vocative case joined to amo. Which you must know."

"Amo, amas, amat," said McCardle.

"Correct. Each distinct as you learned it but not as a poet or anyone else would pronounce it. Who goes around saying 'I love,' 'you love,' 'he loves'? What we have is someone who knows how to say 'love ya' in Latin. If you had learned English the way you learned Latin, you wouldn't have recognized this 'love ya.' "

"I see," said Lew.

"A very interesting story, and I don't know why anyone would make this effort, unless of course the person is British. They do that, but with better grammar. Interesting. Powerful. Here is a man who says the whole world thinks it knows him, and it doesn't know him. It doesn't have his love, and without that it will never know him. And that is good, because the world crushes tender things. The world cannot allow precious love, defended love, love kept away so successfully these many years."

"That's in there?" asked Lew.

"Very much. Crude but powerful. He has got a problem. He delays telling her about something, and then confusion, then that name that keeps coming back with much consternation, Publius."

"Publi, Publius. . . . Oh, my God, Pebbles."

"Dr. McCardle," said the mother superior, concerned for the American losing color in his cheeks.

"I'm all right, I'm all right," he said. He thanked Sister Olav and the mother superior and asked one more question.

"Sister Olav, if you were unconscious, might you not speak in Latin?"

Sister Olav smiled. She nodded. A crucifix on large beads that formed a belt rested on the black material that made her lap. To the mother superior's annoyed concern, the young woman absent-mindedly began pounding the palm of her left hand with the butt of the cross.

"Good question, good question, good question. Would I? I think sometimes I would. And perhaps a line or two or a short poem, but the unconscious does not speak foreign languages. No language learned after five would be spoken by an unconscious person. I take it you didn't hear the language spoken, but are trying to track down who did the tapes, or how?"

"An unconscious person speaks the language his mother taught him, right?" said Lew.

Sister Olav nodded. She slammed her open palm with the cross again. The mother superior gently, but with the certainty of a stone pillar, kept Sister Olav's hands from working over the image of their Lord.

"Thank you," said Sister Olav, realizing what she had been doing. "My language, if I were unconscious, would be Norwegian, not Swedish, although I studied in Sweden so long that I have a Swedish accent."

"I couldn't tell the difference," said McCardle.

"You're not supposed to," said Sister Olav, smiling with much gusto.

"We can," said the mother superior. "A Swedish accent has a soft haughtiness to it. It is an 'I can do whatever I want' sort of sound. An 'I know better' sort of sound. We are not all alike, just as you are not all alike. Not every American is a football player, millionaire sort of thing, if you know what I mean."

Lew McCardle didn't know what she meant. But the mother superior knew what she meant. Some things were better and more charitably left unsaid, she said. She meant this for Sister Olav, McCardle felt.

"What I don't understand," said Sister Olav, "is why someone would work so hard to pronounce the words naturally, and then play havoc with the rules of grammar? And if he is an actor, his audience couldn't be more than a hundred or so of us scholars across the world, or a people which hasn't been here for sixteen hundred years. Interesting thought that the world will destroy precious loves unless they are hidden. Almost Christian."

"Almost," said the mother superior.

"Yes," said Lew McCardle.

He thanked Sister Olav. He thanked the mother superior. He asked that they help him further by not mentioning these tapes to anyone for a while until his study was over. He also made a gift to the convent in appreciation of its help but, most importantly, to continue its good work. The phrase came easily.

And then the difference from his old job came upon him in full, as he left the convent in darkness, the rented driver opening the door for him. He lied, naturally, and it depressed him. He had said he only studied a little Latin, and that was untrue. He had hidden what he knew, prompted by some instinct which told him what they did not know would be to his benefit. He was not sure how this would work out for him, but it could not hurt him. And all he gave up was a little bit of pride in saying, "Why yes, I have had three years of Latin in high school and four in college, and you thought I was some cowboy, didn't you?"

What bothered Lew McCardle most that night was that he should have been happy to hear that there was a great discovery, a window on the great civilization of the West, once thought to be gone forever. He should have been contributing by providing geographical data.

The patient's very existence could prove temperatures never rose above certain levels in certain areas of the world for at least sixteen hundred years. It was in itself a historical thermometer, a great scientific tool.

And Lew had always thought that if there were ever a conflict between corporate profit and scientific advancement, he could find a way to reconcile the two. Now he had such a conflict. And he was not thinking about reconciling it.

He had never entertained doubts about helping to find energy. Energy was the difference between man dying in his thirties or his sixties. It was that basic. It was necessary for civilized survival.

Unlike his daughters, he had never viewed transportation, heat, and power as some right of birth, and oil exploration, which made it possible, as some desecration of the earth. He knew there was a price to be paid for a sixty-year life expectancy.

What he did not know and had successfuly kept from himself when he was a geologist was how ready he was to pay any price, not for mankind's benefit, but for Houghton's assured profit. More specifically, his own retirement.

He was not proud of himself.

He had lied in the convent to the excitable nun. He had studied more than a little Latin. He had three years of it in high school and four at Texas M and C, the only football player in the class.

"Don't you think you might be happier with another subject?" the professor had asked. It was a woman and she spoke with a British accent, and it was known that she had some reservations about teaching the subject to Americans, and more reservations about teaching it to Texas Baptists, and no intention of giving a football player a passing grade because coach and administration felt obliged to keep muscle in the stadium. If Mr. McCardle wanted a passing grade, he should take push-ups, or whatever the requirements were for the football team.

"I had four years of Latin in high school, ma'am," Lew had said.

"Yes. North Springs, Texas?"

"Yes, ma'am."

"That might not be adequate preparation."

"I'll make up for whatever I missed," Lew had said. She had failed half the class trying to fail him, and only at the end of the semester did she realize that he was a good student, disguised in his big body and Texas twang and with parents he didn't want to talk about.

She was also the reason why, after eight full years of Latin, even long ago, Lew had not recognized snatches of the language from the tape recordings.

He had always assumed Latin was spoken with a British accent. And it was a shock realizing now how foolish he had been to think Julius Caesar spoke like Claude Rains or Crassus like Basil Rathbone or any British actor, just because the British claimed the grandeur of Rome for themselves.

Lew McCardle had not recognized the tapes because the subject had sounded—it was too embarrassing even to admit his own stupidity to himself—too Italian.

In Oslo, he found a Latin-English dictionary, bought a bottle of scotch, and stayed up the night consumed with the tapes.

CHAPTER

X

Fifth Day — Petrovitch Report

Condition remains critical. Improvement stalled. Several small lapses. Move to new, special intensive-care unit done without any apparent, harmful effects. Closer observation now available. One word quite recognizable: "Ma." Unfortunately, that is the word for mother in Indo-European, covering every European language from Slavic to French, according to L. McCardle.

It was a good day for the games, sunny, but not draining on the crowds. It would be hot, but not uncomfortably so.

As always, I was there at dawn with my slaves in my cubicle, resting. Before the first of the crowds were there, I was there. Separated, secure, lying on a couch covered with linen, feeling the soothing hands of a body slave work oil into me.

Normally, everything is done for me in virtual silence, but this day was the last day of the arena for me, and the fact was shared with the men.

"Before this day ends, Plutarch is a freedman," I announced, sitting up in the couch. The big slave, who knew every grain of sand in the arena, trembled like a child.

"No," I said. "You are free now. Now you are a free man. This instant. Bear witness, all of you. Plutarch is free."

"To do what, master?" he asked, his giant hands searching the air helplessly.

"To be free."

"But I have not built a peculium. What will I live on?"

"I will make one for you."

"If I did not accumulate money as your slave, how will I keep it as a freedman? I would prefer to remain yours, where the food is good, where I have my woman, I have my wine, I have a place to sleep which is comfortable, and most of all, my skills are always used well."

"So be it."

"You have never beaten me," he said, and he wept. He was a bulky man, having once been trained for the arena. The tears wet his fat cheeks.

"You have never deserved it, Plutarch. I have never complimented you here, because under your guidance perfection has become as sure as the sunrise and as plentiful as the air. And, therefore, just as unnoticed in its regularity."

Plutarch kissed my hands.

"We need my hands, Plutarch. Stop," I said. All the slaves laughed and so, finally, did Plutarch.

"Since I am free, I tell you, seal your mouth," said big Plutarch, his eyes still with the tears of happiness. "Rest."

He pushed me playfully down, face forward into the linen already darkened by the oils from my body. The first joyous shouts of the people came to us in the lonesome cubicle like calls of birds. There is a pathetic sound to voices from people who know that whatever they think or say at that moment will be meaningless compared to the great event they are going to see. Woe to him who fails to provide it. Domitian would be equally invested in that sand with me.

More than a city-state, more than the village of my birth would come here this day.

This quiet time is always set aside for me to empty my mind and then, bit by little bit, to fill it with my purpose this day. From empty to full.

Perhaps it was because there was Publius facing me who could not strain my skills, perhaps it was my son who confronted me with my mother, perhaps it was remembering that I had been distracted by the latifundia in the bad games that led to this, perhaps because this was the last time I would ever lie like this, so quiet, but this time I allowed myself to think and to remember how I came here, how I became a slave, how I became a gladiator whose single presence could fill the biggest arena with more people than the village I was born in.

It was small, in northern Greece, and my mother was the daughter of the king. King? He could lead twenty men at most and this meant, more than likely, that he was the one who had the helmet and the sword. I remember horses, but I do not remember riding them. We spoke only the Roman language, and my mother reminded me how Roman I was, and that my father, an important man and a Roman, would come back to take us to that great city where he was an important man. In this Greek village, I was raised with the mother tongue of the center of the earth.

When the villagers told me about my father, they spoke well of Rome, for the taxes did not appear heavy, compared to the previous great taxes demanded by robber bands. Rome ended the rule of the big cities, cleared away the robber bands, and built the first roads giving us access to the wisdom and beauty of the great city of Athens. This I learned from my mother, Phaedra, whom the king married to a Roman merchant, Gnaeus. Gnaeus sired me, took the dowry, and did not return until my eighth year. I do not even remember what he looked like.

My mother packed things on a cart and told me everything would turn out fine. I had not been aware until that time that there was something coming that needed a good resolution. I was eight, I was trusting, and I do not remember raising a hand to anyone, it being considered unvirtuous to fight friends.

We traveled many days, with my mother and me in the back of the cart and my father driving. He did not play with me as other fathers did with their sons, but seemed to try not even to look at me. He never called me by my name and gave orders to my mother when he wanted me to get on and off the cart, as though I were a pet of hers.

One day we stopped at a large latifundium with more people

than I had ever seen. My father drove off, leaving my mother and me. I would find out when I was older, through agents, that he had lost my mother and me in a game of bones. It was beneath his honor, after the wager was lost, to impose stipulations upon the loss, such as that my mother and I should be used in a city house, that she should weave, and I should be used for reading and writing.

It was the first latifundium I had ever seen. In later years I would have paid five times its worth just to know its name. I do not remember the first night there, but I do remember the second day. I was put on carts, rubbing grease into wheel axles. After a while I grew tired and said my back ached, and I ran away looking for my mother. I wanted to go home because I did not like this place. Another slave stopped me. When I told him my back ached and I wanted to go home, he asked where it ached, and there he hit me harder than I had ever been hit before. I looked for grownups to make him stop hitting me, but they were laughing. I remember thinking this is not happening. This could not be happening. Grownups do not act this way. This is not happening. I went back to the wheels crying, thinking I could not endure the pain.

At night, when I told my mother, she became angry with me, saying these were ignorant slaves who did not know our special status. We would go home shortly. There were stipulations that we were not slaves but only on loan to this place. The slaves could not know these things because merchants did not take the slaves into their confidence concerning business affairs. My father was using us as a point of honor to show the owner of the latifundium he could be trusted while he went out to make lots of money. He was going to return for us and make us wealthy. We were going to see Athens, maybe even Rome itself.

The one thing my father did not want was to return here and see that I had turned into a slave. Then he would never take me out. A person was only a slave if he thought himself a slave. She told me not to associate with others because I would pick up their slave habits.

But I knew better. On the wagons that brought water to the fields, I knew better. In the cold nights that made me hate the cold forever, I knew better. I knew better in the long barns in which we slept surrounded by a stench that at first made me vomit, but then became welcome because it meant sleep. I knew better, when I stole food and brought it to my mother. She would not eat it, because stealing was a slave's way of doing things. She made me return that handful of barley to the wagons hauling it. The slave I gave it to laughed and threw it on the ground, for he worked at the storage houses and had access to wheat itself. There was no condition so low that there was not a lower one.

I told my mother about that, but she said it was not the food or whether anyone needed it or cared about it. The important thing was that we did not eat stolen food. We were not slaves.

She made no secret about what she thought was our special status. One night, the men in the barn, goaded by the women, raped my mother to show her who she was. She screamed they would be crucified because there were special stipulations for her release and that she was only collateral for a business loan made by her husband, her legal husband, a Roman citizen.

At the time I thought the men were beating her up with the help of the women who held her arms. But it was strange because I saw many do it in that large barn, usually without screams. It was, of course, copulation, but I had never seen people do it so publicly. She would not let me sleep near her that night.

In the morning, like all the rest, she was led to the fields. When she complained to the vilicus himself, showing scars about her face and body, she was cuffed back to work. It was harvest, and one did not delay this crucial work or cause commotion in the groups.

A cart was unloading water for the slaves in the field when I noticed a scythe lying at the feet of the first man to assault my mother. He was using his given moment for drink. I slipped between his legs and swung the scythe upward into his chest. It was a wild, sloppy stroke, but it struck just beneath the heart and kept going. I had killed a man. And during the harvest.

He was not cold before I had my first collar on my neck, and I was put in a cart all by myself and driven from the latifundium. My mother, seeing me taken off, ran to me, and only the vilicus and his armored slaves stopped her. The other slaves stood still, and the woman who had led the goading strangely attacked the armored slaves to save my mother, and so both were beaten.

She called out my name and my collar restrained me. I cried, but instead of weeping I should have taken note of the mountains, the buildings, how long the journey was to the sea, how long the journey was on the sea, what the port we left from looked like, and where the sun was at midday in relationship to the land.

I was eight years old and had killed a man. Instead of being punished I was sold to a lanista at Capua where the best gladiators are trained. A nuisance on a latifundium, I was of value in Capua for not every man will kill by nature, and most must be trained to it with molten rods and flogs. Not even for their own lives will some men kill. I had killed at eight.

The lanista laughed when he saw me crying, saying, "This is the killer we paid so dearly for."

The food was good. Where I had been beaten once by another slave for taking a gnarled pear on the latifundium, here in Capua I had all the pears I wanted, provided I ate my barley first, for barley builds bulk. The food was better than my mother's father ate in the big house with all the horses in the city of my birth.

I was the youngest in the school by eight years and most were no younger than sixteen. Not knowing what size I would be to fit which weapons, they trained me in all forms: net and tridens, secutor minor armored, Samnite heavy armored, Thracian dagger, and even the fists of the pugilist, should I turn out to be big and slow. To goad others, the lanista used me as an example whenever I did something right, pointing out that even little Eugeni could do this or that.

This all but exiled me from the others. And learning so young, I learned properly, so that in a time of panic I could only revert to what was right, never having known anything else. Captives, on the other hand, would often revert to what they had learned in their far-off homelands, invariably taught by their fathers who were shepherds or hunters.

When I was twelve, with four years of hard training and somewhat large for my size, Greeks accused me of being haughty because I spoke Latin better than they, always trying to imitate the lanista in speech and manner. I refused to fight, and reported their threats to the lanista. But because it was in my interest to maintain order in his school and because gladiators could earn coins for their peculium in fights, he approved of me and lashed those he didn't.

I told the lanista I was willing to fight one of them, but I did not consider it proper to waste his property for anger which, I said, I truly felt. When he asked me which one I hated, I told him "the slow one." At this he laughed to tears, and I thought I was being most grave. He said I would be too valuable to risk just yet, that I had a good seven or eight years until I began my good strength. He said he would punish him.

"If you fear for my life, then that is the best way to lose it, dominus, for surely the punishment would build such resentment that they would see me dead one way or another."

"And where would you want this match, Eugeni?"

"The big arena in Rome. They free gladiators there for good fights. And they give them money."

"And what would you do with money, little Eugeni?"

"I would buy my mother's freedom."

"You have a mother?"

"Yes, dominus."

"You should not have been separated. While slaves do not have legal recourse and though slavery is a hard, hard thing, we in all our hardness and sometimes cruelty are not that hard. A child is never separated from his mother. This is an infamy, Eugeni."

"Worse than an infamy, dominus. It is a fact."

The lanista thought a moment. I remember standing before him while he sat, and his large grownup's head was eye to eye with me. I would find out later that he was one of the few lanistae who comported himself with respect and was honest in his dealings. But being a child, I thought all lanistae were like him and all Romans like him, for he was the second Roman I had dealings with—the first being my father, who was hardly a recommendation for a people.

"What sort of slave was your mother? What did she do?"

"She could weave."

"She may be expensive, Eugeni. That would be a lot of money."

"She was harvesting when I was taken away."

"Then she would not be too expensive. We can get ourselves a bargain because we know she can weave, don't we? But the latifundium doesn't. That is good. We will make a contract between us. I will buy your mother for a victory. That is our agreement. You have my word."

"Dominus, why do you pay for what is yours already?"

The lanista smiled. I remember he had a scar through his gray hair, and while his face to others was hard, to me it was the glory of the gods themselves. For with him, I knew that if I did things properly, I would be rewarded, and there were rights he granted. They were not the most awesome of freedoms and prerogatives and protections, but coming from the latifundium they seemed great indeed.

"I own your body and rights to punish you. But I do not own your spirit."

"You own it now, dominus."

"Let us say I have earned it now."

The lanista said I was hardly ready for Rome, even if boys were allowed to fight there. I would find out later that Romans considered the gladiatorial combats a sign of manhood. Therefore child gladiators were an infamy, although they readily let captive children participate in the acts where gladiators would represent soldiers sacking a town and killing everyone. They were old enough to die but not to fight for their lives. But in the small arenas there were no rules. The lanista could fight whomever he wished with whatever he wished. Since the slow Greek would have to be a pugilist anyway and not worth much, he had a small private showing for the first patricians I had ever seen.

They were beautiful to my eyes in the way they moved, the way the women wore their hair, and the cleanliness of the men's faces. Their white garments made them appear like gods. I had never seen cloth so white. And of course it was the first time I saw the broad purple stripe.

I could hear their comments on the sand, so small was the arena. I was dressed like a Thracian dagger man, with only a loincloth and sandals, but I had a sword and a light shield, like a secutor. The slow Greek was laden with armor like a heavy Samnite, and his sword hand had enough iron on it to equip a legion. This made him slower still. The woman patrician let out a gasp when she saw how formidable he looked and how bare I looked. Her husband quieted her fears, telling her appearances were deceiving.

"But he is so young," she said.

"Would you wager with me, then?" said the man.

"I would not bet against that poor child," said the woman.

"Neither would I, but I wager he is no poor child. Is that not correct, lanista?"

"Most correct, dominus," said the lanista, and at that time I learned that even the lanista had people he looked up to.

"Then it is not a fair match," said the patrician.

"No. It is not. I would not risk that boy at twelve."

"Settling some problems in your school?" asked the patrician.

"Yes," said the lanista.

"An honest lanista," said the patrician laughing.

"He looks so young. But a boy," said the woman.

"I will wager a thousand sesterces," said the patrician.

"Against what? My husband gives me no money. He keeps me poor," said the woman.

"You are sitting on your treasure, woman," said the patrician, and she agreed.

It was my first match. Men are supposed to be nervous at their first match, but it was then that I first felt the great, cool air in my lungs and the power to run all day. I remember the Samnite armor coming at me so slowly I wondered how a man could be that slow even with his arm weighted down. The sword lazed its way towards my head, and with great ease I was under it and at his neck, almost like a slow dance. His body, falling on me, pinned me, and he bled to death atop me, his life spilling from his throat. I was not strong enough to lift him off and had to wriggle from beneath. I stood above his hulk and looked to the lanista for the signal.

"You have already done your job, little gladiator," said the patrician and he threw coins at me. They were gold.

The woman complained that she didn't see what happened.

The patrician took delight in explaining to her about combat.

"You saw a Roman-trained gladiator execute a slave. I told you before it was not a match, dear. This was not a match. To a trained eye, there was no contest from the beginning. They could have used a cross." He demanded his money back, but the lanista said he had been told honestly what he would see. The patrician said there was no magistrate in the empire who would take the word of a lanista against a patrician.

Terror seized me when I thought that perhaps I would not get my mother if the match were not paid for. I offered another match, and the lanista had me whipped with a rod for my insolence in talking to him and a patrician while they were in conversation. It was not a hard whipping, and it was done on my buttocks where the marks would not show. I hardly felt it. But my terror was such that I would not have felt the hot irons, either. It was agreed, and for more, that I would fight another gladiator, the patrician giving the money first, but also inspecting the armor first. The lanista would not let him select the gladiator.

There was a Briton who had no training but was huge. He was faster than the Greek. But I knew now that a match consummated too quickly might not be paid for. He swung his sword in the wide arcs of a scythe, and it made a ferocious noise going about my head. As with the Greek, it all seemed so slow. But this time I did not take the finish quickly, even though I heard the lanista yelling for it. I knew I could tell him later I heard nothing in the sand, but I heard everything. The woman's shrieks, the man's cheers. I was not strong enough to block a direct blow, but I did not have to. He slashed. He was armored as a secutor and had half his body bare. I took nicks that if followed through would be kills. I danced with him, and worked him towards me. When panting, he moved the sword even more slowly. I opened his belly and caught his right thigh from behind, lowering him to the sand. I mounted his chest looking for the signal which was death. But his huge hand grabbed my leg and upended me. I rolled as he crawled toward me, and, with my own belly on the sand and both of us at the same level, I put my short sword into his neck as his huge hand lowered on my head, pushing it into the sand.

I knew where his body was and got to it many times without seeing, for the sand was in my eyes. There was an Egyptian physician at the school and he washed out my eyes, right there on the sand, as the patrician and the woman screamed my name. The patrician wanted to buy me.

"You could have named a price before this match. Now you cannot have him for a half million sesterces," said the lanista.

"He will be worth a million when he is grown," said the patrician. "I know combat. That is the gladiator the way they used to be. I am the first to see him, and I tell you, lanista, you are a wealthy man. Twelve years old!"

For this I received ten gold coins from the lanista and six from the patrician, which brought my peculium to twenty—the price I had been bought for. Yet even then I knew. I knew I was much more valuable than I could afford. In Rome, they freed gladiators for great performances. Just for a fight they did this. Yet I was not troubled by my own rising worth. For now I would see my mother and tell her how good life was and that she should not worry about me. She would see the food I ate, the magnificence of my couch, how slaves oiled me, and how I relaxed just like a Roman in the baths. And she would enjoy this, too. I had hoped the lanista would take her as a woman, he being so kind.

The lanista showed me a parchment with drawings on it. He said it was a map. A long peninsula was Italia, having first been conquered by a dot that was Rome, the center of the world. A large blob was the sea. I had come that way because I had been picked up at the nearby port.

"Now we bought you from a dealer with the guarantee that you had killed. Today, you proved yourself a good investment. But this dealer is dead, and the problem is latifundium slaves are not recorded as to where they are from and who they are. They are sold in lots. So you are going to have to tell me exactly where the latifundium is, what its name is, what your mother's name is, and what she looks like."

"She was beautiful, dominus. Her name was Phaedra."

"But what did she look like?"

"Very beautiful. I see her some nights in dreams."

"Describe them."

"She is kind and she sings to me in my dreams."

"Yes, but that does not help me, for they are not my dreams."

So, well trained with a sword, I found myself weak with descriptions. I said she had eyes like one slave and hair like another and a nose like another.

"And what was the name of your mother's city? For we can say we want to purchase Phaedra from Thebes or from Pharsalus or from Actium."

"It was called the city. It did not have a name. But I know names of all the other cities, and the one I do not mention will be the one."

"You cannot know all the cities at your age, Eugeni."

"I do. Athens and Iberia."

"Iberia is a country, Eugeni. When you came by boat did you leave the shore? How long did you take? Where was the shore? Where did the sun rise?"

"I do not know." I was crying. "But it was a big latifundium."

"The world is filled with latifundia. Don't you know its name?"

"No," I said. I felt panicked, like a new man seeing his first arena death. We estimated, by my remembrances of mountains as a child and the way it was cold there, that I had come from northern Macedon, Greece. I had high cheekbones, and this might also show a touch of Dacian blood beside my Roman and Greek blood. I did not remember how long the journey was to where my father sold us, but I did remember one of his names being Gnaeus. And yet I did not remember the others.

"He was in Athens a lot," I said. And thus began my quest to find my mother. It never fully ended and it was never successful. They found traces of my father within a year because I knew he dealt in dyes. There was a Gnaeus who had lost his wife and son in a gambling game, and she was from a provincial village.

According to the tales brought back, he was so remorseful about his life, he killed himself regretting every day that he had sold his wife and son. He drank much and blamed the wine for his misdeeds.

"If that is what wine does, I will never drink," I said. "I would not do what he did if hot irons were buried in my belly."

"They say he regretted what he did. And he took his own life."

"That was his to take," I said. "Ours were not his to gamble."

"According to the law in that province they were, Eugeni."

"When I am rich, and I will be rich, dominus, I will buy all the law there is."

Until I was sixteen I was matched for private showings. I assumed the size and the speed to use any weapon, but knowing all, I made the combination of the punching shield and the long spatha with the point the best for my skills.

I earned extra coins not only in the arenas around Capua, but was rented out as a bodyguard to women and men. I drew a high price because they did not want the sword I held in my hand, but the one on my body. After a match, the price was higher. But in those years, I began spending the money freely, for I knew I could never afford to buy my freedom as I became more valuable. I bought misinformation and charlatan's skills at telling me where my mother was: through looking at chickens eating corn and at the shape of a goat's liver. One even looked at a glass vial and said he could not see my mother but felt she was content.

I even bought three old latifundium slaves called Phaedra, and it was sadder still knowing they were not her when I met them. One was afraid she would be beaten for revealing her name was

Lilith. I put them in the lanista's house, where he promised they would be treated well. When I was sixteen years old he said he could not live through another match of mine, because I was just too valuable for his purse to risk. The excitement was too much for him.

I was sold to Lucius Aurelius Cotta for one million, three hundred and fifty thousand sesterces—the largest sum ever paid for a slave. Of course, rumors had it as twice that.

The lanista kissed me on both cheeks when I left. He told the great Lucius Aurelius Cotta, who had young, dark hair then, that I knew more about the arena than any lanista in Rome. He should follow my advice in all things to do with the arena. He should never use me as a bodyguard or waste me as a teacher of his children in the art of the sword. I was better able to choose my opponents than Lucius Aurelius Cotta, although the lanista thought I could defeat anyone now, and most assuredly when I was twenty.

Lucius Aurelius Cotta rented my performances to people sponsoring games for politics. In Rome then it was quite common for gladiators to fight in groups of twenty and one hundred. I told him his investment could be easily lost because I did not have eyes in my back, although for one gladiator to kill another in the back was almost unheard of.

"What we do is limit as much as possible luck or chance, and by that, dominus, I do not mean diminish the quality of a match. It is the appearance of danger the crowds want, not danger itself, for perhaps the most dangerous thing is the poison in a Syrian's hand, but who would pay to watch someone drink a glass of wine? No, we will have the appearance of danger."

And matches were arranged where I fought one gladiator, took his weapons and fought the next, and with the next's weapons fought the next. Considering that I chose the order of which weapon would fight which, it was not as dangerous as it seemed. I would always appear exhausted before the final match and make a great show of insisting the games go on.

The master of the games would say "no," and he would appeal to the people to end the games. Their decision always sounded like a gigantic growl, indistinguishable from a loud wind. But of course, the master of the games always heard "yes."

I learned to fall safely and even lose my spatha safely, sticking the point down in the sand to keep the pommel clean. Invariably my opponent would guard it, and I would walk away and even pretend to chat with people in the seats. So there he was, looking like a frightened fool. The most dangerous thing would have been for him to touch the pommel with his sweating hands and hand it back to me, for at the moment of grabbing the pommel, I would be closest to him and least secure with my weapon. None did. They always had to chase me to the walls where I could run away and eventually get to my dry-handled spatha getting drier in the Roman sun.

Sometimes I would be chased so clumsily I could snatch my opponent's sword from his hands and kill him like a pugilist. Within two years, Lucius Aurelius Cotta earned back his huge investment that some had called him a fool for making. The biggest attraction, however, was the stories: at first created for me by the mobs themselves and then later by myself for them. I was the boy gladiator who had sold himself into slavery to buy his father arms to retrieve, by himself, the standards lost in a battle in the German forests, where three legions had been annihilated.

In my seventeenth year, Cotta sought the lucrative post of praetor for Iberia. He made the proper donatives to powerful senators and to Emperor Vespasian, father of Titus and Domitian who were both to become emperors.

At that time, a German had decapitated an opponent with one blow in games in which one hundred gladiators had been matched simultaneously. He became famous immediately, and just as immediately I asked Lucius Aurelius Cotta to get me a match with him as soon as possible. Cotta hesitated because he feared he might lose me with a blow, and, while that might offer great excitement, many lanistae had advised him that a beheading might also prove dull or dispiriting to the mobs.

"Dominus, a head comes off with a slash, not a thrust. He is a gift. If he were drugged, the outcome could not be more certain."

"He is very big, a head taller than you. They say he can split a wooden beam with his hands."

"Do not let him get away, dominus, for with this one the mobs will beg you to give me my freedom, and what a great gift it will be. Iberia is yours."

He agreed. Already in a small way I had learned to use rumors. I was going to avenge my father by showing the Germans to be barbarians. Since many had been used by Nero to terrorize the populace and since, about fifty years before, three entire legions had been lost without a trace of them and since my own father had already been said to have died trying to recover the standards of those legions by himself, the city devoured this match like a day drunk with a fresh skin of wine.

It was on sand that I won my freedom. I fought him on my knees, announcing that I only fought equals on my feet. While this looked like foolhardy hatred, it actually exposed the poor brute incredibly, and, while trying to take off my head, he reared back each time. I could have written my name on his stomach with my spatha. But I danced on my knees, working at his stomach bit by bit, prolonging the match until the crowds were hysterical with passion. When his blows were tired and his stomach muscles punctured, I caught his last weak blow with my shield and raised his helpless sword as I stood, pushing it up in his own hands.

I put him to the sand with a blow on the side of his neck, and waited for the signal which was death. His body moved, but he was already dead. I made a great show of a strong effort in dispatching him and then panted as though breath could not come fast enough. In the volcano of noise, Lucius Aurelius Cotta, who was to become praetor, ran out onto the sand and broke a disk. I had never worn one to signify my slavery, but it was clear to Rome that I was freed for this.

There was a saying that men condemned to the arena fought for their lives and, given their lives, fought further to live in order to support themselves. I already had money from my peculium, which had grown heavy.

With the money, I began my search for my mother as a free man instead of a boy. I bought myself a grammarian who resumed my education, which had ended at age eight. Knowing that my own mind might be my worst enemy, the first words I wrote with my own shaking hand were what I remembered about my mother: the colors of my mind's sight, the hills around the latifundium, the shape of the barns, the color of the oxen that pulled the carts. While these were most common, I wanted all the facts unchanged, even those I thought would not help. And that was the great gift of writing, for it did not rely on the unstable memory. These scrolls I did not let slaves see or touch. I was sure the latifundium was in Greece itself because I did not remember crossing the sea. I was sure that was a thing I would have remembered accurately. Yet I did not know south from north or east from west, and the latifundium could even have been in Gaul, if we had traveled inland from the Adriaticum. Yet my cunning told me latifundium slaves were so cheap, my father would not have invested in so long a journey. We must have been a very small wager.

With all I remembered written unchangeably, I bought and studied latifundia: the probabilities of lots being sold off, how long each lived in each job, the chances of my mother's weaving abilities getting her to a less harsh labor, which were good except that beaten slaves were not swiftly put in tanners' or weavers' jobs.

I bought latifundia in Greece, once taking six months to go through each. I purchased heavily around Athens. Having been duped by charlatans while at Capua, I was more careful now not to let anyone know what I was looking for. I explained to one praetor that I was looking for women who bred killers, assuming that might identify my mother more easily, without exposing how precious she was to me. But with the reputation of my growing wealth, I discovered there were enough latifundium slaves birthing killers to annihilate the population of the civilized world one and a half times.

My presence proved to be a hindrance to the search and an added torture to myself, for I saw how latifundium slaves toiled without respite, the vilici working their lives out of them with rods. I ordered that my latifundium slaves be given certain guarantees against beatings and more plentiful food.

In one month I had two slave rebellions that required legions to be put down. The praetor insisted I allow every tenth slave to be crucified, the healthy males being sentenced to the arena.

"Do not try to change the world, Eugeni. It does not change but only becomes more of the same, faster if you hurry it," the praetor had told me. "You are a good boy and a great gladiator. Do not let your soft heart bring ruin to your glory and your happiness."

On the day he told me not to ruin my happiness the rebellious slaves were punished, and one of them could have been my mother, for I realized that should I have seen her, I would not have known her. A child's memory is flawed enough without the drastic changes wreaked by latifundium labor. I had been looking for a young woman, and my mother had to be at least thirty-three or -four, woefully old on a latifundium.

Of course I did not know whether I caused her death any more than I knew if I owned her. At twenty-three I already owned more than forty thousand slaves. And I did not know if one of them was her, nor could I alleviate her burdens if I did own her. I was too rich to get honesty and too poor to change the order of the Roman world.

So I buried the pain of my mother's memory in my heart and kept it from my young family as well as I could, Petronius, my son, thinking I hid facts because I was ashamed of her. I was not ashamed of her. I was ashamed of myself that I could not find her, and might have allowed her execution.

It was also why I would become so distracted at a latifundium that I did not press the family which had sponsored the ruinous games for proof that they could afford proper games.

These things I thought about waiting for my last match.

"Eugeni!" The word was sharp and I felt a hard hand slap my shoulders. It was Plutarch. "Whatever you're thinking, stop that. This is the last time. Last fight. Last day. Perfection in the beginning, perfection in the end. Your muscles are tight like an olive press."

"Thank you, Plutarch," I said. But I could not help thinking that of all the games supposed to honor the dead, none had honored my mother.

She had to be dead, I told myself, although never honored in death. Lying on the small couch in the special cubicle, I realized that was a Roman thing. And she was not Roman. Perhaps I should have told Petronius about her, but I feared his sharp tongue. The boy used truth like a scourge.

"Eugeni!" It was Plutarch again. "A little while longer, great gladiator, and then no more. Just a while longer."

"Yes," I said. "I empty my mind now." I stared at my fingers and listened to the crowd.

"Eugeni!" he said.

"My mind is clear."

"Your body makes you a liar, dominus," he said. "You lost control."

And he was right.

But then I was on my stomach. And now I am on my back. That was Rome. And this is beyond the empire, and suddenly I see it. The biggest head I have ever seen. He is the largest man, with red-flecked face, wearing a gray tight slave's tunic. I cannot move my legs.

Somebody calls him. Grunts. Who is and what is this giant Macudal? What is a Macudal? Where am I? Where is Plutarch? Why is everyone in white?

CHAPTER XI

It opened its eyes. It stared.

"It is focusing," said Petrovitch. "Look, McCardle. The eyes."

The lids were open and the black eyes, so black Lew could not discern the pupils, seemed to latch on to Lew's eyes.

It was a strange feeling for Lew McCardle, like a corpse or a ghost. Yet this ghost blinked in apparent terror. Its tannish skin, blotched with white, its lips dry with whitish spittle at the edges, its body living through machines here in the new intensive-care unit Houghton had provided Petrovitch, it looked at Lew. And then it closed its eyes again and was mumbling. This was the seventh day since Petrovitch's team had refused to accept its death. The cheeks so tender once they were savaged by mere gauze now grew whole again, serviced with the life of blood. It also had a beard.

"I think it saw us," said Lew.

"I think you are right, Lew. I think you are right. Now what are you not telling me?"

"You know just about everything. It will take time to get you reports on where it was discovered, but we're in no rush. We aren't even certain it's going to live."

"No. No," said Petrovitch. He stared only at the body gone back to its mumbling sleep. "Who is he really?"

"We don't know, yet."

"There are limits even to my trust, Dr. McCardle."

"This is a great achievement of yours. Why can't you accept it?"

"I would like to accept it. I would like to believe that it was not living and warm but a few minutes before I got it."

"You saw the ice."

"On the outside."

The nurse, assigned to this period of sitting with the living specimen, became more entranced with the doctor's conversation than her novel.

Petrovitch nodded to the door.

"Come. Come with me, and I will share my doubts about John Carter with you. All right?"

Outside the door marked "John Carter," and "Private," Dr. Petrovitch lit a British Oval with a gold Dunhill lighter. The oxygen tent inside prohibited smoking.

"There's a story going around about some Houghton executive playing sexual games in the snow, and your transporting him here for us to save him. Hush hush."

"Yes, there is that story. I didn't start it, but I'm not going to stop it. As long as people believe that, we are not going to have a circus of publicity around here. It protects you."

"And you?"

"I have other interests," said Lew. He carried the tapes with him in a small attaché case. He had yet to tell Dr. Petrovitch about the language.

"Come with me and we will have lesson number one in cryonics: what we have done, what we can do, and what we have yet to do."

"You've done a lot with John Carter," said Lew.

"It would be nice to think so," said Dr. Petrovitch, his thick, doughy features like a gloomy pudding made without sugar or decoration. "So nice to think so."

He sighed and walked down the hall toward the elevator with Lew following.

They took the elevator down to the basement with Petrovitch explaining his lab was here and how spread out everything was. Petrovitch had a key to the lab on a key ring so crowded it could have been worn by a night watchman.

The dull gray metal door had warning signs on it. Petrovitch said they were not just to keep people out. There was danger inside, he said.

The lab was dark and smelled of some dank chemical swamp.

"Chilly in here," said Lew.

"No. Sixty-nine point eight Fahrenheit," said Petrovitch.

"I could take it in Celsius, too," said Lew McCardle.

Petrovitch shut the door behind them. Lew heard a lock click. They were in blackness, and suddenly a harsh fluorescent battery of lights assaulted the eyes with white, as Petrovitch turned on the lights. Lew blinked trying to adjust to the harsh light.

He saw four large white-bellied sinks in the middle of the room. He let his hand drop to one and felt the white lining of the sink was soft. Polished stainless steel boxes, about eight feet high, came out of one wall. Each box had square drawers. There were forty drawers in all, half with small, round windows and all had monitoring instruments in them. Long pipes, some of them sweating moisture, some apparently insulated, came out of the ceiling into the boxes. It looked modern, yet it had flaws so common in Soviet engineering. McCardle wasn't sure what these large compartments were for, but he knew that good engineering did not have right angles in pipes. It was just bad. He assumed this arrangement was designed by Petrovitch for low-temperature experimentation. The man had a good reputation in the field.

"The finest cryonics equipment in the world," said Dr. Petrovitch. "This side of Moscow, of course."

Dr. Petrovitch counted down the drawers from the top of one polished stainless-steel box. He hummed a tuneless garble, assured himself he had the right container, and pulled the drawer. The front plate with the glass panel folded down as the drawer came out. The inside was white and spotless. Dr. Petrovitch raised a hand, signaling McCardle to wait.

"A frog please," said Dr. Petrovitch.

"I don't have one with me," said McCardle.

"The black rubber tanks behind you."

McCardle saw a series of black tubs with lids. He lifted a lid on a middle one. The water was dark.

"Not that one," sad Dr. Petrovitch. "To your left."

McCardle replaced the lid and took the lid off the next one. He looked to Dr. Petrovitch, who nodded. McCardle dropped his jacket on his briefcase. He rolled up his left sleeve and plunged the hand into the dark water. He felt the short, squirmy kicks of fast things against his hands and through his fingers. He cornered something against the wall of the tub, cupping his hand for a prison. He moved the cupped prison up along the side with the skipping, pushing thing still trapped inside. Above the water line he let the water drip out thoroughly then slid his captive to the top, where his other hand waited to make an escape-proof chamber. He felt it jump and splatter around inside his hands as he brought it to Dr. Petrovitch. The water smelled of fresh green algae, like a swampy womb of life. Dr. Petrovitch nodded to the tray.

"Don't touch the tray. Drop it in the center quickly, if you please."

McCardle saw the frog for the first time and only briefly, as he separated the bottoms of his hands. The little fellow was green with yellowish stripes and black circles. He had big black, sad, round eyes. He blinked. Dr. Petrovitch pushed the drawer closed and pressed a switch. McCardle could see into the drawer through the clear panel. It was lit with a purplish light. The frog did not jump. He quivered momentarily, and even the quiver stopped. The black eyes changed immediately to white. The dots and yellow stripes became white: a little white crust of frog. It was still.

"Sixty seconds," said Dr. Petrovitch. He opened the drawer, took an index card from his pocket, slid it under the white little frog, and carried it to the sinks. He dropped it. It hit with a little click and bounced to its nose, where it stayed balanced between nose and left leg. Its back feet curled beneath it as though caught by a camera while diving into the sink. It stayed diving.

"Dr. McCardle, I now offer you my proposition. Anything you want, just name it, if you do me a simple thing."

McCardle was quiet.

"Bring it back to life," said Dr. Petrovitch. "Its systems are much less complex than a human body, and I am sure its freezing conditions were far more exact and favorable than your cargo. You bring this frog back to life."

"I'm not an expert in cryogenics," said McCardle.

"Cryonics, doctor. Cryogenics is low-temperature physics. I am talking about cryonics, biological low temperature. The effect low temperatures have on living matter. An entirely other thing, which is where you made your mistake."

"We found the body eight point two meters down in the ice, Semyon."

"After he fell there in an accident, or what?"

"You saw the body on delivery."

"I saw external ice."

"He was stiff as an iron pipe," said McCardle.

Dr. Petrovitch nodded while smiling sarcastically. "In any case, before we make this a criminal affair, would you please be so kind as to bring this little frog back to life."

"Well, I don't know too much about your discipline, fella. You're the expert."

"Yes, I am. Which was your mistake."

"You've achieved a miracle and you're doubting your own success?" said McCardle. He buttoned up the sleeve. A small drop of water remained on his pinky nail.

A patch of frost at the frozen webbed toes glistened. It was thawing.

"Make it live, Dr. McCardle. Do this little thing for me."

"Can you do it?"

"No," said Dr. Petrovitch, "and neither can anyone else. Take a stool and I will tell you what we can do and cannot do."

They could bring the frog's sperm down to inactive levels of temperature, and bring it back to levels of high enough temperatures to make it active. It could then fertilize eggs. They could freeze human sperm and whole blood. This was common practice now at hospitals.

There had been some notable successes. The small intestines of a dog had been frozen for a week and revived. Not in Oslo, and not by Dr. Petrovitch. His area of discipline had been primarily treating frostbite, the revivification of limbs, skin, and other partial elements of the anatomy, which was why an oil company doing exploration in northern climes would know of Dr. Petrovitch.

"I know of you and know you, Semyon."

"In a professional relationship," said Dr. Petrovitch.

Lew McCardle tried to light a cigar, and Dr. Petrovitch told him there was no smoking in the laboratory. Among other things accomplished elsewhere was the freezing of a calf embryo and the replacing of it by surgery, after the rapid-thaw process, in the uterus of a cow. It was born alive. This was done in England without giving the Soviet Union the proper credit for the rapid-thaw process. A dog's kidneys had been lowered to 58 degrees below zero Fahrenheit, and revived. A cat's brain had been frozen for 182 days, and when brought back to normal temperature, again through Soviet techniques of rapid simultaneous thawing of cells, it resumed electrical activity. That's what had been done.

"And that body upstairs?" said McCardle. "We had to dig to get it out of the ice."

Petrovitch shook his head. "Not that body upstairs. That's too healthy for a trusting Russian."

"There's no such thing as a trusting Russian. So get off it, Semyon."

"There's no such thing as a crystallized body being restored. Crystallization destroys cells. They are like little bombs going off in the body," said Petrovitch, his hands going wide as though pleading for something, his whole manner that of a man exhausted spiritually.

"If it can't be done, why do people have themselves frozen?"

"For the same reason pharaohs were buried with their boats and servants, people light candles and sprinkle incense, while others create societies and art they hope will last forever. We're afraid of death, Dr. McCardle. It is a property of the human animal, as reflexive as breathing. It keeps the human race alive. People who have themselves frozen can't accept death. It is hardly anything more than the eternal myth and hope of resurrection. I leave that to the churches. Look around you, no spires, no crucifixes, no candles. Instruments."

The frog was wet and shiny. Dr. Petrovitch righted it with a finger under its stiff head, like a small statue. It stayed as stiff and as perfect as its last movement in the drawer. Internally, it was still frozen. The little yellow lines had returned and so had the dots. But the eyes were white. McCardle found himself wondering whether it was a baby or a full-grown frog.

"I know of a scientist who had it done to himself, frozen in a capsule, and, from what I remember, he was a highly rational man," said McCardle.

"I know of whom you speak. And his reasoning was that having himself frozen gave himself, what he called, a nonzero chance of recovery. If you are buried in the ground and your body decomposes naturally, there is a zero chance of recovery. When he talked of zero chance of recovery, he really meant death. Zero is death."

Dr. Petrovitch, by the way, was fully familiar with the cryocapsules that stored people. The freezing concept itself was correct. They drained the body and cooled it to 10 degrees Celsius, then perfused the arteries with glycerol. Blood was not a good freezing agent because it crystallized. Once the body was filled with this cellular antifreeze, it was lowered to minus 79 degrees Celsius at which temperature molecular movement ceases.

McCardle said he was aware of that.

"The problem is not freezing a body. That can be done quite well. The problem is in unfreezing. I could freeze you very well now, I just couldn't bring you back to life. Even in single cells, thawing is only seventy percent effective. Which leaves, under the best conditions, thirty percent damaged or, if you will, dead. The human body is so complex with so many billions of cells, it is impossible to perfuse it thoroughly with glycerol, assuming glycerol works perfectly which I do not think it does. And with the brain—hah, hah, hah—you get something that looks like a brain, is composed of brain cells, smells like a brain, feels like a brain, and might as well be cauliflower. People are not frozen dinners, Dr. McCardle. Dead is still dead."

"And when did you change your mind?"

"When it started talking. When it started talking, I would have had to believe that under less than ideal conditions, a brain had been revived intact with more than ninety percent, if not one hundred percent, recovery. All this with all the other organs. I couldn't do it with our little frog here, and yet nature is supposed to do it with an incredibly more complex human body with its original blood?"

"The blood looked brackish."

"No. No. No. What happened, my dear Dr. McCardle, was you thought you had killed him near the hospital and froze the poor person ineptly so that the brain never froze, the organs never froze, and gullible trusting Semyon Petrovitch provided you with the disposal of a body you had just tried to kill. Or maybe the CIA tried to kill him. I am no murderer. I do not know how your mind works."

"So why didn't you phone the police?"

"I want no trouble here. I am on loan to the university. I told my embassy."

"So it's not your problem."

"It is not a political problem, it is a scientific one."

"Well, friend, you have a bigger one right now. You've got a doozy. You'll hear it."

McCardle opened his attaché case with slightly wet hands slipping on the brass snaps. Careful not to wet one of the tapes, he found an early one and snapped it into a slim aluminum recorder, also taken from the case. In the case was a Latin-English dictionary with a few corners already worn.

"I have friends who have heard those ramblings from John Carter, and they declare them peculiar."

"At your embassy, KGB?" asked Lew, although it was a silly question. Of course they had. They weren't going to be drawn into something blind. They didn't run their country like men ran their lives. Dr. Petrovitch had to have their permission.

Petrovitch pointed to the frog. McCardle rewound the tape. Perovitch pressed his finger down on the little frog's back. The shiny skin gave way under the finger. It was thawed. But for the once-shiny black eyes, it looked alive. They were white. The crystallization of water had destroyed them. It had also, McCardle knew, destroyed the brain.

"Dead," said Dr. Petrovitch, "is dead." He clasped a slippery hind foot of the little frog delicately and finally dropped it into a small bucket.

Only moisture and a small black speck with a small red streak remained on the white sink top. Even if the eyes had returned to their shiny blackness, it still would have been just as dead.

McCardle played the tape and this time, listening for it, he heard the name "Publius."

"So?" said Dr. Petrovitch.

"So undoubtedly your friends, who understand the criminal mind, have heard some of the tapes, if not this one already."

"I do not know how they operate," said Dr. Petrovitch, using superiority like a fence.

"They have, have they not?" said Lew McCardle.

"I imagine," said Dr. Petrovitch.

"Let's assume they had copies of the tapes right away, and let's assume they tried translating within, oh, a day. I'd say an hour, but let's say a day, all right?"

Petrovitch shrugged as if it were of no matter to him.

"And let's say," said McCardle, "they still don't know what language it is, because if they did, you wouldn't be here calling me some sort of murderer. I'm telling you your secret police still haven't translated this tape because they're so suspicious. Their own mentality has protected them from the truth."

"They say it is a form of Italian."

"No, Semyon. Italian is a form of this language and so is Spanish and French. It is Latin. Classical Latin."

The tape stopped and the forward button clicked up.

"So it is a dead language," said Dr. Petrovitch. "So your victim speaks a dead language."

"To whom is he speaking, Semyon?"

"Someone else in a Latin class. You have those things. You study Greek, too."

"In a semicomatose state, Semyon?"

"He is reciting a childhood lesson. It happens."

"Seven days in a row with no other language present?" asked McCardle.

He was not sure the person had not lapsed into some other language until he saw Semyon's face, which did not flinch. McCardle was correct. The body spoke only Latin, and Semyon's embassy staff had yet to identify the language, because Dr. Petrovitch himself had assured them the patient could not have been more than twenty minutes in ice. The Russian embassy apparently had examined every tape.

"How old is he?" asked Dr. Petrovitch.

"At least sixteen hundred years, probably older," said McCardle.

"Are you lying, Lew?"

"No. That is too big a lie."

"It is too big a truth," said Petrovitch. He rubbed his balding scalp and sat down on a high stool. He peered down into the waste bucket where the dead glistening little experiment was and shook his head.

"How?" asked Petrovitch finally. "How?"

"That's what you've got to find out. Now you yourself have admitted that one of the problems with Soviet science is its taste for the spectacular. What's breathing upstairs is pretty spectacular. Do you think if this becomes public knowledge too soon, you're going to have the slightest chance of working scientifically?"

Petrovitch gulped for air. He shook his head. He wouldn't, he knew.

"Not at all. Now I need the same thing. I need to be free of the kind of intense, wild publicity that will surround this guy when they find out what you've done."

"If he lives," said Petrovitch.

"Is there a doubt?"

"I do not know. I do not know," said Petrovitch. He stared vaguely at the ceiling. "The blood. Of course. The blood."

"What?"

"The blood," said Petrovitch, as though Lew had been part of the scientist's innermost thoughts. "The blood. At the wound. It did not feel crystallized, although it might have been melting. I didn't know."

"What?" asked Lew. "Is that possible below freezing?"

"Yes. But not for blood. But this blood was different."

"How?"

"We are finding out. The final tests are not in yet. But somehow the bloodstream at one point did not carry completely normal blood. We saved the blood. We'll find out what it was."

"It was whitish, yellowish, sort of, when I saw it first. But wouldn't that be natural for its state of existence?"

"Of course. The red cells were driven out by the temperature," said Petrovitch. "That wouldn't explain it. There was that odor. That blood was not normal blood. Not at all. There was another element in that bloodstream. And we'll find it."

"When the core sample came up with that piece of thigh . . ."

"The gracilis muscle."

"Whatever. When I felt it, it felt sort of rubbery. There was no crunch under my fingers."

"Yes," exulted Petrovitch. He clapped his hands with a loud crack, blew a kiss to the trash barrel with the remains of the frog, and danced three light steps around the table. "Yes. Yes. Yes. There was no crystallization. None. None. None. None."

"We must be cautious with this," said Lew.

"Absolutely. Absolutely," said Petrovitch, his mind still grappling with medical facts, while Lew was emphasizing political ones. "But why is it so important to you?"

"With the kind of miracle you've done, there will be armies of people and journalists and kook hunters running around looking into where I've been and double-checking where I claim to have found him, which won't be the place I really found him, but they'll find that."

"That you would lie about?"

"Semyon. I want oil. I look for oil. We want to find it by ourselves, so that we can get the rights cheaper. Your own people must have told you that. That's why I don't want the great publicity for a while. That is my area of interest."

"Why would your people tell my people?"

"Because, Semyon, in this business, on the project I was working on, the great enemy is not the Soviet Union but Royal Dutch Shell, Phillips Petroleum, Standard Oil. Those are our enemies in this, not you."

"Capitalism," said Petrovitch, as though that explained all sorts of peculiarities and that to delve further would be a waste of time for one would find only more peculiarities.

"So, we share the same interest. You will work with discretion and a shield that I help provide, and when you are ready, and we are ready, we will announce what a great thing you have done. We laud Soviet science and you laud the commitment of an American oil company. We get the oil. You get the prestige."

"It has to be the blood. It's got to be the blood," said Petrovitch. "A maximum of sixteen hundred years, Lew?"

"No. Minimum, Semyon. It could be two thousand, three thousand. Sixteen hundred is the youngest it could be."

Petrovitch shrugged, his dark eyebrows rising with an acceptable thought. "Sixteen hundred. Actually, at certain temperatures sixteen hundred, a minute and a half, ten thousand years. At certain temperatures they become the same. Organic functions like decomposition need heat. Did you know that?"

"I guess you're right, yes."

"We have another problem, small this time, Lew. Who talks to it, if it recovers enough to talk to people instead of itself."

"The woman suggested by the Romance professor, Semyon. She's a nun. I saw her. She identified the language."

Petrovitch shook his head. "They will try to prove some religious thing. They will."

"I think we could use her and she wouldn't have ambitions."

"Then we must extract a promise, she would not try to prove some religious thing with it."

"She has gone to Oxford."

"I don't trust religious things."

"Meet her."

"Religious people make me uncomfortable. I don't like them."

"Meet her first, and then decide. She is quite taken with the language. I just know she is not the sort who would let religious convictions interfere with academic facts."

"Nuns are lesbians," said Petrovitch.

"Do you know any?"

"If they were not lesbians, why would they become nuns?"

"Is it possible," said Lew smiling, "that you are being a bit irrational?"

"A bit," conceded Petrovitch.

"We have benefits if we use a nun. She is not going to hold press conferences or sell her memoirs or go running off with someone who might sell information."

"What about the nurses?"

"They don't know what we have, and only one is with us who remembers its condition when it arrived. Everyone else thinks it's some dirty-minded executive."

"Let me think about it. If recovery continues, then we will interview her. I have sent her a package without getting a reply. One advantage to having a lesbian is that she will not play around with the subject."

"Maybe she is hoarding a passion and will sexually attack John Carter," said Lew.

"Not John Carter. It should have another name. A Roman name."

"Not yet."

"Yes. You're right. You don't think she would rape a patient, do you?"

"I thought she was a lesbian, Semyon."

"You are right. I am being irrational. Let us see her tomorrow in case we need her. I will talk to her. Although I think it is a waste of time. I cannot imagine anyone so religious being scientific, but who knows? I really don't know if she is a lesbian or what or anything. But I do know there has to be some reason why she would live without men."

"You can ask her tomorrow."

"I might," said Semyon.

But the trip to Ringerike the next day had to be put off. What Petrovitch had feared, happened. Screaming "no," the patient went into shock.

The little figure with the dark skin coughed and was quiet. The tormented mumbling calmed to an occasional whisper. The twitching stopped, like a storm leaving a lake calm.

John Carter was dying.

CHAPTER XII

Eighth Day — Petrovitch Report

Condition poor. Blood pressure down. Heartbeat unsteady. Temperature down. Body producing abnormally high white-cell count without sufficient infections or any other normal stimulus for this action. Apparent, now, that despite its semicomatose state, mental process, as with conscious people, effects physical reaction. Heartbeat rose to 180 when recordings picked up the scream of "no."

The giant is gone, and I am warm again in soft and gentle places that beckon me for my final rest. Remembering the beginning of the disaster was only an interlude. What a great relief to go off without the pains of the mind. It is enough that I lived through it once.

Poor Plutarch. He trusted me. And Demosthenes. And my Miriamne and Petronius. No greater danger has anyone than a fool for a close ally. Better a ferocious and a cunning enemy than an unreliable friend.

Plutarch himself went to my body as we waited for the games.

He mentioned no scars on the back and said to all those in the cubicle that the reason I lived so long was that I had cunningly purchased him and then did not let him fight. He knew, of course, that he had been given an ample demonstration that even his good size would not help him survive long, but it was like one of those untested fancies that do no harm while they remain fancies and untested.

My problem that day was that I would discover what I did love and did not love at the worst possible time. It was a day of much blood and vengeance and started well.

The former master of the games, who had taken the bribes not to insist on elephants at the Vatican games that led to the riot, was the first attraction. After the priests had examined the liver of a goat to determine if the day was suitable to the gods—they always were—the man was led out to the center of the vast arena. His body, but for his right arm, was covered with easily inflammable pitch. He was chained in such a way that he could not move his body. Then, with ropes bound to his clean right hand, arena slaves drew it over burning wood. If he could keep his arm there and let it burn off, he would be free and save his life. To move the arm would make his pitch-covered body a torch.

The other slaves asked Plutarch if they could watch from the slip above us. Plutarch selected one, who described everything in the arena. The master's arm was momentarily in the flames, and then he was a torch. He had tried to take his arm away from the flames.

The new master of the games had the next event moving into the arena before his predecessor stopped screaming. Domitian had uncovered another plot against his life the day before among three senators. They were blindfolded, tied together, and given swords. Domitian both fought the senate and yet simultaneously wanted its public approval for his laws.

While one senator struggled free and the other two lay wounded, the bears were sent in. Unlike lions, they were simply starved and did not have to be specially trained to eat human meat. They feasted and the crowd roared its approval. While they were feasting, a large platform like one used to assault a walled city was rolled into the center of the arena with Domitian on top and horses moving it underneath. From there he hunted the bears with bow and arrow.

I would be next, followed by the criminals, Germans, and Jews willing to fight for their freedom. There had not been enough of these last in the city, so Domitian decreed that Jews building another aqueduct were lazy; and to teach them the value of hard Roman work, he sentenced seven hundred of them to the games. Half would dress as Samnites and the other as hoplites; the most valorous of the survivors were to be given their freedom, with the cowards to be crucified and set aflame in the arena. It was not the best strategy—none is that depends solely on force. But Jews were all Domitian had in numbers for such hasty games. He would have preferred to match different people instead.

The cheers were good. I became quiet, and the unctores worked oil into my body as I lay on my stomach. I watched my sword slave prepare my spatha, a longsword. He kept the pommel wrapped in cloth lest oil touch it, the oil with which he wiped the blade. It was of special steel made in Iberia and forged on one of my latifundia there. It was less hard than other steels but also less brittle, since I did not wish to find myself with a stub in my hands at a crucial moment. The spatha, unlike others, used the blade only for deception. The point was what I used for damaging work. My shield of soft wood wrapped in iron straps, the size of a feeding bowl was a punching and blocking tool with which I could wrest some small momentary advantage. That was all I ever needed, preferring to work a small, safe advantage into another advantage and so on, until only the illusion of conflict remained, with my opponent fighting with a shattered knee or ripped stomach tendon. I could also pound a skull into meat with the helmet still in place, so it would look as though a groggy man were still dangerous.

Publius had arrived with family retainers, although most of his friends, as did most patricians, publicly dissociated themselves from him, saying it was a disgrace that he should appear in the arena.

As each wrapping and each piece of armor went on, I was informed. Legionnaire sandals, metal and leather skirt, metal chest piece, and helmet. But it was not an officer's helmet. I had assumed Publius' fancy would endorse his patrician tastes, and he would parade out before Rome like some shiny general. He had come to fight. Good for him.

Perhaps terror had finally made him vulnerable to wisdom. He had the scutum, the large rectangular shield of the legion, which could cover a man's body. Stretched side to side by a thousand legionnaires across a valley, it became a wall. In the arena, it would be little more than baggage. It was too heavy. I could move around it with as much ease as Publius. The short sword—the staple of the legion—was a good instrument, especially in a mass of bodies at the close. In the arena it lacked range, but could still do a craftsman's job.

Publius also carried the pilum, a regulation spear of the legion. At twenty paces, the ranks of the legion hurled these simultaneously, like a descending flock of birds. Then the next rank would move in solid against the stunned opponents. In the arena it had not been used by combatants because one pilum with one man would be a one-throw match. My problem with the pilum was my small round shield. It was meant to deflect and push a thrusting object, not a flying one. The pilum might cause a wound.

But the threat was not to my life. Even if Publius had my speed and strength and my perfect weapons and I but a club, still I would emerge alive. I had walked on arena sand, and Publius had not. There are too many things happening in the arena for a stranger to survive. Not only is the sand different, but brief moments become like long afternoons, and the unprepared mind loses the strength of the body too quickly. A person can watch the games for a lifetime, and yet, when he moves over the wall to the sand below, he enters a country he has never seen before.

There was no question of losing my life in the arena to Publius. None. I feared only a wound, a hurled pilum. One that would either disable me in such a way as to give a bad performance, and thus create the necessity of negotiating another sort of final departure from the arena than the wooden sword, or give me some disfiguring wound to carry as a remembrance of Publius for life. Worried about his being too slow, I now worried about his being too fast at the beginning with that pilum.

"Sweat him," I said, and one slave was sent to Domitian's emissary and another to the new master of the games. He sent back a runner to say that he could not delay the event, even for the great Lucius Aurelius Eugenianus.

Sweating Publius meant delaying our entrance. While he stood baking in the legionnaire armor inside the tunnel, I rested unclothed with the fresh air of my chamber as my slaves kept my muscles limber.

Three times the master of the games called me. Three times Plutarch sent back word that I was on my way. The nervous grumble of the mob was heard. As I received word the master of the games was coming to my chamber, I stood up, my hands wrapped in soft cloth so no oil would touch them. My slaves fastened a pure white cloth around my waist and sandals to my feet. I met the master of the games in a tunnel and suddenly ran past him. Without his presence in the entrance, I was able to come upon Publius from behind. As I was told, Publius stood holding heavy scutum and pilum in full armor, waiting as though on the Campus Martius parade ground.

I slammed Publius's steel helmet with my right forearm. One cannot do this with experienced gladiators or with the master of the games present. Publius tumbled like a sack of apples from the surprise blow. The arena crowd did not see this.

Immediately my wrappings were off my hands. My slaves had the small punching shield in my dry left hand and my spatha in my right, and I trotted out of my sandals into the bright, hot sun of the summer day and before Rome, which greeted me with a cheer of relief as much as joy. Their waiting was over. I signaled towards the entrance tunnel where Publius in darkness was regaining his feet, his shield, and his pilum. The short sword was strapped to his side in a sheath.

I waved my spatha as though inviting him out. The crowd cheered. I shrugged and turned my back on the tunnel. The crowd booed as Publius entered, jogging to catch up. Publius must have looked very funny trying to run on sand in full armor because the crowd began laughing, and I joined too, careful to pump my body so the laughing gestures could be discerned. In this way, we moved towards Domitian, I, rested and warmed in the sun, Publius, in the heat of anger with metal about him baking.

For the crowds, I stretched my muscles as I walked. Little groans and shrieks came from women, young girls, and even the elderly. They waved bits of cloth. It was really a silly display. Miriamne would have laughed me from my peristilium if I had attempted it at home. But in the arena, folly becomes grand spectacle, and grand spectacle was my worth to the people of Rome. Killing was only part of my performance.

You can see faces more clearly from the sand than they can see you, yet there is a feeling of being very far away from them.

Domitian showed the flush of his recent hunt. His wife, Domitia, was not there although I had expected her. She had not attended games since Domitian had uncovered a plot between her and her lover—an actor named Paris. Paris died in the arena. Domitia was sentenced to stay in the palace for a month. I thought she would come for my final performance since one time after a match she had arrived at my chambers herself, demanding to see me fully undressed. As though I were a slave, she removed my garments and touched me all over. I have never been so grateful for a failing erection in my life. Perhaps the terror of it helped me.

Domitia left, saying I should visit her when it regained its youth, referring to my penis, which she had assaulted with hand and lip and tongue. I feared telling Domitian and feared not telling him. But after a week of racking, helpless worry and doing nothing, the incident passed—her vagina was more dangerous than any sword.

We approached the emperor and, looking up, I saw Domitian was pleased. Before we gave the formal salute, he leaned down to us, and I could see that his carefully arranged hair hid great baldness. With a sidelong glance I noticed Publius' family—father, mother, relatives, and retainers—sitting to Domitian's left. I was not sure, but it appeared as though the mother were eating. The father seemed stunned.

"Do you have enough armor?" asked Domitian at full lung. He looked down at Publius.

"Enough," said young Publius sternly.

"And you, Lucius Aurelius Eugenianus, do you not have too much armor?" asked the emperor. By pointing out the disparity in apparent protection, Domitian also won himself approval from the crowd, for they laughed. The arena carries voices very well.

Only a very few understood that Publius had no protection at all.

In years before, all gladiators dressed in heavy armor of Samnite style. But this iron hacking iron could go on for hours, and to create entertainment the masters of the games removed more and more armor until many private arenas featured men fighting nude. It was all entertainment for the seats, from the retiarii with nets and tridens especially invented for the arena to Thracians with sharp, curved daggers. They killed sloppily, these Thracians, and crowds loved it; for a man's insides quivering on the sand was entertainment, too.

"What about your armor, Eugeni?" asked the emperor, addressing me in the familiar term when the laughter had subsided. He knew the crowds and was a master of the dramatic. He had the face and body for it too—a tall, handsome man, made to seem taller because he always brought a small, misshapen boy with him to the games. His voice was that of an orator booming out so all could hear. His face was reddening, and I could see he was already well into wine for the day.

I knew what he wished of me.

"Perhaps I have too much, oh, great divine Domitian," I said and unleashed my girdle to the sand. There I stood in the major arena of the world glistening nude. A roar came from the crowd. More entertainment, as though I were showing something everyone in the arena had not seen countless times before. Such is the madness of crowds.

With a hand, Domitian signaled me to parade the edges of the arena as though in victory. I carefully deposited spatha and shield on the girdle, sure not to let the pommel or shield grip touch sand. Sometimes there is blood remaining in the sand.

I stepped out of the girdle and strutted empty-handed along the wall. This, of course, as Domitian well knew, meant Publius stood even longer in hot, sweaty armor under the sun. He would fight in an oven.

I looked at faces as I walked just beneath the seats and few eyes met mine. All the people saw was my body, but in their faces I could see their minds. Hungry women, envious men, the dissatisfied of the world thinking they were rulers of that world, when they were slaves to their basest passions and most absurd myths. Publius' father looked at my face. Publius' mother's eyes did not meet mine. They looked lower, and I knew I could have her if I wished, even after her son was slain by my hand. That worn face would probably even enjoy it more because of the killing. Roman motherhood.

My face was a mask, a proud, smiling, happy mask to tell the crowd that I loved them and loved to fight for them. As I walked beneath the wall, I let the sun warm my body, and ever so slightly I exercised. Every once in a while I would glance at the bundle of iron standing erect before Domitian in legionnaire salute. The tip of the pilum quivered. The arm muscles were tiring and we had not yet exchanged a blow.

As I passed the seats of the vestal virgins, I covered my loins with my hands, and everyone laughed. A laugh in the arena sounds like a growl. Upon my return to the emperor, I nodded slightly to Domitian. Thus did gladiator send order to emperor, a signal that now would be fine to begin. But young Publius chose to rob himself further of energy. He asked to speak. Domitian granted his wish.

Publius gave a short talk about the honor of his family, the honor of Rome, and the honor of death that is honorably met. This touched the crowd somewhat and I could see Domitian's face anger. He would not allow this little patrician to die with sympathy.

Domitian rose ceremoniously to speak in oration stance. He talked of honor, too. He talked of fair combat with both men armored equally. He talked of prideful boasts not being honor but shame. He talked of the dishonor of wearing legionnaire uniform in the arena, thus robbing the memory of the true virtue of the arms of Rome, of men who often faced many times their number instead of one naked man.

Domitian talked of the true honor of the Roman patrician who would never indulge in arena play. He talked of the honor of Roman motherhood, which he somewhat tenuously tied to the virtue of the legionnaire. He talked of the honor of the citizens of Rome, and by the time he was finished, this former soldier had praised everyone in the arena and showed Publius to be a thief of their honor. This he yelled, of course, since the arena demands things larger than truth.

Before Publius could offer to take off his armor also, Domitian ordered combat to begin. Publius and I saluted, and I, having taken up sword and shield again, marched with him to the arena center.

We separated by the proper paces. The arena was suddenly very quiet as it always is at the beginning of combat to death, like a massive silent gasp. Only in this arena can it be heard. I breathed very deeply; the stench filled my nostrils. I was at home. Publius quickly showed he had a plan of attack. Heavy scutum shielding his left side from assault, as though he were in a line of battle, he raised pilum to throw. It made a line at his ear, and his elbow was cocked for a short throw instead of a straight, open line for the more forceful but less accurate long throw. A long throw would have been nice. I had never seen one in the arena, only on parade grounds, but I half expected Publius to attempt it. He didn't. His feet were not planted firmly either, another requisite of the long throw. I knew he did not intend to release until I came closer.

At this distance and with Publius standing the way he did, it was a good time to provide the crowd with entertainment. I danced around out of his range. I then stood facing him with arms outstretched as though offering a target. I turned my back on him with my head away, listening for his feet to grind in sand. At that distance it meant he was planting for the long throw which could reach me. The crowd yelled its approval, making it impossible to hear Publius' feet, so I turned my head as though scoffing him, but actually to see. His foot was still not set. He was not to be lured into casting the pilum at this distance.

I tried bowing, looking only at his rear foot, the one I would be looking at even if I were standing. This appeared dangerous and the crowd loved it.

I straightened and yawned. Laughter from the people of Rome. Publius still did not move. I would have to draw the throw at closer range. In semicrouch, shield held forward just beneath my eyesight, I closed. To twenty-five paces I advanced. Twenty, fifteen, and with each step Publius' prospects increased, not to advantage but to possibilities.

I knew then in my heart, what I had always known in my head, why gladiators rarely made friends with gladiators. I was thinking as Publius held his throw: Good for you, Publius. Good for you. Smart boy. Good for you, Publius.

Then the pilum came and I was under it and at him in one simple bound. Instead of trying to bounce me back with the scutum as I expected, or going for spatha and ignoring the use of the shield, or even one-handing the scutum to give him protection for his sword reach, he opened the scutum with one hand and reached for the spatha with the other, concentrating on neither. He was an open throat. Not even from a slave had I seen such a thing. He looked at me, stupidly, an open patch of flesh between breastplate and helmet.

I was already going to what I thought was his attack. I hit the pommel of his short sword with my shield and snapped his open scutum arm with a clubbing of my spatha. I slammed my bare head into his helmeted face, knocking him backward and suffering a small cut on my forehead. It must have looked as though I were mounting a woman. Publius went down on his back, and I went down on him, my knees straddling. I was up in an instant. He lay beneath me, belly up, mouth open, feet and hands useless, his short sword off somewhere to my left, his scutum weighting down a broken arm. He looked at me hazy-eyed, waiting to die. It was a bad show.

The rumors of his strength had been a trick. Granted, a trick with little chance of success, but that had been a vast improvement over his previous outlook. The old centurion had used cunning. If I assumed Publius was strong, I might approach him in such a manner that might be vulnerable if ever so briefly to a weak man, when not to a strong one. The former centurion has used my own retainers against me, not as it turned out for his success, but to rob me of mine, leaving a useless Publius beneath me.

"Get up. I'll move back. Fight for your life," I said, the smile still large on my face.

"I cannot."

"You must. Just touch me and I'll fall."

"I have no arms. My shield is holding one. The other pains me, Eugeni. It hurts."

"Move it anyhow."

"It hurts. It hurts, Eugeni," he cried.

I heard a few cheers and then the growl. They were laughing. Not good.

"Hit me with your head."

"I cannot move it. I pain."

"Mars's ass."

"I'm sorry, Eugeni."

"Idiot you. I will cut your eyes out."

"I'm sorry."

"Quiet. I will do you quickly. You will feel nothing."

I raised the spatha in a grand gesture. I could end his pain quickly, getting the bones in the back of his neck on the first lunge down, and then, with him feeling nothing, I could continue pounding at the throat, hoping a thrust would cut and then possibly wrenching the head off. The crowds would think this was a grand conclusion, not knowing I was mutilating a dead body of a person who ended his life as he had faced it, like a little boy.

If that were not enough, I could run to the entrance and have the master of the games send out criminals singly. I would fight each on my knees, taking the weapon from the fallen man and using it against the next.

Domitian would understand what was happening. After the fifth or sixth criminal, I would appear exhausted, and then he could raise the wooden sword above him and the crowd would cheer me home. Maybe ten criminals. It would be less dangerous than walking from this mismatch, for then rumors would start that not only was Publius drugged, but the secutor I had killed days before was drugged also, as had been all my opponents. Then I would be back here to die for certain, with Domitian thinking he would get all my wealth.

I was grateful now for the six million sesterces he had been promised and had yet to receive.

I thought of these things as I looked to Domitian for this signal of death that was certain. I had to wait. Formalities are vital in Rome. I put the point of the spatha to Publius' neck in case his lack of strength be a ruse also. Domitian waited for the virgin's signal. Sometimes it is a turned-down thumb, other times it is a thumb into the heart signifying, "Give it to him here." From the twisted folds of Domitian's toga, I knew it was the thumb and it was down. A thumb up somehow does not twist the folds of the toga as much. The virgins had called death. I barely bothered to look at the rest of the crowd. I knew it would be death there also for the virgins followed the mob. It was really always the mob which decided, and all wanted death.

"Good-bye, Publius," I said.

"My mother," he said. "Where is her thumb? Tell me that last thing, Eugeni."

"It is a big crowd, Publius, and a far distance. I do not think I can tell."

"Look. Please. A parting gift."

"No time."

"Please."

I spotted his mother easily even at a distance, for those around her were looking at her as she stood proudly, her robe a mass of twisted cloth. Her husband's head was in his hands. I would have delighted in splitting her, from lacquered hair to perfumed vagina. I felt at that moment truly proud to be a Greek, and if conquering the world did this to women, then I was glad that it was legion, not Greek hoplite, which proved victorious.

"The thumb is up, Publius. Your mother stands with your father, alone, against the tide calling for your death. She is your mother, truly."

"I had thought so ill of her. I never knew her. Help me stand, Eugeni, so that she may see me take my death in a noble Roman way."

"Roman whelp, the Roman way is why you lie down there like a bug. Death is no more noble than your urine. It is not a big thing. Not a big thing at all. Good-bye."

"What is a big thing, Eugeni? Before you kill me, tell me."

"There are no big things. Shut your eyes."

"Tell me a great thing. You know great things, Eugeni. You are great."

"I am cunning, not great."

I heard the first rustle of boredom. I knew Domitian must be signaling madly by now, and Publius' mother more violently than her neighbors. And at that moment I realized I was proud, not ashamed of my mother. For she had yelled for me, when they took me away. If I were on the ground, instead of Roman Publius, my mother would yell for my life, if the world had come down upon her. My Greek mother, so poor I could not find her, so worthless as to not even have a name in a sale of property, was a goddess compared to the Roman mother.

Was this what I wanted for my son Petronius? Was Publius an example? The finest thing I had done in my life was not marry Roman.

I hated Rome, realizing only then how much contempt I had for the city spawn of my drunken father.

Publius begged.

"A great thing, Eugeni. Tell me a great thing, Eugeni, please."

"Quiet, you poor thing."

"A great thing."

"Nothing is great. There is no great thing."

"A last gift."

A rolling groan started around the arena, gathering strength.

"A great thing. My mother was a great thing. I love my Greek mother. Glory to her forever," I yelled. And the action of my head stilled the crowd. They naturally thought I was yelling curses at Publius. One hundred and fifty thousand people can naturally do almost anything but be quiet.

"For Phaedra, and her spirit, here is a great thing," I yelled. "Mother, for you. Forever." I brought the spatha pommel high over my head, with the blade pointed down. I knew Rome waited now for the anxious little killing, thirsting as a latifundium slave might thirst for water, yet the crowd thought they had rights to blood, where the slave could drink only as a privilege given by a Roman master.

I brought the spatha down with my entire body behind it. A gross stroke. An obvious stroke. A visible stroke.

Away from Plubius' head. In the sand. Quivering.

"No," I yelled.

And in that silence, it was heard.

CHAPTER XIII

Sister Olav was stopped again before class and called into the office of the mother superior. She was asked what she thought of the American who came from the University at Oslo.

"I don't understand the question," said Sister Olav.

"The materials he brought. Did they interest you?"

"Yes. Somewhat. They were very strange," said Sister Olav. She did not sit, but stood beside the chair before the desk of the mother superior. If she did not sit, she thought, then she would be allowed to run along quickly.

"You showed a great deal of enthusiasm."

"Yes. I do get carried away."

"You were oblivious to the crucifix around your waist on the rosary."

"I'm sorry. I did not know."

"Yes. I realize. Enthusiasm and joy are not evil, and the academic life, child, is also a gift to our Lord. I am asking this because this year you take your final vows. Is the cloistered life your calling?"

"I do not know what I am meant for other than what is promised through Scripture and revelation. I, like every other person, am meant for heaven. What you are really asking is which path there. And to that question I can only answer, I hope I have chosen the right path."

"It seems like a waste of your training that the world seems to need now," said the mother superior. "I have had inquiries about your skills, which seem to be wasted here."

"A bigger waste is a soul."

"God does not give talents to be wasted."

"But if the talent becomes an obstacle to reaching heaven . . ."

"You may think that, but I have seen these things work out quite nicely. It is in the grit and grime that He works also. Please think about it, dear."

Sister Olav made her class on time, but she left unfinished the beautiful passage on Roman justice. How fair it was, how inspirational it was, how incorruptible it was as compared, of course, to the rest of the world, and, according to the poet, especially to the Greeks.

In the special intensive-care unit, what was now being called the "cryonics floor," Dr. Semyon Petrovitch awoke to a gentle tug. He had fallen asleep in the chair usually used by the round-the-clock nurses. He had stayed three days with the patient, and now it was breathing easily, and the oxygen tent had been removed. The intense time had taken its toll, however, on Petrovitch, who had not left this room; his underwear was sticky, and his skin itched, and his dark beard was almost as thick as the patient's.

The person tugging was the American.

"Good morning, Lew," said Petrovitch.

"We need a translator," said McCardle. "Soon. Because I said to it when its eyes were open, 'Requiescas,' and it shut its eyes."

"Yes?"

"That's Latin for 'you rest.' If you have ever seen a tombstone with 'requiescat in pacem,' you might recognize the word. It understands, Semyon. It hears."

"Well, you talk to it."

"I wish I could. I know very little Latin," lied Lew. But it was only a partial lie. He really did not know enough to speak it, for Latin had been taught to him as a language for print, for only the written word had lasted. And they needed someone who could think in that language. And that left only the nun at Ringerike.

"The chances are very good," said Petrovitch, "that it will regain consciousness. Very good. I expect it, Lew."

"Then let's talk to the nun about translating, now."

"I prefer a Russian."

"Fine. When?"

"That is a problem."

Petrovitch shook himself fully awake. He looked at his watch. He had slept four hours. He could go on, he told himself.

"Are you still trying to promote that nun who identified the language?" he asked. He took Lew back to his office, where he made them both a drink from the little boy with the red plastic hat who pissed Ballantine scotch when you pressed the hat.

"Yes," said Lew.

"Why?" asked Petrovitch. As a Russian he felt he should be able to drink more than Lew, but this American seemed to have an inexhaustible capacity. Petrovitch decided not to take drink for drink.

"She's supposed to be good, according to the professor of Romance languages here at the university."

Petrovitch nodded, allowing that as an acceptable fact.

"She's near."

Petrovitch nodded.

"I think we can expect the highest scientific standards, and someone who is not going to sell for cash the amazing inside story of the man dead for a couple of thousand years or so. You've got to think of that, Semyon."

"Which is why I want the Russian. But I agree on the Norwegian holy woman, if we can get her." Petrovitch pressed the little red hat as Lew wiggled his fingers signaling Petrovitch should continue pressing. When the tumbler was three-quarters full, McCardle made a cut with his hands.

"I don't follow," said McCardle.

"If I get a Russian, I must apply for one. That will take a while. But they are not going to just go looking for a linguist proficient in a dead Western language. They are going to examine why I would want that particular person, then examine how this whole thing might be a ruse to get that person, then examine the people examining the person, and, assuming that person wants to go in the first place, then there must be people to go with him. And so we will get a group of four translators, one of them speaking Latin, hopefully, and the other three watching him, each other, you, me, John Carter, and then heaven forbid one of these people should decide he wants to see the West alone, and we all get yanked back. You think the KGB is just some people sneaking around with guns and secret weapons, and women luring scientists across our western border, or planting guerrilla movements hither and yon. I will tell you what they are. They are people out to justify exorbitant budgets, fine homes, and heavy consumption of Western goods. And they don't want to lose their cushy jobs by doing anything rash. Therefore they don't do anything quickly. Therefore to get our translator we would probably have to put John Carter back in ice for another sixteen hundred years. Therefore, I accept the nun, but with precautions. We will allow the nun, but under the strictest controls and agreements."

"If we can get her," said Lew.

"If?" said Petrovitch.

They put in a request to the office of the metropolitan of Oslo, and, surprisingly, the mother superior called back, quite anxious to talk to both men. This within two hours of the call to the metropolitan's office. They could come up immediately if they wished, she said.

Lew cleaned his breath with a clove and gave one to Semyon. At first it stung, and then you had the feeling of breathing spiced air. Semyon bathed at the sink.

On the trip up, Semyon drove, despite his weariness, and explained how he got permission to work in Norway. He had to pretend to love his wife and two children.

It was the first time Petrovitch had talked of his personal life to Lew, and as Lew listened he thought how similar they both were in some respects.

"Yes. I do not love my children. They are spoiled. They are ungrateful and my wife has turned them against me. I tried to love them, Lew. And then I thought, why bother? What law says you have to love your children? And yet, I feel bad confessing. But I had to show I loved them to be able to work here. I would die if I thought I could never return to my motherland. I have no intention of flying the coop, as you say. But you see the mentality of the KGB. Back home they have their insurance, which of course is meaningless, but it looks good on paper which they pass from one to another."

"You didn't have to explain, Semyon."

"I wanted to. I also want you to know that I am grateful to my motherland. Without the Communist party, I never would have had a chance to go through medical school, or achieve the things I achieved. I may talk cynically, but I want you to know the nuisances and regulations and things like the KGB are a very small price to pay for what we have. A small price, Lew."

"OK," said McCardle.

"You have children?"

"Yes."

"Do you love them?"

"Honestly, I don't know. One thinks I am as rich as the Shah of Iran, and the other thinks I am some capitalist devil and she's Che Guevara leading some revolution."

"Does she shoot up things?"

"No. She sleeps around with people who talk revolution. Her big thing was sleeping with a black."

"What did you do? People from your part of your country are the biggest racists."

"I think that's unfair. But I didn't do anything. I wasn't there. Kathy, my wife, was there."

"What did she do?"

"I don't know. She just told me about it and then got mad at my answer."

"What was your answer, Lew?"

"I told her it was my daughter's pussy, not hers."

"And what did she say?"

"She called me dirty-mouthed, trash cowboy—a peasant, sort of."

"You were a peasant?"

"Yeah, I guess that would describe my father."

"Was he a good man?"

"No."

"I'm sorry. Mine was a good man. I loved my father. I loved my mother. I wish I loved my children. I wish I hadn't married my wife. She had such a lovely body. She was a beautiful woman. Her family was important. She had everything to recommend her but a heart. And yet that is the last thing a young man looks at. They look at breasts, at asses, at faces, and they do not look at the heart. An eighteen-year-old is a perpetual erection. And when you're hard between your legs you are soft between your ears."

"I kind of examined Kathy's heart," said Lew. "And I got exactly what I wanted when I was a graduate student."

"I take it that it is not sufficient now?"

"I don't know," said Lew. "I'll find out when I retire. I am going to retire soon."

"I would hate to have the kind of job that I looked forward to leaving," said Petrovitch.

"It's all right. Hey, it's a great job."

"Oh, that's good," said Petrovitch kindly.

Petrovitch asked if McCardle wrote his wife.

McCardle said he phoned a lot.

"What do you do for company?"

"I find it," said McCardle.

"Phoning is expensive. Now, I write on the seventh of every month. I do it early in the morning before I shave and that way I don't have to put it off. It's over with. Done."

"Does your wife write to you, Semyon?"

"Always. I stack her letters and then open them all at once, just before I write. It's a good system. It gives the impression I remember everything she writes. A wonderful system."

"Semyon, I don't think either you or I can honestly say at this point there is anything odd about the nun's sex life," said McCardle, and at first Petrovitch didn't understand, but when he did, he laughed so hard he almost lost control of the car.

They did not talk about the body back at the university. There was a gadget by which Petrovitch could be reached from the room, if anything happened. He said it was almost as important to find out what Sister Olav was like as to attend the patient. Semyon had thought about what was happening.

It was an important thing they had between them in that body, he had concluded. It was more important than anything either of them had ever dealt with and, even though they might talk of their families, the body living on machines, hanging on this side of death, warm with life, lived between them as more than a link. Little John Carter was their environment.

"A scientific advance outlives everything around it," said Petrovitch, coming to a stop. And he did not have to tell Lew what and whom he was talking about.

"Yeah," said McCardle.

"I know you have special interests. And so do I, but we also have an obligation to everyone. To people we will never know, generations hence. Even if they don't know who we are."

"I agree," said Lew.

"I have legitimate worries about someone who dedicates her life to a religion, especially one to whom that time of Rome is of vital importance."

"We will talk to her. I think she's honest."

"Honest is not the point, Lew. I would not want a devout Marxist either. Our job, if we can succeed with John Carter, and I think now we have a very good chance, is first to find out the biological key in the blood that allowed his brain to freeze without massive crystallization damage, and secondly, to find whatever historical evidence is available. I am not relegating history to a second place out of prejudice. I am putting it there because if there is one discipline that tends to be unreliable, it is history. It's at the service, usually, of whoever pays for it."

"Yeah," said Lew, hoisting his bulk up in his seat. "It's not a pure science. It's like a big guess. You know I once talked with one historian who studied the entire Middle Ages without ever realizing that it was a little ice age with a temperature drop that was astounding. History is the least important thing."

"And we must keep the religious aspect out. Agreed?"

"Yes. I agree."

Lew shook hands and almost engulfed Petrovitch's stubby fingers.

They first met with the mother superior, who had heard of Dr. Petrovitch and his work. She was not sure how cryonics fit in with geology. Lew explained, looking straight at her, with the crucified Jesus hung up on that four-foot cross behind her head, that they had found certain Roman items preserved.

The mother superior nodded.

"If Sister Olav agrees, and I personally think her calling is academic, she would have to stay at Saint Sabina's, a teaching hospital near you."

"Of course," said Petrovitch.

"Certainly," said Lew.

They were taken to a bare room with several polished wooden chairs and walls of solemn white plaster, and a dark, foreboding crucifix. The mother superior left them and went to get Sister Olav.

"I feel uncomfortable in here," said Petrovitch. He squinted at the crucifix.

"So do I," said Lew.

"You're not Christian?" said Petrovitch.

"Baptist. We don't go in for the statuary."

Petrovitch nodded. "Do you go to church often?"

McCardle shook his head. "I was really raised Church of God mostly, and partly Baptist. You just say Baptist. It covers a lot."

"Your wife and children?"

"They belong to a social center sort of thing." McCardle looked at the crucifix again. Little John Carter, or Julius Caesar, whoever he was, had probably seen real crucifixions. At the end of a rebellion in a province, it was not unknown to crucify thousands. McCardle had once read about Saint Helena finding the true cross, because when she found a cross buried in a building she assumed that was the cross. It would be like Christ being killed on a battlefield and, finding a bullet, you said this one killed my Lord. Lew tried to imagine what thousands of crosses with men hanging from them looked like.

"One thing," said Petrovitch. "We must be firm on keeping that out." He pointed to the crucifix. "She is a translator. Good enough. I am not interested in the cradle of Christianity. I am not interested in which saint met with which saint over what, and who did or did not do what miracle. Or how many of those they had in their homes." He nodded to the crucifix.

"They wouldn't have that in a home at that time. That was an executing device."

"I always thought it looked horrible with all that blood. We have ikons but . . ." He opened the palms of his hands and shook his head. "Frightening. I tell you this, Lew, I would rather have no translator than one working some religious, superstitious sickness on our patient. Yes? You hear me?"

"OK," said Lew. His bulky coat was getting warm.

"None," said Petrovitch firmly.

"I heard you, Semyon. All right?"

Petrovitch's dark eyes narrowed. He stared at Lew with boiling contempt. "I will not have science defiled by the superstitions taught to children to frighten them. I will not."

"Do you want us to leave now?" asked Lew.

"No. We will do what is polite. Politeness, courtesy, yes. That we will give."

"OK," said Lew.

"And no more."

"Get off my back," said Lew.

"What does that mean?"

"It means I said yes. Enough. You got your 'yes.' I'm not the Catholic Church. Don't yell at me."

Petrovitch was adamant until Sister Olav entered with the mother superior. Perhaps it was the smile, so perfect and so bright. Or the pale blue eyes that seemed to dance. Maybe it was the black setting for that gem of a face. But Petrovitch was up and clicking his heels like some Prussian when she came in. He even bowed. Lew McCardle rose out of politeness because men were not supposed to sit when women entered. The mother superior observed like a wary mother goose as her gosling confronted a heel-clicking fox and a big, old, lazy, yellow American dog.

There was a proper order of things that the mother superior oversaw, pointing to seats, making introductions, establishing who was who, and who said what, and needed what, and wanted what.

The two doctors had a project at the university which could use the academic talents and skills of Sister Olav, presumably to the benefit of the scientific community, and therefore mankind. Sister Olav, while teaching locally, had ambitions for the contemplative life. If the mother superior were correct, these men wanted Sister Olav to delay further her total involvement in the cloistered life because of her special skills.

Sister Olav smiled. "I am sorry, no."

"We're not anti-Christian," said Petrovitch.

"I have my reasons for doing what I do. I do not wish to share them with you. I am sorry," said Sister Olav, exposing a cool, gentle wall that was not so much a hot rejection as a fact of life that was not going to be altered.

"Oh," said Dr. Petrovitch. He looked to McCardle. A light had been put out of Petrovitch's face. McCardle raised a hand, signifying there was more to be said. There was a force in him that surprised Petrovitch, a sureness in a shaky world.

"Sister, I know for a fact that when we present our case to you, you will say 'yes.' We are not asking for a long-range commitment. Six months at the most, and you are vital to us."

"I don't think you are fully aware of my reasons for doing things, therefore you cannot say I will do either this or that."

"You have had Latin in your precollege schools, in college, and in graduate schools. You have studied it in all these stages?" asked McCardle.

"Yes," said Sister Olav.

"Then, when I show you what we are working on, you will decide to work with us."

"We are not anti-Christian," said Petrovitch again. "We realize the profound influence of the Christian Church, of the Roman Catholic Church, upon its environment in antiquity. We think it would be a travesty to avoid it." He looked to the mother superior with great sincerity. He avoided Lew.

Sister Olav spoke: "First, Dr. Petrovitch, I never thought you were anti-Christian or pro-Christian. Secondly, Dr. McCardle, you just do not understand me. I seek a contemplative life for my own reasons. One of those reasons, I think you assume, is that I find the academic life inadequate. That is not my reason."

"I know you have studied Latin for much of your adult life, and therefore, there had to be some fascination. Maybe there still is. But what I can show you is something you cannot refuse to work with. I know this because I have studied Latin just a bit, too. And you teach this, also, which makes me all the more certain you will help us. But that is neither here nor there. What I ask of you, and of the mother superior, is that you take one afternoon and observe our project, and then tell us 'no' if you wish. I am certain, technically, that you will not wish to tell us 'no.' "

"Does it concern the tapes?"

"Yes," said McCardle.

"You have found something?" said Sister Olav.

"Bigger than a bread box," said McCardle with a smile and then had to explain there was a guessing game played on the radio when he was a boy, where the typical question was whether it was bigger than a bread box.

The mother superior nodded. Sister Olav nodded. Petrovitch wasn't listening. He was looking at the smooth, white cheeks of the nun. He was thinking that they might never have been kissed. They were beautiful cheeks.

"There would be the utmost propriety," offered Dr. Petrovitch.

"We ask for an afternoon," said McCardle to the mother superior.

"I would recommend it to you, Sister Olav," said the mother superior.

"Do you order it?" she asked. The way she looked up to the standing woman, the total concentration, the honesty, the simple beauty, the exquisite beauty, thought Semyon Petrovitch, what an incredible waste.

"No," said the mother superior.

"Do you wish it?"

"Yes," said the mother superior.

"I must think," said Sister Olav. And she remembered what the mother superior had said about vocations, which was the Latin word itself for callings. Was she being called by this? She thought the arrogance of the American being so sure was amusing. She was not unaware that the Russian was somewhat enamored of her, but that would prove only a little problem, at most. He seemed like a nice enough man.

"Yes. I will see. I have a class in the morning but in the afternoon, if you can provide transportation, I will see what you have to show."

She was all but certain the American had in his possession some valuable scrolls, more than likely encased in some sort of precious jewels. He had had someone read it to see if it could be recognized, and she had only placed the language.

The American, being a geologist, had obviously dug it up somewhere. The Russian doctor? She wondered about that, assuming possibly some piece of flesh, or some fruit, or some organic matter might have been preserved by the cold. But up here? There were summer thaws. One had to go farther north for the year-round, century-round ice. And besides, no Romans would come this far to leave something. This was outside their civilized world.

One of two things had happened. A barbarian tribe had captured some scrolls or objects from a Roman legion farther south in Germany, passed it on as booty, lost it somewhere up here, and the geologist found it. Or the pair of men had been taken by a hoaxer. As she bid good-bye, promising to see them on the morrow, the latter seemed most likely. She quickly dismissed the possibility that they would be so foolish as to believe there were tape recordings back in ancient Rome or that ancient spirits talked.

Outside, Petrovitch wanted to know, demanded to know, how

Lew McCardle could speak with such arrogance to such nice ladies.

" 'Cause I can, Semyon. And what's this sudden conversion of yours?"

"They were nice ladies."

"Bullshit. You had a hard-on."

"What?" asked Petrovitch, suddenly looking down at his pants with a violent jerk of his head that almost pitched him over into the gray snow lining the walk to their car.

"In your mind, I mean," said Lew.

"You shouldn't joke like that," said Semyon recovering his dignity.

"She's only a lesbian, Semyon. They're all lesbians, right?"

"That's just normal misinformation that goes around. She is special, Lew. That is a beautiful woman wasting her life. That is a precious gem. Hidden away, deprived. Innocent. Did you see her smile?"

"No," said Lew.

"It was a smile, Lew, of someone who has put herself away for some reason. If we can find that reason, we can save her."

"Maybe she wants to be there."

"No one that beautiful could want to be there in that cold and frightening place."

Sister Olav arrived the next day in the back seat of a rented car, reading. The driver startled her by telling her she was at her destination.

Semyon was at the curb to open the door. Lew watched from a window in an office he had made his. He drank a beer. He could taste victory. He was glad he did not manipulate people as a career but happier still that he had found this hidden talent when he needed it. Lurking behind that was the fear that suddenly everything was going to go wrong because he wasn't that sort of person. Because of that fear, he dressed very carefully now, every day, to remind himself he was a vice-president of a company.

It was important that he greet Sister Olav outside the room of the patient, so he dropped the half-filled beer bottle in a wastebasket and went up the corridor along the cryonics floor, through the double swinging doors under the red exit sign, to the intensive-care room where signs in Norwegian, English, and French said keep out.

He looked back at the doors under the red exit sign and adjusted the jacket of his gray suit. He wore a subdued blue shirt with a plain black tie and black shoes. He was sorry he left the beer unfinished. He had more time than he thought.

But he had to be here in front of this door. It was this door and what it represented that would convince Sister Olav. He knew she had been told about this door in her first Latin class and that she too had believed it didn't exist.

The corridor doors swung open with Petrovitch leading the pale nun in the black habit, like a court jester, dancing around her, hovering over her, explaining too many things too quickly. He had promised he would not tell her what they had.

"If you do, and not me, we will lose the effect of this offer. So don't tell her."

"You have my word."

"I mean really," Lew had said.

"My word is my word."

"Except when it comes to the nun."

"I don't lie," Petrovitch had said imperiously.

And so now he ushered her to Lew standing in front of the patient's room.

"I have complied with your request," said Semyon. "Not a word."

"So mysterious," said Sister Olav, as though being shown a trick by children for whom she had to show the proper awe.

"Semyon, please wait there," said Lew, pointing across the corridor.

Petrovitch watched suspiciously and quite closely as the large American put a forefinger on the door. He whispered something into the black veil bonnet of Sister Olav. She shook her head. She covered her mouth.

"No," she gasped.

"Yes," said Lew and tapped the door. Then he opened it. Petrovitch could hear the constant mumbling of little John Carter with the scarred body.

He saw her wait a moment in the doorway then turn away, her

blue eyes rimmed with tears. She blessed herself with the sign of the cross and then took a very deep breath.

"I must get a room within this university hospital complex. Now. I am not going back. Not to my class, not to the convent. It will be all right with the mother superior. Please. Close the door, we must get organized. We must have working rules."

Petrovitch was agreeing to everything, as Lew took her to Petrovitch's office where she busily began writing a list of needs.

"How?" asked Petrovitch stunned, as they waited for her.

"Because I come from the same culture as she does."

"No. You don't. You're American. She's Norwegian."

McCardle shook his head. "We are all the children of Rome, without knowing it. Our months are called after Roman emperors or gods; our summer is July and August, named after Julius Caesar and Augustus Caesar. When your people scream fascist at us, you are referring to the rods of authority called fasces by the Romans. The idea of law written down and to be observed equally comes to us from the Romans, and our alphabet comes to us exactly from the Roman. From plumbing to the idea that surrounding someone in battle gives victory, Rome gave them to us. Rome is our common, civilized roots, so deep that many of us in the West do not even realize it unless we are educated to it. Rome is our intellectual father, and we have been living off its remnants for two thousand years."

"But, obviously, Sister Olav knew that before she came here. Better than you," said Petrovitch.

"You're right," said Lew. "I want to show you something that we have talked about for centuries, and only you gave us."

"What?"

"I want to show you," said Lew.

As they walked back up the corridor to the patient's room, Lew explained how complicated it was to learn and teach Latin, how many complex rules there were for this very precise dead language.

At the room he put his right forefinger on the metal fire-retardant door as he had for Sister Olav.

"From Berlin to Paris, from Des Moines to Rome, almost every first-year Latin teacher has told every first-year Latin class how sorry he or she is that they must study Latin grammar in such an artificial and complex way . . . almost like putting together a puzzle. They have said, for centuries now, to almost every first-year class that the student could learn Latin better and faster and more properly if they talked to a Roman on the other side of a classroom door."

Petrovitch nodded. He saw Lew's finger pressed white from the pressure on the door. He already knew what he would hear.

"Semyon, for the first time in I don't know how many centuries, we have found the Roman on the other side of the door. And that's what I told her, knowing she had heard the same thing in her first class as I had in mine. I told her simply, 'We have found the Roman on the other side of the door.' And when she heard him, she knew what we said was true. And she knew what it meant. And she knew it all at once."

"John Carter is more than a body, more than a medical breakthrough. Is that what you are saying, Lew?" asked Semyon, his voice hushed.

"I think so," said Lew McCardle.

CHAPTER

XIV

Tenth Day—Petrovitch Report

Condition fair. All support systems removed, except intravenous feedings. According to Olav report, patient apparently living through period in life, estimated time, late first century. Confirm on cardiovascular system of athlete.

Armor rustled in the tunnels. Animals bleated from the deep rock cages beneath the seats. Someone in a high tier dropped a metal cup, which banged down marble steps on this great, hot day. It was as though the center of the world stopped breathing. One hundred and fifty thousand people were quiet. I had never heard total silence in the arena before.

The pommel of my spatha quivered upright in the sand, and I was running. I could not go back and kill Publius without Rome descending on me anyhow, and I kept running. Through the portal I had entered, past the new master of the games, who was as still as though I had clubbed his skull, past unarmed legionnaires, from the urban cohort who only watched, through the tunnels, and past my chambers. I unsheathed a slave from his brown tunic in a single yank, leaving the stunned man as nude as I had been. I covered myself and ran. Usually, someone running in a slave's tunic would be stopped by someone with a weapon, under the assumption the runner is fleeing his master or someone he had stolen something from. But the silence seemed to still everyone I passed. I was out into the streets and still running when the silence ended with a roar as though the earth had rent.

And I was laughing. Running and laughing and shrieking a lifetime of discipline away, imagining Domitian fleeing under praetorian shields. Our divinity might not live out the day. The thought of Romans erupting on themselves for a second riot at games being held to soothe the passions of the first left me stumbling, giggling, helpless in these streets, like a baby. Prisoners would run, the urban cohorts would run, and the vigiles would run the fastest.

It was not even a choice I made, running through the quiet back streets without a light-colored tunic in sight, only slaves lazing about their duties because their masters were at the games. I knew I could not save either my fortune or my life. But I could save those jewels of my peristilium: Miriamne and Petronius. I always knew I had loved them, but only while running behind the vacant marble baths of Agrippa, forced to make a choice, did I realize they were the only things I had loved.

A few slaves tried to stop me, thinking I fled a master and that they might return me for a reward. They hardly required a break in stride. I had exercised every day of my life since I was nine and the run home proved no obstacle. Yet the coming revenge of Rome showed itself in the empty temples and the quiet forums I dashed through. I had never seen the forums without the hum and clang of business and rhetoric. On the days of the games, I had always been at my home or on the sand.

It was as though some plague had removed all the patricians and freedmen and equestrians from the workings of the empire and had left only the slaves, who did not realize fully that their masters were gone. A pair of slaves, for some reason, were fornicating at the gates of the House of the Vestal Virgins, while armored slaves looked on.

Fortunately, living in the arena and through the arena, I had prepared for a possible eruption of the arena. It was a sword I had always known could someday turn against me. I had not realized I would grab the pommel and do it myself.

As I reached the first high houses of the warren of houses that made the complex of my fortifications, some of my slaves, seeing my dusty, brown tunic, tried to stop me. But when I ordered them to prepare for riot, they realized who I was. There was always a chance they would join a mob, these gatherings excluding no one but its victims. I had prepared for that, too, with all the strategies and tunnels and only I knew them all. In my vestibule I found my armored slaves lounging and drinking wine, which they tried to hide when they saw me, all the while apologizing to me for fear of a beating.

"Riot," I said and they ran to their positions. A slave of accounts sat behind my expensive citrus-wood table as though he were the master and fell off the sella when I ran in.

"Riot," I yelled. "All slaves to the walls." Miriamne, her gentle face confused, ran out to the atrium and saw me sweating in the heavy arena oils and wearing the slave tunic.

"Eugeni, what happened?"

I touched her fine white stola, tugging her gently with me into the peristilium as slaves ran yelling, some with sticks, some with swords, and some with spears, through the passageways of the house toward the positions for which they had been prepared for so many years. Miriamne stumbled and I pushed her upright.

"Petronius," I called out. "Petronius."

A slave ran into Miriamne and I threw him against a wall.

"Petronius, Petronius," I yelled.

"He is here," said Miriamne. I looked behind me and Petronius was following, his cheeks pale, his eyes teary, his white boy's tunic gray with sweat. He was sobbing.

"What happened to you?" I asked.

"I saw. I saw," he said.

"Mars's ass. You were there?"

"I'm sorry. I'm sorry. I saw you take off your clothes, and I ran. I'm sorry, father."

It was a blessing that he had left at the beginning of the match, for he never could have made the run in my time. He had no more stamina than a patrician of his age. I grabbed a bunch of his tunic in my fist and dragged him to the cubicle of Mars. In both hands I took the heavy marble statue and lifted it above my head bringing it down on the seventh tile, diagonally from the north corner. The flooring cracked, and the head sheared along some hidden flaw into two parts. I ripped at the ground with hands becoming bloody until I found the edge of a blackened, heavily oiled cloth. I dug around it and eased it out of its burial place along with a dagger that was underneath it, a precaution. For who knew when I would want to give death, not jewels, while I pretended to get jewels. It struck me that I had taken precautions against almost everything and everyone but myself.

As I showed the jewels to Miriamne, who still appeared not to understand, and to Petronius, flushed with his run, his tender young cheeks so red from so strange an exercise to him, I told them I had failed to kill Publius, and all Rome would be down on us. This did not mean that we could not escape, but it meant that from this moment forth everyone would have to think coldly and logically, and do exactly what I said.

"We will be slaves," cried Petronius. "I had a dream. We were all slaves and Publius owned us."

I slapped Petronius across the face to bring him to the problem at hand.

"That is a patrician fear. You cannot afford those things now. There is enough to fear without creating more things. You will not be a slave if you think and act with cunning. People do not easily become slaves, and there are different kinds of slaves, and there are worse things."

Petronius said he had a dagger and showed me a jeweled pin no more useful than the one Miriamne used to hold her stola in place. I gave him a teak one with a solid blade.

"Hold it. Not that way," I said seeing him caress the pommel. "Hard, like you want to strangle it. When you strike, thrust. Never slash. Thrust and do not stop thrusting. People do not die as easily as young boys think."

He nodded.

"Always hide it and do not show it unless you will use it. Once that blade shows, you must kill. It ends all negotiations. Do not threaten with it. You have no friends but your mother. I want her alive. If you lose her, I will kill you. The world is not small enough for you to hide from me."

"Do not say that, Eugeni," said Miriamne. "You cannot kill your Petronius."

I slapped her face. I had never done that before. She was more surprised than hurt. I showed her the contents of the purse. It contained coins of gold and silver and several jewels, a large ruby being the most valuable. I told her she was a Roman citizen from Judea, named Gor. It sounded Hebrew. Most importantly it would sound Hebrew to Romans. She was to board a vessel at the port here, Ostius. To Athens, then to Jerusalem where her own people were. Petronius would be her Roman cousin. They were not to be mother and son. If she felt she needed legal protection, she should marry a weak man and use his name. The empire was descending on us like a great timber upon three small grapes. I could maneuver better knowing she and Petronius were safe. Two going one way and one going another had a good chance.

"Should I sleep with him?" Miriamne asked. She rubbed her face.

"Who?"

"The man I marry to use," she said.

"Of course," I said.

"You would have me give my body to him?"

"I would have you alive for me when I get to you. I would have you alive. I love you. I love Petronius. I most love you."

"You never told me that, Eugeni."

"I am telling you now, ignoramus."

Over this she cried. It was very difficult giving instructions for I cried also. I kissed her where I had slapped her and kissed Petronius where I had slapped him and told him I could not kill him but was lost for what else to tell him to make sure he protected his mother.

"I love mother, too," said Petronius, and there we were as the sounds of the mob far off came to us in the cubicle. We embraced, and I told them how proud I was of them both, and of Petronius, not for his Romanness, but for his good mind and courage, for being his mother's son, and mine.

"You love me?" asked Miriamne.

"Of course I love you. I freed you. I married you legally and put it in the records of Rome."

"But you never said you loved me."

"I am saying it. I am saying it. I love you, ignorant house slave.

Quiet. I must explain the difference in the jewels."

"I know, father. The ruby is the most valuable."

"But as valuable as it is, you cannot spend it easily."

"Of course, the value fluctuates," said Petronius. "We will use the coins and the other jewels to keep us until we can sell the ruby at a propitious price. The ruby itself is a fortune. I know that. What do you think you sired, a latifundium slave?"

I kissed Petronius again. We entered one of the passageways that bore us under the ground towards the outer perimeter of houses. Petronius carried a small oil lamp, shielding it with his hands from going out.

Miriamne had a question.

"Maybe there will be no trouble, Eugeni? What law have you broken? The Romans are famous for their love of laws. You have broken no laws by refusing to slay Publius. They may just never match you again, which I would love. You must break a law in Rome to be punished."

Petronius answered better than I. He laughed.

"There will be a law," I said. "One will be found. Rome needs one. I have robbed Rome of a fond myth. This thievery is one that is always punished."

We climbed up rock stairs by the little dodging yellow light of the lamp and entered through a storage room of an ironworker's shop—one of the many merchants to whom Demosthenes rented the periphery of my buildings, cheaper to them because they also served as gatekeepers to the area.

We startled the large ironworker, whose shoulders were like boulders, his face sweaty and black from his forge. I think he was a freedman. His face was as dirty as the leather apron he wore. He put a hand on an iron bar, but when he recognized us, he fell down kissing my hands.

"Go," I said and embraced Miriamne and Petronius a final time.

"Good-bye," said Petronius. "Good-bye forever and hello. I know you now, and never have before." He whispered that he knew I was going to my death.

"Maybe not," I said. "There are ways. But you are a smart, smart lad. Smarter than I thought. Remember always your father thinks of you as a blessing."

He tugged crying Miriamne into the street, and, seeing some

exhausted people, obviously crazed with mob fever, he pointed in the direction of our house behind him.

The ironworker vowed upon his household gods that he would never say what he had seen this day. He also mentioned that he was a very poor man, and his silence was a very important thing he was doing.

"I understand," I said.

"There must be people willing to pay me five thousand sesterces for saying what I have seen. But I will never talk."

"I know," I said and had my hands to his throat before he even saw them move, and I squeezed his voice into eternal loyalty. It was the second murder of my life, the first sentencing me to a life in the arena, the last after I had left the sand forever.

I found a sharp cursi—a vicious little knife—in his shop and ran out into the street with it. I only needed the dagger long enough for Rome to capture me alive.

Petronius had wisely known that I had no intention of escaping. I brought no wealth with me, and he had seen that. It was not the most secure of all plans, but I had neither the time nor the certain influence to build a better one. I would not know for a while if anyone would remain loyal.

And all my allies with any sense would be running themselves as soon as they heard the news. Until Rome found me, there would be a hunt of such magnitude that Miriamne and Petronius would surely be caught. But having found me, Rome would hardly hinder a woman and her young Roman cousin from sailing safely to their destination within the empire. Once Rome had what it wanted, it would not be poking into every purse and bale and bag to see if Eugeni was there.

It was not a bad plan. There was an invincible limit to what Rome could do to me, and when that was reached I would be free. I had seen too many men mutilated and dragged around the arena to worry. Nothing hurt them after death, no order from the mobs of Rome was loud enough to bother dead ears, or flames to burn once-burned limbs, or rods to whip flesh that had been whipped enough. The greatest horror was in the mind. Living men suffered more.

When I saw large groups of people, I joined them—the most dangerous thing in the face of a mob was not being a part of it. I ran, I walked, I hid at times, but street by street made my way to the most likely place to be captured. There were several people I could go to: Tullius, Galbas, many. I chose the home and countinghouse of Demosthenes. Domitian and his praetorians would most certainly look there for me, under the assumption that I would attempt to save my fortune.

The door to his vestibule was open, a good sign. I ran into the house waving my cursi, calling his name. A frightened slave said Demosthenes had left. Neither the urban cohorts nor the praetorians had arrived yet. If Demosthenes had stayed, they surely would have had him over the coals or under the whip until his paining body made his tongue disclose the last copper.

I loudly accused Demosthenes of being a wily Greek, untrustworthy in a crisis. I went through the account rooms. I went to a storage room. There was the six million sesterces bagged for Domitian and little else. Good. Demosthenes had cleaned the house of any massive wealth. Smoke came from the kitchen. Piles of scrolls were burning. Good for you, Demosthenes, I thought.

"Wily Greeks. You cannot trust them," I yelled and assisted a few scrolls, that had failed to catch, toward the embers and blew them into flame.

"Wily Greek," I yelled again and returned to the account rooms. Many scrolls remained, and I thought briefly of lighting them, but if Demosthenes had left them, he probably wanted them left. Perhaps enough to fill Domitian's mouth and stay that appetite for wealth from finding the greater fortunes. Perhaps to confuse Domitian more.

The emperor would get most of the known lands, but it would take him much time, and I was now sure Demosthenes had left exactly what would delay our divine Domitian most, while giving him the least. The jewels and gold he probably would never get. The shares in my Egyptian wealth could be sold, even to Domitian himself, without his knowing to whom they belonged. Such is great wealth, so big and so vast that it is harder to find than a small gold coin in a field. I not only had properties in most of the civilized world, but offices as well that stretched from Alexandria to the northernmost boundaries of pacified Britannia.

I was not completely helpless. There might be something worked out. It was not as though I had stolen a cloak because I was cold, where simple justice would punish me without fail. I had breached a contract which, because it involved the most politically sensitive arena games in Rome, now threatened the empire's stability. It was, in truth, a form of treason against Domitian himself. But punishments are meted out not for the severity of the crime but for the helplessness of the criminal. Yet Domitian might himself be helpless not to punish me, for this was public crime.

I sat down to think in the room I had teased Demosthenes in just days before. If the praetorians or urban cohorts were not here yet, then Domitian had either been assassinated, or he did not know how important Demosthenes was to me. The longer they looked for me, the greater danger that Miriamne and Petronius would be captured. Frightened slaves brought me drink while I waited to be captured.

I did not wish to think. For then I would have to say to myself that I had ruined my own life and sent Miriamne and Petronius into flight for something no sane Greek would ever do. My mother, Phaedra, was not here to appreciate the honor, and even if she had been in the arena earlier in the day, she would not have liked it. My mother would have said live, Eugeni. That is what my mother would have said. Defiance for some passing thought and the risk of welfare for that thought was not only a Roman thing, but a patrician one.

And there in the room, the torture began. I looked at the small cursi, for I could end my pain now. Let Demosthenes have all the money, he loved it so. Let him run with it. That was what he would do if I were dead, and possibly even if I were alive.

But I could not do it. Rome needed me. And if it did not have me, it would seek out Miriamne and Petronius. Surely it would. Rome needed my punishment.

I put the cursi in my lap. I would satisfy the Roman appetite for revenge. They would feast on me. But why so long?

Finally, the praetorians arrived with pilum and shield and the glory of their muscled cuirasses—chest shields that were sculpted to the muscles of their bodies and in other units used only by generals or wealthy tribunes. The series of plumes atop their ornate helmets was like a gentle crimson sea flowing up the street.

When I heard them, I had run out to see them. Upon seeing their great number I realized what had delayed them. There must have been twenty continubrium, or one hundred and sixty men, almost a double maniple. They were delayed because they could not risk small units to simultaneously search all the places they thought I might be—the small units being vulnerable to this seething city. Therefore they sent this large unit, and their having been delayed meant Domitian had estimated other places were more important to me.

I made a great act of running back into the house and slamming an iron lock on the door. Then I hid myself in the room where the bundled gold for Domitian was. When the praetorians reached me there, I offered them half the gold to let me go free.

"The gold and you belong to the wrath of our divinity," said a praetorian officer. He had a likeness of Domitian upon the center of his finely muscled cuirass, the face of the emperor being the standard upon which they swore all sorts of religious and military oaths.

I bemoaned the fact that all my wealth was gone and that all I had was this meager gold. I swore vengeance upon Demosthenes whom, I said, I had always distrusted and now was proven right.

The officer ordered me shackled and told me that I would be unwise to think of the praetorian as some slave gladiator I could trundle with. The praetorian was the best of all the legionnaires of the empire, and the legions were invincible.

"Is that a threat or an invitation to join?" I asked.

"The praetorians slaughter Greeks, we do not accept them, Greekling."

"Yes, you're too busy perfuming yourself and decorating your bodies to accept anyone who can get to a fight on time. Or did you have trouble with the armored slaves at my entrance here?"

"We checked all your money places, the only question being which you would run to first," he said, telling me for certain they were not looking for my wife and child.

Relieved, I could not show it.

"All my money. The slave ran away with all my money," I cried.

"A Greekling, no?" laughed the praetorian. He tapped me contemptuously on the back of my head, slapping away my cursi with a following blow. He wanted me to stand and follow. I was roughly pushed out into the street and shackled to a young praetorian who made threats for me to keep pace.

We avoided the major forums and outlying shops where large mobs tended to congregate and marched behind the House of the Vestal Virgins, the Julian temple, the temple of Mars I had donated to the city, and came upon Domitian's palace from the rear, skirting entirely the Forum Romanum and the nearby senate. I smelled the smoke of great fires, and the sky was gray with burning cinders blowing in from the Vatican arena. Even the port of Ostius might be aflame now, and I worried for the safety of Miriamne and Petronius.

At Domitian's palace, the vigiles, who were supposed to be containing these flames, were huddled behind the massed cohorts of the fully armored praetorians and the urban cohorts, who were also fully armored. The urban cohorts were supposed to be quelling the riots. Friends of Domitian were hurriedly moving their families and portable wealth through the soldiers into the palace, bringing only their most valuable slaves with them. The praetorians stripped everyone entering of weapons. A few people saw me and shouted curses. It was an army of wide purple-striped togas. The patricians now needed Domitian as an ally—common disaster being the greatest peacemaker of them all.

Although Domitian and I had had many dealings, I had never visited here nor had he been to my home. We entered the palace through a vestibule the size of a small arena, except it was rectangular. There were enough statues lining this entranceway to make the finest, most perfectly carved marble a drudgery to the eyes. I was led by the same praetorians to a large room with a couch, three sellae, two tables, and delicate murals of fields and streams and birds with gods and women playing through them.

A slave brought me wine and bread of pure white, the finest there is, all the darkness milled from it. There were also plums and apples and garum sauce for crushed chickpeas. I drank the water, not the wine, and ate the bread and chickpeas. It was good garum, the fish fermented just right and seasoned properly to make a smooth, brown sauce. At home, mine had been as good.

Domitian's emissary entered the room and I saw the hallway was packed with praetorians. They were my guard. The emissary's face was taut, with a jerkiness around the eyes. His body was stiff, and he poured himself wine in a silver cup and watered it by but half.

"Well, Eugeni. We have a problem."

"I have been robbed," I said. "That Greek stayed loyal until the first crisis. Then he was off with my wealth. All of it, except the six million sesterces you bargained for. Domitian's money. It is his."

"We have it. Thank you."

"You are welcome to it."

"Things can go more easily for you if you cooperate," he said, and his face was still grave. Did he think I was some schoolboy who had stolen a peacock with his friends? "I will not lie to you. You are going to die, but how you die can be up to you. There are fast crucifixions and slow ones. Our divine Domitian is not a vindictive man. We will find out everything you know anyhow."

"Tell Domitian I have never known of anyone able to enforce an agreement from a cross."

"Dead, you will have no need of money."

"And if I am dead, you will not have it."

"We will get most of it."

"Then why are you here?"

"For your cooperation. You have done Rome a great disservice this day. Perhaps you can make amends."

"I am willing to pay what I have, whatever I have, if you will give me something for it."

"What?"

"My life."

"Impossible. You wouldn't believe it if I promised it anyway. Is that not true?"

I nodded.

"So let us begin from there. We can make sure your wife and son whom you love will live and with a reasonable pension from Domitian's own treasury."

"They're probably dead now. The mob was heading towards my house."

The emissary nodded. What he really wanted, I knew, was to find out for certain how much Miriamne and Petronius meant to me in terms of cooperation Domitian could trade for. Wife and child for my fortune. Knowing Domitian, he would probably have them crucified before my eyes once I had given him what he wanted. Their safety was in Domitian's belief that I really did not love them as I loved them.

"I will confess," said the emissary. "I lied to you. They were mutilated by the mob near your house."

He watched my face like a priest examining a goat liver for the secrets of tomorrow.

"Too bad," I said lightly. "They should have proper funerals. I would like that. Although I don't know what I could pay for mourners. I have nothing. That Greek abandoned me. Took everything." And on this I clenched a fist and showed great anger in my face.

"Will you help us find him?"

"Only if he dies with me."

"Done. We can promise that." He finished his wine and poured himself some water. There were no slaves in the room. "Now. Who was in it with you?"

"Me and Publius."

"No. No. The plot to create the riots. One does not create two riots consecutively without a plan."

"You mean assassination?"

"Yes."

"That is in Domitian's mind, not mine. As you rightly stated before the match with Publius, I did quite well with Domitian as emperor. It was not in my interest to see him replaced."

"But what if you thought Domitian would confiscate your property after you left the arena?"

"And therefore I offended all Rome so that his successor wouldn't? This is foolishness."

"We did not believe you were part of a plot. But who knows? Rome is treacherous today. The old virtues are dying. The senate is a foul sewer. The patricians, from whom one would expect the most virtue, show the least. Domitian loved you, Eugeni. He sent three gold swords for your son's ceremony. Still he holds no anger. Look at the fruit. Look at the wine. Is this an enemy you deal with? He could have you burned as a torch this very evening, if he wanted."

"No, he could not," I said sharply and slapped the table to emphasize this. "He could not. If he burned me to ashes, there would be people who said I had bribed him for my life. They would say it was a slave who was burned. Whatever our divine Domitian does to me, he must do before Rome publicly so it will not be said that the wily Greek bought his life."

The emissary sighed. "Eugeni, you overestimate yourself and underestimate our Domitian."

"He did not come down here because he could not look upon me without killing me. Until the execution, I am as safe as in my mother's womb."

"He could throw you to the mobs."

"And the first hundreds would see me, and all the rest of Rome would swear I had bought my life and it was a slave who was torn apart."

"Only a fool thinks he has power he does not. Good-bye. You will never see me again. When I leave, I leave forever. Be good to yourself for once. Use your cunning."

He rose, standing before me. At the door he begged me to reconsider, for he was never going to return once he left this room; he was my last chance.

"Help us find what you do not need and things may go easier for you."

I took a red plum, both sweet and tart.

"Then I must say good-bye forever. The last friend you have with Domitian."

Forever was by nightfall. I knew it was night because when the door was open the lamps were flaming in the hallway. No light from the sky. The emissary had prevailed upon Domitian to give me one more chance. I had not had the advantage of a Roman upbringing and therefore lacked the logic and reason of a Roman. I could not be expected to see things clearly on first examination.

There was but one question. Who really controlled my funds? Tullius? Galbas? Some other clerk? Domitian did not believe I would entrust the bulk of my fortune to a Greek.

"I said Demosthenes."

"All right, Galbas then," said the emissary.

He returned in the morning to tell me it was not Galbas.

"Tullius, then."

"It's not Tullius," said the emissary.

A young girl came into my room. She had large breasts and smooth skin. I did not touch her. She left, and later a young boy entered with even smoother skin. I did not touch him.

And then Tullius entered followed by slaves. He looked worried, but there was not a mark on him. Galbas was dead, he said somberly. Tullius had managed to win his freedom and even a small stipend by telling our good friend Domitian everything.

That was why he was able to walk away free now. He was sorry he gave up part of my fortune, but it was his life. There was one thing I should understand about Domitian. He was not a vindictive man. As emperor, he was a veritable slave to reason.

That afternoon I was taken to one of Domitian's baths, first the caldarium with its warming steams and then the frigidarium with water cooled by shade and rocks. There was another prisoner in the baths. He followed me from hot to cold. He too had offended Domitian once, endangered the whole empire, he confided. He was so ashamed of what he had done that he would not repeat it. But Domitian, he discovered, was not a vengeful man. He only appeared that way to the mobs to keep order. If a person were cooperative, Domitian would keep him quietly in his own palace. He was an emperor, not some besotted youth in the street venting anger at problems. He had an empire to run. It was a heavy burden. Domitian could not indulge in wreaking vengeance for every slight. There was not enough time.

"Our poor emperor," I said. "He does have great burdens, and I am afraid I am one of them. My fortune, by right of offense, belongs to him. Yet I am stubborn and selfish. He could beat me and burn me to free my tongue. But he has a problem there. I am a gladiator, and I was trained on whips and burning iron. He would have to bring me near death to get what is his, and I believe he needs me living. Our poor divine Domitian."

The praetorians delayed me before taking me back to the room. The man in the baths was a foolish attempt. It was obvious the man was not a lounging prisoner. He had calluses on his right hand and left forearm—hand to hold sword, forearm to hold shield. Was a prisoner going to practice with weapons daily? His cheeks were red from recent sun and his chest and arms were muscled. His legs showed the sharp work of long marches. The palace was big but not the Appian Way.

When finally the praetorians returned me to the room, it smelled of recent defecation, as though the slaves had failed to remove the pots. On the sleeping couch, a large white linen cloth covered what appeared to be sacks of apples. The marble floor beneath the couch glistened with fresh scrubbing. Two small red dots appeared in the center of the linen and grew larger. The praetorian officer made to it first, so that he could remove the linen with a sudden flourish. There was my recent bathing partner, the pink in his cheeks drained out of his neck. His head had been severed. His dismembered arms were crossed over his belly, and his body ended at his loins. Those hard legs had been sawed off and his trunk rested on the stumps.

"That's you, Eugeni. Here you go," yelled the praetorian, and two men seized my arms and two my legs and they laid me on the table. The praetorian raised his unsheathed sword. It was smeared with blood.

"No. No. Domitian needs him. He will not allow this. He wants him to live." It was the emissary.

"I want his liver," yelled the praetorian.

"You cannot. He knows things."

"You have gotten nothing."

"We can get something. Let him live," begged the emissary.

"No."

"I promise you. He loves Rome. He will help."

"He hates Rome. He defies the gods themselves," shouted the praetorian. His face was positively imperial purple above me.

"I will tell all," I said.

"Not enough," said the praetorian.

"I order you to let him. Domitian demands it," said the emissary.

"I want his life."

"It will be yours, then."

"I do not care."

"Then your honor and virtue. You will lose it, if you harm our Eugeni, the emperor's ward."

"Only if this Greekling pays back his debt to Rome."

"He will," said the emissary. "Eugeni, please. For your life. Who helps you? Who has the maps to your wealth? Who are your allies?"

"Actors," I said.

And this excited the emissary even more. For an actor had been the empress's lover once.

"Actors?" said the emissary.

"Yes. Dressed like praetorians," I said. "See how good this one is? One would believe he is going to kill me."

And I laughed the gross arena laugh which has no joy in it. The praetorian officer raised his sword as though to chop wood and brought it down near my head so that I heard the air whistle.

But I had heard swords before. When you hear them, they are no danger, for that means your opponent is slashing and has lost control.

I might even live.

CHAPTER XV

The patient was in extreme danger and all three had to prepare for it. This from Sister Olav, as she and Dr. McCardle and Dr. Petrovitch met in a bright sun porch down the hall from the room. Workmen had just finished putting masses of large houseplants around a small stone pool, as Sister Olav had ordered.

"I don't know if our patient can survive discovering where he is. I think it will be like falling off a cliff for him. I think it might be fatal."

Her manner was even more grave than usual. She had been here two days, and Lew had gotten several calls from Saint Sabina's Hospital nearby because of the brevity of Sister Olav's visits to the place where she was supposed to live. She worked twenty hours a day. She typed faster than most secretaries. She had done a Herculean job with the tapes. When she wasn't organizing the bits of verbal information into typewritten form, she was visiting the patient's room and making notes. She was always attentive, sharp, and definite.

She was not someone Lew wanted to be near with his massive hangover, with his body thirsting for relief, with his mouth dry and foul, and his head a prison that must be kept perfectly still, or great ringing alarms would punish his skull. He wore a dark brown suit with a soft white shirt and dark brown tie. He wore polished brown cordovans.

He put his head in a position of attentiveness and tried not to move it too much. The sun beat into his left eye. Semyon wore a blue blazer with a dashing white cravat. He assumed Sister Olav's gravity.

"Please explain," said Petrovitch.

Sister Olav sat between them on a pea green couch without a back, but with two curving padded arms.

Semyon and Lew sat on backless chairs. Semyon had said how much healthier a chair like this was for the spinal column. Sister Olav had said it was not for them but for the patient. He would find this sort of chair more familiar.

"I have done the transcripts of his talkings, mumblings, ravings if you will, whatever. I agree with you, Dr. Petrovitch. There can be no question now of a link between his physical health and what he is thinking. In Rome of his time there were violent games, one of the less commendable, perhaps least commendable, aspects of that civilization. Our patient at the time of his severe shock, the one that almost took him, was at these games. Either as a slave or a soldier or a gladiator or whatever capacity he had."

"He has scars, healed by cauterization," said Petrovitch. "Do you remember me pointing that out, Lew?"

"Ummmmmm," said Lew in agreement because he had to answer. His hands lay on his lap and his back hurt. Semyon leaned forward, his left forearm against his thigh. He was so close to being on his kness, Lew would not have been surprised if he dropped to one and proposed.

"The patient is reliving. And he is highly susceptible, physically, to his emotions. I believe that discovering what has happened to him might send him into shock again, and this time, Dr. Petrovitch's genius and commitment might not prevail."

"You might be right, Sister Olav," said Dr. Petrovitch. "What do you think, Lew?"

"Ummm," said McCardle.

"What we are going to do is, if at all possible, to soften his fall from the cliff—provide a cultural parachute so to speak. We won't impose anything more strange on him than we have to."

"Very good," said Semyon.

"Ummm," said Lew.

"I have prepared some suggested guidelines as to how we should treat our patient," said Sister Olav, giving Dr. Petrovitch twenty-two typewritten pages, and Dr. McCardle the same. Petrovitch, too, had brought materials—X rays, his abbreviated daily reports (three days omitted during the period of shock), his lengthier reports that lacked final analyses of the blood that, he had explained, had retarded crystallization in the remarkable physical specimen which Dr. McCardle had so thoughtfully saved for science. Lew McCardle had brought only a package of gum, which no one else chewed, and the sweetness of which proved too much even for him. His stomach told him that if he continued to keep that sweet taste in his mouth it would come up with everything from the night before, and then some. He put the wet stick in his pocket.

As he silently prayed for a beer, Sister Olav went point by point over how they would provide their cultural parachute, looking to him for his assent.

"I would suggest that we change our names for use with and in front of the patient. Dr. Petrovitch, I think Semyonus, a Latinized name I made up, would do well, if you would agree. Lewus for Dr. McCardle and Olava for myself."

"Olava, Olava is beautiful," exclaimed Petrovitch. "Olava, Olava, Olava. I love it. Love it. I never felt comfortable with Sister Olav. It sounded so, so, well some might say masculine. Olava is beautiful and fits you. Pure Roman."

"No," said Sister Olav. "Lewellyn is Welsh, Olav is Germanic, and Semyon, Slavic. But he will be able to talk to us more easily, because he can treat the endings more easily in his language knowing how to say 'to us' and 'from us' and 'for us' and things like that."

Then there was the problem of what everyone wore. No watches, no lighters, no gadgets. Pens would be allowed because they contained ink, as had styluses then. Semyon would have to give up his cigarettes in front of the patient for a while.

"It's going to be hard," said Petrovitch.

"This too is hard," said Sister Olav, and she removed the crucifix and rosary beads from her waist. "This is very hard. I would like to wear a fish to replace them, but that would attract the sort of attention we deal with in section five which I will talk about later."

"No. No. You may wear all your religious trappings. I would fight to my death for your right to wear these things as long as you wish. I would never request that."

"Not for you, but for our patient. The crucifix, as an object of Christian symbolism, came into public veneration centuries after the probable life period of our subject. At his time it was an ugly execution device. The Christian symbol was the fish. But I forgo even that. And I must recommend to both of you here and now, from the bottom of my heart, that neither of you seek publicity and that you forgo on behalf of your government, Semyonus, and your corporation, Lewus, the fame and approval of the world."

Petrovitch accepted this admonition with a nod and visible rising of his chest.

"Ummm," said Dr. Lewellyn McCardle, vice-president of Houghton Oil Corporation, Houston, Texas, USA. It was hard to tell his ringing ears from the occasional jet engines of the nearby airport.

From now on, it was agreed, no nurse was to be allowed to bring a radio or television set into the room, which had not happened so far, but might. While the working language could not be Latin, because all three had only English in common, everyone would try to limit conversation around the patient, although, if he were from Rome itself, he would not be shocked by different languages, since Rome was the center of the world and had many peoples as guests and residents. The windows would be shaded.

"He would be shocked by glass?" asked Dr. Petrovitch.

"Not at all. They had glass in Rome, but he would be shocked by a window facing outside. The Roman house faced in. It kept the world out. Just a little thing we're doing here, too, with our imitation peristilium. Now the diet, when he gets off intravenous, is all wrong. I see meat scheduled once a day. A regular diet with meat was not considered healthy. The Roman wouldn't even like it. If our Roman is typical, he covered everything with a sauce called garum or alum, types of a fermented fish product which they used on almost everything. Like you, Lew, might use ketchup."

"I don't use ketchup," said Lew. He took a big drink of water.

And he readjusted his position on his backless chair, which he knew was a sella.

"I meant it was a common sauce," said Sister Olav.

"That's what I meant, too," said Lew. He wanted to yell out he not only knew everything she had mentioned but just might, if he had put in as much time intensively as she had, if he didn't have to earn a living, just might know her subject better than she did. But somehow, that she did not know that he knew, no matter how grating this was proving, could well help him. Lew felt this in his bones. But it did not make the cup he drank much tastier.

"I didn't mean to offend, just explain."

"Do we have the recipe for the sauce?" asked Petrovitch, trying to muffle conflict.

"Not that I know of, but I think if we give him wheat and barley products with plenty of fruit and cheese, and, of course, the staples of the ancient world, olives and olive oil, we will provide an adequate diet."

"Possibly even better than ours," smiled Petrovitch. "But what about our ties?"

"Leave them on. He will think you won them. They didn't have medals but they did have necklaces called torques. He will think your ties are some kind of badge, especially since they have no use. And if you want to, wear white and let the nurses wear white, also. He will think he is among the established class. My habit will remind him of a stola, but black like Lewus's dark clothes would make him think we are the lower class. They were not all that different in judging people by clothes."

"Us ketchup dunkers sure do dress right peculiar, ma'am," said McCardle.

"If I have offended you, Lewus, I am sorry. I really do appreciate your contribution to this project. There is a need for someone to get things done. I appreciate your arranging for a replacement for me at the school in Ringerike. It's not easy to find a civil Latin teacher so readily."

"It was very easy," said McCardle. "I phoned our public affairs people back in Houston, and I said fly one in. And they did. In a day."

"Yes, well, that's fortunate."

"They just had one of our vendors go to an employment agency in Great Britain. They're plentiful. No difficulty whatsoever. No one even knows Houghton did it. Because no one cares."

"Lewus!" said Petrovitch angrily.

"Please. Please," said Sister Olav. "We have important work to do. What was the structure the patient was found in? I don't see your report on that, which is important, because there might be other artifacts in the frozen cave, although none could be as important as our patient."

"No cave, glacial ice. Eight point two meters down. I'm working on it. I had things to do last night. I had to phone home last night," he said, remembering how he had reached his wife, Kathy, who said Tricia, their daughter, was now planning to do something violent to change the world, and he had asked if that meant sleeping with a triggerman instead of a philosopher, and his wife had said he should rise above his beginnings sometime, and he had hung up. He had drunk quite a bit and met someone in the lobby. In his hazy stupor, he finally realized she was a prostitute, and that her airfare back home was not a friendly gift from a beautiful, sexy older man to a helpless woman, but a payoff for a screw. To be exact.

So, today, Sister Olav asked him if everything was all right, and he said yes and wondered whether he could get a drink this early in the morning without arousing curiosity or contempt.

"We have another curious fact here," continued Sister Olav. "Romans didn't come this far. Never did. The empire ended in Germany, which was considered wild, barbarian country, and farther north here was even more frightening to Romans. There was cannibalism through what we know now as Scandinavia."

"Maybe he walked alone. A great trek," said McCardle. "He's a tough little bugger by the looks of things."

"I doubt it. Nude, at least hundreds of miles beyond the borders of his civilization. I doubt if he walked alone. I don't care who he was, he just would not be going to make this sort of trek through this area. You're looking now at what is the more civilized part of the world, that is, in the sense of safety. Africa in your most extreme thoughts was never as wild, though, as this part of the world at his time."

"What were Roman methods for freezing things?" Petrovitch asked. "Maybe that's a key."

"They didn't have freezing, to the best of my knowledge, and if there were evidence they could have frozen things, I would have known. No, they could cool things and warm things, and their baths had a frigidarium for cooling and a caldarium for heating. But they never froze things. The closest they came to using ice was having runners bring it down from the mountains for banquets."

"Cooling would not do," said Petrovitch. "The action had to be immediate. Both in bloodstream and thermal reduction. Immediate. No one ever had these sorts of things until recent history. I don't know how it was done."

"We'll find out, Semyon," said Lew.

"Semyonus," said Petrovitch.

"Yeah," said Lew.

Sister Olav suggested that they continue on the morrow because Lewus seemed a bit under the weather, so to speak, or as the Romans would say, his liver was acting up.

"I second the motion and vote yes," said Lew and got up, his mind somewhat relieved by the thought of a cold beer, followed by a cold beer, followed by a cold beer.

"One more thing," said Sister Olav. "When do you think the patient will recover complete consciousness?" She asked this of Dr. Petrovitch.

"Any day now. It might come in bits. He might just open his eyes and say hello."

"Now I have a problem," said Sister Olav. "What are my first words to the man who might have spoken with Vergil or Juvenal? What do I say to the man who knew Saint Peter or Saint Paul, as we know each other? This man, who may have personally known those who administered their known world. What will be his thoughts when he sees us? I sometimes feel it is beyond me."

There was little question what the patient was thinking in his deep sleep when all three visited the room on their way out. It was visibly apparent. Petrovitch and McCardle looked away in embarrassment. Rising underneath the light covering blanket, like a pole under a tent, from the horizontal form, was a full erection. Lew withheld the comment that if the patient were reliving something, he certainly wasn't suffering.

CHAPTER XVI

Fourteenth Day—Petrovitch Report

Condition good. Brief periods of apparent consciousness. Swallowed a mouthful of food, but did not chew. Blood pressure normal. Temperature normal. Heart normal. We await his arrival.

When the senators began appearing in groups and singly to question me, I realized Domitian's problem. In but three days, he had run out of time.

The city boiled, I was told. After the first day and night of riots, Domitian decreed I had committed maiestas, offending the gods of Rome. For this I would be tried by the senate, neatly focusing the mob's attention on the senators, instead of on him. He didn't get a decision, but a windy debate, while whole sections of the city declared war among themselves. The praetorians and urban cohorts huddled around the palace for their protection, not Rome's. Domitian had tried sentencing a whole area of the city to crucifixion, hoping stern measures would set an example. But he couldn't spare the men to seize them, assuming the likes of the urban cohorts or vigiles would follow a dangerous order, and he wasn't about to let the praetorians stray far from his body.

The senate leaped on maiestas like a dog on a kidney, scarcely realizing Domitian had forwarded his massive nuisance to them. Guilt hardly received investigation. It was the punishment that was debated. The noble senators surprised even me with their inventiveness. I should be blindfolded and set in a box with starving rats, with only my spatha for protection. This was rejected because a closed box would hide my agony.

Another senator, who had devoted his life to scholarly comparisons of the city-state and the empire, offered that this battle between rats and gladiator could take place in a pit. He suggested covering me with pork fat, lest the rats decline living meat.

There was a faction for crucifixion, but there is always a faction in Rome for crucifixion, as though hanging a person on two beams were an all-purpose governmental solution. It supposedly reduced crime, inspired morality, and made slaves more productive.

They had faced, during those three days, what I thought confronted Domitian alone—the problem of showing my agony to enough people. It had to be most public.

There was a suggestion that I fight ten gladiators simultaneously, thus enabling the people of Rome to see the match to the death that I had denied them. When Domitian heard this, one senator told me, he threw chairs in rage.

"And what if he wins? What then?" the emperor was supposed to have demanded.

There was the suggestion that I be bathed in pitch and forced to hold a clean arm in flames. This was dismissed, because it had been done on the day that started the major riot—the one that came after my secutor's being killed, now called the minor one. Finally, I was told, Domitian sent word that the arena was out. He did not trust me there, having had two performances and two disasters already. Rome could not survive a third.

Factions within factions were forming with a good deal of basic, mindless fury that fuels any contention people deem to be a moral issue. A faction of freedmen armed with clubs wrecked goldworkers' shops when a rumor started that the goldworkers thought I should be allowed to fight for my life against a single gladiator chosen by the senate. It did not seem to impress the senate that it was the goldworkers who were attacked for their views and not poor people who were on the bread dole. This of course was not lost on Domitian, who knew that the most wealth was stored in his palace, thus his desire to get the matter before the senate and not himself.

Should Rome have been faced with a resurrected Hannibal marching again, there would have scarcely been a harsh word. The people would have prepared to defend the city and themselves, the only question being how. And that would sensibly be left to the generals. But given something that had absolutely no bearing on whether they would eat or be housed or live safely, the people tore at themselves with more passion than many men defend their very lives with. People I had known would say it was the Roman mind. But while Rome seized most of the world, it did not hoard all stupidity.

Witness men throughout all lands who freely squander their lives and fortunes to be remembered by history, seeking accolades from people they have never met or ever will meet, because by then they will be long dead. Such pain and deprivation so that unborn schoolboys will be forced at the end of a rod to remember their names, probably incorrectly.

As each senator came into my room—the praetorians had already removed the couch they had used in their little charade, real only for the unlucky man I had met in the baths—I found out more and more about their position and Domitian's.

"You look tired. Were you delayed?" I asked of one who did not appear all that tired.

"No. Not tired, just saddened by an offense against our gods, gladiator," said one senator.

"Ah so, the praetorians are back in the barracks and they did not delay you."

"By Jupiter's balls, no. They are thick around the palace for what you have done, ungrateful Greek," said the senator.

"You just happened to meet some on their way to the barracks. Things are not that bad."

"Not that bad! They have not left their positions since your atrocity that day. And this, after all that Rome has given you. Taken you from a slave. Brought you into its homes. Made you wealthy. Made you famous. Made you fully Roman."

I lowered my eyes in apparent shame. Domitian still felt himself under the sword. Things apparently were turning back in my favor.

Almost all the senators in their august, judicial process asked me why I did not slay Publius. To an old general I said I could not thrust my spatha into the armor of the legion that I knew protected me and my estates from the barbaric hordes. To another famous for his boy friends, I confessed Publius and I were lovers. One senator, whose children had him watched over constantly by slaves, was known to believe the sun was the robber of life. He wore a heavy brown tunic under his toga, and a slave bore a heavy parasol behind him. He asked why I failed to slay Publius.

"There was the brightness of the sun, and then the sun, and then the sun was taking me," I said, "and I thrust the spatha into Publius."

"You did not thrust the spatha into Publius but into the sand."

"Did I really?"

"Yes. Undressed you were to the fullness of the sun."

"By the gods, this is a surprise to me. No wonder I have been charged."

Unfortunately, this senator did not have much of a following. A full third of the senators who came to interrogate me trusted no Greekling. To them I was stone. Yet they told me which streets they could not travel, and how long it took them, and how many armored slaves they brought with them. All this told me Domitian's problems with the city remained ominous, day after seething day.

Lucius Aurelius Cotta came, with several relatives and a small following of other senators. He told me how I disgraced the family, bringing shame to a name borne by two praetors and, in the ancient days, a consul. He turned to his following, his white hair so immaculately placed in small lines over his forehead, his toga white as the finest bread.

"I will take this offense we see before us from our family rolls. No longer will he bear our name. No longer will he share in the treasury of virtue which is the Aurelii. No longer will he enjoy our protection and influence."

Several spoke approval. The old patriarch said he must disown me alone, however. Face to face. One man to one man, to show me how Romans did things, not with cunning helpers and spies, but alone.

When they were gone, fully gone, for one tarried and impatiently the patriarch motioned him from this room in Domitian's palace, Lucius Aurelius Cotta, who had once so publicly freed me, now privately told me I was no longer an Aurelius.

"And we lose the best blood we ever had, Eugeni. No. Do not embrace me. Things might be seen even though we do not see the seers. Thank you for not mentioning me to Domitian."

"There was nothing to mention," I said, still surprised that he thought me the best of the Aurelii. Petronius had only told me what I had felt before, which was why I had been sad that night. And now I discovered I was wrong.

"Many men in fear give Domitian what they think he wants. You could have sent me to the arena with a word."

"I had other problems at the time, dominus," I said.

"Your adoption by us was political. And you had few friends, but you were the first Aurelius who did not buy his honors. Today was the first day you did not look enviously at my patrician piping on the toga. Good for you. In my heart you will always be an Aurelius, the best of us."

This shocked me, as though seeing a stone statue move. Did he mean it? And if he meant it, why did he mean it?

"They say you went first to your money and abandoned your wife and child. They laugh at you for your Greek mother. But I tell you, they would leave their wives and children and me, this I know, for their fortunes. You are cunning and brave and good. Thank you for being part of us for a while. We are the better for it. Not you."

A sudden weeping seized me that I had not known since I was a child. So deep, the sobbing had a life of its own. I cried, and the tears were full upon my face, and I was not all that sure why I cried, only that it was as deep and true as anything I had ever felt.

"Good-bye," he said, and then loudly, "you may never use the name again."

Domitian may have had as many problems as I had. I tried to concentrate on his situation to give me respite from thinking of Miriamne and Petronius. With good fortune and cunning, it now became apparent I might even be able to get back to them.

With me and my money the focus of Domitian, barring some chance misfortune, they would make their way to Jerusalem. There, she might be happier than in Rome. Although she loved me. She would find another. I had given her all I could.

These thoughts again became tears. When another senator wanted to see me, I was relieved. This one grinningly told me he was himself going to vote for maiestas, for indeed the very gods roiled at my desecration.

"The gods, senator, are only offended by what the senate knows," I said. When he left, I refused to allow any thoughts of Miriamne and Petronius to cut further. Rome had me. It would not look further.

Maiestas was a good charge. Domitian's problem was not the charge or the conviction, it was the punishment. I doubted that he feared me loose in the arena winning again. As his captive I could be sent in drugged. These things happened. No. Our divinity was unable to stage the games now, and probably for weeks. He could not get the animals through the city without dispatching armed men he kept around the palace. And even if he should be able to organize games on such notice, which was impossible considering the tumultuous state of the city, the mob might riot immediately, just by seeing so many of themselves together.

Nor could he keep me here safely much longer. Those armed cohorts were not on the parade grounds of Campus Martius. He was not going to keep something that required that sort of protection much longer. He couldn't kill me safely, and he couldn't keep me safely. He might just publicly get rid of me. But how?

A princeps of the praetorians, one of the two commanders of that guard, interrupted my thoughts. His handsome face was well oiled, and his muscled cuirass must have cost a small estate.

"Lucius Aurelius Eugenianus, we have a fine showing of slaves for you," he said. "Come."

If I had wanted to attract more attention to myself, I could have owned a palace like this with as many rooms as this, and, marching through this gigantic structure, I was glad I didn't. One does not own a home this big, but occupies a small piece of it, and hears only partial reports about the rest. I was lost by the time we reached the entrance to a vast peristilium with the natural opening to the sky almost as big as an arena. But this royal peristilium was a shock. Instead of the flowers and little trees and graceful statues and seats, there, inside Domitian's palace, was a scrounge of a slave market. I would have been less surprised to have seen oxen grazing here.

There was the wheel on which a slave was shown, and small stalls in which they were stored. There were the poor wooden bowls for their meals and a few chains for the recalcitrant. Women, some with their legs chalked white to show they were fresh from the provinces, stood in the places of slaves.

But they were not slaves. They wore coarse slave tunics, some with breasts bare, yet they were not slaves on sale. One only had to see the well-cared-for faces, the brightness of the stance to know these were not property. For a slave on sale has the expression and droop of a person telling himself he is not where he is. He is there as little as possible. And these women were all active in the sharp movements of their heads. Some even giggled.

"This is the great Lucius Aurelius Eugenianus, premier gladiator of all Rome," announced the princeps to these women. "He has come to loose his will on you. If you are lucky, he will ravish you. If you are unlucky, he will feed you to the lions he keeps in his house."

Lions in the house? Ravish?

In a whisper, the praetorian told me to make my selection, starting on the right.

"Touch all the parts as though you are buying," he said.

"I never touched parts," I said.

"You owned slaves. You married one. Touch parts," he said.

"I looked at slaves. I bought slaves. I didn't play with them. They are not toys."

"Do it."

"You do it."

The princeps of the praetorians, the most prestigious officer in Rome, equaled only by the other principes in military affairs, went to a matronly woman with hair only recently disheveled, because it was still crusted with expensive lacquer, and he ripped off the rough tunic. The woman's breasts sagged like cheap wineskins. He played with them, squeezing here, poking there. The nipples rose hard. She liked it.

"Examine her vagina," he told me.

"I'm not your vilicus," I said.

So he did it, roughly poking his finger into the triangle of dark hair flecked with gray. "Too old," he said. "You do the next."

He took my hand in his oiled fingers, and I felt his calluses on his palm. He worked with a sword. He was still a praetorian. He placed my hand on the rump of a young woman. This supposed slave wore delicate cosmetics and jeweled rings.

"Squeeze," he said.

I removed the hand and turned in disgust. These were wealthy women who for some reason were playing slave in Domitian's palace—a state they would have worked their whole lives to forget if they ever had tasted the true dregs of the wine of it.

"Eugeni," called the slave on the wheel. "Don't run. Enjoy yourself."

One of the praetorians had stripped a young woman in chains, and she writhed on the floor of a stall, moving her naked body as though a man had mounted her. He teased her with a finger. Another supposed slave helped.

"Harder," moaned the woman on the floor, and then for spite they both stopped.

"Touch me. Harder. Please," she begged.

If they wanted to fondle themselves, they could do it in goatskins, for all I cared. Chains or goatskins were both confessions of lack. A ripe plum did not need gilt embroidery, nor did fresh bread need a heavy sauce. Neither did the clear, good water of the north country need wine to make it drinkable.

I had other business, even as a prisoner.

"Eugeni," called out the slave on the wheel. Her feet were chalked with white gypsum, and her wrists were fastened with heavy chains, too heavy for a recalcitrant slave. If one were to believe all the chains and shackles abounding in this peristilium, this was the most rebellious lot of slaves since Spartacus. And not a whip mark or iron burn on a one of them.

"You used to do these things for money, Eugeni. Now that you are a traitor, are you too proud?"

Most of the supposed slaves laughed.

I looked more closely at the slave on the wheel. Yellow German hair had been woven into her own—a fashion among the wealthy to imitate what they thought were their inferiors. The face was hard with a strong, proud nose, dark eyes, and contented flesh of forty years or more. The hands were smooth and delicate, the nails unchipped by labor. She had noble, thin lips. It was Domitia,

Domitian's wife herself, which explained why a princeps of the praetorians was her servant.

"Empress," I said. "My respects to your divine husband."

"You're such a bore," squeaked Domitia. "I told everyone you were really a bore, but no one believed me. They remember the games and that body of yours. They didn't believe your manhood lagged like a tired stew."

"Now they know their empress never lies," I said.

"I'm not your empress. I'm a dirty German slave girl. You can take me like the slave you married. I'm dirty. Our empress is a beautiful and fitting wife of our divine Domitian. I bed even with gladiators."

"Then buy some. I am but a traitor awaiting his end."

"I'm a slave. I can't afford gladiators."

"My respects to our divine Domitian," I said.

Of course, Domitia was not about to let her plaything escape. She had me brought to another room with pillows on inlaid marble floors and a small cool bath in the center of it. Into this room she entered as empress, clothed in a delicate stola, her hair woven high and regal, her fingers jeweled, her neck hung with large diamonds set on small chains of gold. She came with the wind of Egyptian musk, and we were alone. The gypsum had been cleaned from her legs, and she wore sandals of cloth and silver.

She ordered me to pour her wine. I did, although I didn't know the proper portions of wine to water and took only water myself.

"I would like to thank you for the other day," she said, sitting in a cathedra—a chair with a back which women favor. "It was the most exciting thing in years. Years. The praetorians ran back from the arena, Domitian himself running with them. You should have seen him screaming himself into the palace. Eugeni, it was the greatest show ever."

"What do you want?"

"That," she said pointing to my loins.

"It seems to have an unwilling mind of its own," I said.

"You could make it willing. You used to do it for a few coins."

"But then I had a future. I have little need of money now."

"I am so lonely, Eugeni. He keeps me here, and I cannot leave."

"You seem to have adequate amusements."

"The same faces and same walls. Eugeni, I have such a hard life.

I am a loving woman, but I have no place to give my love." She placed a smooth palm on my wrist.

"There are three full praetorian cohorts," I said.

"I must choose carefully. I am empress. I have just a few selected praetorians. Domitian would not allow wantonness to be known, for I am empress. Let me have your body. You are not using it anyhow. I will pay you gold. Domitian will not mind."

"He is my emperor."

"But he will not mind. He knows he has forfeited his rights to me."

"I cannot believe that."

"It is true. We are modern. He has accepted that he owes me what I owe him."

"You have met another Domitian. All you see in the arena is not real."

"No. He has a different problem. He is afraid. He keeps a sword under his couch for fear of assassination. Then he is afraid that while he sleeps I will take the sword and cut off his manhood, so he has not let me sleep with him for years."

"Why is he afraid of that?"

"All men are afraid of that, no?"

"It is a fatal wound, but so is the heart or head or upper belly."

"What I want to know is why you would do it for a few coins when you were a slave, and not now?"

"I was building my peculium for my freedom."

"You will still need money for the soldiers."

"I am given everything here."

"But you won't be on your march."

"I am going to be banished?"

"Why should I give you anything? You give me nothing. You are selfish with your body."

"Not so," I said and placed a hand on her thigh.

She smiled like a little girl surprised by attention from a man. She claimed I only wanted her for the information she would give but did not really want her body. I protested. Of course I wanted her body, I said. I had always hungered for her, I said. I had dreamed of her. I had thought of her face when I slept with others. I had wanted only her since I had first seen her but was afraid to ask, I said. She also demanded that I mean what I said, and I begged the gods to drop fire on me if every word I said did not come from my heart. This accepted, she allowed herself to be serviced, and I found out that banishment was forced on Domitian by the praetorians as the only sensible solution to a bad problem. They had all told him that he could not keep the praetorians and the urban cohorts and the vigiles fully armored around the palace indefinitely, for then the people would realize the palace felt besieged and make the attack that was still only in Domitian's mind.

Domitian had suggested calling in a legion from Gaul, one from Iberia, and one from Africa. Both praetorian principis said he would not be inviting his safety but three possible new emperors, reminding him how, when he had combined two legions several years before, they found they had a treasury sufficient for a rebellion. Since then no two legions could be combined. He was now suggesting that they bring in three. This was too dangerous.

So it was agreed I would be marched through the city and out of the empire, and the entire city would receive donatives, as though they were legionnaires, the bread dole would be increased, and there would be games in a month. They had already been selling off my lands and slaves and could pay for this now.

"Under what law does he seize my property?" I asked.

"Ah, your love of money. What passion!" said Domitia. She lay beneath, her wants met, her smooth, stocky body the polished product of years of care. Her bellybutton, however, was no different from Miriamne's, except Miriamne's was in the center of a stomach behind which was Miriamne, and from which had come Petronius, and in which I had spent myself many good times, easily and with all the natural glory of a bud opening to a spring sun.

I had begun to think of life.

"I said your money is your real love, Eugeni," said Domitia. "Where is your mind?"

"I did not fight because I liked to feel my sword in someone's throat."

"Money is excrement," said Domitia. She pouted. I stroked her cheeks.

"It is not easy being the wife of Domitian. It is not easy living plots, and plots against plots, and being accused as regularly as a harvest of conspiring against his divinity."

"And I thought slaves had hard lives."

"Not as hard as mine, Eugeni. Not as hard as mine. A slave considers a piece of fresh fruit a victory and celebrates. What is my victory? To become empress? I am empress. To find a lover? I have so many lovers I have to buy new ones like you. You don't love me, Eugeni."

"Of course I do, Domitia."

"No. The game is over," she said and pulled up her stola, pushing me away with her shoulder. "You know Christians believe all life is a game, and the real life comes after this one, and it is always beautiful."

"I am not that familiar with the Jews."

"Your wife was a Jew."

"Yes. I think so. Yes. Correct."

"You never loved any woman, did you?"

"You, Domitia."

"Did your father really die trying to retrieve the lost eagles of Rome in Germany?"

"No. That was what the mobs liked to believe."

"He was Roman, wasn't he?"

"Most Roman of them all, Domitia. Sold me and my mother into slavery to pay a gambling debt."

"Dice or bones?" she said referring to games which required luck in the way square cubes or animal bones were thrown.

"I do not know. I was the bet, not the bettor."

"Were you old?"

"Eight."

"They say you killed a man before you were ten?"

"I was eight."

"How did it happen? You must have been very ferocious."

"I was eight. It was a lucky stroke."

"It must have been exciting. Tell me about it. Tell me."

I caressed her breast and kissed her neck, but she pushed me away.

"No, Eugeni. You want to make love to me to stop talking."

"Yes. Slightly, but only slightly less odious."

"Hah. Hah," she said gleefully. "I've hurt the great Eugeni. I've gotten through to you and I've hurt you."

For servicing her, Domitia gave me fifteen gold coins with Domitian's head on one side and his triumphs in Germany on the other. She asked if they reminded me of something, and I told her they did not. She said that was the price I had charged when I was a young man. She said my body had not changed, but was even more beautiful now.

"I do not remember, Domitia."

"And now you have returned the hurt, Eugeni. May the gods give you a happier life than mine."

My sleep was stopped that night when I felt the cloth pulled from my mouth. A praetorian grabbed the gold, but got only thirteen pieces. I had kept two in my mouth. He did not see them, apparently. I was taken out of the palace. I was not good at judging numbers of men that accurately, but the cohorts must have been at half-strength during the dark night.

I was marched through the night to Campus Martius where the great military ceremonies are held. My clothes were stripped from me and an iron brace put around my neck. Someone said I should be left my sandals in case I could not keep up the march. The ironworker attached a chain to the brace, and flying hot cinders burned my cheek. It was covered with salve. If they were going to kill me, they would have placed a cosmetic not a healer on the wound. I was going to live. One of the praetorians helping the ironworker saw the glint of gold in my mouth and wrested out one coin. The ironworker got the other.

Two praetorians oiled my body. There was going to be a display. At least a full cohort in armor with sixty-pound marching packs assembled in the night under torches. The tribune spoke to five centurions who returned to their centuries and talked to the men.

They were drawn up in neat ranks. The tribune told them they were to be addressed by the pontifex maximus. They would not cheer, nor make sounds. This was to be done in silence, therefore there were certain words on which the signifers were to move the standards, as though in battle. Signals were sent by standards because hearing is the least accurate way to receive a proper order in the fury of war.

They marched out of the Campus Martius and back, and then they marched out again and back again. I heard some wheezing from the heavy packs. These were urban troops. A legionnaire in the field could march thirty miles and then build a camp without tiring.

Someone suggested that the packs be left off. The tribune refused, saying they had to show a long march was coming and it was not moving the cohort through a little parade.

"Into Domitia's cunt," yelled a voice. The cohort laughed.

A loud order came that the packs should be lightened. The axes and saws and extra sandals should be kept, but the tenting leather and the tenting poles were to be discarded. The extra sandals were to be carried outside the backpacks. A continubrium was told to remove its helmets because they were parade helmets.

"This is a long march," yelled a centurion.

The signifer of the continubrium said it only had parade helmets, and that they were perfectly suitable for a long march and a battle. The centurion yelled it did not look like a long march. The tribune said that they were all actors pretending to be legionnaires but by the end of this they would be legionnaires. The signifer said their helmets were worth a thousand sesterces apiece and that the men did not want to give them up. Besides, no one was getting nail pay anyway, which was an extra bonus for a long march. It was called nail pay because legionnaires wore out the nails in their tough sandals on a very long march. At first it had only been for nails, but then it had been paid on every long march —even a sitting trip across the sea.

The tribune said the helmets had to go. He wanted good Roman iron on their heads, not some merchant's gold. The centurion said they had an ironworker here and he might be able to wash the helmets in iron. The ironworker said he could not do it all in one night. The signifer suggested that the men wear hoods. It would look like they were even more prepared for a long march. Hoods were acceptable. The tribune overruled this. Everyone must wear battle helmets for this somber occasion. They could change to parade gear if they wished once the march was under way outside the city. But in the city everyone must look like a legionnaire in the field.

"We're not going to a festival," said the tribune.

The chain on my neckbrace was attached to an ass. A legionnaire explained that I was to follow the ass as though being led by the chain. No one would touch the chain. I was to be exposed as an unclean thing. The men were told to rest. The extra gear, along with the gold-inlaid helmets, was carted off. The legionnaire told me no one would speak to me inside the city so I would have to watch him for signals if there were any. He said the mobs might fall on me but the legionnaires would collapse around me and make a turtle of their shields, which is another virtue of a heavy scutum—men can make a marching shell of them.

The sun came in red streaks and then a ball. It would be a hot day. At the movement of the standards, the entire cohort rose to take their neat rectangles, and this way we waited as crowds came to the edge of the Campus Martius to watch.

I was in the center along with the ass, which was given water and grain. I was thirsty and wanted its water, and when the sun was baking at midday I also would have stolen its grain, as I had as a young boy. I had never thought I would be hungry or thirsty again in my life. Perhaps a hard death in the arena, but hunger never.

I heard the horns and saw the priestly procession in purple. The pontifex in his tiered crown addressed the gathering crowd and the legionnaires.

"This morning the senate of Rome unanimously voted a gladiator guilty of a transgression against maiestas. An offense against the gods of Rome, a more grievous crime never having been committed. That gladiator's name shall never be spoken or written or carved again in Rome. Those statues of this abomination, still staining Rome, shall be smashed. Those scrolls with his name shall be burned. Those letters in clay and marble that make up this abhorrence shall be broken. The punishment for speaking his name, writing his name, or carving his name is crucifixion."

The word "crucifixion" worried me briefly until I realized it had to refer to anyone using my name, not to me. For as the pontifex declared at the bequest of the senate, I was to be banished from the civilized world, my money and my lands to be confiscated in the name of the people of Rome by Domitian, their divinity on earth. I would leave as I had come, with nothing but my spatha and shield, for they too were unclean things, and the city must protect itself from their being reforged and contaminating other weapons.

At this, a centurion marched with my spatha above his head and placed it on the back of the ass, then publicly washed his hands. A legionnaire did the same with the small shield. They had either retrieved them somehow from the arena that day, got reserves from my armorer, or made new ones. It did not matter. That the people of Rome thought they were the ones I had failed to use against Publius was the important thing.

The standards moved. The cohort moved. A legionnaire led the ass, and I moved. It took us the full afternoon and into the evening to march through Rome. Several times the crowds packed in the streets attempted to get at me, but the legionnaires collapsed around me with their shields, and I heard rocks and garbage and pots bang against the Roman iron.

Several hard things hit me during the march from the city, but I showed no pain. If the crowd saw me weakening, I knew the legionnaires could not contain them from the kill. There are times when showing weakness means death. Nothing inspires like the belief that something can be accomplished. So I let the pots, the rocks, and the garbage bounce off me, when the shields were not there to protect.

The cohort looked magnificent, as though it had walked off a chiseled column. Pila erect, shields at proper chest height, iron helmets cracking along, as even as buttons on a stiff board. Rome impeccable, Rome immaculate, Rome with its legions that moved with the precision of construction machines with great wooden gears whose spokes would no more think of moving independently than would the great Roman legionnaire who had conquered the world by first conquering himself.

The city had seen me. They had seen the cohort in its stern magnificence, ready to march me off the end of the world because there was an order to do it. No speeches, no bribes, no games. A job to be done. The virtue of Rome. The legionnaire was doing it as he had done it against Greek, Syrian, Parthian, Iberian, Carthaginian, Jew, Scythian, German, Egyptian, and Gaul.

The Romans might indulge themselves more today, but they were still Romans, men of iron. No frills. Discipline. Let the world look at that.

This is what the cohort told the people of Rome by their dull, sturdy uniforms, methodical pace, and silent march. This was why the gold-inlaid helmets could not be worn. The cohort was showing them their virtuous past alive today and to be believed in as they believed in their triumphal arches with just such scenes carved in them.

Outside the city, the whores and merchants and slaves were

waiting at the first camp, along with the impedimenta carts carrying the supplies, including the accounts of the unit. Five of the gold-inlaid helmets had been stolen, as the legionnaires had feared. There was a dispute over compensation. The signifers put down the standards they carried so nobly and began settling pay disputes and allowances for this new unit.

There was a speech by the tribune in charge, Gnaeus Cornelius Macer, who said that he would crucify any man who spoke my name. And to show those who lived within city walls all their lives what a real crucifixion looked like, he would make an example of two men who had, he said, spoken my name.

One trudged out in chains, his massive belly hanging out over a loincloth. The other, even in the twilight behind him, showed his ink-stained fingers. They had gotten Demosthenes and Plutarch, who had obviously been my most loyal friends.

"Forgive me," I cried, and I yelled it as the legionnaires dug the holes for the crosses. They were not road or display crosses, which are high off the ground, but little taller than the men themselves. My two slaves and friends were standing there facing me, while legionnaires laid the crosses down behind them: the crossbeams far, the bottoms lying just over the recently dug holes.

Two legionnaires kicked the legs out from underneath Plutarch and Demosthenes, while another pushed them back, so they went backwards like falling boards and landed with a harsh bang that briefly immobilized them. With smooth practice, the legionnaires immediately broke the arms with hammers and drove spikes into the forearms, pinning them there. They smashed one leg on each, and rammed a sharp spike first through the unbroken one and then into where their hammers had broken the other. Thus were the legs secured.

Two legionnaires at each cross yanked them back with their suffering cargo, then up with a heave, and the crosses were planted with my friends' legs just above the earth. Plutarch let out a massive cry, and Demosthenes bit through his lips.

"That is how a crucifixion is done by men who have served with me in the field," called out Macer. He ordered the men into formation to watch and put me in front of my good friends, eye to eye.

"That, for just mentioning the unclean name. I am going to execute one out of every twenty-five of you. One of the easiest ways will be talking to the unclean thing, taking one of its bribes, or even brushing up against it in a manner I do not approve of. Just so an execution doesn't come as a surprise."

Plutarch wept and called for his mother. He called for me, he called for mercy, he called for water, and all the time I begged forgiveness. Demosthenes would not yell, so they poured boiling dinner oil over his head. But he had also bitten off his tongue and choked on it.

Plutarch took longer, calling out to an Eastern god, which reminded me of my wife and child.

"Jesus," he said. And one legionnaire answered him, "Same as you," and was flogged for the breach of discipline.

"Forgive me," I said.

"Forgive me," said Plutarch, which must have meant he had gone mad, for what did I have to forgive him?

"Forgive me, Jesus."

And then the breath was out of him, so they broke his ribs that he might die faster from the bleeding.

CHAPTER

XVII

Sister Olav was euphoric, Dr. Petrovitch confused and depressed, and Lew McCardle was surreptitiously gathering all the Latin textbooks and history books he could without attracting attention. He had gotten one public relations man fired for giving him lip when he wanted to know what a geologist would want with Jaeger's *Paedeia*—"We digging in ancient Greece or something?"

The subject had sat up in bed, very sudddenly, showing good use of stomach muscles, had focused briefly, and said what sounded like spitting, which, explained later, was a soft J—a breakthrough in sure understanding of the pronunciation in Latin, unless of course the subject should have a speech defect, which would have to be checked against other pronunciations.

"He said 'Jesus forgive me,' " said Sister Olav. "We may have an early Christian on our hands."

"I didn't hear Jesus," said McCardle.

"Because it sounded like Hesu. But that is Jesus."

"We're not sure what he's thinking. As you know, he is apparently repeating things said to him also."

"I know. But this is a great day. I am tempted to ask a non-Christian to assist me, just so there will be no doubt."

"I'll assist. We don't need more people."
"I mean more non-Christian than a nonparticipating one, and someone who knows Latin."
"I had a bit of Latin. Rusty, but I can revive it."
"Perhaps you're right. I just didn't think of Americans, especially Americans from your part of the country, with a background in Latin. But isn't this a wonderful day, nevertheless?"
It was 8 P.M., outside it was especially black, darkness even shrouding the stars.
"It's night," said Lew.
"No, only here, only briefly, but somewhere it is as bright as yesterday on the sun porch when you could not focus it was so bright. The darker the night, the brighter the sun shines on the other side of the world."
"Yes, ma'am," said Lew McCardle, for the first time in his life actively putting Texas in his voice. "You sure do say some mighty pretty things."
"Prettier because they are true," said Sister Olav.
"Dern tootin'," said Lew and gave a big old wink.
Petrovitch was too deeply depressed for a drink. Besides, he had hidden the little boy who pissed Ballantine scotch because he didn't want Sister Olav to see it in his office.
"What's the matter now, Semyon?"
"The lab report came back about what our patient vomited up."
"What? What's so bad about what's in him? Did you find out it was Coca-Cola?"
"Worse."
"What could be worse?"
"Poison. Someone poisoned him. He vomited up an extremely effective poison."

I deserve to die. I deserve to be eaten. Let the barbarians feast. Why do they wait? Has a life in the wilderness taught them to tame their hunger? Have they dined on Tribune Macer yet?
Demosthenes and Plutarch are safe. But the manner they died was their punishment for loyalty to a fool. A barbarian in black, like some Eastern magician or some sneak thief in the night, assures me not to worry. She hovers over me, huge head and ugly

grin and grunting the language as though she heard it in some cage in Rome.

Let her eat. I will join Demosthenes and Plutarch. She has a black hood. Macer the tribune had a red hood. I had been sure I would be able to work something with the cohort. Many of the men had been the worst bribe-takers in the city, which was probably why Domitian wanted them out.

Macer was a stocky man of light brown hair and weak nose who exposed himself to the sun whenever possible to make himself appear more Roman. His tonsor scraped his face clean every morning, and every morning he sacrificed to the gods, including Domitian.

We marched north, to the sound of floggings and men with heavier packs. I should have suspected where we were going because of the size of the escort—a full cohort—and the heavy baggage, which I overheard one of the legionnaires say contained heavy furs. One of the men stole a fur, tried to sell it, and was executed before the cohort drew up in ranks.

Macer marched the fat off the cohort. He marched the wine out of them. He marched the whining out of them until one day, when cracking along at its regulation legion pace before the mountains that separated us from Gaul, he drew the cohort into a parade formation and he addressed them.

"You have called me Vercingetorix, after the leader of the Gauls, defeated and long dead. And by that you mean, away from my hearing, that I am more Gaul than Roman. But let me tell you, I have been twenty-two years as a legionnaire in the Twentieth Rapax, that legion which sweeps all before it. You have heard of it back in Rome. When his divinity told me I would be transferred from the Rapax, I wept. When I saw whom I would lead, I laughed. But after these recent days, on the march with you, I now salute you, most Roman of them all. I will this day, by my hand, and by the authority invested in me by our divinity, the spirit of the senate and people of Rome, present you with your standards."

The standards had the usual eagle of Rome above them, and the abbreviation SPQR, which stood for the senate and people of Rome, and beneath them the head of Domitian. The cohort would be called Domitian's own.

Men who had once owned brothels and would set fire to a man's house for a fee cheered these hunks of iron atop poles. By common knowledge it took fourteen years to make a legion, but Macer had these men believing themselves legionnaires in twenty-two days.

We were hitting the regulation legionnaire thirty miles a day even through the mountain passes. Still the furs were not unpacked. I walked now with a loose chain around my neck behind an ass with my spatha strapped to it along with the small shield. The heavy brown tunic had itched at first, but by now I felt nothing.

Here in the provinces, I could see the reason for Roman power, hidden in the center of that power itself. Roads. Roads of stone, marked roads, leveled roads. Romans built roads everywhere. Port to city. City to cities. Arteries of an empire. Other peoples might have one or two roads to their capital that lazed where oxen had chosen to walk before. Romans sighted and leveled where the engineers decided.

Into Gaul we marched and then east towards the borders of the empire. We camped the last night in civilization at a garrison on the border. That night, even I had wine.

Heavy bags and barley were loaded into carts, the men mumbling that when this went there would be only meat. Meat for who knew how long.

An old barbarian woman, living with the garrison as a slave to a centurion, told fortunes, but the men were warned not to ask her. Naturally, after this warning she did a wonderful business, but it stopped when she predicted nothing anyone wanted to hear. Then they paid her to predict for the unclean thing, which referred to me. She threw her bones, with hands scarcely more than the bones she read. She threw them many times, each time seeming most confused. She confessed an inability to read my future, and the legionnaires of Domitian's own said it proved the charge of maiestas was true because the gods refused me a future.

The next morning we went east into the wilds of Germany where there were no roads but paths, and every night the cohort would build a moat and wall from the bountiful forests of this uncivilized region. Without mileposts I could not count the distance. Even away from senate decree, the Roman legionnaire honored his word. None talked to me or mentioned my name.

A large German band came upon us, and Macer had the cohort

fortify a hill. We waited there a week until the band, like some herd with little patience, moved off. When the sun was on my right in the morning three days in a row, I knew we were marching north. With the cold, I saw the reason for the large carts of impedimenta. Furs and leathers for the feet and body and head. So many furs that this cohort now looked like barbarians themselves from a distance, if one did not realize they all had the same regulation pilum and scutum and short sword.

It was here in the first frosts that I noticed an uneasiness come upon our columns. And I overheard men talking about the horrors of the barbarians, as though in Rome they did not have the arenas. Now I saw them draw lots for those who would comprise the small bands that went before us so that we should not be trapped by sudden assaults.

It was here that Macer made a mistake. A small group of the cohort that had gone before disappeared and finally was found, its bones stripped of flesh, its furs and weapons gone. They had been eaten, and several legs had been left smoldering over charcoals when the barbarians were surprised by the full column. Macer allowed the entire cohort to march past without burial or ode. He should have stopped the column and made a great speech about the courage and discipline of the legionnaires, and said that here, in the unknown wilds of most barbaric Germany, these men, who had gone before, represented that courage and that discipline far greater than any legion marching in triumph across the pleasant and paved Appian Way. He should have made these deaths seem significant and worthy. He did not.

Undoubtedly afraid himself, he let each man nurse his fears privately as we all walked by. That night, the moat was not fully dug nor were the walls set deeply into the ground, and men talked to me for the first time since the senate decree. It was no use telling them there was no difference between funeral pyres with trumpets and priests and answering a barbarian's hunger.

I told them they were superior to the barbarian as long as they remembered their training. I told them I had fought barbarians, and they were but children to men who let their logic rule.

They answered that the very pale yellow-haired ones could not be felled by the pilum because of their size and their inability to feel pain.

I told them the pilum used in waves had conquered the world.

They said a barbarian when hungry would eat his own arms. I told them that a long time ago this was thought of Aetheops, too, because their skin was black, and this was found to be not so.

They said barbarians were especially fond of the hearts of young virgin girls, and that they would go insane over the liver of a Roman baby.

I tried to speak to Macer, but he himself held true to the senate decree. He would not talk to me. I wanted to tell him the men were stripping their minds of armor.

A young barbarian boy had been caught outside the camp, and, like wolves, the legionnaires fell upon him, cutting out his liver and trampling it. During that night, as the cohort became a mob, I found out none of the men or centurions knew where they were going or my destination. Snows came that night, white as hell and cold.

One of the poorly planted walls caved in. The men did not form for march nor would they draw lots to precede the column. Macer spent the morning threatening crucifixion and decimation—the killing of every tenth man to restore discipline.

We were all lucky he did not get himself murdered by these actions. Lucky for the men, because without a leader—no matter how inept—they were nothing more than frightened children with overgrown muscles. Many went to the wine that morning.

I could have left the camp then, but my destination would only have been a barbarian's belly. And it occurred to me I might live through this if I were cautious. The barbarians were around us shortly, in great mobs, with furs and hair so light and skin so pale it looked as though the dead had come to collect our bones. Some legionnaires tried to form a maniple. Knowing their plight they now looked to Macer, but, even as they formed, the barbarians with their women and children became numerous and their grunts and growls filled the hills like a storm building.

We were, in any way I could divine, dead anyhow, so I took a short sword and had someone wrap my left hand in leather with a piece of iron strapping, and I went outside the little log walls and stamped out a circle in the snow. My arena weapons were unwieldy in the cold. I made laughing gestures at the barbarians in the hills. I beckoned for company. It took a while, but a large one with his hair like snow and the sun wild on his face and body, huge in muscles, ran down at me with a club the size of a good sapling.

There was little skill needed and absolutely no subtlety or misdirection. I skewered it as it went by, making an explosion in the snow, screaming its last and spreading its blood like a child attempting to make a picture with its hands. I signaled for two, and two came down with many cheers from the hills. Instead of pinning me between them, they crossed into each other with a bang and fumbled around on their knees. I finished them.

Thereupon I made a speech to the barbarians in the hills. Of course, it was not meant for them since they undoubtedly understood nothing I said. It was for the legionnaires. And I demanded to know how they, the barbarians, dared entertain thoughts of meeting Roman steel on any equality. I told them to get other tribes, for they represented barely a morning's entertainment for a Roman cohort. I said the men needed greater training, and they would grow fat on this garbage that surrounded them now. Look well, for behind the logs of your forest set in order behind a moat are not men who hide behind walls, but use these walls to keep out your smells. Look well, for you see before you the greatest military blessings of all times, past and future: Roman legionnaires. Invincible. Men of iron.

Cheers came from the camp, and the log walls came down, and there was the cohort in battle order. Macer had good timing. The barbarians charged full from the hillls now, but the spirit was with the cohort. The barbarians left many dead. During the battle, I stayed inside the lines of men, always being the farthest from the fight.

In the goodwill of a victory, I suggested we all march now back to civilization, perhaps even Greece where I would make every one of them rich. They had more than served Rome so far. But Macer, expressing grief, said he was Roman and under orders, the most noble thing being the following of those orders when, in all likelihood, no one would appreciate their success or even know about them. Nor could I turn the men against him as we marched north every day, into heavier snows and the colder weather. Macer wisely kept to himself, the only one who knew where we were.

But he did speak to me and confided that I had not saved Publius that day in which the city went to flame. It seemed long ago because life here required so much thinking, I could not dwell on Rome, but on what was at hand.

"According to our divinity, he was collected by scavengers who came to the arena later and found him living under a pile of bodies, and he was brought to his parents, who demanded he fall on his sword because of the shame. Apparently he was too weak, from what I hear, gladiator, and his parents had slaves do it for him. So in the end, you did not save his life."

"You don't understand, and I don't think you could, Tribune."

"I don't know the arena. I don't know politics. I know my orders. I shouldn't talk to you. But I have."

"Where am I going?"

"You'll find out."

"I know that. But will you tell me?"

"No. But I want to thank you for giving the men back their spirit against the barbarian."

"And thank you for the information about Publius. He probably was not too weak but fell on his sword and missed."

"People have said that if I saw Eugeni fight I would not wish to see a sword in any other man's hand. I saw you fight. It was magnificent."

"You are emperor here, Tribune Macer. You could grant me my freedom for the fight I gave you."

"I owe you something, but what you ask is Domitian's to give, not mine."

Human bones with the flesh gone no longer bothered the men when we came upon camps of the barbarians. One could smell the grease and odors of their bodies miles off, even in the snow that dampens odors.

As we marched further north, the marching became more difficult. The cold was unlike any I have ever known, even beyond the depths of winters in my early youth, when I would long for the first sun smiles of delicious spring. This cold slowed and numbed and made the cohort a bobbing, loose collection of men stomping through knee-high snow. I managed better than the others.

The entire world was cold—a true hell, as the Persians saw hell. It was in this cold that my hope of ever seeing Miriamne and Petronius—a hope resurrected when I had heard the decree of banishment—fled my mind.

One day we marched into a bitter wind. Even in the recent days there had been nothing like this. A wind of knives and blades and points. I cried for mercy. Not since boyhood had I cried thus.

This, despite my gladiatorial training. The tears froze on my face.

Macer yelled into my numb ears that I should open my eyes.

"I cannot. I cannot," I yelled back into the wind.

"A little bit, open them. Domitian demands you look out upon the German Sea."

With great pain I opened my eyes to a vision of horror. All was white but for the black sea, whipped at foaming points to a froth. My mouth tasted of blood and my ears heard a constant, roaring hum. I could even smell the pain of the cold.

"You are here," said Macer. "This is where we must leave you with your eyes on the German Sea. Domitian has ordered that I give you this. You do not have to look. It is your spatha. The emperor bade me relay to you that you may fight the cold with it."

"If I had the strength I would fall on it," I said, and even the words came with pain.

"We do not like this task the emperor set before us, but we must follow it to the letter. There was nothing in the orders that said you may not have a drink before we leave you, and it is my suspicion that this drink is drugged to remove pain. Officially, however, I know nothing of any drug. Drink, gladiator. Drink away the pain."

I felt something barely touch my lips and realized it was the spout of a flask. I felt bitter, cold liquid fill my mouth, and then it went down my throat, burning like fires. Blessedly, he was giving me an easier death, dying himself. I ran full and naked to my death.

I saw myself going down to the black sea beneath me, and then I was very warm and felt quite good about leaving the world. I had had my time, and I had loved Miriamne, and I had heard my son call me father, and I was through. It was no great thing at all.

Even my mother was there, and exactly as she had looked back home in Greece, very young and very beautiful, and singing me songs I only now remembered.

There was no pain, but a deep floating into a wonderful darkness. Even my father was good and proper as was everything.

And then the incredible pain and the burning flesh and a giant bird beak stuffing down my throat and barbarian grunts.

The barbarians were back.

CHAPTER XVIII

Fifteenth Day — Petrovitch Report

Hail the Soviet Socialist Republics. Hail the Houghton Corporation. Hail the Dominican Order. Hail the Scandinavian–Soviet Friendship Pact. Hail man. Hail twentieth century man.

I vomit.

I live.

Hands wipe at my face, and I cannot lift my head. Large barbarians reach down to me and grunt their yellow-haired grunts and point. I am captured. I am high from the ground and linen surrounds me. White linen. I am on an altar. But, if I am on an altar, where are the worshipers to witness my sacrifice? The room is white, and there is sun coming in through cracks in a curtain. A summer sun, a spring sun.

I smell their foul incense. They wipe me so that I should be prepared for their gods, clean for their gods, whatever gods they may be.

Their priests are white. Where are the people? Am I to be eaten alive or burned? Where is the cohort? Have they been ambushed? Are they filling some barbarian's belly? How long are they gone? A day? A half day? Moments? It is spring. Why is it spring? That is a spring sun. A barbarian woman with white cloth helmet above her head plunges a ceremonial dagger into my arm. It is glass so they must have some contact with civilization. The point is a small metal spike, beyond barbaric crafts. If they have such ceremonial instruments, they must have contact with Greeks or Romans or Egyptians.

Perhaps they trade gold to Scythians. Their faces are so frighteningly pale. They are so large. But if they have fine instruments, then there is a way back to civilization and from civilization to the provinces of Judea. If I am not eaten, I will see you, Miriamne and Petronius. I am far craftier than any barbarian. I feel good and sleepy, and all is right with the way of things. I have won. I have beaten Domitian. I have beaten the world.

Why do I allow such foolish confidence? They are madmen's thoughts. I will be crafty. The darkness of sleep is good.

"Roman. Roman," says a voice.

I am awake. A woman speaks. But she says it as though she is talking about me, instead of to me. She is big and her skin pale white and eyebrows as white as the most northern German. Yet she stands stiffly, composed rigidly within herself. The eyes are blue. She does not smell like a barbarian, no rancid animal fats, no human flesh decomposing in a satchel on her side. She wears black. Her teeth are good, white and even. Barbarians always have good teeth, the better to tear human flesh with.

Yet there is a quietness in her voice.

"Roman, please be excusing me, Roman. We are friends. Friends we are of you and your people. Helpful we wish to be."

Two giants of men stand behind her. They wear tight-wrapped tunics of dark colors. A strand of knotted cloth hangs from each neck.

"What is your name? Who are you? Say now this thing to us."

The two men dog-bark their grunts to each other and then to the woman. She wears a small black cap, and a black loose tunic with round clasps holding it around her breasts. The round clasps are in a row. They are quite orderly. Have they captured Greeks or Egyptians or Phoenicians who serve them by making these? It is always said of barbarians that, should they get their hands on the finest sculptor, they would enjoy him to the last morsel. Yet these people obviously let the craftsmen live as slaves. Otherwise, where would they get the clasps of such perfect roundness and in such order down the front of their tunics? I have never heard of barbarians saving craftsmen, however. Yet who knows what happens in the far wilds of Germany.

"We know you talk. We have heard you in your sleep."

How strange this one talks. She pronounces the words with hard, growling sounds, yet the order of them is relatively good. Barbarians always have trouble with this. She does not.

"We are your friends. Friends."

They are confused. They talk among themselves. How constrained are their hands, as though they have been drugged. Perhaps they are slaves themselves, secretly educated by Domitian. Then, even while appearing to banish me from Rome, Domitian would get me back.

The men seem excited. One smiles briefly and quietly. Had I not negotiated with many like him, I would have lost sight of this. I have never seen that sort of smile in a barbarian. Yet there it is, so briefly and so quietly, like someone selling a lot of rebellious slaves while the buyer forces the bad deal. He must be Domitian's man. The woman is frightened and ill at ease, so she has no power here. The smaller one with the heavier features and dark hair seems honestly joyous.

My thigh pains. I cannot move my right big toe well.

"Hello," I say.

The woman gasps as though copulating. The men smile broadly.

"Who are you?" says the woman.

I open my mouth and the word comes hard. "Eugeni."

"What is your full name? Eugeni who?" she says.

"*The* Eugeni. You know you are talking to me."

"Yes. Yes. I know. I am talking to you."

"*The* Eugeni."

"Yes."

"Lucius Aurelius Eugenianus, *the* Eugeni. Rome's Eugeni. The Eugeni." They give me some more water. It is cool and good. My mouth feels as though someone has scraped it with steel brushes. The water burns as though coming into cuts. But it is good.

"Hello, Eugeni. Hello. Hello," says the woman.

"I am Lucius Aurelius Eugenianus, citizen of Rome, servant of our divine Domitian, singing chastened praises to his name. Would that I could look upon his face again, cleansed of my sins."

They babble.

"Hello. Hello. Hello, citizen of Rome. Welcome. Welcome. Welcome. Hello," says the barbarian woman with the dead white skin.

"And greetings to you," I say.

"How are you? How do you feel?"

"I feel weak. It has been a long march. Is this a temple?" I say.

"No," she says. "This is not a temple. This is a place where people get well."

"A training area. I will be fit for training shortly." I try to raise my body but can only lift my head. I clench my hands and curl my toes. I breathe. My reflexes are there, although quite diminished. And the right big toe barely moves.

"We just want you to get well."

"What tribe do you belong to?"

"Rest, Eugeni. There is much we have to talk about. Know you this, we are your friends, and we wish to give you comfort. My name is Olava. This is Lewus and this is Semyonus. We are your friends."

"Why?"

"Because we want you to be well," she says.

"Why?"

"We have our reasons, which we shall tell to you at the times proper for such telling. You must eat and exercise and rest."

"I never get fat and tender no matter how much I eat," I say. "I am good for the arena."

She says this does not matter. She growls her dog-bark German to the two men, who leave. She stays with me, smiling and showing her big teeth. It is a horrid large head she has draped in black. I am dizzy and I sleep.

I awaken and she is there. It is night. She asks me if I wish food, and I say I do. She has a bowl for me and I pick a lump of meal in the darkness. Outside there are lights I see through draperies. But I cannot discern what they are. Their tribe may be camped there. There is a small piece of meat in the bowl, too. I ask what the meat is.

"Liver," she says.

"Of what?" I ask.

"Calf. Young cow. It is the liver of a young cow."

My jaw hurts and swallowing feels like little knives ripping my throat. The room smells of strange bitter incense. The linen covering my very high couch feels well made. They weave here or know where they can capture cloth from civilized towns. Perhaps they trade for it.

"I saw the sun earlier," I say. "Have I been carried far south?"

"That depends where you were."

"I was at the German Sea."

"No."

"Did you see the cohort? There is a Roman cohort about. They are fierce, but I know things about them that can help you."

"We did not see the cohort," she says.

She is interested in my teeth and asks me what sort of care they had in Rome. I tell her the best, Egyptian. She asks what that is, and I tell her offending teeth are poisoned so that when they are pulled there is no great pain, although I never allowed that sort of drug to be used. I had two teeth pulled when they became poisoned of their own humors. Without drugs I had this done. She does not allow herself to smile freely. I lift my head and can sit. My thigh itches. I feel a wound but, strangely, someone has put thread into it. Olava explains it is a curing technique of her tribe, but she does not explain what her tribe is, or where we are.

I sleep and eat and stretch each painful muscle. Lewus is a giant of a man, with fierce orange hair and maws for hands. They want me to wait. I wait. I am alive. I will find out what is happening.

If I can move, I can escape. Greece or Syria must be south of here. From there to Jerusalem and Miriamne and Petronius. Or perhaps back into the empire at the Danubius. If it is summer, then there has been at least a year for Rome's passions to dissipate.

But how could it be summer? I remember winter. Has something happened to my memory?

Wait. I will wait. I will know everything if I wait and watch.

The days come and the days go. I get out of this high iron bed. My legs collapse beneath me. There is great pain coming up my knees into my belly.

Semyonus, the physician, hoists me back up, easily. But I force myself out again. It is good that pain is an old friend. Olava asks me about my daily life before the long march. How shrewd and cunning to have a seemingly innocent barbarian ask innocent questions.

It is not the obvious thrust that kills, but the one that looks harmless.

There is a gash in my right thigh. Olava assures me no one has eaten from it, that a machine did it, and she will explain later.

Why does she wear black, I ask.

She will answer that another time.

There are so many questions she will answer another time.

One morning, I feel strength come back to my legs. I exercise. Olava asks me where I learned my exercises. I tell her from the lanista who is famous because of me.

"What is that one?"

"You don't know?"

"I ask," she says. "What is that gentle one with right hand going forward? It doesn't seem like an exercise."

"It is a thrust."

"But the body isn't behind it. It looks strange as if it comes from nowhere. It is just there."

"You have never seen someone kill with a sword? Or do Germans still slash wildly? This is proper. This is right. Slashing is wrong. I can teach your tribe. I can make you famous."

But there is no answer.

My flesh has burned off in places, and the skin at first did not bother me. When it tingles and burns Semyonus, who admits he has never even read a scroll by an Egyptian, tells me it means the skin is getting better.

Lewus, the giant barbarian with red in his face and old wine on his breath, stays with me regularly before dawn. He says nothing. He reads things on strange papers, and hides them when Olava takes his place in the morning.

Semyonus always comes early to be with Olava, who tells me Lewus and Semyonus do not understand my language. They will get me anything I want.

"I want to leave."

"Anything but that."

"I want to leave the room."

"Later. How do you feel?"

"Do you care?"

"I ask."

"I feel sad."

"Is that all?"

"That is nothing?"

"It is important how you feel, of course, but how is your body? How are your pains?"

"My pains enjoy themselves immensely. I do not."

"Is there anything else?"

"Yes, I would like to see an emissary from Domitian. I have information he can use."

"We can't do that."

"Why not?"

"We will tell you later."

And the days pass, and through pain and will, I make my body mine again. How long these barbarians kept me until my senses returned I do not know. It could have been weeks. On that question, too, the answer I get is "later."

"Is there nothing I get told now?"

"What do you want to know?"

"Why do you wear black?"

"I am mourning a death."

"Whose?"

"Later. We want you to make yourself fully well first, and when things are right, then you will know everything."

"Nobody knows everything. When what things are right?"

"Your blood pressure, for instance. And by that, the force and frequency of your blood within your body which was very bad, even dangerously erratic. It is getting better. When it is fully better, we will tell you."

"How do you know what goes on inside my body?"

"Later we will tell you."

My urine and excrement are saved. My spit is saved. My beard grows longer. For the first time in my life it grows. I let it, although there must be tonsores here because I see Lewus's and Semyonus's faces are clean.

I sleep less and I exercise more. And the days pass without an explanation. Olava talks mysteriously.

"Eugeni, the eye cannot look directly into the sun. But a little bit of light is necessary and good. You will know as much as you can know, and eventually you will know everything we know."

Already her speech improves as though she rapidly learns from me. She is barbaric but she is cunning. I ask about the wound.

"You were found in deep sleep, and a digging tool did that."

"I did not feel it?" I ask.

"Did you?" she asks.

"I do not remember. What tribe do you belong to?"

"Eugeni, a single thread of a garment can unravel the whole garment. And you are not ready to see what is underneath."

"Underneath garments is what is always underneath. Garments are worn to make one believe there is something special or unusual or of great hidden value underneath. But underneath is always the same."

In the morning Semyonus, who is supposed to be a physician, asks me questions through Sister Olava. I ask if he is German, and Sister Olava says he is not but sounds German.

He has many questions about the poison that Macer gave me. I am told I spoke in my sleep. I tell him I was probably imagining that I had been given poison because the cold suddenly became warm. I tell them not one legionnaire spoke to me until my clothes were removed at the German Sea, and then I was told I was to fight the cold as I had fought Publius. They want to know who Publius is specifically.

"He is a patrician. But dead by now."

At this, Sister Olava asks quite sharply why I say he is dead by now.

"Because he was trying to commit suicide even before he tried to fall on his sword."

She asks about Miriamne.

"Who?"

"Miriamne. She was your wife."

"Yes. I lost everything. Even the gold I had was in such quantity slaves could not count it all."

The physician Semyonus wants to know more about the officer's poison.

"I remember no poison. Why poison?"

If I am supposed to believe this, there is a pale-skinned physician, supposedly good, not a trace of Egyptian in him, asking me, very concerned, about how one of Domitian's men carried out his orders. It is like the man executed for my benefit by the praetorians back in the emperor's palace.

Domitian has not given up.

Of course. I know what this means. Domitian never found out Demosthenes was the key to my major wealth and knows there is more. Oh, how our divinity dances in his arena!

Slaves here all wear white and are female. The physician Semyonus owns them. He is a physician of great renown, yet he has never studied in Egypt nor has he even been to Rome or Athens.

By the afternoon I walk with good balance, and by next morning I push my pained body to better training regimens. In pain I build strength. They still do not tell me where I am or how long it has been since the cohort left me. Olava tells me only that it is a long time. Cunningly, they ask about Domitian, and, with the shield of innocence, I tell them he is a great man and a great emperor. And nothing more. I do not abandon my reason even among barbarians.

The food is meats and fishes and vegetables with strange breads that are like cakes, and some are shaped as square as marble. Apparently, there are even more slaves here than in Rome, for who could fashion so many exact squares of bread? And it gives me thought. Who would want to?

Yet the food is without spice or life, and tastes like slave gruel. Why do they deny me garum, if they have such good pale bread?

Semyonus the physician visits often, and there is some contention between him and Olava. He wants her, says Olava, to ask me more questions. She says this will come later. She assures me I am not a slave or captive. She says there are no slaves here, but this is an absurd lie, for with my own eyes I see the white-capped slaves run here and there upon the bark of the physician, Semyonus. They do not even speak.

I ask why the couch is so high, since people would fall off it during sleep. She says people do not do this.

They have cleverly shielded with drapes the finest glass I have ever seen. Clear it is as water and uniform in squares like the bread. And then in the observation of the glass, I realize a shocking thing. These people in some way have mastered a uniformity either equal or superior to us in Rome.

They are not barbarians. Somehow, for some reason, possibly

known to Domitian himself, they have discovered a way to make their skins pale. Dyeing hair is easy. But how did Olava and Lewus achieve such barbaric noses? Where were the doctors to do this? I have yet to see an Egyptian. The Egyptians who perform these intricate operations must be kept somewhere else.

But why so much trouble for me? Perhaps it is not just for me? Perhaps it is for others, also. A hidden Domitian weapon.

But if this is a Roman place, I would have known of it. One does not keep such a fact uncirculated when at least five people know of it. Back in Rome I would have heard of such civilized barbarians. A legion outpost would have heard the tale from some German tribe it negotiated with, and it would get to Rome, especially something as exotic as this. How Publius would have loved the rumor, for he had a theory that all men were basically the same, and should a barbarian be raised in a Roman household, it would be Roman in mind. This, when wine had not convinced him that Roman blood came from the gods to rule lesser peoples.

I eat, I rest. I move my muscles, and slam breath into my lungs, and run around my room, and get strong. I live. I will find out where I am, get to know these barbarians, and then make my way safely from here to Athens and then to Judea and Miriamne.

The cohort last left me at the German Sea. Men do not sustain themselves in the semideath that I obviously suffered for more than five days. Seven days at the most, for the body needs water even in this forced rest.

Yet they say they have fed me through the wounds in my arm, which is of course great medical magic. And this, swearing there is not an Egyptian within miles. They do it themselves, they say.

In seven days at the most, during winter conditions, I could not have moved far. And I must still be outside the empire. The problem is the German tribes. I will have to go through them alone. I will have to wait for the beginning of spring, the first breaking of the ice, so that autumn will find me well south.

Yet, if I endured the semideath seven days, why do I catch glimpses of spring outside?

And where is that cohort? The drink they gave me had some drug. Now if the drug put me to sleep, and they wrapped me in warm furs, then transported me to this prepared place, why is that a spring sun coming through the glass? And who puts a sleeping room next to an opening to the sun or valley or whatever is outside? If this is truly spring, then I must wait through the summer and their winter to start my journey. Being fortunate so far, I should not risk a winter travel through the Germans. It might even be summer now, and then for sure would I be trapped in the cold.

If I knew where the cohort went, I would know where Domitian stands. The night torches outside may be their camp. If all this is Domitian, then he has not left me an open gate to walk through. It is a trap. It is a time for balance, not for lunging.

Olava brings me dinner in my food bowl. For light, she uses hardened oil with a strand of cloth in it instead of normal oil with the wick floating in it. She says the physician Semyonus finds me in good health and surprisingly good condition, that my exercises have produced truly amazing results.

"You wish to match me?"

"We don't have arenas where men fight to the death. We are glad that you become strong so we can tell you something that we understand will be very hard for you to hear."

"What is that?"

"In a few days, Eugeni."

I tell her the lamp with hardened oil is a fine product. She says she uses it because I am not ready to see a better product. I ask her if she is free or slave. She says she is most free. She has not known men.

"You are a virgin then?"

"Yes."

"Then where are the games?"

"We have no games."

"Then why do you bother with virginity if not to decide life or death? What is the name of your people?"

"Norwegians," she says. "It is time to tell you more."

And then the terror begins. She takes a rod from her tight tunic, which she claims is a stylus, and on some incredibly uniform parchment, runs the rod, leaving a trail of thick blue blood. The rod makes the form of a map. I see Rome. I see Latium. I see Gaul and the Helvetian lands. There is the blob of Britannia. With as much authority as she has outlined the world, she outlines the German Sea in the north place. She makes a circle in the northernmost part of the German wilds.

"We are here," she says.

"The most northern Germans," I say. How pale she is. How smooth is the skin. What flesh of child went into the grooming of her body? What mother's liver eaten raw gave her size and strength? I smile politely. If I must eat human flesh to live among these people, I will eat human flesh. I have taken it with the sword to preserve myself, now I will take it with the spoon. I will live.

The gentle of dusk comes and she talks about life and asks about the cohort and Domitian and the senate and where my house is in Rome. I am careful with her, saying that while I remember most things, my mind does not hold things perfectly, yet each day I remember more. She asks about a Jewish sect. As she asks about it again, she draws the fish with that rod. And just as she is completing the design, the room lights in flame. Bright bonfires of roaring intensity blind me. They are cooking me. That was the preparation. She screams in her howling bark. They cook her, too. The room burns. And just as suddenly as it burned, it becomes darker than it was before, the solid oil lamp giving less light.

"Eugeni, it is safe. It is safe. It is correct. It is safe. Don't scream. Don't scream. Don't scream. You are safe. It is a product. We produce that light. It is a product. A safe product. Don't scream, Eugeni."

I slam an elbow into her giant stomach. It surrenders quickly, unlike a barbarian. There is someone standing at the door: a cannibal priest. And he is joined by another cannibal priest in white. They may be savage, but they cannot fight. One drops with a kick into his groin. I push it hard for he is so big. One would think he is unprepared. They will not get this fattened dinner without combat.

They moved slowly for those who like human flesh. I lunge upward to smash him in the face. The bone breaks under my hand. The other throws his own yellow-haired hands in front of his big-toothed face.

I am in a corridor with the entire ceiling aflame. Yet the people do not burn. I hobble through it, my bare feet on marble, the coarse, white toga flying about me. Marble, blessed marble for my bare feet. Stone I know of, touch I remember, feel that is mine, of my life.

The corridor smells strange of that sharp incense. Suddenly, a metal door with no hands or pulleys opens like a giant mouth.

Inside are people held in a small cubicle. They look strange in multicolored tight tunics, some priests with cloth badges around their necks. And then something stranger up ahead.

I had seen writing in strange language on Olava's parchment. The forms of the letters were Roman, but the words had not been. Yet this word on a red board above a portal was in Roman language. It said, as clearly as though inscribed in the stone of the very Forum itself, "He leaves."

I go through it. Strange iron stairs going up and down. I go down. More stairs. I go down. More stairs and more stairs and these I go down. These barbarians are awash in iron. Iron for stairs. What wealth! At last there is a portal with a door that has a square of glass in it.

I push through this door into a large room with very bright flames. Light . . . like limbs of brightness on the ceiling. People in strange nonwhite vestments stare at me.

I see a tree. Through a portal with doors of glass, entire doors of glass, I see a tree. I run to it, careful that the glass of the doors does not cut me. Across a smooth road I run, and my feet touch grass in the cool dusk. The bitter incense is gone and I feel cold in my loose, white robe, but I feel good.

A low roar from above. A giant fat pilum with iron wings and iron body comes down from the sky, bellowing like bulls. It breathes fire from its wings. I run to the tree and cling to the bark of the trunk, making my body small beneath the bare boughs with their beginning buds. I will hold. If it takes me in its mouth, yet I will hold. I will hold as it swallows me, and all I shall remember will be holding.

It passes over me and goes away. And I cling to the tree, even as I get cold out here in the coming night.

"Eugeni. Do not be afraid." It is Olava. She is behind me and above me.

CHAPTER XIX

Lew had the answer, but, even as he explained it, he knew it was only a matter of time before he would not be able to sustain the scientific seclusion he needed most of all.

"You see," said Lew, "what we hope to achieve is a physical, low-temperature cure for emotional illness."

"Cure, Dr. McCardle?" a university official asked suspiciously.

"Not exactly a cure, but a treatment rather. You have physical surgery on the brain, you have analysis and various other therapies, this is cryonic therapy. Cure was an inappropriate term."

"I have heard stories."

"You mean sexual excesses by a Houghton executive?"

"Things to that effect, and also that he came in frozen in a block of ice."

Lew laughed. "As for being frozen in a block of ice, you can touch him yourself. He's living. So much for that story. As for the sex story, back in America they think of Scandinavians as being sexually promiscuous. This whole story came about because indeed he was undressed, suffering frostbite in major portions of the body. What Dr. Petrovitch found was a simultaneous altering of the mental state. We at Houghton think this might be an important breakthrough. That's why we fund it. That's why we give it support. That's why we support you. It's no secret that today oil companies, because of the energy crisis, are considered in some quarters as scavenger ghouls. We need to be involved in the betterment of all mankind, and we at Houghton think mental illness is the great crippler of man."

Lew paused for proper solemnity.

"Perhaps someday, because of the work we do here, people won't go running around exposing their entire bodies to the snow. Some may think it amusing that a person is so mentally disturbed he will disrobe in winter weather. I don't. Neither does my company."

"I don't either," said the university official. "Not at all. I hear he speaks a strange language."

"No," said Lew. "Italian. A dialect."

"Yes. Well, of course. Of course. Good. And continue the good work. We hope the work, uh, continues. Yes. Thank you," said the official. It had gone down. This time.

Lew found Semyon on the sun porch, exulting, describing the damage done to the hospital attendant.

"Do you know what it took to throw a punch like that, Lew, twenty-two days after consciousness and thirty-seven days after the first brain wave? Lew, our Eugeni is beautiful. I was so proud, Lew."

"Our scientific seclusion is being jeopardized, Semyon. Severely. I have only one solution."

"If only I could smoke, I'm so excited. I feel sorry for the injured attendant but, Lew, do you know what goes into throwing a punch like our Roman did? Eh? Are you aware of the human body? Everything has to work."

"Go ahead and smoke."

"Here? We have agreed this is forbidden."

"He's seen electric lights and an airplane. Do you think it's going to shock him to see you smoking?"

Petrovitch lit up, inhaling with deep satisfaction. Outside it was dark, but for the blinking lights of the airplanes coming into the nearby airport. Now he noticed them. Now everyone noticed them. Now he realized they should have taken out the light switch instead of taping it over. Now everything was clear.

"What we need now, Semyon, is total seclusion. We can get a cabin with everything you need. He's physically perfect, you've got to admit that. Then we continue our research in proper seclusion."

"I don't know. I don't like to be spread out. Thanks to you, we're just beginning to enjoy having everything in one building."

"What about the blood? Have you isolated the poison yet? What happens when people start hearing about the eternal life fluid you've got here? If you think people acted funny about cryonics before, I'll wager you can't keep a sample free and clear. And then you'll never find out what it is."

"We know what it is. It's a glycerol compound. I've had that for days. It's a sort of cellular antifreeze."

"I thought it was poison."

"Absolutely. They would use this as a drug in ancient days, as a very effective poison. I want our Roman to verify he was given poison. But he was reluctant to talk about it, and we decided not to press the issue."

"Do you want the storm of publicity while you delicately try to determine the exact compound, the exact formula used in the ancient world?"

"We know it better than they do. We know exactly what glycerol compound was used. That's not what remains to be discovered. What we're doing now, and with discretion I can assure you that, is having various laboratories check out the rate of thermal reduction. In other words, at what exact point does the temperature stop the killing process. This is being done with organs, cells, et cetera. Sort of farming it out, so to speak, with, of course, discretion. No one knows the magnitude of our achievement. When the results come in, we feed it into our computer, and we get the probable time and temperature. You see, there is a point at which different cells will accept this formula. It is the point we are looking for. It is not the solution. It is the point. I don't think notoriety could hurt us now. I don't want it, but it is beyond the stage of damage."

"That's too bad for Olava," said Lew.

"Why?" asked Semyon, a sudden chilling to his warm glow.

"I thought that in a cabin, Olava might let her hair down a bit. I think she likes you, but living at Saint Sabina's with all those nuns feeding her horror stories about Russians . . ."

"How do you know she likes me?"

"I don't. I just sort of sensed something."

"What did you sense?"

"Nothing, Semyon. Look, she's a nun. She's probably a lesbian as you said."

"No. No. Many normal people are nuns. Olava is a nun. What makes you think she likes me? I know professionally she respects me."

"Sort of a feeling, Semyon."

"No," said Petrovitch. He dismissed this with all the finality of a beggar with his hand open saying it was the last chance to give.

"I think so, Semyon, and I think she could use a vacation. She hardly sleeps. She works all the time. She's all business. I think that poor girl needs a rest, or we may have a mental patient for real."

"You didn't say why you specifically thought she liked me," said Petrovitch.

"It's no on the cabin?"

"If Olava thinks it would be a good idea, I could go along with it. Exactly why do you think she is attracted to me?"

With Petrovitch's conditional approval, McCardle broached the idea to Sister Olav and got a wall thicker, harder, and more impenetrable than anything even a Roman engineer could build.

It was impossible at this time to expose the patient to any further confusion such as moving.

"Dr. McCardle," whispered Sister Olav, who had dismissed the nurse and taken over the night attendancy herself, "our cultural parachute has broken. I am going to explain everything as soon as he wakes. This is no time to go gallivanting about. Impossible."

The building was called a hospital where people went to get well from diseases. Yet there was no wine or cheer here, only whiteness. I was not to go anywhere without Lewus or Semyonus or Olava. But if I did, I should show people a plaque pinned to me when I got lost. They assured me I was not a slave. There were no slaves any more. I should answer questions as well as I could. I could have whatever I wanted. But I should not wander alone and, if I felt any illness, I should tell them immediately, especially the physician Semyonus.

I had slept in the ice of the North for nearly two millennia. And they, through science, awakened me. All my friends were dead and so were my enemies. My son was dead and if he had issue, they were dead as were the children of their children, and their children's children: grown old and dead and decomposed so that not even their dust remained to mark their passing. No one was alive who knew their names, nor was anything they felt or thought or did remaining except by some artifact, if that. And even then, people would not know them, nor even their names.

The endless legions that ruled the world were gone. Time had done completely what no foreign general dared fancy in his wildest hopes. The senate was gone. The emperors were gone. There was no patrician class or plebeian class and, most of all, there were no more slaves. Only some stone remained.

Olava wanted to know about my daily life, the physician Semyonus about anything I might have eaten at the German Sea, and Lewus just wanted to know how I felt and kept advising me that I shouldn't speak to anyone but Olava. Both the physician Semyonus and Lewus spoke through Olava. Other women, those who did slave work but were not slaves because there were no more slaves, wore cosmetics. Olava did not.

My thigh healed well. It was not beyond belief that Semyonus had studied in Egypt. He said he had not, but in a workers' paradise where all men owned everything and there was justice and hope and security for all. I asked why he did not stay there, and Olava translated with a smile. Lewus's smile was a mask over worry. Even on a barbaric face, one could tell when a smile ended too quickly or stayed strong too long as though following orders.

In many different ways, the physician Semyonus kept asking me what I ate or drank the day before the German Sea. And I repeated how the cohort marched me to the sea, stripped me, and left me to fight the cold. He said he had found a poisonous substance within me. How did I get it?

"A man dying of cold does not record his menu of the day," I said. "It was legion food, not peacock's tongue." If Macer chose to save me pain, who was I to risk his career?

Of course, if I were to believe everything, Macer was centuries upon centuries dead. And today growling monsters in the sky are chariots with a new form of power, and the burning ceilings were another form of power. And waste was flushed away by the flick of a handle that sent it into a plumbing system superior to Rome's

—for the barbarians no less. And there were no more slaves. Of course, I would believe what I would believe, and until then, less than a fortnight ago, a Roman tribune showed me mercy, and I would not betray him now.

They brought me to a porch with much glass and screens of iron, where the sun, blessed sun, unchanged, warmed me as it had always warmed me. We sat on chairs with supports that went up to the shoulder and I ate cheese and small hard cakes with salt and drank water.

"How did you feel about killing other people?" she asked. She always wore the black robe of her cult. She was a sort of virgin priestess.

"I didn't kill people," I said.

"Didn't you say you killed more than twelve score in the arena?"

"In the arena, yes. If you want to call that killing."

"What do you call it?"

"The arena."

"You do not consider that killing?"

"Where people make fortunes, where whole political groups stake their future, where entire legions scour the world for animals and captives, and where spectacles unimagined in more barbaric places occur. People died of course, but I would not call a good match killing, any more than I would call harvesting wheat stealing from the ground."

"Are you angry?"

"I am a bit annoyed suffering the stupidities of a barbarian who insists I am not a slave."

"You are not a slave, Eugeni."

"Then farewell. I go."

"But no one here speaks your language but me."

"One chain or another, this freedman sits here to do your bidding, master."

"I wish you wouldn't do that."

"I am sorry, but it is the truth."

"Please don't do that."

"Truth is truth."

"No. What you're doing."

"I am sitting."

"No. That."

"What?"

She nodded to my loins. I removed my hand that had been stroking them. I wore tight white pants, fastened by a lever that pulled up, and a white shirt. The round latches on the blouse were called buttons, and when you learned to slip them into the hole sideways, they fastened easily.

"Good," she said, but suddenly she looked perturbed again and asked that I stop stroking my loins. This I did not understand, since I could understand her objection if it were her I were touching, not me.

"I have slaves, or had slaves, they were sold, and they could touch whatever part of themselves they wished, Olava."

She explained it was custom in her civilization not to touch certain parts in public. I asked if I could touch my knee. It was acceptable to touch the knee and face also.

I could see the chariot clearly through the glass. It was far off and made of shiny steel. Its steel wings did not move, and it made smoke behind it. People rode inside, like in a ship's hold, I was told. It stayed up without falling except when something went wrong. It always let the people out once they wanted to get out. It never let them out when it was high up. Men steered it from inside.

"You have not mentioned your early life, Eugeni. How did you become a gladiator?"

"I was a slave," I said. The machine run by men that went through the air disappeared. It was not burned by the sun because it was too far away. The lights from the ceiling were operated by a lever that was very simple. I pulled it, and the ceiling lit, yet not so brightly because it competed with sunlight. Lest a slave be above the ceiling watching to manipulate a hidden torch, I brushed my hand lightly over the lever not touching it. No light. Then appearing to walk away, I suddenly pushed the lever, and the light went on simultaneously. The light was not done with slaves.

"You said you knew how to read and write."

"My mother was Greek," I said.

"Was she born a slave?"

"No, and neither was I."

"You sound angry."

"I am not angry. Anger is a luxury no man can afford."

"How did you become a slave?"

She asked this as though she talked to while away the morning hours. I could not believe the presumption of the woman, unless of course a barbarian is a barbarian, never to understand. Then again, perhaps in her mind this question was just another one of a thousand questions asked me. It occurred to me then that Domitian might truly be a genius. Given a man with hidden fortunes, given my former political value in the cauldron of Roman politics, and given Domitian's cunning, why not this awesome charade just for me? That might be the key to all of this.

It was logical. Why waste a gladiator of my public worth in some petty vengeance at the German Sea? My death alone could be a fortune. Given that it was a charade, how did Domitian make all this work?

Probably I was in a drugged state. The poison given by the officer was on Domitian's orders. It made my mind susceptible to manipulation. I had seen a young girl lift a heifer under this sort of influence. It happened in Capua.

I concealed my excitement with a yawn. This would explain the interest of the physician Semyonus in what I ate before the German Sea. He wanted to make sure I was fully drugged lest I realize where I was. I could be in Rome for all I knew. The march to the German Sea could have been in my mind.

And why do all this, Domitian? To remove my cunning, to strip it away neatly so that I babble away as to what I love and hate and fear and as to where my secret monies are? What a wonderful way to find out that I would trade it all for Miriamne and Petronius. What a wonderful way to make me a slave. What a brilliant thrust. Perhaps it was because I had acquired instant cunning or that, if I were not born with it, I would not have lived so long. But my attack against him should be instantaneous. And against it, Domitian had to be defenseless. The more he believed he succeeded against me, the deeper I would cut.

"How soon after I left Rome did they get Domitian?" I asked.

"Quite shortly," said Olava. "I see you know about Roman conspiracies. They murdered him with a sword kept under his pillow. Nerva succeeded him."

"He must have outfoxed the real conspirators who had me not slay Publius. They were supposed to slay Domitian in the ensuing commotion. They failed but said if I disclosed their plots, I would die. They were my guards while the senate debated maiestas. I tried to get word to Domitian, but his very emissary was one of them. There were so many against him, and they had so much power. So much power. Yet if Domitian had known them in time, poor man, he could have moved. They had so many weak links. That is why they did not succeed on the day I let Publius live."

"So in the arena, in that fight that led to the charge of maiestas against you, your real motives were political. You failed to slay Publius as part of a plot."

"Correct."

"I see."

I pushed the light lever. I always believed the mind could create paradise, just as it did the fearful places. I had seen too many disemboweled men calmly watch their life leave, contented as men after a woman and a good meal.

"I suppose there were many conspiracies," said Olava.

"Rome is gone for centuries. Let us not talk of the dirt of conspiracies. They are vile things. There was even the woman close to Domitian who was going to cut off his penis with a knife and display the penis in the arena," I said, with enough, but not too much, horror in my voice. If that didn't get the old purple suet, I did not know my emperor.

I let Olava know of three small hidden treasures, saying I wondered what had happened to them over the centuries. Then I was tired, I said, and needed my rest. My head felt funny. I could not remember names or places or specifics. Yes, I remembered the drug now. At the German Sea. The officer gave me something. As I had figured, the physician Semyonus arrived quickly and I gave him every detail through Olava of what I ate. And what the liquid tasted like. And all other things.

"He says you were poisoned, Eugeni. The thermal reduction—the sudden lowering of your body temperature—stopped the action of the poison. You have been kept at near death, in a suspended state. You were, in effect, in a solution. Medically, he saved you from poisoning. He pumped out your stomach. I don't think you know how lucky you are, Eugeni."

Good fate, of course. One year ago I was one of the wealthiest men in the world, and today I was struggling to be free of an emperor's net.

"If you had been discovered at any other time more than fifty years ago, you simply would have died of the poisoning," said Olava.

"You mean your miracles are only recent? They have not been built carefully, like Rome?"

And at this, the man who called himself Semyonus the physician became excited. Olava had to talk quickly and sometimes to interrupt Semyonus to keep up with him.

"There is no such thing as magic," she translated. "There are scientific principles, which scientists discover and write down, and these principles are followed by engineers who invent such things as what you call the flying monster or the electric lights. Scientists discover principles, engineers act on them. Yes?"

"Hail the priests of Science and their temple slaves the engineers," I said. "Truly the god Science is a great god. You worship a great god."

"It is not worship. It is science." Semyonus angry, Olava smiling.

"I am sorry to have given offense to the god Science but you must understand this is a strange land to me. Will your god understand?"

Semyonus was very angry. Olava translated for him.

"Science, Eugeni, is immutable. It understands nothing and forgives nothing. It is what it is."

"A mysterious god, great for the Pantheon."

"Science is not a god. It would not like you calling it a god. If you think of it as a god, it will never let you know its mysteries. You must approach it in the scientific manner, with an open mind. Men devote years of their lives to it, their entire lives. It has given us everything we have today." Thus said Olava for Semyonus.

"Hail Science, giver of things," I said. "Let us sacrifice to it."

Lewus joined us and there was much talk. There was gloom on his face. They brought me to what was Semyonus's laboratory. And they expected me to believe this was not a creation of a Roman mind. Oh, Domitian, too much. Too much, Domitian. Who but a Roman would keep frogs frozen solid? These barbarians?

Another disclosure of their methods was the smell of the special incense. It was bitter. This, Olava admitted, was the smell of a drug that made people numb: ether.

"I don't think you fully comprehend where you are or what

has happened," said Olava. She held her hands clasped in front of her, as though bound by an inner chain.

Semyonus stood at some sort of martial attention in front of tall boxes made of solid steel, polished it was and apparently harder than the eating implements. There were square basins coated with a strange material like resilient wood, a new product called plastic. There were the lights above. Another thing, these lights gave off no smell. The physician Semyonus showed me a small orange fish swimming in a clear glass bowl. It was called a goldfish. Lewus looked at a metal disk on his wrist. By this he could tell the divisions of the day, like a sundial without the sun.

"Wondrous," I said. They put the fish and the water into a solid vessel because they said glass would crack in the cold. They put the vessel and the fish into one of the boxes and after a while removed it. The water was ice, like the German country.

"Wondrous," I said.

The ice melted.

"Now you will see the fish swim," said Olava. "This is important because you will understand what happened to you."

"Wondrous," I said. The fish swam upside down, the white of its belly showing.

"It didn't work," said Olava. "But these fish freeze during the winter and thaw out during the summer and swim. They do it all the time. If it had lived, this would have represented you."

They showed me worms. The worms became hard, then soft and wriggled.

"That's the general principle," said Olava. The physician Semyonus looked disturbed.

"Wondrous," I said. "Tell me, when Domitian was murdered, did that woman cut him where she said she would?"

"We have no record," said Olava.

"He was not a bad emperor. He deserved better," I said.

"Do you miss Domitian?"

"I miss Domitian, I miss the arena, I miss Rome and my position."

"Do you miss your family?"

"Women and children are plentiful. Gold is not," I said most disdainfully.

"You do not miss them?" asked Olava.

"Not much."

"Was that common in Rome, for people to feel like that?" she asked.

"Not uncommon."

"Did the Christians feel that way?"

"I did not follow the cults."

"The Jewish sect."

"There were many Jewish sects."

"The one that believed in the resurrection of the body. The fish. Fishers of men?"

"Yes. Yes. Publius was one of those."

"The patrician you did not slay?" asked Olava. Her pale face flushed with excitement. Her stone hands fluttered briefly.

"Oh, yes. One week he worshiped the bull, the next the god of the water, the next the unseen god of the second life."

"An early Christian," she said.

"Wondrous," I said.

"You have been given a rare opportunity. We have been given a rare opportunity."

"And science, also," I added. Domitian would make himself known when he was ready. The ceilings here appeared very high. But the magician's drug could have made them thousands of miles high, if they wished.

Lewus, the giant, said I seemed to be rather calm, Olava translated.

"The arena teaches us control," I said.

She translated back to him, and he gave me a short nod, looking down on me as though I were some sort of a lying child. I poked the belly of the fish. It was still. Lewus left. Semyonus placed a large hand on my shoulder. He smiled. I smiled. Olava smiled. Why did they seem so casual about the plots against Domitian? Undoubtedly, we were many miles from Rome and it might take a long time for word to go both ways. They might even be part of a real plot, although barbarians are usually too crude for this. Then why was I sure they were really the giant barbarians? They could be Roman and only barbarian in my drugged mind. I reached up and touched Olava's right breast. She gasped. Semyonus lunged at me. I moved around his slow-moving body with ease. Olava screamed at Semyonus. Apparently she tried to stop him from assaulting me.

Another flaw in their armor. Touching could somehow break the spell, obviously. For everyone here avoided touching. It was apparent now because of the commotion. That was why I could not even touch myself without alarming Olava. She might not even be a woman, although the breast felt real.

She explained that in her civilization they did not touch. That night, as she probed further into my daily life at Rome, how I lived, what I ate, what I believed, she cleverly circumvented the plots, but returned to my casualness about Miriamne and Petronius.

"Why is it, Lucius Aurelius Eugenianus, I cannot believe you?"

"I am not proprietor of your thoughts, woman. Why do you ask me?"

"Why do I believe you do not believe what you say?"

"Am I to explain this to you, woman?"

"I don't think you believe you are where you are."

"I have noticed some peculiarities, yes."

"What?"

"You are a virgin, yet you associate with me. This is somewhat illogical."

"I am trusted to keep my vows."

"Wondrous," I said.

In the morning she showed me artists' pictures of such exactitude one would swear they were real objects. There was the Flavian arena already in decay. There were the few stones of the Forum, as though demolished by a thousand barbarians. There was Hadrian's column chipped away here and there.

"Time did this, Eugeni."

"Time is invincible," I said.

"I am sure you do not believe me."

"Yesterday I was supposed to sort out your thoughts. Today you judge mine. I propose guardianship of my thoughts and you of yours."

"You seem so sure of yourself in such a strange place."

"All places are strange and dangerous, woman, it is the fancy of the human mind to confuse familiarity with safety. A man can be a stranger to his own time and to himself."

"You seem quite thoughtful for a gladiator."

"My mother was Greek. I told you."

"Yes, you did. And nothing else about your childhood."

"I was a slave."

"What was it like?"

"Wine, dancing, leisure."

"Seriously."

"We were latifundium slaves. Does an ox enjoy life? He lives. We were oxen with hands. It seems to give you some pleasure to dote on my slavery."

"Was your father a slave?"

I was quiet.

"Was your father a slave, Eugeni?"

I looked out of the clear glass at the trees and grass and people going in their tight tunics and all the miracles I was supposed to believe.

"Was your father a slave, Eugeni? You've gone into details about everything but your mother and father. Was your father a slave, Eugeni?"

"No."

"But you and your mother were slaves, correct?"

"Yes."

"Why was that?"

"Because it was."

"And what happened to your father?"

"He died before I could kill him with my hands. He cheated me of his life."

"I'm sorry. I'm sorry for you, Eugeni, not that you did not kill him."

"He is dead; like Domitian, like Publius, like the legions, like the senate, like all the slaves, and all kings of foreign lands, dead, Olava. For they all lived two thousand years ago but I, because of the god Science, live today. So dead is dead, and no more talk of the dead. Let us talk of you and Semyonus and Lewus and all the big people who dare not touch each other. Why?"

She offered a hand and said I should touch it. I did. There were no calluses on the pads of the palm and fingers. She turned on the magic light, she turned off the magic light. She asked if Domitian would not have these things, if Domitian could. I said yes. She asked if Domitian would not have the machines that flew, if Domitian could. I said yes. She asked if Domitian would not have a plenitude of iron, such as was in the bed, if Domitian could. I said yes.

Would not Domitian have machines that lowered him, if Domitian could? I said yes, even as we rode in one. She asked me to repeat every detail of the march to the German Sea when it became cold. She asked me of all the cold times I remembered, and how it felt. She asked me how the cold felt at the German Sea.

Then, she led me into the room Semyonus the physician was so proud of, where the goldfish died and the worms lived. Semyonus was there. She spoke with him. He chose the box in which the fish became ice. They opened a small door. Mist came from it. Its sides had icy snow like the German winter. She took my hand, and placed it on the cold. It stung, but the pain was good. It burned, as I had once burned. My hand became numb, as I had become numb, becoming even warm before the nothing I so well remembered now. My flesh adhered to the cold.

"It is real, Eugeni," said Olava. "Take out your hand now. Take out your hand now. Let me help."

"Miriamne. Petronius. I love you," I wailed. Semyonus the physician helped Olava the cult woman ease my flesh from the ice. They could have left it. I did not care.

CHAPTER XX

Sister Olav's Report

Subject shows a deep monogamous attachment to his wife and son, typical not of imperial Rome 79 C.E. but of the early Roman citizen farmer, this despite the fact of mixed parentage: father Roman, mother a provincial Greek. Subject is highly familiar with political intrigue—who was in whose pay and who was on whose side—which was of crucial importance at that time, but meaningless today.

His earlier statements before realization—if he has fully realized where he is—must be viewed with extreme caution. Tales of conspiracies and names of minor officials support a brilliant lie designed for Domitian's ear, not historical accuracy.

Today we know Domitian was the father of the secret police. Yet the subject apparently used Domitian as much as he was used. As a gladiator, subject was a showman, and the show was political. They served each other's interests quite well until what the subject calls the second riot, most likely what we call today the fires of 80 C.E.

Subject reluctant to discuss motives for his causing the second riot. Motives are most intriguing because subject had to have understood the meaning of his actions in the one place he was most in command, the arena.

Yet he turned the arena against himself, and Domitian, at a time when he could have left as its most successful participant in the long history of the games. Nor was this an emotional man like Publius (see earlier references), who might have been seized by some fancy. The subject, Lucius Aurelius Eugenianus, was a cunning, practical man, whose emotional involvement was directed almost exclusively to his immediate family, except for feelings of guilt towards two loyal slaves (see earlier references).

There is a garden here, like gardens that had been centuries ago, with grass like that grass, trees like those trees, new leaves like those new leaves, and the hot sun that has seen it all in a yawn. The sun does not share time with us in our meager portions, our brief dollop that seems so big when first served and so little when done that we wonder where it has gone. Was it so big to begin with? Did I miss something?

Mine was interrupted to end at a later time. Olava talks of purpose and of journeys. She will not accept my stupidity or hubris as a cause, when it is most apparent that I did a stupid thing, Rome did a vengeful thing, and nature performed according to its laws.

There are grander purposes, intriguing ironies, accidents that are beyond accidents.

I have already reanswered her questions about Domitian, now that I know he is truly gone. Ceasing to be a threat to my life, he loses his glory, but strangely enough he does not become especially evil, rather a bit cunning and a bit silly and, most of all, overwhelmingly unimportant. Not to Olava, however. This barbarian never tires. I dig my hands in earth. Petronius' great-grandchildren, if he had them, are not even bones. It is a hard thing to think about and cuts the belly like a dull sword. If I had lived the whole time of their passing, I could accept this more easily, but in my feelings he is but a little boy and Miriamne my warm woman. I hate. I hate the fool Eugeni.

Olava, soaring into her private pleasures, tells me she is going to tell me of a most exciting thing. I ask if it is about her own cult, but she says she has taken a vow not to discuss it at this time but first to serve science, which is not a god. This large, pale woman has more binding vows than a tribune. What excites her most is a great irony concerning what she has studied for her major recognition rank at a great academy in Britannia. People now study in Britannia.

"Be prepared for a great irony," she promises me. "I studied the comparison between Aeneas and Ulysses. Is that not amazing?"

"I am not aware of modern things," I said.

"Not modern. Homer was ancient Greek even in your time and told of Ulysses and the Trojan War. Vergil wrote the *Aeneid,* about Aeneas, the traveler who founded Rome and came from Troy. You knew the story of Troy, didn't you?"

"The destroyed city?"

"Yes."

I nodded. Olava's joy chipped her composure. She jumped lightly, and I saw her sandals were black.

"I've heard of the poem of Ulysses and the Greeks. That's a story."

"Yes," she said.

"It is one of those fanciful things men seem to need to justify their wants. Domitian and others who lusted for the games said they made good politics. In a way they did, but not to the extent he followed them, because in my last years they had become as much an incitement to the mobs as a palliative. And of course, the siege of Troy by the Greek cities did not happen because someone robbed someone else's wife. No one could keep the cities in a long siege for someone's wife, even an emperor's."

"It was Agamemnon's wife, King Agamemnon."

"I do not know what king or what city. There were many cities. And this was long, long ago, even in my time. But I do know there was a long siege against the city that taxed the tin for bronze. That's how long ago it was, when bronze was used for sword and plow. And that siege gave rise to the tale of the theft of a wife and great justice in a war."

"Perhaps because love of wife and family had declined during your era you cannot understand it, Eugeni. Is that not possible?"

"I loved Mir—my wife. And my son." I could not say her name without sudden weeping. Without saying her name, I continued. "I loved her and my son. I told you I didn't because I thought you were an agent of Domitian's. If he had known how much I loved them, he would have fed them to animals."

Olava nodded. She understood.

"With my love for my wife and my son, I truly would lay siege to any city, were there a city that I could lay siege to to get them. I would expend my fortune and my life to see her and touch her and make her happy. This I would do. Many years. Yet, Olava, what you don't know or seem not to want to understand is that I could not get other people to join me in such a siege."

"What about loyalty?"

"Loyalty is strongest when there is common self-interest."

"What about Greek honor?"

"You sound very Roman in that. Honor is sufficient for an afternoon's endeavor, especially against a weak and untroublesome opponent. It suffices to send a legion somewhere while you sit in the baths. Honor is a ship that floats best on seas of wine. It is not something that can keep armies in the field for many years. Tin kept the cities there. You cannot make bronze without tin. That is how a king could keep other cities with him. Not for a woman or honor."

"It is a great story, Eugeni, read today by schoolchildren."

"I am not judging its meter, woman, but its truth. It is one of those lies people use to justify doing what it is profitable to do. All do it. It keeps them occupied and safe from thought."

"What lies do you tell yourself?"

"That somehow things are with me that are not with me."

"Like what?"

"Do you care?"

"Yes."

"Why?"

"Because it is important."

"That is your lie, Olava."

She thought this quite amusing and even chanted a praise for me saying, "Hail Eugeni. Hail Eugeni."

I told her that I once had many scrolls, and works of Vergilius were undoubtedly among them. The name sounded familiar, especially the *Aeneid*. Publius knew the poets.

Olava had a box that reproduced sounds exactly. A similar box reproduced pictures. The box reproduced her voice almost exactly. On mine it faltered, lacking the true lilting resonance of my words.

Of course, if her voice sounded correct, there was no reason mine should be incorrect—other than my perception of my voice. I asked her if this were so, and she said yes. So much for human perception. I pointed this out to her.

She said that if I were not too tired, we should go over the same subjects we covered when I thought she was part of Domitian's plot. She understood now that, if Domitian had known how important Miriamne and Petronius were to me, they never would have had a chance to escape.

I stood up, my thigh still creating pain, and I did my exercises under the tree. She asked about the exercises. She asked where I had defecated. She asked what I owned. She asked again about Domitian and what people thought, as though, like a slave, I had kept an accounting of what every person thought about everything.

She explained again why everything was so important. She pointed to the top of the high tree and said that I should imagine the tree as time, the bottom being ancient Rome and the top being now, and all that has passed beween then and now, centuries upon centuries. With her fingernail in the bark of the tree, she made a small scratch.

"That," she said, "is a lifetime. In all this tree but one small mark is a human life. Imagine these small marks going to the top of the tree. That is how many generations have passed. Most records are lost, and we have but stones, small works, to re-create what once was. Here you are now to tell us. That is why I ask."

"And you, who are you that you dress in black when others dress in white, that your head is always covered, and your body always tight?"

She belonged to a cult as old as I, a few marks beneath me on the tree. This had survived, just as the word "to leave" had survived in the sign that I had followed when the lights had terrified me.

When asked to be translator for me, she had been living a secluded life with other members of her cult.

"To be a virgin?"

"No. No. You can be a virgin without seclusion."

"Seclusion helps," I said.

Virginity was not her major temptation but rather her love of my language. She began talking of life and death and love and eternal life, and I interrupted to say I was willing to talk more of Rome.

We talked until sunset, and I realized this big, pale thing was as disciplined in her skills as the best of gladiators. She would sense when I had difficulty with something and go past it onto something else. We spent the afternoon talking of Roman politics, the mechanics of money and property, of slave management, and of the correct pronunciations of words, though I told her I was not sure of some because they were only the way I knew. My langauge was not the best, and I had given up trying to improve the sounds because it would sound stilted. I was strongest being what I was.

"And what was that, Eugeni?"

"You're rather cunning in your questions."

"It is a simple question."

"As simple as taking off a head with one stroke."

"Did you see that often?"

"No. No. There are very strong muscles in the neck, and the head will move with the blow. I've seen a head taken off, but it must rest on a rock or something solid, and the blow must move faster going into it. You cannot take a head off without the blade going faster at the moment of striking. Many try it. It does not succeed often. You'll see Germans try it a lot with two hands on the pommel. Only once did I see it succeed with a man standing. And a German did it. The mob loved it. There were cheers for him. The head rolled and he picked it up and ran the arena with it. I had finished a match at the time, and the Aurelii had just bought me . . . are you all right, Olava?"

She was bothered by the blood. And I promised I would not talk of the arena anymore. But, she said, I should since it was historical and valuable.

So I explained how that German was a perfect match for me because he looked so ferocious and was really not dangerous at all. More importantly, the Aurelii could sponsor a match between us cheaply, and thus introduce a family member to politics with much fame and glory, without an exorbitant drain on the family's wealth.

I showed her how I fought the German on my knees, which looked even more dangerous than it was. Olava, at my request, played the German and I myself. And it occurred to me, as I showed her how vulnerable she would be trying to cut my head off, that she was the first person I had ever explained the arena to.

"Cut my head off. Pretend you are cutting off my head, you who are so large," I said.

She looked down at me, her body sagging.

"Do it. Do it. No. Imagine you have a big sword in your hand and you must take my head off clean. You're not doing it."

I asked permission to touch her body to get her in the proper position. She said I could touch only her back. That was enough. I got her weight on her rear foot and her hands lowered behind her.

"You see, at your size you cannot come down into my neck without getting into the bony shoulder or chest. You must come level because, while a blade will go through bone, it also loses power in bone. A good thrust rides a bone, it doesn't hit it. Do you see?"

I showed how I disemboweled the German and what his innards looked like on the arena sand, for he was a big, big man. As I described laying his giant yellow head on my shield so I could appear to sever it in one blow, Olava suddenly started to vomit. We had to fetch rags for her to wipe herself off with. She apologized for vomiting, but I told her it could happen to anyone, depending on the food eaten.

We ate their big evening meal with Lewus and Semyonus, who was happy when I described taking the officer's poison. Lewus was quiet. Olava produced a short oration for them. She said every classics scholar had been told when studying Latin—a difficult language for her time—that it would all be so much easier if they could produce one Roman who sat by the door answering questions. She told me these men had produced that Roman, a gift to historical and linguistic research.

Semyonus gave an oration. He said, according to Olava, that his people, the Russian people, were happy to welcome me into a new age of mankind—an age when oppression was dying with a new form of government in which all men shared in the wealth of the land, and knowledge belonged to everyone. A land in which, the physician Semyonus added, all religions were allowed. He smiled at Olava and offered her wine. She refused.

She asked something of Lewus, and he responded, and then she asked me how I felt. I told her my liver was alive and bubbling. Lewus said he would have some questions for me later on, said Olava.

Olava explained that Lewus studied the makeup of the earth: geology. The earth, she said, was round. People had walked on the moon—people from a new land beyond the Iberian Sea, which now was called the Atlantic. They had machines that shot out beyond the clouds to other stars. Stars were really very big. People did not fall off the bottom of the earth, if I were interested, because of gravity. Gravity held people on earth.

"People walked on the moon?"

"Yes."

"Then I believe the earth is round and the moon is big."

"The earth is not the center of the universe," she said. "Did you know that?"

"I know that now."

"The sun is the center of our solar system."

"This dessert is good. What is it?"

"It is yogurt, made of milk, fermented."

"It is good."

She said perhaps tomorrow I would be more comfortable talking about my father and my early days in slavery and why I did not slay Publius. She had missed nothing.

Semyonus asked Olava something. She did not translate until I requested it.

"He asked to see me to where I live now. I told him thank you, but that it would not be necessary."

"I think he wants you, Olava."

"No, no," she said. "He is very nice."

"If no one sees, you would still be a virgin," I said.

She said that was not funny. Semyonus asked her something else. She answered briefly. I asked what he said.

"He asked me to translate what you asked about his translation. Now you know."

Semyonus was always attentive to her. He made sure she was offered fruit first. He listened closely, and he waited for her to speak.

Lewus seemed to smile much, but there did not seem to be enthusiasm in his smiles. He drank his wine unwatered, as did everyone in these days I was told. He drank many cups. He was watching Olava and Semyonus, not obviously staring, rather like someone looking for something in them, and discarding things they said as not the thing he wanted from them. It was as though he sought for them to give him something to use against them. They chatted on, oblivious to Lewus.

And then his look. I had seen it before. It is not strange on so massive a face. It is a glance totally divorced of malice or fear. The muscles in the face are as unused as death. Neither smile nor grimace nor frown. The eyes do not blink and are open wide. There is a silence in the mind.

I had seen it only on the arena sand, when another gladiator saw me for the first time. And it was there across this table from me, the table where only eating was supposed to occur.

He looked away quickly, and then I realized, seeing that opponent-estimating stare, that I, out of training so early and so thoroughly, had returned it. Death eye for death eye.

Olava said Lewus had to leave for a few days but would be back.

That night I spent alone under the scrutiny of a slave called a nurse, who was of course not a slave. She was big and yellow-haired and smiled at me whenever I looked at her. I went to my room, and she went with me. I went to the sun porch, and she went there. I pointed to my mouth, and she ordered someone to bring water. I pointed again, and she ordered someone to bring food. Perhaps she did not know what was proper food, but there was a slab of almost raw meat dripping its blood.

I cringed. She ate it for me, like a wolf. The slab of meat was too big to come from a human unless it was a buttock. But Olava had assured me cannibalism had not been practiced here for many centuries.

The woman sucked up the blood with great enjoyment, making slurping sounds with her red cosmeticized mouth. Every few mouthfuls she offered me a taste. I refused, shaking my head. She offered me some wine. I refused. She offered me vegetables. I took a leafy thing with the taste of good cabbage. She ate enough for three men. She was taller than Olava, who was taller than I. She had massive shoulders.

She shut the door. She giggled.

She pointed to my loins and giggled more. She pinched me

playfully. But the raw, heavy meat odor from her breath made me raise my nose. She guzzled more wine. It helped the smell. She sat down on the high bed. I felt her wants. She was there. I was there. It was there. Why not? I embraced this large woman, leaning her back down on the high bed, when difficulties began.

Under her white tunic was a network of webbing to confound an engineer. Straps went from a loose mesh surrounding her legs to a cloth and wire cinch around her loins. So tight was this reinforced cloth around her vagina that it felt like the lining of a snug helmet. It did not go up but was caught about her heavy, pale legs. She helped by pulling it down, and her flesh stuffed in it flowed out, like a punctured winebag pressed with white suet.

I was not aroused now so much as challenged. She grunted as she pressed down the white and pink cloth barricade to her entrance. She got it to her massive knees, and, with a yank, I had it off her toes. She unfastened her tunic, and there was more defensive clothing, this time around her breasts.

Metal buckles and two tenting cloths, with straps as though each breast had to be contained from fleeing the body, hung from her neck and buckled around her back. She loosened this protection, and her white pink-nippled breasts were released to the air, full and already wanting. It was a rich flesh banquet of a body with strong thighs and moist entrance. She groaned as I worked her to a crescendo and then entered, ramming home a civilized thrust into a barbaric body. She moaned softly and pressed her lips to my forehead, and I started her passion at her breasts again, and then took it with my tongue to her navel, and then again brought her to crescendo, and then again, before I spent myself.

But there was a sadness in it as much as pleasure. It was not Miriamne. She made soothing sounds with her grunting language and embraced me. A small, thin gold chain hung around her neck and I played with it, rubbing the links between my fingers. I felt a talisman on the linen beneath her neck, attached to the chain. I felt its corners, and then a small figure in the middle of it.

I did not believe what I felt. Not even Domitian with blood lust roaring would wear something so ugly. When I brought it around from behind her neck, I saw it was what I felt. And gold no less. They would make it of gold in this world? What creatures! Perhaps the games were gruesome to some and were most certainly bloody. But no one back in the city wore a dying man in gold around his neck. Yet this sweating hulk of a woman had one made of gold, hanging on a cross.

She seemed confused when I moved away. She offered a hand to touch me. I slapped it away. Her wild blue eyes teared. I motioned her to stay. I took the little knife from the tray. She might be big, but I could whittle through the flesh.

The door opened, and the woman covered herself. Olava stood in the doorway. She said something in the barbaric tongue and then to me:

"Oh. Oh. Oh. I am sorry, Eugeni. I did not know. I am sorry. I guess this is natural. I'm sorry."

I did not know why she was sorry, but I put the knife down next to the bloody plate the big woman had eaten from.

She was stunned there, as though struck. The big woman managed to throw on the complicated and intricate strapping quickly and cover herself, hiding all the things, including the abomination around her neck. She fled the room.

"Let us go to the sun porch," said Olava.

"Good," I said. "You say things have changed and people are milder, but this is not so. Killings go on. Crucifixions are loved even."

"That is not so," said Olava.

"That woman wore a figure of a man being executed."

"I see," said Olava. "Yes. Of course. My God was crucified. In remembrance of his death, people wear the re-creation of the crucifixion around their necks. It is a way to honor Our Lord. That is my cult, which I am not at liberty to discuss with you now."

"No," I said. "No honor. There is no honor in that."

"My God transcended death. He conquers death. I too wore one of those things, but took it off so as not to frighten you. I replaced it with an earlier sign, this fish, fisher of men."

I was quiet. She said many years had passed since people were crucified.

"That must be so, because if you had seen my slaves and friends, Plutarch and Demosthenes, die you never would have worn a remembrance of that death."

"Not the death, the man."

"I remember the deaths. Choose what you will."

The next day we discussed this on the sun porch with Semyonus, but I was more interested in this land. I saw a hill in the distance, and Olava said we were just outside the city, on the edge of it.

It was a great city of the north people. Nurse slaves brought us things to eat and drink, and I wanted none of it.

Olava told me she was telling Semyonus about the sexual encounter. A rigid woman normally, she became taut like an overstretched thong on a bow, smiling suddenly every once and a while, like a cup breaking, and with the crash of the grin over, the smile going too. But the eyes never smiled. It was a great strain for her. Perhaps because she was a virgin by calling.

Semyonus, speaking through Sister Olava, asked what I thought of the sexual encounter, comparing it to Rome. I didn't understand the question.

"Were there any differences between the woman last night and women of ancient Rome?"

"Many."

"What?"

"Underclothes of webbing are different."

When Olava translated this, both she and Semyonus laughed.

"You said something funny."

"What?" I asked.

"Undergarments."

"What do you wear?"

"Well, I wear different things because of my cult."

"What?"

"I wear a scapular around my neck underneath my black stola, and that covers my front and back. I wear a crown, and around my ears a gimp, and a bib over the scapular in front. On my wrists here are cuffs. The veil over my head is symbolic of something in my cult."

"Why aren't they funny?"

"I don't know. I'm not sure. Perhaps it is something in our culture that cannot be translated. We are trying to determine what you felt about sex, and what it was to you."

"It was sex."

"But what did it mean?" asked Olava.

"Mean?"

"In some cults there are rites of sex, in other cultures it cements the family, in others it is the right of the man, and he has ownership of the children. What does it mean to you? What did it mean to others? What we want to know is your feelings towards sex and its ramifications."

"Ramifications of sex, woman, are children. Unless precautions are taken."

"You had precautions?"

"Oh, yes. There were two kinds. One good and the other not so good. Not so good were potions. They would mostly work. There was one best one, of course."

"Which was?"

"Celibacy," I said, and at this they both laughed, so I added the ever-popular "Underclothes." And this time they didn't laugh.

"What was sex like in your home with your wife, with Miriamne?"

I tried to answer, but when I thought of Miriamne not even being remembered by anyone but me, not a kind word said of how she treated others, and all manner of things people say of those who are good, I wept. I wept for her and for Petronius, not only dead, both of them, but with no one to remember them but me.

Semyonus offered that if I so loved my wife and son, I should know they felt no pain at this time. And that was a kind thing to say, but my heart wanted something more. Olava spoke with Semyonus.

Their builders here were good. The glass was quite even, and the sun came through without distortions. Far off in the very air, the big metal air chariots like slow, shiny blots in the eye of the sky moved down toward where they gathered near here. The economy was such that the giant latifundia no longer existed where carpenters and ironsmiths produced things, rather there would be a whole latifundium which did nothing but produce things like air chariots or those that went on the ground, and other devices in which there was great commerce between these nations. One could buy shares in these latifundia, called corporations. In Semyonus's land, east of the middle of Germany which was not civilized, everyone owned everything. Unlike Olava, Semyonus took offense when I referred to eastern lands as barbaric.

"I have the permission of my friend and yours, Semyonus," said Olava, "to have my cult perform holy ceremonies for your wife and child, who I believe were early participants of my cult. At least I think your wife was."

"Good," I said. "That feels so much better. Although Petronius did not believe in those things. He was a smart boy. There was much slander against that little Jewish cult. There were those who said they drank the blood and ate the body of their god in horrible symbolic ritual sacrifice, but there is no lack of bad things said about the unknown, hence the stories about death."

A red flush galloped across the pale face of Olava. She adjusted her big body. The words came hard to her.

"Eugeni. You are describing the Mass, but it commemorates God offering up his son in sacrifice for all mankind. The wine and bread represent his body and blood."

"Yellow-haired people adopted this religion, yes?"

"You don't understand, Eugeni. It is love, not cannibalism. What greater love can someone have than to die for someone?"

"Live for them. Any idiot can die. Would that I had lived for my Miriamne and Petronius. She would have had the comfort of my love, and Petronius my strength. I cast them adrift because of a moment's insanity."

"Because of the patrician Publius?"

"Because of me. Let us talk of sex. We, in our strange and now ancient manner, performed secret and unusual sexual acts."

I waited for Olava to translate. Semyonus leaned forward, nervously eyeing Olava.

"There was this special way to do sex that drove women so mad with passion that they would voluntarily cast themselves into slavery just to have you touch them once again," I said.

Olava concentrated on her book of papers with lines, in which she would write now and then. Semyonus said something, Olava did not translate.

"What did he say?" I asked.

"Nothing."

"It was one word. What was it?"

"The word was 'really,' signifying great interest."

"I can only show these great sexual feats if I know I will be rewarded in some manner, because the act itself drains, not so much on the virility but on the fat, and I do not have the fat to spare. Now Semyonus would be left with glistening muscle from this act and look like a god."

Olava translated, but I could tell she explained more, and I was fairly certain she told Semyonus this was a bit of a game I was playing.

"How much will this miracle be?" asked Olava.

"Did Semyonus ask that?"

"No," she said. "And stop selling sex stories to him. He is a good man, and his only crime is believing too much."

"Only crime," I asked in amazement. "Good woman, you may not be punished for murder or for stealing, but gullibility as certain as sunrise will get its price. It is always punished."

"You don't want to talk about sex with Miriamne?" she said. She understood.

"Correct."

"Then we will talk of other things. You are free. What was your daily life like? I would like details this time. From the beginning."

"I do not understand the question."

"What was your daily life like? What was a typical day? How did it start? What was the absolute first thing you did?"

"I awoke."

"And then?"

"I urinated."

"And then?"

"I bathed."

"Every day?"

"Yes."

"With what?"

"In the tears of a thousand Parthian virgins carried by runners bathed in the oil of the essence of roses."

"Water, correct?"

"Yes, unless oils were on the body, and then they would be scraped off."

"We know you had hot baths and cold baths, but what did the average Roman bathe in?"

"Average?"

"The typical."

"I don't understand."

"If you were to go out in the street and stop the first passerby, who would it most likely be?"

"I don't know. I didn't go out in the street to stop people. I only went out for public occasions, and then surrounded by my retainers and armored slaves."

She said there had been enough questions for the morning. The heavy woman with whom I had copulated brought fruit on a tray, and I saw she had taken the abomination from her neck. So I smiled. When she bent over, I patted her buttocks. She jumped with a giggle, spilling an apple and a few grapes. Semyonus looked to Olava with shock, apparently for her.

"Was that a common public occurrence, the pat with the hand?" asked Olava. She flushed during this subject and made up for it by becoming even more tense and concentrated.

"With the average typical Roman of the street?" I asked in response. "The one your god Science loves so much?"

"Yes, was it a common gesture?"

"I would say it was done often."

"How often?"

"As often as there was a man's hand and a woman's buttocks."

"Did women do it to men?"

"Yes."

"And you wouldn't know the frequency, I suppose. All right, I see in your face you are tired." The slave nurse gathered the fruit and took it away with her.

They had machines that did the work of artists called "cameras" whose product I had seen before as a demonstration that time had done so much, even to the stones of Rome.

At my leisure I could examine these pictures, I was told. I glanced briefly and laughed.

"Who are these people?"

"They are actors and actresses in costume in a play. You had plays, but without the sort of costumes we use now for realism. This is a play about your time in Rome."

"Ridiculous. The picture is ridiculous."

"Historians helped in the costuming. Where did they make mistakes?"

"Everywhere."

"We have records and paintings of the manner of your clothes. What details did they miss?"

"Everything."

"In what way? You don't have to answer now."

I told her what was wrong with the painting. These people who could fly in the air seemed to lose their senses at times. In the painting there was one man wearing armor for war, another for the arena, another for a parade, another for a formal speech to the senate or at some forum, and the women were dressed for formal occasions and for going to bed. All these people were crowded around a giant dinner, and someone was dancing while they ate.

"The costumes are wrong. What about the dinner?"

"More than three people at a formal meal is really improper."

"What about the orgies and feasts?" asked Olava.

"Some people did them. Some people slept with animals too. Some people will do anything," I said.

The slave nurse left, giving me a surreptitious smile. I had questions of my own. Who provided the monies for this? What would the information be used for? If the god Science was the purpose, where was his temple? Who was the chief priest?

The answer, that sunny day in the north country spring, was that different peoples of different beliefs all got together in support of the truth and learning.

If I believed that one, I would have been most surely punished for it.

CHAPTER XXI

Lew McCardle at times had been caught looking before, but never had he felt so stripped and so challenged as in making eye contact with this patient. He had drunk seven or eight glasses of red wine, and suddenly the mild little glow was gone, replaced by chilling sobriety. It was as though two dogs had met suddenly in an alley, and one of them had to back off.

Lew McCardle was a full foot and then some taller than the little fellow, and more than one hundred pounds heavier, but when he caught the dark, cold glance of the patient, it was like being stripped of the secrecy of his mind. The little fellow at dinner was looking through him.

It was not like the stranger to the century being awed and trying desperately to absorb and digest his strange surroundings. Lew had been gauging Sister Olav and Petrovitch at the meal and was just about to lock in on the little fellow when he looked back, gauging McCardle.

And Lew excused himself from the table.

"Good-bye, Semyonus. Good-bye, Olava, give my good-byes to Eugeni. I will be back in two days at the most."

"Good-bye, Lewus," said Sister Olav.

"Take your time, Lew," said Petrovitch. "Say hello to Rome for Eugeni," said Petrovitch.

"You're going to Rome?"

"Just some research," said Lew.

"Geological research in Rome?" asked Sister Olav.

"No. Something very important that I think I have discovered."

"What could that be? Why didn't you tell me?" said Sister Olav.

"You were too busy, ma'am. You all don't have time to rest as it is."

"I can make time."

"Two days, and my regards to Eugeni. Good-bye," said Lew. He did not want to continue this conversation with the little fellow looking on. He had been reserved with his questions, secretive with his studies, and quite casual with Sister Olav on the suggestion that they move to an isolated cabin somewhere. When she had said "no, the patient is doing fine where he is, why change it?" Lew knew he had to find the reason why they would all change it.

If they didn't remove the patient from this cryonics floor to some distant place, the whole ball of yarn would come unraveled. And when the world found out that through an accident of poison, the function of nature, and the committed skills of a Russian doctor, not only had a body been suspended in time through cryonics, but that it was Roman and the premier gladiator of the imperial period, there would be a circus from Oslo to the drilling site and beyond—a greater circus than even Rome would stage, because now there was electronics instead of slave power.

Everything Houghton was trying to do would be lost. There was no chance it could be saved under those circumstances; Lew's retirement going because the world wanted to be amused. They would have it all, only later, Lew thought, leaving the cryonics floor and going to his small office where he packed the stacks of typewritten reports from Sister Olav. These reports had Lew's pencil markings on them, like intellectual graffiti. Questions to be answered but, after days, none big enough. Not enough to make Sister Olav want to move the patient away from the university hospital complex. He needed something very big, and he was going to Rome for it.

While both Petrovitch and Sister Olav sought seclusion, as each day went by there was less reason why they should maintain it so closely, as their solid scientific studies became firmer and more thorough.

Moreover, the hospital was beginning to get a scent from the cryonics floor. It was not the administrators who had showed Lew his deceptions could be punctured, but rather a simple general practitioner working in emergency who had treated an attendant assigned to the Petrovitch cryonics floor. He wanted to know about a strange fracture.

The doctor, in white coat with stethoscope hanging around his neck, puffing on an old pipe and speaking English with a singsong accent one could almost put to music, nearly punctured all of Lew's cover stories that had worked so well with the administration.

"What are you treating the patient on the Petrovitch floor for, if I may be so bold to ask? I am just a doctor, not a great scientist, and everybody seems to think only you can answer questions, Dr. McCardle."

"As I told the administration, mental destabilization. It's a form of cryonic therapy we're doing."

"That is your business, Dr. McCardle. But when your patient or subject becomes lethal, it is mine."

"Lethal? Is someone dead?"

"No. We are lucky, considering the punch your patient threw."

"How could a punch be so deadly?"

The doctor pressed an X ray into clips on a metal box, then flicked on a light behind it, showing a side view of a human skull.

"This is an X ray of the attendant's skull," said the physician, and with his mottled pipe stem traced a very thin dark line running up through whitish bone halfway up the nose. "That's the fracture, but look here . . . a splinter driven towards the brain." The pipe stem stopped at a dark eye socket. Lew couldn't tell the splinter from normal bone, but he took note.

The physician continued. "If that splinter were driven into the brain, we would have had a fatality on that cryonics floor that is sealed to everyone as though you were kings or something."

"I would say we certainly are lucky, especially since an accidental blow almost killed. We will do whatever we can for the attendant, and let me say whatever extra might be needed, please provide at our expense."

"You can't buy everyone. You people should have found that

out in Vietnam. We are not talking about an accidental blow. The attendant was lucky because your . . . whoever he is . . . hit him twice. According to the attendant, one blow with the fist broke the nose, as you see here, and the second with the heel of the hand coming immediately afterwards, drove the splinter up toward the brain."

"Lucky?" asked McCardle.

"Lucky he's alive. That was a killing blow, a blow designed to murder."

"Can you prove intent?"

"If I could, police would be up there. You can bet all your money on that, I tell you."

"Well, we certainly will do what we can to avoid anything like this happening again and, on behalf of the Petrovitch floor, I would like to say I'm sorry. I'm very sorry. I really am."

"Perhaps," said the physician. "But you corporate executives are such practiced deliverers of sincerity."

"I have a Ph.D. in geology, doctor," Lew had said.

"Not as good as business administration, eh?" said the physician, with his departing cut.

For eighteen hours straight, Lew stayed in his little office, building a collection of empty beer cans as he went through the transcripts Sister Olav had so painstakingly typed herself after each laborious and meticulous interview with the patient.

He made notes on the transcripts, such as—Sex—Domitia . . . Peristilium . . . Demosthenes . . . Tonsor . . . Plutarch—why Plutarch? Latifundia? No. Who did Publius strike in arena chamber?

It was 4 A.M. when he reached Petrovitch at his apartment by telephone.

"Is everything all right?" Semyon asked, worried.

"Sure. Sure," said Lew. "Do we know for certain if the patient has recovered one hundred percent?"

"Why do you ask?"

"I'm working on something."

"That's not an explanation. Is something wrong?"

"I think so."

"What?"

"I'll tell you later. Maybe show you. Brain damage is the one thing we are not certain of, correct?"

"Yes. Because if it forgets something, how would we know what it has forgotten, and besides it could be normal memory lapse. Have you found something?"

Lew held the receiver a long time. Finally he said very softly, "Maybe."

"Do you think Olava loves him?" asked Petrovitch, apparently little concerned with whatever Lew found.

"I don't know. I don't think so. No. It's four A.M., Semyon."

"I answered your questions, and it's only a few seconds later."

"All right, my answer is no."

"Why do you say that?"

"Because I don't think she does."

"She spends all the time she can with him."

"That's her job."

"She doesn't have to spend all the time with him."

"She doesn't. Haven't you read her reports?"

"Do you think I care whether he urinated when he got up in the morning two thousand years ago? Lew, do you think Olava has ever known a man?"

"I don't know. I don't think so."

"I don't think she has either. Have you ever been to bed with a virgin?"

"Yes."

"Your wife?"

"No. Someone else."

"My wife was a virgin, I think," said Petrovitch. "Maybe I should write her even though it is not the seventh of the month yet."

"No."

"Why?"

"She'll get suspicious," Lew said.

"So you have been in similar situations."

"When my marriage was better, it was as bad as yours, Semyon."

"Mine is not that bad. It doesn't bother me anymore. Goodnight, Lew."

McCardle made reservations for an early morning flight to Rome with a changeover in Paris.

He returned to his hotel and napped until midday, when he called the public affairs office of Houghton in Houston.

"That's pretty short notice," said the man at public affairs who had been assigned to give him what he wanted. "How good does this historian have to be?"

"I don't want anyone famous. No one who has written anything. Just someone to save me some time running through all these books you sent. Have him at a suite at the Excelsior Hotel and make the reservations for me on that. It takes forever with these operators."

"If you're looking for something maybe we can find it out in Houston, Dr. McCardle."

"I am looking for something," Lew had said. "And if I knew what, specifically, I wouldn't need you."

And so saying, he prepared for dinner with his two colleagues and the patient. He was going to stay longer dining with them on the cryonics floor, until that predatory look from those black eyes. And then he just didn't want to be there anymore.

The next morning the flight took hours to cover what had supposedly taken the subject months. Beneath Lew were the roads Rome had built, and they had paved the world with only slave power. And a road meant more to people than all the philosophies, he thought. Roads let people see other people. Before Rome, men were born and died never knowing there were other languages and other peoples, or even growing more food than they could eat.

"They built the roads, the little bastards," thought Lew, on his fourth drink. Somehow he felt it was exceedingly unfair that the world remembered the emperors and poets but not the men who made Rome Rome, for every little tribe with a club and a crown had poets and kings. But Rome had roads.

Lew signaled an attentive stewardess (they were so attentive in first class) for another drink. He nestled his big body back in the wide seat. He was riding on the new roads.

The airplane was the new road of the new Rome. Lew looked out the window and saw the tops of the Alps in the spring morning, late with snow, and he imagined the legions tramping over passes to extend an empire, bring civilization, take slaves and animals, give law, take freedom, and ultimately leave the alphabet, the Roman alphabet, throughout Europe. The "A" that the subject's son Petronius learned was the same "A" that Cara and Tricia, Lew's daughters, learned.

All this because of roads.

Even today a road meant getting produce to market. A road

meant an iron plow instead of a wooden one because you could buy things, too. An iron plow instead of wood meant you lived past thirty. It changed more than the depth of a furrow.

Lew was proud of Houghton Oil. It was not pretty, no prettier than a Roman engineer. But it gave life. It gave leisure time.

When you wanted to go back to nature, more than anything it proved that you were not born in the wilderness. When you wanted to rope cows or shovel grain, it meant that you were born in Rome or Chicago or Paris, not North Springs, Texas.

People hungered for the natural life when they lived in apartments cooled by air conditioners and sealed from the rodents and bugs that competed on this planet with you for food and space and air.

Lew hoisted his last drink to the company he served, and the stewardess looked confused because she did not understand the language.

"It's a language that's not used anymore," said Lew. "It's old. It's gone. It's dead."

Lew realized he was drinking too much when they were slow bringing fresh glasses. He dozed, thinking about the peristilium and atrium of Lucius Aurelius Eugenianus, or whomever they really did have back at the cryonics floor.

At the hotel in Rome, near remnants of the walls the subject had left nearly two thousand years before, Lew found Public Affairs had done its job better and faster than he expected. Not only was there no trouble getting him a suite, but waiting in the living room of the suite was a middle-aged man with sweaty hands, in a worn tweed suit with highly polished shoes that could not hide the cracks of age. He rose when Lew entered, thanking him and his company for providing the pecuniary aspects of his trip.

He had been to Rome before, of course, but not in such lavish surroundings, and he had written a poem in Latin for this occasion and for the possibility that Houghton might fund a classics program.

"Later," said Lew brusquely, and got down to business as soon as the bellboy had left the bags. He had never realized before what an impression clothes could make, and at that moment he regretted a life of careless dressing.

Lew sat on the edge of a hard chair, leaning on his left knee with an elbow.

"Please sit. I would appreciate no digressions," he said suspecting this was just the sort of person who could go on into meaningless nowheres with enthusiasm and little regard for time. The man was in his early sixties and could not sit down fast enough, apparently trying to please Lew.

This was just the sort of person Lew had once planned to become, until Kathy had become pregnant, and Lew found Houghton Oil was the highest bidder for his doctorate. Lew could not imagine now what he was thinking then, or during most of his career.

"Have you ever read of a Lucius Aurelius Eugenianus?" asked Lew.

"Gracious," said the professor. "It's such a strange thing to rush into, concerning such an ancient subject. It does not lend itself to rush, so to speak, but I would imagine that is a digression."

"Yes," said Lew.

"No," said the professor, referring to the first question.

"All right. Have you ever heard of maiestas?"

"Yes. An offense against the gods, but you pronounce it incorrectly."

"No. You do, but that's neither here nor there," said Lew. "Could the senate decree maiestas?"

"Oh. I don't know. Let's see. Yes. I would imagine. I don't know. You see that is an offense against the gods and—"

"Yes or no?" said Lew.

"Uh, probably. Yes. Of course. A thing on the name you mentioned. That's not a pure Roman name, you know."

"Beautiful. What's wrong with it?"

"Lucius Aurelius is Roman, of course. But Eugenianus is Greek. It would be like someone raised in Russia being named Ivan, and then coming to America and changing his last name to Jones. Ivan Jones so to speak. It was a common practice in Rome, Dr. McCardle."

"You are familiar with gladiators?"

"The politics of the games, yes," said the professor.

"Were there any famous gladiators?"

"Certainly."

"A single premier gladiator?"

"Oh, yes. But at different times. You've got to realize these games in the arena were unlike anything you understand today. They went on for centuries. Although in the latter centuries, there is no record of any single great gladiator."

"After Domitian's time, correct?"

"Why yes. We have records of a few gladiators famous among the city mobs before Domitian, but his reign seems to have ended the idea of one man being important in the games. Interestingly enough, it is Domitian, I believe, who is the most underrated emperor in Rome. He brought the armies under control so that they would not be prone to rebellion. He did that interestingly enough by never letting two legions share one treasury. Sort of keeping the treasury low, so to speak. One might say we classics professors share the same fate."

"Could following through on a charge of maiestas have caused all records on a certain subject to be destroyed? Could a religious crime do that?"

"About the only thing that could. Yet there's no record of it. Then again, there wouldn't be, would there?"

"Riots in Domitian's time?"

"During the imperial period, almost all emperors had riots. I suspect one of the most severe was A.D. 80, known as the great fire during Domitian's time, except for my theory on the gap."

"What gap?"

"It's my theory. It's a digression."

"C'mon. C'mon," said Lew, closing his fingers indicating he wanted whatever was coming and wanted it now.

"The Domitian gap is sort of a historical record process, and by that I mean, oh, gracious, I am just not used to answering questions like this, as though I am in some court for a living current case."

"I am sorry," said Lew. "Take your time."

"Rome was a great record keeper, as were Roman administrators throughout the world. Much was destroyed through time and barbarian invasion by Vandals, Goths, et cetera. But this was not like a single civilization being destroyed, such as ancient Egypt where everything was in one place. No, this was like a bowl of spaghetti. One could burn entire cities to the ground with their libraries and administrative offices, and it would be like only removing a spoon of spaghetti from a whole bowl. Well, there would be other strands. You really couldn't destroy records of an incident because of the great extent of record keeping and references here and there."

"So how could there be a gap?" asked Lew.

"Because I found a single strand. In an excavation in Tunisia, a fragment of a will by a vigil who was responsible for the fire and police . . ."

"I know who they were," said Lew, glumly. He also knew how much they could be bought for, in detail.

"Well, he refers to the fire, but he calls it a riot. We have known it as the fire of 80 A.D., or the C.E., as they call it today. He calls it specifically the 'great riot' after the 'disaster games,' now the games—"

"I know the games. Where's your fucking gap?"

"Oh, sir. Well," said the professor, feeling strange pressure and heat coming from a topic that had always been discussed in a leisurely way. And never had anyone asked a question about Rome with the angry word "fucking."

Nevertheless, the professor forged onward, gathering his wits and resolve. "Sir, I came to believe in the gap when I came upon this single strand of spaghetti. The will referring to the disaster games and the riots and a parcel of property damaged during the riot proves the gap."

"How?"

"Well, where in bloody blue blazes were the rest of the strands of spaghetti?" the professor yelled out, and then wrestled control of himself, back down to where he felt comfortable.

"No other references?"

"We haven't found them yet. Just the references to the fire. But Rome had endured smaller fires before, especially the one romanticized by Nero. Almost the whole city burned down under Domitian. Where were the vigiles?"

"They were corrupt and incompetent," said Lew.

"But why weren't they blamed for the fire? Why weren't they blamed for letting the fire get out of hand? During Nero's fire they had to blame someone, so they blamed the early Christians. Whom did they blame after the bigger fire in A.D. 80?"

"I don't know," said Lew, feeling weakness throughout his body. "I don't know," he said, and desperately wished it were not a lie.

"We don't know whom they blamed. So around the world, we

pick up references to a blameless fire, and not blamed are the firemen for letting it get out of hand, and only one reference to its cause. We have found a single strand of spaghetti in a desert and not a plate within a thousand miles, or a thousand years if you will. That is the gap."

"Thank you," said Lew, weakly.

"I'm sorry for raising my voice."

"No. You did a good job. A very good job."

"If I may say so, Dr. McCardle, you appear very disappointed. I don't know what I could do to help, but I feel an obligation, even an indebtedness, to your Public Affairs Department."

"Just stay here a while. I'll be back. I want to see the city."

"I could act as a guide if you wish."

"No. Thank you. I've got to do some thinking. But if you would wait, I may have something. But I'm not sure. Not sure at all."

When things went wrong they went wrong without end. Lew found he couldn't even get the right kind of cabdriver. He had come here looking for enough flaws in the patient's story to help convince Petrovitch and Sister Olav to remove the patient from any possible public scrutiny. But first he had to find the flaws himself, those things that might possibly create enough doubt to make his colleagues see the wisdom of further scientific isolation until that doubt was resolved.

He had been assured by the hotel that the cabdriver spoke English. So why did he look so confused?

"I am most sorry," said the driver. "I do not know any Flavian, mister. I don't know it at all."

"I'm sorry," said Lew. "The Colosseum." He had used the patient's term, the proper name for the Flavian amphitheater, which of course the patient would always call the Flavian, for his divinity, his emperor, the man he knew almost two thousand years ago, the man whose father had built it.

Lights played off the Colosseum—a shell of what the patient had known, just portions of the bare understructure without the statues in every opening to the street, or the fine marble skin. Auto traffic scurried around on new, soft asphalt, at a dizzying pace. Lew told the driver to stop.

They probably never had night games here, thought Lew, such as he had known. He had played in the first night game of his college, and it had drawn much excitement. He remembered running into the stadium with the banks of lights shining down and after the first hit, not feeling any difference. You were so tired at the end of those games you could have played them at the bottom of the ocean and happily drowned for the relief of knowing you didn't have to go on.

He had been afraid of that first night game because it was new. Just as he had been afraid of his first college scrimmage, just as he had been afraid so recently of a managerial post in a delicate situation.

He remembered that first practice. There was a halfback from Santa Fe, who was five foot three inches tall and had been famous in high school for scoring more touchdowns than anyone in the history of that city.

There were wind sprints in the first practices, testing speed. Lew and the little fellow were matched, and they ran ten-yard windsprints together. When they had gone the hundred-yard field, he could see shock on the little fellow's face. Lew McCardle out of North Springs was six foot three and a half inches tall, two hundred and fifty-eight pounds, and every bit as fast as the smaller halfback. What had been sufficient for high school ball was woefully inadequate for college, because when there was so much money involved, you could always find a good big guy who was better than a good little guy. That was the law of money, and that was the law of athletics.

Lew McCardle clapped his hands and let out a Texas yahoo that could have awakened the ghosts of Domitian and Nero themselves. He had found it. He had found the flaw.

He had been thrown off by the size of Romans. Eugeni was the perfect size for the average Roman. But not for the arena, not to be the premier gladiator during his time. That size would be more appropriate for Plutarch, the arena slave who kept being mentioned in Olava's notes, the one who was supposed to have been crucified and was supposed to be inadequate for the games.

While Romans were rarely over five feet by average, a foremost gladiator had to be at least the size of Plutarch, maybe even as big as Lew himself. There was just too much money involved. Too much.

He looked for the last time at the Flavian. This was the smaller arena, and it was so big to centuries of men who came afterwards that they copied this misnaming of the Flavian for their stadiums, calling them "coliseums," not even knowing they referred to a statue that was no longer there.

Too much money. Too big. Eugeni, too little. Had to be.

Back at the hotel, Lew found his professor drinking sherry and reading some Latin poetry.

"I have something for you to do. It's sort of a rush project, which I will explain later, but you are not to tell anyone you represent us until later. Right now, you are just doing research for yourself."

"Why, thank you."

"We are interested in the finances of the games, their effect on the economies of the provinces and how far they reached, and how big financially they were."

"The greatest testimony can be borne by the European lion," said the professor, somewhat confused but very happy at this moment.

"I've never heard of a European lion," said Lew.

The professor grinned wickedly at his little joke.

"Of course you wouldn't. With only spears and swords and nets the Romans made more species extinct with their games than we have with helicopters and guns. The European lion was just such a one."

"One more question. A gladiator wouldn't be trained as both a pugilist who could throw a killing blow and a swordsman who could use, let's say, a spatha."

"Absolutely not," said the professor. "Your common gladiator was a trained slave. No lanista—an owner of gladiators—would invest money in training a slave in something he wouldn't use. No more than a coach would train one of your football players, Dr. McCardle, as a tackle suited for some other position—one of those other fellows."

"A halfback, said Lew. "Or a cornerback. You know, back home people watch a lot of football on television. And they see these little cornerbacks running around so quickly and getting hurt against big fellows. Those little fast cornerbacks are usually six feet tall."

"Fascinating," said the professor.

"In my studies," added Lew, "I never read about sizes of gladiators, that is, of their fighting according to sizes, like our current boxers."

"Of course not. This was life and death. They weren't going to see someone disemboweled and then worry about his weight. Gracious. They had them fight animals with their teeth. You're thinking of the Marquis of Queensberry, not Rome. Weights. By Jove, never."

CHAPTER XXII

Semyon Petrovitch got his answer early and from a computer. He knew what had happened, and why a man could walk alive two thousand years after he had been frozen.

An American computer had told him. An American system had helped, and he had heard Americans did their election returns like this, by early projections. He knew his work, and what he discovered very early and by calculations was what he did not want to discover.

He had farmed out certain experiments with the glycerol solution to universities with which he had liaisons—such projects as the effect of the solution on organs, cells, et cetera, in variations of thermal reduction speeds and temperature levels.

He often shared experiments. Those who carried them out, of course, did not know what the larger meaning was. He set up a program for the computer to receive this information, which was very much akin, although on a more complex level, to his program for measuring oxygen disbursement in thermally deprived tissue. It was the burning oxygen experiment on a larger scale.

He did not want the answer that quickly, on just eight experiments. But there was the projection with the results; he understood.

What they had accomplished was saving a perfect human specimen from poisoning. The scientific process was akin to pumping out someone's stomach, with the action of the harmful product delayed by thermal reduction.

Was it a breakthrough? Semyon Petrovitch asked himself. The glycerol substance was still too unstable for human use. He had several dead animals whose corpses would testify to that. The substance, since it could easily kill, had been used as a poison. How often things had been used for destruction, when they could have been used to save, Semyon Petrovitch did not know.

But Petrovitch did know his great discovery was not all that great a discovery, in that new knowledge for mankind would follow as a result. Given a perfect specimen—the gladiator—with an uncontrolled substance at a certain temperature, body functions could be delayed and started again.

Which was the theory, before a thought had crossed the patient's mind, two thousand years after its last one. It could be done. But they always knew it could be done someday when the state of the art was more advanced. And that was exactly where they were now with this supposed breakthrough. They had learned nothing from the body other than that it could be done.

If they were to take ten thousand healthy people now willing to risk death, they could, or might, with many experiments get five who would recover, possibly one as well as their subject.

To control this substance was like creating a car powered by atomic energy and ensuring that its reactor would not leak in the event of a crash. It was simply beyond the state of the art. It was a thing for tomorrow.

Dr. Semyon Petrovitch had supervised a medical accident and a physical rarity. It was no big thing at all. Perhaps the beautiful Sister Olav was right that the miracle was life.

Still, it had been done. Something worthwhile could be gained, if only in establishing the limits of this substance and establishing what further controls would be needed. And, he realized, he would need even more scientific rigor to define those subtle limits.

At this time he was grateful he was not back in Russia, because there would be someone from some bureau ready to blare out to the world that Soviet science had raised the dead, and it would go along with the two-headed dog and psychic phenomena into the circus of scientific entertainment.

It was not a final conclusion Semyon had reached, but a projection he believed. He felt it his duty to tell Olava and Lew.

Olava. What a beautiful name, he thought.

She was in the room and the room was dark, and he saw her blink when he opened the door. A nurse was with her.

He signaled her.

"I was just watching him sleep," she said.

"I have some news for you," he whispered.

"What?" she asked. And her lips were so pale and fine, Petrovitch momentarily couldn't think of anything else but how fresh and clean and beautiful she was standing close to him in the hallway, not moving, within reach of his arms, so close. And he was kissing her. He had his arms around her and was kissing her.

But she didn't kiss back, and he felt her spin away and wipe her mouth.

"You should be ashamed of yourself," she said.

"Olava. I love you."

"You don't even know me."

"You are beautiful."

"You had no right. You should be ashamed."

"I want you. I loved you from that first moment. I think of you whenever my mind wanders."

"What a stupid, stupid thing to do. A man of your stature. A man of your intelligence. A doctor."

"A man, Olava," he said mournfully, the smell of her body still with him.

"You may have cut my lips," she said, running a forefinger across the lip and blinking with pain.

"Let me see," said Semyon.

"No."

"I am a doctor."

"I know," she said crisply. "Silly man. I have not led you on. I haven't, have I?"

"No."

"I didn't think so. You are such a renowned physician. I am disappointed."

"So am I, Olava. Do you love that, in there? With the muscle?"

"Of course not."

"It tortures me to see you waste your life."

"I am not wasting my life. I am investing it."

"What if there is no God, then what have you done with your beauty?"

"Lived with it. What should I do with it? Serve it with paint and perfume, and let my mind and spirit die? I do not worship my beauty, Dr. Petrovitch."

"I must look at your cut. Hold on, don't move."

"I am sorry, I tried to be as scholarly as possible. I am sorry," she said, staying still while the physician examined her lip.

"I am sorry," said Petrovitch. It was only superficial.

"I did not want to make you sorry. I am ashamed now."

"I am more sorry now," said Dr. Petrovitch. "Do not tell Lew McCardle."

"I would be most happy to forget this and consider you still a man worthy of respect. One cannot help one's passions at times."

"I come with bad news, Olava."

"Yes?"

"The breakthrough in cryonics may not be as massive and clear-cut as we thought. So much further work remains in cell permutation that we have raised more questions than we have answered."

"Yes?" she said.

"What we have discovered is not a method of suspended animation, but a proof that we should consider in our research."

"Yes?"

"It's far short of what we expected. Medically, my action was in stopping the effects of a poison. Still, I am glad I was there because I doubt many doctors could have done what I did. I am glad I saved the man. Yes. I am glad."

"That's so nice," said Sister Olav, with withering condescension. "But let me tell you some good news. Today he made an oblique reference to Martial."

"Yes?"

"He used in his speech one of the epigrams of Marcus Valerius Martialis."

"Yes?"

"The epigrams. From the Silver Age of Latin poetry, itself."

"That's nice," said Semyon gloomily and heard her asking if he wanted to hear the epigram and heard himself answering that he most certainly did and waited until she was finished before he returned to his office to look for the bottle of the boy who pissed expensive scotch whiskey.

Lew McCardle had to charter a plane to get to Paris. By phone Public Affairs in Houston had gotten him the small jet, in less than forty-five minutes, and assured him that what he wanted would be there in the morning, somehow.

They would give him the address at the Hotel Lutetia, where he had a room.

"You people are amazing," Lew had said. "How on earth did you dig up a fencer so quickly? Is there anything you can't do?"

"Yes. Please Mr. Laurie."

And Lew heard his contact laugh over the phone.

"Seriously, the jet was more trouble than the fencer. And you'll find out what I'm talking about, and good luck with whatever you're doing, Mr. McCardle, sir."

That little "sir" meant Mr. Laurie was approving what was being done. At first Lew had thought he was as bad a personnel choice as the young superintendent back at the site. Now he knew he wasn't. Perhaps Mr. Laurie was a better judge of Lew McCardle than Lew was himself.

Lew liked the room with the highly polished wood clothes closet, a night view of the Boulevard Raspail, a bathroom with a deep tub, toilet, and bidet, and an elegant little writing desk at the big bay window. He had been in Paris once when he was young with Kathy, and they lived on sweet crêpes and cheap wine and slept in a cold flat owned by someone she had known at school. She was pregnant, and she had said she had wanted to see Paris one more time before she was a mother. It was winter then, and they had seemed to be unable to get enough of each other's bodies. A long time ago, when he was young.

He had the operator put in a call to his home in Houston, Texas, USA. He took a warm bath because he was tired. What luxury, a tub big enough for him, with warm water all over.

He remembered the showers at high school; he had spent so much time in them an assistant coach thought he was a homosexual, the coach not knowing those were the only showers he got.

He didn't have his first hot shower until his freshman year on the football team. He had thought it was such a luxury then, coming from buckets of well water so hard the soap barely lathered. Once when he had taken Kathy into an intimate shower with him, she had turned on the cold water at the end of it, at the end of the hot lather and the lovemaking when he held her so comfortably and so naturally to him. It ruined everything for him, and she couldn't understand, because a brisk brush of cold water against the skin invigorated the blood. Physiologically, she was right. But when you had had to dump cold buckets of water over your head to get clean so other students wouldn't laugh at you, you did not turn on cold water for health reasons, even many years later with the woman you married.

The warmth was good and his body was tired. It had been a long day. He had left Norway looking for something and had found it in Rome. Now he would prove what he knew to Sister Olav and Semyon.

He would rent a cabin sufficiently secluded, with hot baths of course. And television. And cases of beer and scotch. He was not a quitter. No matter how much it hurt in the fourth and final quarter, he never dogged it.

As the Maky coach had said: "If you quit on this field, you'll quit on life. They put walls around stadiums only to make people think life isn't as hard and dirty as it is on the playing field. Well, it's dirtier, boys. And when you quit here, you quit everywhere." The old Maky coach. It was a dramatic speech and it preceded the game in which Lew twisted the knee that thereafter pained him before all storms; and sometimes when he was physically very tired it locked, reminding him that when they separated the men from the boys, he had gone with the men, and paid.

The phone was ringing, and he forced himself from the bath, grabbing a handful of towel. It was Houston on the phone. His call had gone through. His daughter, Tricia, had accepted the call.

"You're in Paris. And you didn't send for us? Thanks a lot. Thanks a lot, Dad."

"Let me speak to your mother, Tricia."

"Go fuck yourself."

And that was his daughter who wanted to save the world. And she had hung up. He would have tried to reach Kathy again, but he knew she would not have all that different a response, and he was tempted to call James Houghton Laurie just for a kind word. Or his old coach to hear somebody say something nice. But the old coach was dead. And maybe it was good that he couldn't reach the man. Because Lew McCardle knew that if the old man had said, "Lew who?" and Lew had to say, "Your right tackle from '43 to '45," there would have been a wound so deep that night in Paris there would be no recovering.

So why was he feeling sad? He was in Paris, and he was rich—at least rich by a geologist's standards and everyone knew what Paris was good for. He dressed and got a taxi to a place he'd always wanted to see.

He wanted to see the Crazy Horse Saloon, which the driver knew of right away, and Lew paid vast amounts for little drinks, and when he had gone through two hundred dollars in drinks which would have been less than fifteen dollars in a bar back home, although the bar back home wouldn't have had beautiful young women dancing nude, nor a table so small the top could balance on your left knee, Lew McCardle left and got one of the taxidrivers outside, all of whom were pimps, and proceeded to purchase an act of sex.

She was a pale little thing who talked of making love, and Lew kept telling her "not love, fucking."

"Fucking, yes?" she said. And Lew tried, but it didn't quite work, and he paid her. Still doing her part, she told him he was a wonderful man, and would she love to have such a wonderful man inside her when he had less wine, yes?

"You really think I'm nice?" asked Lew.

"Oh, yes. Yes, of course."

"Thank you," said Lew. "That's what I really wanted anyhow."

And the operator woke him in the morning, the phone being a jarring rasp at his ears and not stopping until he picked it up and said thank you for the service. She also had the address he wanted in Paris.

He got a wake-me-up shot of liquor at the bar around the corner along with his coffee and the international edition of the *Herald Tribune*.

Unjarred, he faced the day, and whomever and whatever was coming up. He kept the appointment with the French firm—consultants in electrical engineering. He thought there must have been a mistake.

He apologized to the president of the firm, Monsieur Pierre d'Ouelette, a man so impeccably dressed that reasonable men would have to realize clothing itself was a craft and not a function of staying warm or safe from the weather.

"My apologies," said Lew. "We don't need an electrical engineer. I'm looking for a fencer, and I guess our Public Affairs Department fouled up."

"No, ours has. You do not associate our name with fencing, no?"

"Well, no."

"Well, then, hundreds of thousands of francs have gone to the air in smoke. Unless of course one appreciates the sword."

At that moment, in the modern office with the expensive woodgrain desk, clear of everything but d'Ouelette sitting on it, one leg on the floor, two hands clasped over the resting knee—like a photograph for a clothing store—Lew McCardle realized that this man was a source for fencers. He was not the fencer himself.

"You sponsor fencing?"

"Yes," said d'Ouelette laughing broadly. "You just might say with an awful lot of emphasis. We have brought two gold and four silver and seven bronze medals to France in the last eighteen years. The Hungarians hate us. Hate us."

"I am looking for a fencer."

D'Ouelette smiled, nodding. He had one of those sharply lined faces that looked so sophisticated on Europeans, and so haggard on Americans.

"First let me say, I am happy to do a favor for Houghton Oil, with whom we have had a wonderful, lasting business relationship, which we treasure. Treasure. Secondly, asking someone for a fencer is like buying an airplane by writing McDonnell Douglas or Dessault or Boeing, 'please send me an airplane.' "

There were, of course, many kinds of fencers and many kinds of swords. There was the épée, the foil, the saber, each one requiring different skills.

D'Ouelette refused interruptions as he explained the nuances of each weapon and each requirement and how each was scored. Lew sensed he had the man's cooperation because of Houghton, but that Houghton Oil's influence could not buy this enthusiasm. He followed carefully.

Over lunch, served in the office, but with an elegance Lew had not seen in private homes, Lew explained he wanted someone to show someone else he was not good with a sword.

"A braggart, yes?" said d'Ouelette.

"Not exactly. Someone whose memory has been injured. It's a demonstration for his friends to bring them to their senses."

"Before he is hurt, correct?"

"In a way. I don't want him hurt though. Under no circumstances must he be hurt."

D'Ouelette understood. There were always people who thought it looked easy until they tried it. Just outside of Paris was their school. Would Dr. McCardle care to look?

Lew did not dare dampen the man's enthusiasm. He canceled the afternoon flight. He went to the school in the back of a chauffeur-driven Citroën with d'Ouelette, who did not stop talking about matches in different cities.

"Monsieur d'Ouelette, you are lucky I am not your auditor, because I know you do not have fencers to make your firm famous. You have your firm in order to sponsor your fencers."

"So true. So very true. It shows too much. Too much. An obvious thing is never a good thing, yes?"

Lew nodded although he was not sure what d'Ouelette meant.

There was training as for any other sport, but additional tasks for reflexes and nerves. In one room with dull light coming through metal-laced windows, Lew pointed to one man off by himself in a room of men in white fencing padding.

"Why did you pick him?" asked d'Ouelette.

"Because you gave me a choice."

"No. Why that particular one?"

"I don't know. He looked good. I don't need anyone special. I know what I need."

"Well, unfortunately you have chosen someone very, very special."

And Lew had to sit through a very bad thirty-minute movie, called *Man and the Arms,* and there was the boy he had picked. In front of d'Ouelette conduits and fixtures, the young man was shown fencing, talking, exercising.

He had short hair, high cheekbones, and brown eyes that seemed to flicker like hummingbirds.

He was five feet nine inches tall, weighed one hundred and

fifty-eight pounds, was twenty-eight years old, and was the finest with épée in the world, according to the last Olympics, and, d'Ouelette assured, the next. His name was Ferdinand d'Ouelette.

"Your son?"

"Legally, my son. Yes."

"You adopted him and raised him. Well, that was a pleasant surprise that he turned out to be so good."

"No. The good came first."

"I see. Is that a common French practice?"

"No. No. Not at all. But we are not a common French family. Now you know why I was so shocked when you failed to associate our name with fencing. You see, it would be like me saying I am Babe Ruth and you saying 'so sorry, I need baseball players.' "

"Yeah. I see. I guess you have the Super Bowl champion."

"Whatever that is, yes."

Ferdinand did not speak English. He would go with a coach in two days. There was a contest tomorrow in Paris, which was why all the fencers were at the school.

"Could I get someone a little less famous?"

"No. I insist."

"I would prefer someone who would not necessarily attract a crowd."

"A crowd, no. Recognition, yes."

"I'd like someone else."

"No," said d'Ouelette, with the same passion with which he had dismissed secretaries talking about business. "On this I have made up my mind." There was no use trying to get someone less famous, although an average fencer would have proven Lew's point better. Still, Lew knew this could work.

"Every fencer has a flaw, but Ferdinand's only flaw is that he has never had anyone to make him excel. He has a temper, but it doesn't matter. There is no one good enough to punish him for it."

"Please, I ask only that my subject not be hurt."

"There is all sorts of padding. You wish him embarrassed, not damaged, correct?"

"I wish to show he cannot use a sword. That is all."

"That is most simple and guaranteed," said d'Ouelette.

Lew's leg locked that afternoon and required a yanking out. He had to be helped onto the plane back to Oslo.

There he spent a full day renting a cabin and stocking it. He told Sister Olava that he wanted to see her, the patient, and Semyon on the morrow.

In a newspaper account that afternoon, Lew McCardle saw a familiar picture. There was d'Ouelette grinning and holding a metal bowl. He had won his match. The big sports story was at the top of the page. Eight people had been killed in a riot at a soccer game in Rio de Janeiro. Here the paper called it football. And Lew wondered why more people weren't injured tearing down the goalposts.

CHAPTER XXIII

Sister Olav's Report

Subject adjusting well to technological environment, although he appears to misunderstand many things, which is logical. This does not indicate a lack of intelligence, however. In his own environment the subject functioned in a superior manner, influencing and understanding his surroundings in a highly competitive situation.

Subject shows great ambivalence about Rome. Subject loves Rome, admires Rome, despises Rome. Consequently, he also loves its Greek heritage, but is woefully ignorant of Greek culture, which at that time dominated Roman culture itself and, by most classicists today, is considered the artistic giant of the ancient world, much as Rome was the political, military, and engineering ruler. Of his Greek ancestry, the subject is defensive and, we suspect, somewhat ashamed, while he is also proud. In the Roman world this mixed ancestry was common since Rome was the center of the known world, drawing in many peoples. What we hope will be determined, if possible, is whether the subject's great conflicts —these diametrically opposed feelings of love and hate, pride and shame—were common or just the property of Lucius Aurelius Eugenianus. We believe that his marriage to a non-Roman is highly significant, since a marriage to a Roman citizen certainly would have made his upward mobility easier. It is hard to perceive a precise structure to his moral system because of the differences in modern and ancient cultures, which in some areas are larger than anticipated. Despite the knowledge we have of ancient values—morality being an easy topic to write about—it is still a shock to bridge the gap.

For someone who was a virgin, who had taken vows of celibacy, Olava had many questions about sex. I was tired of being inside so long. I wanted to go outside. So before I would answer another question, I insisted we walk outside.

Olava agreed, but said there was an important meeting this afternoon with Lewus and Semyonus. Most important, she stressed.

Few people wore capes nowadays. I was given clothing that conformed tightly to my body, and clung to my arms. It had light woolen lining, was well colored, and had a metal device that closed it by hooking small, almost invisible metal clasps, its name sounding like arrows landing through torn leather shields. Zipper.

A zipper closed the jacket over my shirt, which was buttoned. The pants went over my legs, and socks went under my shoes as lining. I could have a tonsor, but most men shaved themselves. There were ointments that pressured out like froth and made the beard more cuttable. There were no sharp knives anymore, but in the last hundred years shavers had been developed where the blade was encased in metal so that one could hardly cut oneself, yet freely shave away facial hair.

"You pull it across your face, Eugeni, and take off your jacket. You don't shave off beards with jackets on," said Olava.

"I'm doing it."

"You'll cut yourself."

"You said you can't."

"You can if you do it wrong. Let me hold your jacket?"

"No. No. We'll go outside now."

"Not with lather on your face."

"Get me a tonsor."

"We don't have slaves."

"What do you call people who take off facial hairs?"

"Barbers."

"Wonderful. Get me a barber who is not a slave."

"We must go to him."

"Buy him and then he will come to us."

"Is it that hard to understand there are no more slaves today, Eugeni?"

"Quiet. This is fun," I said. The beard came off with easy strokes, but like initial successes, it led to overconfidence and a cut on my cheeks and chin and just below my nose. Olava attempted to stem the blood with small papers, cold water, and finally allowed time to let the blood congeal.

This blood was not my own, although I could not tell the difference. It was someone else's blood. My blood, which had enabled me to stay in that cold state, was actually a poison. It had been taken out of my body and replaced with someone else's blood, although not from one person but from many people, because one person could not give a whole bodyful of blood because they would die—people not being able to lose or give too much blood, which I had known.

The poison was of substances similar to those used to keep blood in a state whereby the body would not be destroyed by being cold and hard. Macer could not and did not know of these things back in my times. In my times it was just a poison. But by its attributes it was also a chemical which prevented the blood from becoming ice as in the mountains or the snows such as we marched through with the cohort.

But the substance was uncontrollable, like this new form of energy made from pieces of things so small you cannot see them. Atomic energy it is called. It is very powerful. It was discovered so tens of thousands of people could be killed with it at one time, but there was no way anyone could watch them being killed, and recording devices that made pictures of things like real life could not work in the heat of atomic energy.

There had been an argument over this, which I didn't understand. I had told Olava that to make pictures of ten to twenty thousand people being burned out of existence, where even the shadows were burned into rock by the power of atomic energy, was a very valuable, entertaining thing.

"That was horrible. To watch it for entertainment would be vicious and cruel."

"Yes. We can pack arenas."

"No. People would not come. I do not think they would come to that. I hope they would not want to see it. Yes, I hope so. That is accurate."

"You also hope that the dead come back to life. So much for your hopes."

But who could argue with the benefits of her god Science? And we let that subject go. There were some things I could not understand right away. One of the problems was that I was not sure I wanted to.

I enjoyed acting as my tonsor very much. It felt good to do something, even slave's work. It had been a week altogether that I was aware of where I was, and more than a month that my body had been active. Sometimes when I went to sleep, I thought it might be nice to drift off and not wake up. I could not get back to Miriamne or Petronius or really anyone I knew. Who could I talk to here?

Talking with Olava was burdensome.

It was good to walk outside and see the spring come to the north country and see buds and mud and grass and people and see them operate their machines that went on the great gas power.

Olava explained why she asked about sexual matters. She was looking for attitudes toward sex, she said. This was supposed to explain things to me. It only confused me more.

"I don't understand," I said. I felt the tree bark and chipped some under my fingernails. It felt good. I chewed on it, not for nourishment, but just to chew on bark. It was bitter. The northland sky was clear blue like Olava's eyes. I could see how she would be beautiful among her own people, if one were used to death-pale skin.

"Concerning homosexuals. Now you had relations with men for money, yet it meant nothing to you. You went right ahead and enjoyed not only a heterosexual marriage, but one that was decidedly monogamous when it was in your power to keep it that way."

"Yes?"

"Well, don't you think that's unusual?"

"No," I said.

"Exactly," she said.

"I don't understand."

"What you're telling me is that people in your age did not believe it was wrong to sleep with men and women and whatever for money. That there was no effect on later life, and when a prisoner again, as you told us, you slept with Domitia for information."

I still did not understand. And Olava tried harder to explain.

"How did you feel about sleeping with men?"

"I didn't like it."

"So you are against homosexuality."

"Against?"

"Disapprove."

"No. I don't like it. I liked Miriamne. I loved Miriamne. It was good with Miriamne. But if I don't have Miriamne, then I will allow passions their service elsewhere. It is not Miriamne, but it is serviceable. As for what other people do, I leave those pleasures to you."

"I ask about your sex and attitudes because of science," said Olava.

"I did not accuse you."

"I thought you had."

"You do not hunger for me?" I asked.

"I don't mean to be insulting, but you are not attractive to me."

"What a shame," I lied. "You are so pale and beautiful."

"You don't think that, do you?"

"No, good woman. You are really too much like Tribune Macer in your spirit. Everything with order. Everything with diligence. I think if you had a man, a good man, perhaps one time, you might take life with more grace and ease."

"How do you feel about that?" she asked, pushing the device that recorded my sounds to my face, like I once used to use my little shield. It was a punch as much as a block.

"I feel I want to mount you, just to say hello," I said angrily and grabbed her left wrist.

"Please release me," she said.

But I held.

"Please, Eugeni. Please. I am a scientist."

"I am a person."

"All right. All right. You are a person. Let go. Please."

She did not look at me, but at the ground like a maiden ashamed. Veins bulged in her cloud-white face. She could not look at me. "Please," she gasped with softness. Her chest heaved under her black robe, and she did not move her feet. She waited.

I released her wrist, and she kept it there out in front of her until she finally let it drop.

"Eugeni, I have made vows precious to me, and I have determined them to be in my interest to be kept. This is my chastity. If you are my friend, you would never put me to trial. I think I would pass, but it is a test not to my liking."

"I am not your friend and you are not mine."

"I have been kind to you."

"People are kind to their horses. Friendship is another thing."

"What thing?"

"Friendship is caring, not because your god Science says, but because you want to. Friendship is protecting. Friendship is knowing. Friendship is liking."

"Did you have friends?"

"Rome?"

"Yes, Rome."

"How do you ask that question?" I said.

"You mean as scientist or friend?"

"Yes."

"As a friend, but I must use it for science."

"I don't want to tell you."

"Are you hurt?

"Hurt? Hurt? You have heard my story and you ask me if one of your questions hurts? Hurt, woman, is not something you can do. Annoy, perhaps."

"You are annoyed. Why? As a friend, I ask. As a friend."

"I am annoyed because you are most Roman of them all, always to the grave matters, always to business, always to discipline. Yellow hair, violent blue eyes, frightening death skin, like snow, yet Roman. Roman in your belly, woman. You have a spine of steel. You are a Macer."

"Macer was the artful tribune who crucified your slaves," said Olava.

"You would follow your orders, too. There are worse things, woman."

"I would never crucify anyone."

"You don't know."

"Yes. Yes. I do."

By the way she answered I knew she hoped she wouldn't.

"Are you an official virgin or really a virgin?" I asked.

At that she laughed.

She said she would like to talk about it someday with me and explain, but now she had work.

"Friends talk, Olava. If you know everything about me, and I know nothing about you, what friend is that? I would as soon talk to an arena stone."

"Did you have many friends?"

People seemed very busy in the immense garden between the large buildings, all like palaces looking out. Some people were wheeled by the nurse slaves, in backed chairs like low one-person carts. Spring was here and yet there was a taste of chill. Olava, being of the complexion less prone to suffer in cold, did not mind being out. We had an appointment soon with Lewus who had been gone a few days to visit Rome in the speeding air machines. He was back with something important.

"I asked you a question," said Olava.

"If you want an answer, flog it from me. Burn it from me."

"If Domitian failed, how could I succeed?"

"By offering me what I want, and what I want is an end to questions. You have one last question to be answered. Agreed?"

"Agreed. For the hour."

"For the week."

"The day," said Olava, and it was done. The question asked was this:

"Did you have any friends in Rome?"

"No. I never had a friend, I think. There was Miriamne, whom I loved, but I would not rely on her for many important things. There were my loyal slaves, who had a fool for a master. I had amusing affection for Publius, but he was no friend. No, Olava. I never had a friend."

"If you never had a friend, then what would one be like?"

"That is a second question."

"No. It is part of the first, and, besides, it is not about Rome, but about everyone."

"A friend must be an equal. It is more than liking. You can like a tree, but it is not a friend. A friend must be someone you can rely on, but not use. He must be honest, but also reticent with that honesty because of fear of losing you. Honesty is too strong a drink to be unwatered all the time; rather it should be given in doses. No, I am not sure what a friend is, Olava. But I think perhaps it is someone you laugh with a lot, not by making jokes, but by seeing the world together. A friend is someone you laugh with regularly. That is a friend. And of course cry with. It is a simple thing. I think it may be a great thing. I have not thought about it before."

I did not like this garden or this spring or this air or this time. Semyonus in a white jacket ran to us. Olava translated that he was saying we were late for Lewus.

As we walked with him, I realized he was subdued towards Olava, and the ready smile was not there. I felt a sadness in him in his little quick nods, as though if he moved his head too quickly the tears would fall out.

"Did he offer his love, and did you turn him down, Olava? He is not loving towards you."

"That is my personal life."

"And so will be my answer to you, woman, when you ask of me. I claim similar rights."

"He did, and I did," she said brusquely, hoping to escape.

"You should have given him what he wanted, so little if any discomfort for you and such satisfaction for him. Look at his sad face. I have seen happier swamps."

"It is my body, not yours," said Olava burning. "Or his. I have given it to my God. And I do not pass it out like little party cakes for the momentary satisfaction of those who happen to be around me. It is neither a sedative, palliative, reward, or bribe. It is my body."

"If I might have succumbed to fancying you, know that you have cured me in advance, woman. A disease uncaught is the best cured."

"And it has nothing to do with you," she said with even more anger. "Me. It has to do with me."

Semyonus asked something, and Olava spat back a single answer —the interchange being Semyonus asking what she was telling me, and she telling him "nothing."

I would have told him everything, but we did not speak each

other's language. Of course, I was equally confused on other matters.

Semyonus said something to me and patted me on the head like his favorite dog.

"Don't worry, he says," said Olava.

"Don't worry about what?" I asked.

And the response was: "Whatever happens."

"What does he think he is going to do to me?"

"Nothing," said Olava.

I thought that was very funny, and no one else did. Semyonus expressed faith in me and his science. He looked to Olava as he said this. Olava said something. I had to ask for it.

"I told him I had faith in him also and in you, Eugeni."

"You reassure with confidence wonderfully," I said.

"Thank you," said Olava. "And Semyonus thanks you." They were so grave in this matter, I did not want to hurt their feelings by telling them their reassurance was like waking someone to teach them to sleep. It was not reassuring. But what could anyone do to me now?

They took me to a room like a small indoor arena, cut in half with a flat side, like actors might use. The lights went on and all three of us sat on chairs on the floor of this arena. Lewus was late. He arrived, smiling that smile I used for the arena. He wore dark clothes, as did Semyonus, dark and colored being a sign of wealth, and white being worker clothes, but only in places like hospitals, and physicians were not workers but were on higher levels. Although colors themselves did not tell rank always, not even the expense of clothes, which was a hard thing to judge sometimes, even for those who lived in these times.

Lewus carried machines in his arms, and Semyonus explained to Olava who explained to me that these machines were the machines recording the pictures that moved that I saw. Upon further questioning, I found out the ones used for dramas were bigger.

Lewus made adjustments. The machines purred like a cat with a rusty metal belly. Lewus asked Olava to stand. He asked Semyonus to stand.

"And he wants you to stand also, Eugeni," said Olava. "Between us." It felt like a family, although we all would have had an argument over who was the parent.

Olava related that Lewus said he did not know all that much

about ancient Rome. He was from a small provincial community where the schooling was not as good as in the large cities of his country, a country which did not even exist in the time we were talking about. He would look to Olava and Semyonus to assist him. They had great educations, he said. Olava, with somber countenance, assured her help. Semyonus did the same with haughtiness.

Only I was alarmed. Olava told me not to worry. I told her I would worry less if she worried more. She asked what alarmed me.

"What sort of a person tells you he is weak, and why does he want you to believe so? That is the danger."

Lewus asked what I talked about, and Olava translated into the almost indistinguishable grunts of his language, a language which Olava had explained lacked order. Through Olava, he asked what I should have to fear of him? He asked this several times, and only he and I knew he was already drawing blood in his battle. The interrogation was not long and it went like this:

Through Olava, he established the great costs of the arena games in man-hours worked in gold, in silver, in animals, in blood.

Essentially, I said, Lewus was correct, very correct for someone who had lacked great schooling, someone who, despite his lack of schooling, carried the academician's highest title of doctorate, something which Olava, with all her great schooling, lacked. This warning to Olava to be aware went like rain upon stone. It landed and went away, as though it had never been at all.

"If this man," translated Olava for Lewus, "were premier gladiator of Rome in Domitian's time, I think that's about 80 C.E., he would literally be worth a city. In farmland, let me try to explain, he would be valued at most of the Ukraine or roughly one and a half times that of Iowa, plus you could throw in the worth of the Suez and Panama canals. Or if one likes cities, he would be worth, literally to the penny, the combination of Dallas and Marseilles. Astronomical."

Of these places I did not know.

Then he said that, according to Olava's reports, I had been given my freedom by the Aurelii. Was this correct?

"It was," I said.

"Could they afford such a great gift, tantamount to letting General Motors run itself for itself?" said Olava for Lewus. She explained General Motors was a gigantic latifundia organization which produced machines instead of grain.

"The Aurelii were wealthy in heart as well as gold," I said.

Olava thought this a wonderful answer, translating for Lewus with a warm smile. Only I noticed that he began his next question before Olava had finished her translation.

Was it correct that I had been convicted of maiestas with my name stricken from all records?

"It was."

So that if I did really exist as such a gladiator, premier gladiator of the entire empire, I would not be known of today in any of the multitude of records.

"True."

"You seem to have an excellent understanding of the politics of the imperial period of ancient Rome. That and finances."

"I knew enough to keep bread and wine in my house," I said.

"And after killing, oh, a hundred and twenty men I guess, even knowing the disaster you would create, you decided not to slay one Vergilius Flavius Publius. Correct?"

"Correct."

"And this Publius was a loudmouth, correct?"

"Correct."

"And you, who were supposed to have known slavery, and now knowing we are not Domitian's agents, admit you loved your wife and child, yet risked their lives to possible slavery, correct?"

"That is correct."

"And a whole cohort takes you out into what was then barbarian lands far north, then poisons you, and then leaves you to die of cold. Correct?"

"Correct."

"One more question. Why didn't you slay Publius?"

"In all honesty, I am not sure."

Olava entered into a discussion with Lewus in his own language, and he became heated on one question. And asking what that was, I was told he asked where the European lions were. And I said I presumed in the forest, and Olava said I had missed the point.

"Lewus says, and correctly so, that games were so important to Rome that with nets and spears only they made an entire species extinct, something the world could not do until recently with the help of great motor-powered machinery. The European lion is the example."

And Lewus said two words and Olava said one.

"Stand."

I stood.

"And we are to believe that the energies of the known world could not find something more deadly than that, even though men were smaller then? No, too much. Too many things do not conform to logic." And to Semyonus, according to Olava's translation, he mentioned something about a frog. Semyonus, raging, yelled at the large man who, like an innocent child, suddenly looked upon the entire world with innocent wonder. Lewus knew only what Lewus knew, he said.

This from Olava, who translated.

So Lewus had created great doubt about my story, not the least being because of my size.

"He didn't prove you were a liar, Eugeni. He didn't prove that at all. He only created some doubts. That's all he did."

"Perhaps that is enough," I said.

"For what?" she asked.

"For whatever he wants," I said.

She explained he had come from a provincial place and, despite his schooling in science, was still a simple peasant sort of person, as were most from his area of his country. She suffered from the common Roman notion that provincials always told the truth, because they never learned to lie like civilized people.

But in the arena, which drew from all places, we knew that lying was most natural to the uncivilized, even though civilized man had perfected it as an art called "oratory." One only has to look at a child to know that lying is quite a natural thing, like breathing. The telling of the truth is something that has to be learned like any other painful training. And this is so.

CHAPTER XXIV

Lew McCardle felt the sweat on him when he left the operating room with Dr. Petrovitch yelling after him, Sister Olav stunned, and that little olive-skinned fellow smiling. He could have sworn the short, muscular guy was the only one of the three who understood what was happening. But of course, he couldn't know. Probably.

McCardle returned to his office and dropped the movie camera and the tripod upside down, camera first, leaning against the wall. He wouldn't need the film. The camera was there for Sister Olav and Petrovitch to have seen him use. So they would think about their size and the size of the subject. It was their minds Lew was working on.

A small refrigerator, slightly larger than a bread box, balanced atop a Jaeger's *Paedeia*—a book on life in the world of classical antiquity. Lew opened the door and put a hand around a chilled bottle of imported Schlitz, which he needed. His throat was dry and his body perspired, and the cold beer felt good going into his belly and easing off the tingles from the night before. He knew he was drinking too much, but after this he would moderate it. Things were just going too quickly to work on not drinking.

He cleaned manila folders off the two leather chairs facing his desk. The desk was covered with notes, beer-bottle caps, and a Latin-English dictionary, opened, covering the phone which Lew made sure was not on the hook. The room smelled faintly of beer and last week's whiskey. It had been spotless just a few weeks ago. It was small. It was cluttered. And it was a great place to work.

Petrovitch and Sister Olav should be coming right away. It was trickier to play with people than with rock formations. He reminded himself he had not wanted this and felt very good that, once faced with this sort of thing, he could work it quite well. Not the least asset for this being his size and down-home Texas attitude, which could be so deceptive. Lew took another beer.

Dr. Petrovitch and Sister Olav came into the office without knocking. Lew offered Semyon a beer, which was declined. Lew cleared papers off his own chair and, with a beer in each hand, sat down, resting his legs on his desk, creating heel marks on notes he would no longer need.

"What's going on?" demanded Petrovitch. Sister Olav blinked nervously.

"I don't know. You tell me," said McCardle. "I'm not the expert. I look to you people to clarify things. I just had some questions."

"You have cast a pall of doubt upon this project," said Sister Olav.

"I was sharing my own doubts, Sister. Again, I'm not the expert."

"I believe Eugeni," said Sister Olav. "I believe he is what he says he is. Religious, Dr. McCardle, does not mean naive. I have run several tests myself, not the least of which was having him listen to an old tape recording of Vatican Radio."

"What did he do? Translate all of it?" said Lew, who knew better.

"No, he barely understood a word here and there, which would be a sure sign that he did not study Latin, because then he would have undoubtedly come across the Vulgate used by the Church. No, I believe him."

Dr. Petrovitch had one question. Was Lew McCardle, Ph.D., now claiming the subject was not discovered eight point two meters in the ice? Is that what Dr. McCardle was now claiming, because if he was, he should get his honest cards on the table.

"No, that's not what I'm claiming, Semyon. I just know that back home when someone comes up with something super ring-ding, it's better not have no hay between the ears," said Lew.

"And by that you mean what?" asked Semyon.

"If you say you cured a head cold, nobody is going to care whether the patient fibs or not. But in something like this, they're going to, excuse the expression, Sister, look up his ass with microscopes, and when we say not only have we successfully managed a resurrecting process, if you will, but that the subject is nearly two thousand years old and, wait a second, ladies and gentlemen, not only a gladiator, but the premier gladiator, I mean, we had better have our facts straight."

"Eugeni is not a liar," said Sister Olav.

"Neither am I," said Petrovitch.

"Gee," said Lew, shrugging his massive shoulders. "I didn't mean to say that. I'm sorry if I gave that impression. Real sorry. I am just one of three. I have only one vote. I'll do what you say. But you know and I know there are serious questions here, which I wouldn't want to attempt to answer in the fanfare and glare of publicity."

"What publicity? We are working in scientific isolation," said Petrovitch.

"Not if you listen to the crazy talk around the university."

"What sort of talk?" said Sister Olav.

"That we've got Julius Caesar or Marc Antony in that private room," lied Lew. "That we resurrected some great historical figure. I don't know who's been talking or saying what to some young nurses, but the word is out that Dr. Petrovitch has produced a miracle."

Dr. Petrovitch shook his head sadly. "Just what I didn't want."

"What I'm saying is, all of us are going to look pretty damned foolish academically until these questions I've raised have been answered. I'm not only talking about me, but your department, Semyon, and maybe your church, Sister Olav. It's gonna look like, excuse the expression, some bullshit hustle, and by that I mean we're going to look like frauds. And maybe that won't be the worst part of it. There's going to be more international noise around us than the biggest circus. We can forget any honest scientific inquiry once Marc Antony here gets on that television station in this town and starts beaming his nonsense around. Your reports, Sister, are all over this place. That's one effective little liar we've got."

"He's a showman," said Sister Olav. "They staged bloody shows then."

"That's neither here nor there," said Petrovitch, obviously realizing that a showman and television were not exactly combined guarantees of scientific integrity.

"If your reports are correct, Sister Olav, and I believe they are, our little fellow in there was at one point giving Semyon, or trying to sell Semyon, a special lurid sex technique in which you lost weight, too. This is not a person who can be let loose upon the world just yet."

"He is not a liar," said Sister Olav, standing firm beside the chair, refusing to sit. "He is not a liar."

"We have no evidence but your supposition, Lew," said Semyon, forgetting his politeness and sitting down despite Sister Olav's standing. "Besides, I am offended by all the dramatics, camera cross-examination, and everything. You hardly take part and, when you do, you try to cast doubt on this achievement."

"Yes. I did. I did try to cast doubt. Because a lot smarter people will do it outside, when this becomes public, and it's becoming public. A lot smarter people with great backgrounds in Latin, who don't have some interest in protecting the patient."

"What does that mean?" asked Sister Olav. Petrovitch looked up at her with some wonder. His left eyebrow cocked. He was quiet.

"That means, I, a geologist, a North Springs, Texas, boy, provincial, if you will, have found out that not only didn't gladiators get trained in many weapons, but that a normal-sized little fellow could not possibly have been the foremost gladiator of his time. Impossible, even if he did have agents making sure of who and what he met in the arena. It's an economic impossibility, and even I can prove it. And I'm not a Latin scholar."

Petrovitch had a new gold cigarette case. He removed a French Gauloise cigarette and lit it with his British Dunhill lighter.

"I don't know," he said somberly. "You might be right."

"Just a minute, Dr. McCardle, I think you're herding us like some of your cattle on your ranch," said Sister Olav.

"Never had a ranch, ma'am. Never had cows. Never even had a shootout. I earned a doctorate, not a notch on a gun."

"Not all notches, Dr. McCardle, are carved in gun handles."

"I'm yours to command, ma'am."

"I doubt that," said Sister Olav. "But was what you have put forth in your cross-examination of our charge—and it was a cross-examination, and Eugeni is our charge—reason for us to believe he is lying? I don't think this is so."

"Neither do I," said McCardle. He finished one beer and balanced the bottle behind a plastic case that was supposed to organize file folders. Petrovitch finally took a beer. Sister Olav declined an offer of one with a shake of her head.

"I think he believes what he is saying. That's not the point. The point is, and this is the crucial one, he could not possibly have been, what is it, the foremost gladiator of the empire at his time. Impossible."

"He would be about the average size in ancient Rome, not small," said Sister Olav.

McCardle agreed. She was correct except for the crucial economics of things. He pointed out the vast amount of wealth connected with the games. She agreed that was correct. With that sort of wealth, they were bound to get larger, faster men in the arena, McCardle said. Many were six feet tall in a civilization where five feet was average, if not a little bit tall. While there were no records of this, it was basic logic that a five-foot man was not going to regularly defeat what must have been an unending flow of six-footers.

Sister Olav pointed out there were no records of the numbers and sizes of arena people. McCardle shook his head. With the kind of economics that went into the games, there had to be a flow of incredibly fast and skillful giants, with longer reaches than Eugeni.

Sister Olav said she had read of fights where smaller men ruled their fisticuff divisions. Dr. Petrovitch said Muhammad Ali had beaten bigger men.

"Have you ever stood next to Muhammad Ali? I once did. He's like a building. He only looks small compared to some other giants he fights. The best boxer, pound for pound, was Sugar Ray Robinson, another American, and he literally would be killed if he stepped into a ring with any of the heavyweights. In America we have a game called basketball. The short, fast men are six feet five inches tall, six feet four, six feet three. That's short. And they're incredibly fast. In football, those speedy little quarterbacks we see are brick buildings, and those linemen are giants and run faster than you can believe. And that's just American sports, and today with all the millions of dollars we put into our professional sports, we have yet to build an arena the size our Julius Caesar says he fought in."

"The colosseum in Rome held only fifty thousand people," said Dr. Petrovitch.

"That's the small one, Semyon," said McCardle. "The big one was where the Vatican is now. It held one hundred and fifty thousand people, larger than many of the city-states at that time, built without gas engines, electricity, or any of the power tools we know today. And that guy ruled there for what, ten, twenty years? C'mon."

"You seem to know quite a few things for someone who says he is not an expert, Dr. McCardle," said Sister Olav.

"I know our Nero was not foremost gladiator. And I don't want to be laughed out of the scientific world as some hustler when you people try to pass him off as that."

Sister Olav said there were worse things to fear in the world than ridicule. McCardle chugged the second beer. He should have ordered Rocker City beer for Semyon. It was the cheap, local beer drunk in North Springs, but here it would be imported. He took another Schlitz from the icebox without getting up. Semyon liked imported beer, hence the Schlitz.

"An economic impossibility for that man to be what he says he is. And that's just one strong point in a whole peck of peculiar points. More than ridicule," said Lew.

Semyon put out his cigarette with finality. Dark suspicion crossed his glum face. He was looking at Sister Olav, wondering why she defended the patient so fervently.

"I'd like to hear how a person can lie and not be a liar," said Sister Olav.

"Let me take this risk," said Lew, looking up to Sister Olav and then across to Semyon. "I think this theory I have is true, as wild as it is. I think our subject has already told us what happened, but we didn't see it or want to see it, any more than he did. Now the human mind is a funny, funny thing, even without bringing in the shock of an entirely new age. And we don't know the effects on the brain, although there don't seem to be any, but, as Dr. Petrovitch can verify, there had to be some brain damage somewhere.

"Given that the body was found frozen, and given that it tells the truth, and given that it cannot have been what it says it was, and given that Latin is its first language, we can therefore assume it is indeed nineteen hundred years old, but not that it was what it says it was, even though it tells the truth. Now how could that be?" said McCardle, holding up his beer bottle, looking at the bottle-darkened foam, but his mind was not on the foam.

"I believe something happened in the ice, to its mind," said McCardle.

"Nothing happened," said Dr. Petrovitch, "otherwise he'd be dead. The slightest ongoing act would have caused the body to react to the poison if not to time. In which case you would have recovered the remnants of a corpse."

"No, Semyon. I am not talking about an entire process, I am talking about some small area in the brain which might have crystallized. One crystal. A million cells among billions gone, unnoticed. That area unpermeated with your glycerol substance. You, more than anyone, should know how unstable the substance is."

"Quite true, Lew. What else?" said Semyon.

"So let's look at something else, also. Let's look at what it remembers and specifically does not remember. Very little have you been told about its slavery. Why?"

"I didn't want to press it with him. It was painful for him," said Sister Olav.

"Correct. It was painful because that was its daily life that would never change. When it was dying, it changed its life. It invented someone it wanted to be, someone it knew and envied. I think we have recovered what was probably an arena slave. Look, since it's all conjecture, let's even get riskier. I've got a feeling that who we have is the slave this patrician Publius couldn't get by to warn Domitian to leave the arena the day of that first riot."

"That is conjecture," said Sister Olav.

"Let Dr. McCardle continue. He seems to know a bit about psychology, too," said Petrovitch. "We can't fall in love with the patient."

"Well, let's say Publius demanded he be punished, and there undoubtedly would have been some kind of imperial inquiry as to why Domitian didn't get word to leave the riot early. OK, so it comes down to this poor slave. Not to make a bigger fuss over the thing, because Rome was political dry wood, if you will, they just quietly shipped this poor guy north with the next legion leaving for the Danube borders. Nobody missed him or cared. There, they traded the guy to some German tribe. And in some way we don't know yet, but I think we will find out, the slave ate some poison and, being property of much less value than a good dog, he's left without a stitch somewhere it's cold. The German Sea, maybe."

Sister Olav listened, stunned. A flush came to her pale face. She felt a lightness in her head and steadied herself.

"That sounds possible," said Petrovitch. "Very possible."

"Who this guy believes he is was created during the trauma of our bringing him back to consciousness. And what did he become? Someone vastly superior to this patrician Publius. And what did he do to Publius when he had him in a weak position? He showed he was better than Publius and to all Rome, that had made him feel weak all his life. He wasn't half Greek. He was all Greek, what they called 'Greekling' all the time with impunity. And he was going to die that way. And what does he do in his re-creation? He becomes the great Lucius Aurelius Eugenianus, and he brings his Hebrew slave woman and son along with him in his imaginary social rise. Now what man in reality, after fighting his way to the top of imperial Roman power and society, is going to legally marry another slave? Come on. He named his own son Petronius, which is a Roman name, which shows how much he wanted to be Roman. More than anything this poor Greekling wanted to be Roman. And more than anything he hated the Romans. And if he had died his natural death, all his problems would have been resolved the way all problems are ultimately resolved. By the worms in the warm ground. He lived, and he became the great Lucius Aurelius Eugenianus, hero of Rome."

Lew McCardle finished his third beer. Funny how everyone could hear the little refrigerator hum now.

"What about the scars?" said Petrovitch.

"Let's say you had a slave being trained for the arena and he wasn't big enough. They started them early. Maybe he was one of those boys who start out big and stop growing at thirteen. So what are you going to do with a tiny pugilist? That's where we get the English word from. It's the first fighter. We found out in the hallway he could use his fists, no?"

"True," said Petrovitch.

"All right, we need more time," said Sister Olav.

"We don't have more time," said Lew. "That's what I am telling you."

"I will not vote for moving the patient because of your conjecture and your fears," said Sister Olav.

"I can prove he is not what he says he is. I can prove it is not conjecture."

"How?" said Sister Olav, but it was an accusation as much as a question.

"A match with blunted swords."

"Never. We are not Romans."

"He will not be hurt."

"No. Even if it proves he is not who he says he is, the revelation might be too much for him. No." Sister Olav trembled as she tightly gripped the back of the chair she had refused to sit in. "Especially if Eugeni was an arena slave do I not wish to see him confronted with this, like this."

"And I vote yes," said Lew. "Semyon, what about you?"

"If he is not what he says he is, what then?" asked Semyon.

"Isolation for a period necessary to find out for certain who he is, or to find out what we don't know."

"I can't approve," said Sister Olav.

"You have made your vote," said Semyon. "I make mine. I find no valid reason not to give this test. As a matter of fact, I am suspicious of motives of those who would vote against."

"Two to one," said Lew humbly.

"Wait," said Sister Olav. "What sort of fencer?"

"An Olympic champion," said Lew, directly.

"I see. That is unfair, of course," said Sister Olav.

"Yes," said Lew. "We should, for three or four centuries, offer purses like ownership of Kuwait, Idaho, the Panama Canal, and then match our little fellow against what would be competing for them. That would be fair. An Olympic fencer; fencing isn't even a major money sport. If Moscow tomorrow decided to have one single sport, and no others, with which it would compete with the world, that would be fair."

"I still vote no," said Sister Olav.

"That is your problem," said Semyon Petrovitch. He finished the beer Lew had given him and left.

"Is there any way I can change your mind, Dr. McCardle?" asked Sister Olav.

"No."

"That's being obstinate. May I ask why you are being obstinate?"

"Semyon might say that about you."

"I think he has personal reasons for his vote. What about you?"

"The match is on."

"I hope Eugeni will understand. I hope he will forgive us. I am not proud to be associated with this project anymore."

Lew so desperately wanted to tell her to get out in harsh and final terms. Instead he just nestled his big body deeper back into his chair. And she left without being told to.

He was lucky Petrovitch was no longer in love with her. He might have gone against him in that case. Maybe luck mattered. He opened another beer. He used to drink a lot of beer. Rocker City beer. Good old hometown beer. He remembered the summer nights. Hot nights. Cold beer. A six-pack of Rocker and Ginny Jackson.

"Rocker, Rocker City," he hummed. *"The Texas beer that's gosh darn pretty. Drink Rocker, Rocker, Rocker City, the Texas beer from the Arkansas city. Rocker. The real beer. Rocker City, yeah."*

Tasted like piss. Always had.

Whatever happened to Ginger Jackson? They drank Rocker City together. They had sex in the backs of cars. And he knew she didn't give it to anyone else. It was good with her. It was easy being with her.

"I know you'll never marry me," she had said one night, parked behind the stadium, her bra dangling free from her shoulder.

"That's not true, Ginny, I just don' wanna get married now. But if I wanted to get married now, I sure would think of you. I sure would."

"You're such a liar, Lew McCardle."

"Don't you ever call me a liar."

"You're a liar, Lew McCardle, 'cause you don't think I'm good enough."

If he remembered correctly, that conversation had taken place before sex. Afterwards, he avoided telling Ginny Jackson she wasn't the kind of girl he would marry, just admitted that she was right, he wouldn't marry her.

"If I was rich. If I came from Hill Springs or some fancy place, you'd marry me."

"Yeah? Why?"

" 'Cause you love me, Lew."

"I like ya."

"Nah. Ya love me. Love's becoming one with someone, livin' day by day with them, and havin' a niceness with 'em. It takes more courage to love than you have, Lew McCardle."

"Shit. I'm All-Conference tackle."

"You'll never see me again, Lew."

"What are you doin'? Get your mouth out of there."

"I want to show you what you're missing."

"Not with your mouth."

"I want to," she said.

But he had seen her again in Austin, and she hadn't gained that much weight, and she had a boy of nine, and she wore a cheap purple print dress that made her body look lush with the extra pounds.

And all they did was say hello, and she had introduced her son to a football player who used to be her beau, and there wasn't a chance to get her phone number, and he had forgotten to ask her married name and, besides, his marriage at the time of that meeting in Austin was just beginning with Kathy.

Opening another beer in Oslo, Norway, he remembered reminding himself how Ginny was just not the sort of girl you married if you were going somewhere.

And he had gone somewhere.

And now he would retire successfully, shortly. A little more successful than he had anticipated. He was doing all right. He was doing fine. He could have phoned home from the office and it wouldn't have cost him a cent. He could talk to Kathy for hours if he wanted. And Houghton Corporation would pay.

He opened another beer and felt a strong urge to ask the little fellow about his marriage in Rome, one slave with another. If Eugeni was a slave. Which he probably was.

Lew McCardle didn't phone home that afternoon and got very drunk.

CHAPTER XXV

In this time, when there were no slaves and no arenas, I found myself matched again. Olava explained that no matter what happened, I should remember that I not only was important historically, but more so as a person whom she respected.

Olava said I was more important than all the gladiators who had ever lived because I had been chosen by the unseen god of her cult to bring history to these times. I begged her not to trouble her spirits over me, for what had happened was a good thing. And I told her to inform Lewus of my gratitude.

"What we need is a price. Now, you say Lewus represents wealthy patrons. Can we get four of the large flying machines with their slaves that run them? I know everyone is a freedman today, but I would find the machines useless without their slaves. So I am sure some sort of contractual arrangements can be had whereby those who run the machines will be paid by the sponsor of the match for a period of, let's say, five years."

"It is not that sort of match, Eugeni. There will be no payment.

"You don't have crucifixion today?" I asked, to reaffirm what she had told me before.

"No," she said.

"Then I will not fight."

"No one is forcing you, but if you are willing, then a demonstration would be most useful to my work."

"I would be happy to be useful to the god Science for two machines and their crews. And the currency for their sustenance. Is gold and silver still the main currency now?"

"I don't think you understand, Eugeni. It is a match, not for political and economic gain, but for you to show you are telling the truth."

"If Lewus does not pay the price, he will never know," I said. "There should be great interest in the man brought back from the dead who fights again for his life. The small man versus the giants. Does this little man have the secret of eternal life? Can he be killed at all?" I said. I wanted to show her the benefits of such a match.

"There will be no blood, Eugeni. Blunted weapons," said Olava.

"People can be killed with blunted weapons," I said.

"Everyone wears padding," she said.

"That is silly," I said.

"That is what we have today. It is called fencing."

"Then think how much better a real match would be. You cannot tell me people have changed so much that blood draws no interest. Real blood, Olava. I would wager that even members of your cult would love real blood."

The first drops of tears, hinting a reservoir of them held back by a dam of will, appeared in Olava's eyes. She obviously felt sad for me.

"I will not take less," I said. But I knew nothing was offered, even as I entered the building that morning on which the match was planned. There were polished wooden floors, which meant no blood was ever spilled. The arena was square, with a high ceiling. There were wooden seats, which meant it was not built to last. There were few seats.

Lewus spoke to a man dressed in white with a small red patch over his left chest. A thin metal basket rested atop his head. Olava said the basket was a helmet to protect the head and face. The red spot was supposed to represent the heart. When you touched it with a blunted sword, you won. The man was large, but much smaller than Lewus.

There was an offering of weapons on a wooden table. There

was a thin sword with a blunted tip which, if the tip were sharpened, could be very effective for thrusting but would require great finesse in blocking. It would be a disaster in close, because the pommel did not have nearly enough weight for smashing. That, according to Olava, was the épée.

There was a slashing blade of such uselessness it belonged in a field for harvesting. This, Olava said, was a saber. I could fight épée or saber, whichever I chose. The épée was the blade that allowed only the thrust. The metal was exceedingly fine.

Semyonus wrapped a gray bag around my arm and pumped it tight to test the caliber of my blood, as he explained. Someone had done this every day along with gathering a sample of my urine.

The physician looked at me and tried to say something. But he only patted me on the back and said something to Olava.

"What did he say?" I asked.

"He said you'll be all right."

Olava spoke to Lewus. She told me she told him that it was not only immoral but unfair, because of my age and the quality of the fencer and also my leg wound, which was healing.

The fencer had won awards for worldwide contests called the Olympics, similar to those of the ancient world, more ancient than I.

"Greek games," I said.

"Yes," said Olava.

"My mother was Greek, but I don't know Greek games."

Semyonus, through Olava, said that if I would make a respectable showing there might be a reward for me. He could assure me of a sizable reward. Sizable, as he described it, would not even buy the metal wing of one of the machines. I spat.

Through Olava, Lewus explained he was conducting this exhibition for the benefit of Semyonus and Olava and myself. I smiled up at him when I heard this. As far as he was concerned, I was not who I said I was. But because of his nobility and love for us all, he was allowing me to stage a free exhibition for him.

I spat.

Olava refused to translate what Lewus said. Lewus picked up a weapon as though strangling it, then poked it around the air. He handed it to me pommel first. I let it drop. Semyonus did the same, despite some words with Olava. I would not take the weapon.

He offered me the machine on his wrist that could tell what time it was, day or night. I knew it was of little value because so many people here had them.

He pleaded with the man in white who came forward. He touched the blunted weapon to my stomach. He touched it to my face. He gave me a short slap across the face.

For some reason he did this without protecting his testicles. I dropped him with a kick, and this supposed modern gladiator rolled on the ground in pain, and thus did Lewus's match end in farce—a match that might have made all of us famous if pursued properly.

Olava was disconsolate. She said there was much work we had to do in remembering. She was worried what would happen to me. I told her that I was always very lucky, and there was nothing to fear in this world, especially since there was no crucifixion or slavery.

"No one starves here, so why should I?"

"It is not that you will starve, it is that you will not be believed. If you thought these questions and tests were difficult, there will be others. And in truth you should have more freedom than that."

"But your god did not have freedom," I said. "And he is the greatest of all gods, greater than Rome itself." He had to be, in their minds of course, because years were numbered from his supposed birth until recently, the years being called "Before Christ, B.C." and then after his birth, "Anno Domini, A.D.," until the god Science, which did not like to be called a god, was given homage by calling years B.C.E. and C.E., meaning Before Christian Era, and Christian Era. And by that it meant you did not have to believe Olava's cult had produced the single god when you counted years. We were in the twentieth century. Domitian's reign being in the first century from here, but in our seventh century because we dated everything from the founding of the city, the city being Rome, of course.

My attempts to comfort her brought her to tears. She told me how good her god was, and that often he was so mysteriously good, we could not perceive how good he was. Basically, he knew what was better for us than we did ourselves.

"As you said, good woman. So do not grieve for me, but grieve for those who are not under the protection of the great god." And truly great he was, for he had survived Mithras and Juno and Mars and all the other gods. How could there be any worry with a great god like this?

"You do not believe that. You only say that because you are so good. You are a good person, Eugeni. I know that. A better person than many who sing songs of love. You have goodness in your heart."

Again, she confused me greatly for this god was supposed to reward those who had goodness and, if I were to be rewarded, what was the worry? At this she wept.

We talked through the morning and afternoon, and she asked me about my early life, not as someone recording, but as a friend. So I told her. But I told her a lie because she was already so overwrought. I told her of the good of my mother and father and how, while slavery was a poor way to exist, there was much love and always food. For why would a master deny food to those who served him?

I even told her why I did not slay Publius. When he mentioned the name of the Jewish god, I knew then that this man's blood should be spared because her god was greater than the empire itself.

"I went to Oxford, not Saint Tweedledum's," she said in a new assault of weeping. "You are beautiful, blessed, good-hearted, and you are a liar, Eugeni."

"I am not a liar, good woman. If you are my friend, you would not call me that."

In explanation she said Oxford was a school of great discipline and Saint Tweedledum's was not a school, but represented a somewhat overly pleasant and simplified view of the world, the sort of school her cult sometimes supported.

"But I tell you, Eugeni, my God shines brightest and most glorious in the blood of His cross, true and painful. He is beyond pain and is truth, and while at first He may seem to be discredited by the truth, yet the full truth shows Him more glorious than any schoolgirl wish. This know you, when you said He is stronger than Rome, as but comfort for me, you said true. And don't patronize me, Eugeni."

"If you want the truth, Olava, let me ask you why so fine a person as you wastes her learned life in that slave religion? True friend, you abstain from men, but what is your reward? You do not dress as well as a proper virgin should, for our vestal virgins dressed with jewels and splendid whiteness, even the slaves who did their hair cost more than all the garments you ever wore."

And this made her happy, for she liked combat of wits. We were too late to be served food, and we went to the food-preparing area, called a "kitchen" in this Germanic language. It was on the lowest floor of the building. It had large boards for cutting and storage boxes which preserved things through cold, and when I saw the knives hanging above the wooden workbench, I laughed.

Olava wanted to know what was funny, and I climbed on the bench to reach a blade, which, barring the thin, smooth pommel, was one of the best designed short swords I had ever seen. Well pointed for thrust and sharp for blocking slash, if that should be open, and solid for a block. I pressed the point into the wood. Flexible, too. Beyond belief. One would not find oneself holding a useless pommel with one's life ended at the crack of the blade. Not this one. And it was strong.

"Eugeni, are you sure you were a gladiator?" Olava asked. She prepared fruit and bread and cheese herself.

"Yes, why do you ask now?"

"The way you handle that knife. You seemed unable to stick it far into the wood. You seemed, well, slow and weak. Have you lost your strength?"

"I would say I am almost up to my peak, not far off it."

"But you moved so slowly with so little force."

I put the blade horizontally into the wood.

"Yes, that's it. It seems so slow and lacking in force. There is no force in it. It looks like no movement at all."

"It is deceiving, Olava. Come. Mark where the blade went in."

"Eugeni, sometimes the mind plays tricks. Perhaps you wished to be a gladiator, and after so many years in the ice, I don't know what happens to the mind, but perhaps you adopted some way of life that would be appealing to you. You were in a comatose state for a long while here in this hospital. And you are not all that muscular, in truth."

I looked at the blade. How did I know she was not right? I did not even know the difference between today and tomorrow and yesterday and centuries before. The thrust seemed good to me. I pulled out the blade.

"But I remember the training," I said. "Even my muscles remember. How could I remember the training? The training was harder than the others. Much harder. I was a murderer at eight. They didn't care if I survived. I remember the training, Olava, and have scars from fights."

"Do you, Eugeni?"

"I remember remembering."

"Do you, Eugeni?"

"Yes."

"Are you sure?"

"I think so," I said, and what a grand time it was to doubt myself, for suddenly I faced a man who wanted to kill me with a blade. Olava had thoroughly stripped me in that instant of the armor of my mind. The large man I had kicked to the ground had entered the culina, called kitchen, and approached with the tip of his thrusting blade without its blunted tip. Lewus and Semyonus, trying to restrain him, but at a distance. Suddenly his movements seemed incredibly fast, he was formidable in his rage. He threw me a weapon. I almost picked it up for defense, thinking he knew better. I backed away quickly from his rage, tripping on the weapon he had thrown.

I tried to keep one of the backed chairs between him and me. He was going to kill me. I knew it. I had but a meat knife in my hand.

And then he drew blood from my cheek. And where my mind had failed, my muscles remembered. One does not survive the arena without some skills as deep as bone.

Lew McCardle stumbled into his hotel suite, his shirt front covered with vomit, his body trembling. James Houghton Laurie was talking to three subordinates around the large coffee table in the sitting room of the suite.

McCardle told the subordinates to get out. There were things they weren't supposed to hear. He took a drink out of one of their hands and gulped it himself.

"Move!" he yelled at them. "Get the fuck out of here." To Laurie he raised a hand for silence. Then he took Laurie's drink. The speckled sausage skin on Laurie's face sagged. He stood up. McCardle signaled him to sit. McCardle got a bottle of bourbon from the bar and poured his glass half-full. It had just contained gin before.

"Everything's going to be all right. OK," said McCardle. "Get out of the country, and don't phone me again. It's my trouble."

"Lew, I thought everything was in a nice, safe seal. We were going to celebrate. I only came because you had said in your message that, quote, 'the egg is in the shell and will be in the country for months.' Did I misinterpret?"

"No. Something happened. Terrible. I miscalculated. Goddamn. I never want to see that again. I've seen men killed. I've seen death. Jesus, I've seen the state troopers pick up pieces off the railway tracks. Those were accidents. Oh, God! God. It was awful!"

"What happened?"

"You don't want to know. You're not involved," said McCardle. "Just go."

"So I'll have to lie on some witness stand somewhere. I won't remember a word you say."

"You don't have to know this, Mr. Laurie."

"I want to," said Laurie.

"I wouldn't if I were you."

"You're not me."

When McCardle told Laurie the revived patient had said he was a gladiator, Laurie looked up as though presented a giant Christmas present.

"Really," he said and demanded all details. General information would not do. How big was he, how did he move, did he have any unusual sizes to anything? This, from the chairman of the board of Houghton.

"Eugenianus is small by our standards."

"In everything?" asked Laurie.

"I don't know. I don't remember."

"Well, what happened, Lew? Just settle down."

Lew tried to explain. His eyes blinked uncontrollably. He kept focusing on nowhere.

"There was sufficient data to indicate he was not a gladiator and, in order to get him and the Russian doctor and the nun out of the hospital where rumors were growing, I staged an exhibition, and one thing led to another, and we have a mutilated body on our hands. I had to try to get them the hell out of that hospital because publicity would ultimately compromise our bidding atmosphere. I thought it would work."

Laurie wanted to know more about the mutilated body, exactly how it happened, who did what to whom, where Lew was standing, was the nun there, what did she do? Sometimes women went sexually crazy at the sight of blood.

"Mr. Laurie. Please get out of here. I ran here myself. Jesus, get out of here."

"You should have phoned. It would have been faster," said Laurie. "You worry a great lot, boy."

The red-crease smile appeared on the tan-blotched face. James Houghton Laurie wanted to hear everything, now.

Lew sat on a couch near the table. He had staged a match with an Olympic fencer against the subject. The subject refused to fight and kicked the fencer, who took it to heart and later found the subject in the hospital kitchen. The fencer had a known temper. Lew and the doctor had tried to stop the fencer, who had sharpened a foil. The fencer was dead now. There was massive readjusting to do now. And that was it.

"From what ah know, Lewellyn McCardle, Jr., a boy from North Springs ain't about to puke up his clothes from seeing a fatal sticking."

The old man was enjoying this, Lew realized. He was playing Texas Ranger again.

"No one should ever have to see how a gladiator kills," said McCardle.

"From the beginning. Who was standin' wheah? Ah jes wanna get the fixings on this here brawl."

And Lew gave him the fixings and all:

"Eugeni was in the kitchen with a large meat knife. The fencer entered, chased him to a corner, and cut a cheek. Then, Eugeni smiled very big in a large, comic gesture, and proceeded to dismember and ultimately disembowel someone fencing for his life, all the while smiling and bowing."

"Like what, what first?"

Eugeni had appeared to move slowly; he caught the tip of the fencer's foil with the tip of the salad knife and, as though the two weapons were soldered, he moved it with the tip until everyone could see he was dominating and directing the fencer's foil.

"Like you would hold a two-year-old's hand and move it around. That easily," said McCardle.

Then Eugeni, who was half a foot shorter, did the same thing with the two fingers of his left hand, while his knife teased the genitals of the fencer. No, Eugeni did not cut him there. Still with a big grin, he pushed his belly into the fencer's belly, then turned around so that the fencer's sword arm was under his own arm. He was showing the fencer how to move. He yelled into the fencer's ear that he should practice more. He accused the fencer of not listening properly, took one step back and took off an ear. The knife seemed to move slowly, just touch the ear. Then the ear was off clean, and there was a hole surrounded by blood on the side of the fencer's head. Then he accused the fencer of talking too much. That was the fault of his poor training. He took off the upper lip and part of the nose. Then he looked as though he slipped, and the desperate fencer lunged, and Eugeni opened his belly like a surgeon and with a skillful hand yanked out his intestines and dragged him stumbling around the kitchen. He looked to the nun for the death signal, and getting none, he finished off the poor man, spinning him over the butcher blocks and taking off the head.

"I saw a head go in Riyadh once. The Saudis did it with one stroke. It's not like you imagine. It's not that easy taking off a head. They had this African, black as a mine shaft. I mean it was black, and it was crying," said Laurie.

"Mr. Laurie, please."

"Yup," said Laurie. "You're right. I've got to go. You've troubles on your hands, and we're just going to have to do whatever the hell we can do. The tight, exclusive find is gone. It's going to show. But don't feel all that bad, Lew. Nobody knows for sure but us."

"I don't understand," said Lew.

"Well, we've got to rush. Cat's got to be out of the bag soon, and if we rush, we can't drive the kind of bargain we want. We're not dealing with fools nowadays. Everyone knows oil. It could have been nice. It could have been seven, maybe eight points."

"What?"

"On the American Stock Exchange. Houghton Oil. It's sixty-seven and three-quarters. If we had the right bidding atmosphere, with plenty of time to haggle and not rush, we could have been sixty-four, sixty-four and a half, without the market doing anything."

"Eight points? Is that what 'big' was?" asked Lew McCardle in horror.

"If you're Houghton people and you're talking Houghton, it's more than ten percent. Give us as much time as you can, Lew," said Laurie, picking up a little overnight bag and checking for anything else in the room that might be his. "You know, when you're blocking on a pass play, you keep the other guys away from your quarterback. You don't try to stop them completely, only sort of misdirect them. But I don't have to tell you, Lew. You're an old Maky tackle and you're gonna give us your best. You'd kill to protect your quarterback if you had to. Because you know Houghton takes care of those who take care of Houghton."

Laurie shook hands, winked, patted Lew on the shoulder, and was out of the room. Shortly thereafter, a man in a business suit entered, put a pistol on the table near Lew McCardle, and was leaving when Lew said:

"What the hell is that for?"

"I don't know. And I don't know you," said the man.

CHAPTER XXVI

Perhaps it was Olava's hysterical shrieking. Or Lewus's vomiting. Or Semyonus staring open-mouthed, emitting the same low grunt like a chorus of deep-throated birds sentenced to a lifetime of a single note. My body was already in its dance of glory to share the triumph with them. But there was no yelling of approval, no stamping of feet, no cheers with my name for a match that would have glorified Rome. If Publius had had the strength and quickness of this slain gladiator, I would now be surrounded by my wife and child and wealth and power, living a life devoted to my wants. I would have been manipulating a good marriage for Petronius. I would have been sharing my wisdom with Domitian, but not too much. I would have been moving my wealth to even stronger positions.

Instead, I was jumping up and down in a slave work area for a cultist, a physician, and, from what I could understand, someone akin to one of my wealthier slaves who managed my affairs under my close scrutiny.

I ran. And when I started running, I realized it was what I wanted to do. I ran for the running of it, as though if I ran hard enough and long enough, something I desperately wanted would either catch me or fall in front of me. I searched for a way away. I was running home. I was running.

Running hadn't changed.

Through the corridors I ran and down the iron steps I ran and, unlike the streets of Rome, here I did not know where I was going.

People let out startled little gasps as I crossed the big hall to the glass doors that opened to the night. I ran, seeing the fast-moving lights of what Olava called automobiles. Out into this strange land of machines I ran.

I ran towards a wooded hill I had seen from the sun porch. The roads and cities were the barbarians' arena; the forests, I felt sure, were more familiar ground. It was good that this was at the edge of the city, for cities are confusing to strangers.

I was clumsy through the trees, for, in truth, I was a city person all my life—except for the years of the latifundia and those first precious moments in the hills of Greece, when I was with my mother and grandfather as a family.

I collided with a tree and paused in the darkness, smelling the freshness of the forest, feeling the chill finally come over me, my weapon hand bloody to the elbow. I was cold. Behind me I could see the lights of the hospital far off and, in my isolation, could hear yelling, made faint by distance. My breath stayed with me, but weakly. I sat down under a tree on what felt like a leafy patch of ground, and for the first time since I had entered the arena before Domitian, I was free.

It was delicious. Through the leaves above, I could see the white specks of the heavens. Lewus's people had taken the gods from these very heavens by walking on the moon.

It was chilly, but the chill was a good discomfort. I was free. I shut my eyes in the joy of my escape. When I opened them, the good chill was a gnawing cold and I was hungry. The blood of the swordsman was now clotted on my tunic and my weakened right leg pained. The stars were no longer in the sky, for the infinite black background was now a close gray blanket in the time before the sun.

I was in a wooded land where leaves from a previous autumn covered the ground. If I had fire, I could burn the cold from me, and then I realized that I did not know how to make a fire. Since

I had entered the lanista training school, slaves or others had always prepared my fires.

In the forests I would not be on even ground with the people of today. Most of my life had been spent in the city, being served for my minor needs. I realized then that my long-ago dreams of the hills of Greece were just that. I belonged in no hill country; for I, who had imagined myself as an innocent lad from the hills of Greece thrust into a cruel Roman world, was in truth a Roman. In my habits, in my comfort, especially in the scheming of my mind, I was inescapably Roman. Not because of my father's blood, but because of my mind. A Greek lad of the hills would have had a fire by this time. A Roman of the city would sit helpless, shivering, waiting for a slave—a Greek slave—to do the work for him.

I realized only then, separated by centuries and miles, that I was not only most Roman of them all, I was the only Roman of them all. Eugeni, the Greekling.

And it was not the best century to be such. The barbarians had civilized themselves, and why not? The patricians were now less than dust, and even the tombs of marble could not keep their bodies from becoming part of the air and land. Was that what tombs were for? To keep the bodies from feeding the ground? To keep your bowels from contenting a dog who would defecate your remains for the afternoon glory of a lily?

It was no big thing at all. Even without the senate voting me guilty of maiestas, what would I have been? Had they made me a god, and had marble images lined every road for every mile in every land, who would know me today? Only to reproduce the sounds of my name and recount happenings they did not understand?

Domitian was remembered. Olava knew his name, his birth, his death, and some triumphs attributed to him. And what did he have? The unflawed stupidity of exerting oneself for later generations, called posterity, banged me like bound rods across the nose. Many great men talked of it as the most significant achievement. Men who would not so much as lift a piece of bread for someone sitting at their side would march themselves and thousands of comrades to destruction, just so that other people, who could never possibly know them or even return so much as a seeable nod, would think approvingly of them.

With a fingernail I made a scratch on the bark of the tree I leaned against. The tree would grow that mark away, as though it had never been. And why not? I should not have even intruded myself upon its skin.

There was nothing here for me, not even hate. In a time when there were no slaves, I did not even have dominion over my urine, which was taken away daily to be examined.

I allowed the moments of the long night to pass, and I understood how I could in a small way make things right.

There was a place I could go to where I would be home. I rubbed leaves on my blade to make it shiny. I rested its pommel on a rock lest it sink into the ground. And I knelt before the rock and touched the point to my chest.

I faced south. I knew, because the new blood sun was coming up from my left, unless of course it had changed. Many things change in a long, long time. I would have to plunge myself down in such a way that the blade went up into my heart. A small animal moved through the dead leaves. I smelled the trees and listened to the sharp, seldom-heard sounds of morning in this north country. I lifted myself away from the blade and examined the point. I had time now. There was no need to rush this. I tried to sharpen the point against the rock, but I only dulled it.

Demos, a slave I once had, could take a blade even of raw iron and craft a point and edge on it to slice cloth. Not improving the blade, I put the pommel back on the rock and prepared to die.

I made myself quiet within myself and waited for my body to suddenly do the rest in a solid lunge to earth. When the sun was yellow, and the morning heat came upon me, I knew I was not going to kill myself. I was not Roman enough. The Greekling and gladiator were too much in me to end my misery in so Roman a fashion. I was a slave to my desire to live and, surrendering to that, a slave to the wants of my body. There was no Aurelius to free me from this bondage. I descended the small hill and found a stream with water. The taste was horrible. It had been either poisoned or infected with some putrid substance. Near the stream was a road, not of good rock, but black and soft to the foot, that stretched like dark, flat honey up one hill south and down another north. Should I take this road to its farthest extremity in either direction, it would not lead me to where I wished to go.

On these roads, built for enclosed chariots that needed no horse and were called "automobiles," meaning things that moved by themselves, did I rest, careful to stay off the road itself. The automobiles moved faster than horses and probably required less skill to operate, once one knew what to do. Everything did today.

Suddenly I noticed one had stopped. A large man opened a front door and came towards me. It was Lewus, and I was happy to see this face because I recognized it.

He was grim, and I could see distaste and determination on his face. In his right hand, he held a metal bashing piece with a tube. How I knew it was a weapon, I do not know. But I knew he was prepared to kill with it, and assumed so with the way he carried it, for it was not a package, and one knows by the gravity of step that a novice is ready to kill.

He looked down at me, and I rose to my feet, and he still looked down at me. I motioned to him that it was all right. I pushed my thumb into my chest to tell him that he should strike there. Did he want me to fight in order to kill me?

I made menacing motions with my blade. He remained as a statue, face and body carved by some barbaric sculptor. I struck my chest lightly with my blade and nodded to his metal weapon. I smiled to show him it was what I wanted. I frowned to show him I was a menace. I put the point up to his throat to indicate he would die if I did not. But he shook his head and put the thing in his pocket, and put one of his large arms, with the yellow hair on the back of his hand, around my shoulder and said sadly:

"Come, let us go."

"You speak my language. Then listen. Kill me now. Do it. Do it for me."

"No," said Lewus, and I knew he wouldn't. Some men cannot or will not. No big thing.

In the automobile, Olava and Semyonus were in the back.

"Eugeni. Eugeni. Are you all right?" Olava asked.

Semyonus also wanted to know how I felt.

"I feel sad," I said.

"But are you all right?" asked Olava.

"For someone who is alive when he wishes to be dead, yes."

"Semyonus wants to know if you suffer any dizziness?"

"Leave him alone," said Lewus in my language. He was angry. His massive neck reddened, and his teeth grated.

"I didn't know you spoke Latin well," said Olava, surprised.

"Four years in younger school, four in older school. Along with other languages."

"That surprises me," she said.

"Because all bigotry doesn't hide behind a white sheet or a swastika," he said.

I asked what white sheets meant and what that hard-to-pronounce word symbolized. Olava said there were groups that excluded people and fostered hate for the excluded people for being inferior.

I ignored her because I never was all that interested in religious cults anyway.

The automobile moved quickly, but with such ease that it did not appear quick. The comfort was like sitting in one's own peristilium. A wheel steered the automobile. There were three levers on the floor and a stick with a handle that came up to the wheel. The right lever released the power, the one next to it applied brakes, and the other had to be worked in conjunction with the stick. The automobile worked on gears operated by the stick, but to get the proper gears into readiness for alignment, one had to press the far lever on the floor, without looking, of course, because one had to use one's eyes for the road.

Automobiles were stolen often, but not as often as they might be, because they required a key for a lock to start the car. Lewus owned the key.

Olava said Semyonus was afraid of my carrying the blade. He wanted me to give it to Olava. She reached for it but I refused.

"His absurd fears are his problems, not mine," I said.

"He is afraid because of what you did to the other gladiator in the culina."

"He was not a real gladiator in the real sense. He never killed before or walked on sand. I knew that. Nevertheless, Semyonus and I are not matched. Does he think I walk about killing people? What is the matter with him?"

I was hungry, but Olava refused to give me food or drink until I handed her my blade. I did so, and she gave me apples and cheese and wine she had brought with her in case they found me. Then I took back the blade.

I did not drink the wine, but ate the apple quickly, down to its core of black seeds. I looked at the dark seeds a long time then threw them through an open window. This window had glass that went up and down by rolling a lever. I hoped the seeds fell on good ground. And where was my seed? On what ground had Petronius fallen or planted his seed? This bothered me, although it is hard to isolate that you are bothered when you would willingly discard your life. Yet this thought had discovered an as yet unused area of misery for me. My seed was out there, unprotected by me, unadvised by me, upsupported by me, loose and free and probably victim to any passing disaster of life; if Petronius reproduced, and if his seed reproduced, and so on.

"Why did you not kill me, Lewus?"

"You knew?"

"Yes."

"I couldn't. I didn't want to. I don't know."

"You were going to kill Eugeni?" asked Olava.

"It doesn't matter," said Lewus.

"You said the gun was for our protection," said Olava, bruised justice resonating in voice and face.

"I said lots of things, idiot."

"I thought she was a scholar," I said.

"She is, and the second biggest fool in the car, the first being me."

"Lewus, you would not kill Eugeni?" said Olava.

"I didn't, did I?"

"Why would you want to?" said Olava.

Lewus said it was complicated.

There were many trees and the land was green and all about us was new, fresh life. I watched Lewus's feet operate the levers on the floor.

We left the dark road for a muddy dirt one. That brought us to a house made of unfinished wood. Despite its rough appearance, it had glass and inside the floor was covered. There was the power of electricity for the lights, and a finely finished large box which made heat for cooking, a larger box for cooling things, and a black thing that looked as though it had a handle, which I was told not to pick up, because it was complicated and I did not know how to use it. On this thing, you could talk and hear voices from it.

I was told to be careful here, because there were not the safeguards that were in the hospital. I should ask before I touched anything.

Olava told me not to touch the square box that was the hearth.

She said it was all right to touch the box that made things cold. I asked her what the argument was about. She said it was about nothing, which did not mean it was about nothing, but meant there was something she did not wish to discuss with me.

"It's about me," said Lewus.

My right leg, from so much strenuous running, hurt again. It had subsided in pain after that first month of awakening, but the night of running had aggravated it again. Semyonus examined it, worked his hands around, and patted me on the face.

"He says you will be fine. Can he look at your tongue now?" said Olava.

"No."

"He is your friend."

"No more than you are, really," I said.

"She has been your friend, your only friend, Eugeni," said Lewus.

"I don't feel warmth for you," I said to Olava. "I don't. I don't know why, but I don't. I just don't. I like you, but I need more for a friend. I never had a friend, not even you."

She thought about this a moment, and she said that was all right. And for some reason, that it was all right was the very reason I could not feel warmth for her.

"I tried to feel warmth. I thought I did. I don't," I said.

"I understand," she said.

"Is there nothing you don't understand?"

"I don't understand Lewus," she said.

Lewus was at the white-painted box that made things cold. It had a door. It was almost as tall as Lewus. It was well provisioned, and from it he took a cup of glass with a metal top that made a sound when it was pried off. The cup was so plentiful, even poor people would discard it, I was told. The drink was mead, called beer. I did not want any.

Lewus slumped into a backed chair, as most chairs were in the room, which, in the modern custom, also faced out to the outside.

He took the object he had pointed at me, and put it on a table in front of him. Then he wept, his giant body sobbing.

"I don't know how it got this far. I don't know how it got this far."

"You were going to kill Eugeni," said Olava angrily.

"Yes. No. Never. Maybe," said Lewus. He tried to talk to her in my language, and then he gave up. Olava quite skillfully translated into a language Semyonus understood, but which was not his. It was their common language, much like my language would be a common tongue for Greek and Egyptian. The new common language was English, made up partly of Latin and partly of a Germanic tongue, although it was woefully hard to recognize words.

"Fuck it," said Lewus, the "it" being in my language, the "fuck" being his, which was a negative response to things, even though the literal translation would have been copulation—copulation in certain circumstances having negative connotations, although the word itself did not imply only negative copulations. It was a swear word like *"Mars's ass"* or *"breast sucker."* Lew needed to say that word. He apologized to Olava for its use, it being a breach of manners to be said before a woman, especially one of her cult. The problem was that a murder had been committed.

"Who was murdered?" I asked.

"The gladiator you killed," said Lewus.

"Yes?"

"That was a killing crime," said Lewus.

"The glaiator with the sword, the thin one? The thin sword with the heavy pommel and the clever hand shield for the sword hand?"

"That one," said Lewus.

I looked to Olava and shrugged.

"How is this a crime?" I asked.

"It is not a crime, Eugeni. Don't worry about it. We'll worry," said Olava.

"We don't have games today," said Lewus. "Not your kind. And outside of the arena, even in your time, what you did would be a crime or, at least, warrant some action by a magistrate."

"And if my blood spilled in your kitchen?"

"Then he would face trial. Ironic. If it could be proven that he initiated this action, he would have been charged."

"If there is no crucifixion, how would he be punished?"

"He would be kept in confinement for a long time. We confine people today for punishment."

"And he would be starved and beaten?" I asked.

"No," said Lewus.

"Perhaps people have changed," I said, although I suspected there were further explanations to be had on this matter, otherwise cities would be unsafe. Of course, Rome was never safe either.

"It is unfair to try Eugeni," said Olava. "He was only doing what he was taught and doing it well, because the only person who ever loved him or showed him love was his lanista. That which he did better than anyone else was entertaining in the games."

Semyonus had a discussion with Olava, and he was furious. He was not going to let me go to trial. He would put Lewus on trial. Olava agreed with him. Lewus should go on trial. Lewus belched a deep, gaseous resonance and got himself another metal-topped goblet. He said the swear word again.

Semyonus was so excited by all this he did a thing he had tried to avoid or limit in my presence, he lit a small paper-covered tube of herbs and smoked it. It was supposed to calm his nerves. It smelled awful. It did not burn his throat but was bad for him physically. He was addicted to it. He hoped I did not mind his indulging. The habit was new. Two hundred, three hundred years old at most. A tenth my age.

I examined the glass goblet, it never ceasing to amaze me how common evenness was, so cheaply produced also, machines providing much of the slave labor.

I also did not care that much.

"Silence," I said. "Now hear me. I did not ask for this resurrection, nor did I seek it. I died my death, and if I had been left alone to sleep painlessly until the ice thawed and the poison took effect, as you said it would, it would have been over as it should have been. I do not belong here. I don't even have any enemies. Lewus, you found me, you kill me."

"Fuck you, you kill me," said Lewus.

"That was my next threat," I said.

"I figured. Look. Maybe I'll kill you tomorrow. We can always kill you. With even better things than guns. We've got pills that are poison."

"I wouldn't take it. I don't want to die. I want to be dead. Do you understand? Pills are often slow."

"Yes," said Lewus.

Olava said one should never surrender to despair. She wanted an explanation from Lewus about his violation of trust, and she wanted to know what his real interests were.

Semyonus seemed to agree. And Lewus, with the tedium of a beaten man, explained. Olava and Semyonus seemed to have difficulty understanding very clearly.

The fuel of this world was oil. Lewus scientifically looked for this oil. It was very valuable. They were looking in order to know what to bid on land. If everyone found out what they knew, they would lose a bidding advantage.

Unfortunately, Lewus found me. More unfortunately, Semyonus performed a great feat of medicine.

At this, Semyonus interrupted with gravity and said that it was not that great.

"Tell him, Olava, it did not have to be great, only that people think it is great," I said.

As things went, should it become known what had happened to me and what I survived and then where I came from, and then who I was—these things making Lewus's problems worse all the time—there would have been such great interest that the clamor would have uncovered this extra find Lewus was working on.

Fearing exposure, Lewus tried to get us all here to this secluded house. He used the inept gladiator to convince Olava and Semyonus—who at that time would follow Olava—that their work would be jeopardized because I was a liar and would embarrass them, making their believability suspect.

What he failed to do, I explained to Olava, was get a good gladiator for this purpose.

"He was our best."

"Not a good test, Lewus. Not someone I would have represent your age. I cannot believe that is the best you could buy."

"I realize now we should have had a few centuries and millions of dollars. Pugilists might have been better. Yet the man seemed so fast," said Lewus.

"Useless," I said.

"Just a moment," said Olava, addressing Lewus. "How did you expect to keep this secret forever?"

"He didn't have to, woman," I said. "He only needed time until the proper donatives were given to the proper officials of the nations in which the oil was."

"I don't know about bribes," said Lewus. "I've heard of other companies but not us."

"Of course you have. If one person does it, everyone must. You have to provide monies just not to be hurt by others. A bribe is a loose thread pulled out of a cloth. Once you get one, others must do it also, and only a rare public official fights determinedly against his own wealth. Your latifundium had to do it, Lewus, if anyone did it."

"Yes. Our goodwill ambassador going from country to country. He was the head of our latifundium."

"I had Demosthenes. Ah, was I lucky to have him. What he could do with the sort of secret advantage you have. He was a good slave, but he had a bad master. Me."

"What about the authorities?" said Olava.

"Whom do you think we talk of?" I said. For she did not understand still. I pointed to the seclusion of the house. I pointed to the stock of supplies. To the rooms we had. Everything Lewus had done was to get us here, I tried to explain.

Upon this, Lewus rose and went to one of the rooms, returning with a statue of a little boy urinating.

Semyonus looked to Olava. He was embarrassed.

Looking at the statue, from what I gathered, Lewus used it as proof that he had planned this all well, even to this object, which I then realized belonged to Semyonus.

"Where did you dig it up?" I asked, and Olava explained something at length to Semyonus.

"She's telling him," said Lewus, "that you think the statue is ancient. He thinks it's a new thing, even though you had statues like that. She says not everything in Rome was in good taste."

"We didn't have the hat. It is a cute statue, don't you think?" I said.

Semyonus showed how it urinated a dark drink, which was the unwatered wine of the barbarians. I had heard of stories of wine like that, distilled so that human stomachs could not tolerate it, and only the coarser intestines of the Germans could down it. Yet Semyonus seemed civilized and, in truth, an intestine was an intestine. I had seen many.

"And the purpose of that?" she said pointing to the statue.

Semyonus gave the hat another tap.

I nodded approval. It was good to see something I recognized again.

"The purpose of the statue, Olava, is to show everything had been arranged," said Lewus.

"I understand you arranged it. I understand that. I am beginning to understand very peculiar behavior. But I do not understand what this has to do with the authorities," said Olava. "I cannot believe complicity of everyone."

And still she did not understand, although the woman had a good mind, except when she willfully refused to use it. And I explained again about vast wealth, about responsibilities of governments, about people who make decisions, and about how, when there is a great amount of wealth depending on cooperation, then all men are friends.

"This is not the politics of the arena, Eugeni. Two thousand years have passed. It is a long time. A very long time. While we still have corruption, there are some things that cannot be bribed for."

And again the woman threatened revelations to authorities, and said she would not be surprised if Lewus's own company would be very interested in this information and peculiar behavior. Lewus pointed to the modern weapon.

"They gave me that," he said.

"Why?" asked Olava.

"I don't know," said Lewus.

"Because they are close to making their arrangement for the valuable materials," I said.

"I don't understand," said Lewus.

"It is complicated."

"I'm not a fool."

"I never said you were, Lewus, but you certainly have run your life into a tangle."

"I have. All I wanted was to retire with the guaranteed salary they give people when they retire from latifundia. And now this. But you are worse, Eugeni. You were rich."

"Don't you dare call Eugeni 'worse,' " said Olava, who for all her gravity and strength now reminded me of my old talkative acquaintance, Publius. Perhaps it was her tone that reminded me of Publius talking to the lanista, telling him how he should address me.

"Why did they give me the weapon?" he asked again. "Do you think it was to kill you?"

"And possibly these," I said pointing to Olava and Semyonus.

"If you had to. Only if it would give them time. Perhaps it would be just me. Whatever they would need."

"Am I in the wrong job!" said Lewus, shaking his head sadly.

"It is not your fault. It is theirs. I would wager they often assigned people to things that were beyond them. Why did they choose you? What foolishness was it?"

"I was there."

"So often the reason, so often the disaster."

"I can't believe this," said Olava. And then Semyonus said that he would inform his embassy, which had relations with this country we were in.

"Have you been translating, Olava?" I demanded to know angrily.

"Yes. Almost everything for Semyonus."

"Then how can he be that stupid? There is a great amount of wealth here. Why don't you understand that your masters work together? You are working with Lewus, by your masters' permission."

"Not to kill people," said Olava.

"No. That is left to the idiot Lewus, who has left his arena and found he does not belong out of it."

Olava was quiet. She mentioned that she was not familiar with some workings of large organizations. She translated for Semyonus. He pressed the hat and the boy gave him the strong, brown wine. I looked outside at the young afternoon, with the trees and the very blue sky, and I was sad beyond reason. I was more a slave now than I had ever been even on the latifundium. Not to have any place you want to go is the greatest manacle of all.

The house smelled of fruits in bowls, and there was a sharp odor of recent soaps upon the wood. I found myself leaning back in the chair, expecting the back to be there now, and I became sadder still.

The three of them did not know what to do. Lewus mentioned that all of this meant only a small amount of money to his latifundium, and he said it as though that were something illogical. Obviously he had once believed his life was more important to his latifundium than their profit. On that silliness I did not answer him.

"How did it get this far?" he asked again.

"It was always this far. It is like a flawed statue. There are pits and cracks that are filled by wax and never noticed until heat is applied. Most often they escape heat forever. Yet the flaws are still there."

"Who would have known?" said Lewus.

"Most people do not know themselves, let alone their masters."

Lewus pointed to me and laughed. "For someone as smart as you, you are the biggest fool idiot I have ever had the honor to meet in my life. Hello, idiot."

"Hello, idiot," I said, and in his manner of greetings with clenched hands.

"Hello, idiot," he said.

Olava protested the name calling. She wanted to know how I could pleasantly go ahead with a conversation with a man who had deceived everyone here and had entertained the possibility of killing me, and whose machinations had led to the death of the bad gladiator in the kitchen, which was a crime that would have to be contested—I being the accused—although it was manifestly clear who the guilty party was. All this was said glowering at Lewus.

CHAPTER XXVII

They could not decide on what to do with me. There were many accusations against Lewus for deceiving them about his intentions and his knowledge of my language. When the accusations reached the level of full throat and became overwhelming in their annoyance, I stood between all of them, Lewus drinking, Semyonus drawing smoke into his mouth from a tube which fouled the air, and Olava, ever disciplined, sitting erect on the edge of a chair, needing neither drink nor food nor rest.

"You two blame Lewus because you are afraid of your real problem," I said.

Lewus laughed uproariously, his massive orange-haired head bellowing to the ceiling. He had been quaffing great quantities of his beer, making the goblets seem like drops to his throat.

"And you, Lewus, let them, because you also cannot do what you must do."

And Lewus asked what that was, as did Olava and Semyonus, the physician.

"You must decide what to do with me, and you cannot. None of you is capable of making that decision."

Olava denied this.

"You should be in a place conducive to your health and well-being," she said.

"And that is?"

"At this point we will have to work on that," she said.

"Because you don't know, woman."

"And Semyonus says you should be happy; in a place that would make you happy."

"I was, until he disturbed it," I said, pointing to Lewus, "and he performed his genius," I said, pointing to Semyonus the physician.

"We will find a way. We will first take care of you, Eugeni, and then pursue the proper legal things and notify the authorities," said Olava.

"The authorities? The authorities?" I laughed. "Why is it people think the authorities are some form of gods with either great justice or great, cunning evil, rather than the same plodding fools they see in their daily lives, and most of all in their mirrors? What is the matter with you people? Authorities are people. They are like seeds and latifundia and every living thing. Every thing living serves itself. The purpose of an authority is to remain an authority, not dispense justice."

"They will do the proper thing. Eugeni. There are people who do what is right."

"When it serves them," I said. "Only if the proper thing helps them survive."

Semyonus and Olava disagreed, but Lewus was deeply quiet.

I told them what I told my son about the fruit, and how it made sweet meat, not for our pleasure, but for its seeds, and we only interrupt it.

"I can see how you would be cynical, Eugeni," said Olava, but I did not let her finish.

"What is the matter with you people? We came here in a chariot that runs on fuel. I am told flying machines run on fuel, the lights above run on fuel. Everyone uses it. Its discovery is so secret and of such enormous wealth in a land where people are not executed that Lewus, the server of the god Science, finds himself with a weapon to execute someone. He doesn't even know who. And your cult, Olava, and your wonderful government, Semyonus, give you so easily to this man, and you turn around and blithely tell me you will report this to the authorities. Who do you think the authorities are?"

Olava said her cult would never endorse killing. Semyonus said the same for his government.

"In previous times," said Lewus, "Olava's church has ordered people killed, and Semyonus's government now does it. You should know that. I am not the only person with a sin."

"You think I needed to be told these things, Lewus?" I said.

"There was a bad period in my church when men did evil things," said Olava.

"They did what they thought served their interests, those deeds now not serving yours, woman."

Olava bit her reply short. Her kindness was like a cloak of stones to a swimmer. It reminded me of myself, of the me who always thought he had controlled events more than most men and was now so controlled as to be exhibited as less than an animal in the arena. For an animal will be allowed to fight. I was not even allowed that.

"You don't know what to do because you don't know yourselves," I said. "And by that I mean what is valuable to you. Right now, I vote for the grave, to which I tried to return, but could not overcome a too-well-trained lust for life. You, Olava, talk of Lewus's sins because if you dwell on that, you can delay deciding what happens to me after that."

"You are right, Eugeni," she said, clean and courageous as ever, "for to admit a flaw in crisis requires enough strength to know the rest of you will not follow to the depths."

"And the same for all of you. This crisis now confronting you—a fine performance that is by some quirk of time now called a crime—has put before you what I had to face by my quirk in the arena. The world is coming down on all of you. What do you want to save? I was lucky. I had my loves. For most people those decisions are never made, the grave ending the debate before it begins. But not for you."

"You were lucky," said Lewus, "And Semyonus says so too, but I think you are wrong, gladiator."

"How?"

"About you. Your time of decision was not running from the arena, for those are the immediate problems of life whose answers are apparent. You cannot tell me, gladiator, that running for your life is a decision."

And I laughed. For he was right.

"Your decision was whether you would kill Publius, and you made the wrong one. I think."

"There is nothing to think about. It was wrong. I know why I did it, but it was still wrong. I said no to many things that day when I said no to Rome. I said who I was. I was Lucius Aurelius Eugenianus and how dare they put this piece of trivial nonsense beneath my sword for their imaginations. They never knew how really good I was, because they wanted their dreams satisfied. Only a few knew, and I served the mobs. They did not know my mother, who was a good woman, and better than all of them. She would never, for someone else's approval, signal my death, as Publius' mother did his. Neither would Miriamne.

"My mother was beaten in the fields when they hauled me away in chains. They had to beat her cries out of her. My mother, who was so unimportant she did not even have a name in a bill of sale, was better than all of them. I was ashamed of her. Yes, I admit it. I was ashamed of her because she was beaten.

"That day, my last day in the arena, the horrendous day, I was proud of my mother. I was proud of me. I was proud of Miriamne, whom I loved and love today, strong as the day I left her. I, the only one with memory of her, love her this day as I did in my last thoughts in the German Sea. As I did Petronius at the German Sea.

"For I confess to you now, as a child I did not hate those who beat my mother, but in a way hated her for making me ashamed she was beaten. I was sorry. But am sorry no longer."

In hot tears, I took my blade and threw it quivering into the wooden floor as I had thrown it into the sand.

"No," I screamed. "No."

And if Rome could not hear it, that was all right. They had not heard what I was saying when I said it. That was why they had to find so many reasons for why I did what I did.

"Semyonus says," said Olava, "that now he believes in his form of government more than ever. For his government, he says, has freed the masses from slavery."

"Masses?" I asked.

"The lower classes, the bulk of people," said Olava.

"If that is some form of advanced government, we are back on the latifundia. For that is how my mother was treated. You call people 'masses' when you treat them as a lump, as a hundred slaves more or less, as an army if you will. Nobody ever knew a mass or loved a mass or even paid the respect of hating a mass. In a small way, being treated as the Roman given to you, I have suffered my personhood going, a living death adding to my great sadness. An emperor looks upon his lower classes as a mass, a patrician looks upon his latifundium slaves as such, for his house slaves usually have names."

"Semyonus says you do not understand. He is part of the masses."

"If he has a name, he is not. If he is human, he is not. That is the convenient lie he tells himself. I have been wrong. All of you can continue your self-deceptions; this crisis just makes them a little bit more difficult to sustain. However, with perseverance, you can keep them comfortably to the graves and never pay the price."

As was natural, Olava, the strong one, spoke first:

"My self-deception—my lie—was that I loved a language so much that I feared losing my soul. It was not the language I loved so much as it was escaping from the world my Dominus, my God, had given me. I liked my world better than His."

As was natural, Semyonus did not know what I was talking about, which meant he had chosen the warm, easy way. But Lewus, with a great sob in his big body, gave himself to tears.

And thus the three of them began talking with an open heart I had never seen between them before. They did not invite me into this but talked deep into darkness outside, as I watched. My blade upright from the floor stuck solid between them all, as if they all shared it.

When I tried to interrupt, Olava answered that all three were serving themselves and their interests and that it was not my concern.

"With you three, it is my concern," I said.

I dozed and was roughly awakened by Semyonus. His eyes were ringed with red, for he too had been crying. Of all of them, Olava was without tears; rather, her grim determination was even more grim.

"We have all decided what we will do," said Olava. "We have decided that we want you to know what we have done, and who we are."

"I know."

"No, you don't," she said.

"I understand the machinations of your masters better than you."

"To a degree, yes. But we are talking of what we are. We want you to know that none of us thinks those we serve are evil. Semyonus believes his government is the great hope of what governments can be and is on a road towards that. Lewus points to his latifundium as enabling man not to be a pack animal and to live past thirty years. I believe my cult is the path that everyone should take, for the one right destiny for every man, and that is God, my God, whom I believe is the God for all. This we want you to know because we do not hate whom we serve."

"I did not hate Rome. Rome, too, was good. There were bad things, but there was much good. Much good. Roads and water and governments, as corrupt as they were, were better than what was there before the legion planted its standard."

"Good. On behalf of all of us, we ask that you do not attempt to take your life again, so that you will know what we have all accomplished."

"You have given me a second life."

"There is more and you will see. It cannot be explained in a picture or word. You must see and feel to understand. Now each of us has one question we ask of you. If you will give us an answer, we would appreciate it."

"Why one?"

"Because we have burdened you enough with questions, and we had set rules on ourselves that we should not ask personal questions, but treat you as a scientific thing."

"I felt like a thing," I said. The three had not removed the blade. I left it there, still not touching it.

"Do not use this on yourself for a while. Let us show you first what we have done. It will take days, but give us your life for that time, as a gift."

"And then you will kill me at my request."

"We cannot. None of us can do that or promise that. But we are certain we may show you a great thing."

"There are no great things."

"We think we can show you a great thing, and in doing so you will know what we have done, and a bit more of who we are who have done this."

"Done, if I get an answer to my question. Not one given to an exhibition of science, but to a person."

And they all agreed. And my question was:

"Why are you doing this thing, whatever it is?"

"Because we are who we are," said Lewus, and Olava translated for Semyonus. And all three agreed.

"Do you think your masters, whom you all praise here before me this night, will lose their self-interests for your convenience?"

"No," said Olava. "We will take care of it."

"You? You three? Olava, the legionnaire who follows all orders with discipline; Semyonus, falling in love without perception; and Lewus, the orange-haired giant who works his entire life for a master and does not know who that master is or exactly what it wants, until, like an imbecile, he finds a weapon in his hand and does not know he is standing on sand? I cannot conceive of any of you succeeding in blunting a plan by your cult, Olava, your government, Semyonus, and least of all your latifundium, Lewus."

"We have worked things out. Every master will be pushed aside or fooled. Do not worry. I will handle my latifundium."

"You? Least of all you. None of us would be here if you were not some clumsy oaf. You?"

"I am not stupid, Eugeni. I am not."

"Then why are we here?"

His massive hands closed on my shoulders and, like some brute ox, put me into a chair.

"All my life, Eugeni, I have dealt with people who thought I was some form of stupid trash in some manner. Now you, after two millennia, stab me in my biggest wound. My parents were not people I was proud of. And my home village school thought I should not study your language, which in our age only the better students studied because it is difficult for us today. Yet I knew it. In a more advanced school they thought that, since I was a gladiator, I should not study this and, most recently, Olava assumed I was deficient in this language because I came from an area of a country she looks down on. I allowed her that because it served what I thought were my purposes. But I want you to know I am an intelligent and perceptive person. And I am offended at being thought of as some sort of big package of garbage."

"You were a gladiator?"

"Our kind. Games. But people got hurt, not killed though. We threw ourselves at each other."

I nodded, but did not add, for Lewus's feelings, that his size would make him good at such a contest.

"Please do not call me stupid any more for I am not. I have a title that bestows on me a certain level of intelligence accepted by others. Perhaps like your son Petronius, who felt he had to be more Roman than others, I needed that title, but I have it. And my plan is sound."

"What is it?"

"It is something you would not understand."

"Try me."

"I am going to take that which is precious and make it unprecious."

That might work, I thought. That might be the one thing that could work.

"Now," continued Lewus, "I have my question I ask of you. And that is, what is it like to live with someone you love? When Olava's reports showed you ran back to save only your wife and son, I so envied you having that. So did Semyonus."

"Did you, Olava?" I asked.

"No. I thought it was nice but quite natural, even though during your period, for political people, it might have been an extraordinary act."

"That is a lot of words to say what?"

"I think I am saying my own parents had such a good love that your good love was not all that enviable, because as a child I had come from a family with love."

"And it was so."

"Lewus," I said, "it was no great thing, until I lost it. Then the love Miriamne and I had was most clear. Of all that I have done, marrying Miriamne, legally, was the happiest and best thing I have done."

And I knew he understood. I removed the blade from where it was sticking up, pommel high, from the wooden floor. I had to exert pressure, for it had gone in a goodly depth, and the wood clung.

Semyonus wanted to ask his question with Olava not listening, so the stalwart woman went to another room. He was ashamed of the question, but he wanted to ask it anyway. Lewus translated. They spoke in hushed tones, like conspirators.

"Eugeni, Semyonus wants to know about slavery. Specifically, if you bought a woman, if you owned her, could you do anything you wanted to her?"

Semyonus hung on the words.

"I don't understand," I said.

"Sexually," said Lewus. And then he repeated the word to Semyonus who nodded enthusiastically and added something.

"He does not mean with your wife, the woman you married, Eugeni. Rather, generally," said Lewus, Semyonus adding other things to be translated by Lewus. ". . . like tie them up . . . and do whatever you wanted . . . or anything you wanted . . . chain them to a bed . . . or things."

"Could or would?" I asked.

"Could," same back Semyonus's answer through Lewus.

"I suppose. I guess. There were slaves you bought for sex. And there were prostitutes. What does he mean by could?"

"Legally."

"Slaves did have rights, although magistrates who were slave owners did not pursue those rights with zeal; they pursued their own, of course. Female slaves were generally willing, and if masters did that, they usually added some coins to a peculium. I honestly cannot answer that question well. Does Semyonus have sexual affairs with nurses?"

When he heard this, Semyonus glanced nervously at the room Olava was in and then nodded back to me.

"But they are mainly for work, and if they do not wish sex, he does not ask it," said Lewus, translating.

"So too with slaves," I said. But Lewus did not translate Semyonus's response.

"What did he say?" I asked.

"He said 'oh.' "

"Which means?"

"Which means he was disappointed," said Lewus.

"What did he expect?" I asked.

"Probably the other side of his romantic coin, that which was not what he has known. Another thing. A strange thing. Something in his imagination. Perhaps a bit Roman in his entertainment, for as you have said, the arena is in the mind of the mobs."

And Lewus said this was so with his game that he played, sponsored by the schools of his country for fame and finance—the myth being that the gladiators fought for the schools instead of their own interests.

Semyonus, after asking me, through Lewus, never to let Olava know what he had asked, called her back into the room. And with this he gave me an embarrassed wink, and I winked back.

Only Olava did not have a question to ask me, for as she said:

"I will have more time than Lewus or Semyonus, and I will have many, many, many questions. And, if all works well, time to ask them. Much time. I hope. I pray."

But they insisted she ask a question, and she said most of her questions were religious, which Lewus and Semyonus would not be interested in. So she thought a moment and asked a question she said might interest her colleagues:

"Who was the most famous person you knew personally, and tell us about him."

"Most famous person," I said.

"In all Rome, outside of Domitian, of course."

"I didn't know our divinity personally," I said.

"All right, then you have no problem."

"Famous. Famous. Famous." I thought of the men I had dealt with, all the senators and tribunes and the like. I remembered incidents with them, but all I remembered was how I had calculated what they would do.

"Famous, outside of Domitian," I repeated.

Olava and Lewus nodded, Olava translating for Semyonus.

"Quintus Cornelius Fabius."

"Who?" asked Olava, looking to Lewus. Lewus shrugged.

"Never heard of him," said Lewus.

"You never heard of the phrases left over from my age, 'rich as Fabius,' 'pure Fabius,' 'I am not as Quintus Cornelius Fabius'?"

They hadn't.

"His donatives to Domitian not to seize his fortunes were as large as most fortunes," I explained.

Still, they had not heard of him. And this was possible because he had never built monuments to himself as other rich men did, rather he had spent all his time collecting more fortunes. He lived alone, somewhat like Demosthenes who had known him better than I had, his fortune and mine doing business.

Lewus and Semyonus drank, and I went to sleep alone, and Olava went to her room. In the morning, Lewus was dressed in the formal manner of his times with a cloth around his neck and his face shaven. He smelled of men's oils, and his orangish hair was combed back and neat and tonsored with grace.

He had awakened me to say good-bye. He used words identical to those of Lucius Aurelius Cotta, my patriarch, who had said good-bye to me in Domitian's palace.

"And so, brother, forever hello and good-bye."

And by that Lewus meant we had just really met each other and were saying good-bye forever.

CHAPTER XXVIII

Lewellyn Mc Cardle, Jr.,
son of Lewellyn "Slim" McCardle, Sr., Purina
Mills warehouseman, dead;
and Dottie Shanklin McCardle, resident of
Beaches Senior Citizens Home, St. Petersburg;
graduate of Texas M and C with highest honors;
holder of a Ph.D. from the University of
Chicago;
former senior geologist of Houghton Oil Corporation;
father of Cara and Tricia;
husband of Katherine Hooper McCardle;
owner of one home and two cars and small
shares of the great Houghton Corporation,
said good-bye to a friend.

"Atque in perpetuum, frater, ave atque vale," he said, quoting the famous poem of Catullus to the muscular, dark little fellow who had so changed his life. And then he embraced him that morning with spring all about them, and life coming green in the little hills. He remembered the dark ice and the still form, so long ago, less than two months ago, and how he had come alive to remind him of his education—a word which itself came from Latin, almost unchanged, "to lead out of," meaning by that to lead out of darkness, into the light, into knowledge.

He understood now, hoping it was not the great amount of alcohol he had drunk, that he too had a heritage. The very act of learning was a heritage. Before Eugeni, it was, and after Lewellyn, it was. Bound one and the same, a man was a man because he thought, and all the cheers and all the illustrious parentage could not add one whit to any of his meaning. Neither could the jeers nor a father like "Slim" McCardle take that away.

So when Lew said hello and good-bye, he was not only greeting Eugeni, whom he now knew as a brother, he was greeting himself. And while he knew he had done good in his lifetime—man needing energy—he also realized he was worth more than that. He was better than that. And this was so.

So it was good-bye, and Lew regretted one thing that morning, and it was that he had not told Eugeni how much he had enjoyed Ginger Jackson and was sorry, now that so many things were coming to a close, that he had not married her and seen what might have happened. She was his Miriamne, and he had not taken her to wife.

Lew looked back at the cabin. Eugeni stood halfway up the door, a giant of a little man. Lew saw him tap his heart, and he knew he had something to live for, whether he understood it or not. Lew had something to die for. And he was not all that sure who was luckier.

By noon, Lew was in the major Oslo television station talking freely with a television interviewer and feeling the very big lens on the camera devour him. He had not thought it was that big, or that round, and it was dark like eternity behind that glass. The drink came out in sweat under the lights, but his voice was steady. The metal chair seat bit into his fleshy thighs and he did not care.

He talked of the great future of the economies of the Scandinavian countries, especially because of the new, large deposits of oil in excess of the current ones discovered at this point.

He did not mention his friend. With a polished stick, he pointed out on a map just where the deposits were and described scientifically the earth formations under the ice that encapsulated them. He was telling the interviewer this because he wanted to live and invest in an ever-growing and more prosperous Norway. He said this with a straightforward, fresh-washed, honest face. He was retired from the oil business.

At his hotel suite, he put in a phone call to Kathy in their Austin home. It took twenty minutes for the operator to get through. Kathy was groggy. He had awakened her.

"Honey," he said, with delicious malice, "I never loved you. Banging a Yankee is like sticking it in wet cardboard. Put on the girls. C'mon. Don't delay. This is costing money. It's from Oslo, Norway. Hello, Tricia, listen, honey. You think you're some kind of radical progressive, but, sweetheart, you're just an insignificant piece of shit, and you're not all that different from your mother whom you call a pig, honey. You're the pig and the insect, and you know it. That's why you're clawing at people who do things. You never put so much as a biscuit in anybody's mouth. Put your sister on. Cara . . . hello, honey. Look, you tell that shrink to go suck. You happen to be one of the finest human beings I've ever met. Sorry I didn't get to know you better. But being responsible for someone's welfare is no way to get to know her."

"You drunk, Daddy?"

"No. Stopped drinking early this morning. I'm going to rest for a while now."

"Do you want to talk, Dad?"

"Honey, there is not a seventeen-year-old living, including you, no matter how decent you are, who can tell me about anything that matters. And this is the truth. Seventeen, especially your kind of seventeen, just hasn't been around long enough. Good-bye."

The phone was ringing as soon as he hung up. It was the long-distance operator from Riyadh, Saudi Arabia. He recognized the smooth patrician voice with one word:

"Why?"

"Hi, Jim," said Lew to the chairman of Houghton Oil.

"Why? Why? Why? Why?"

"Because," said Lew, and all he could think about was his father coming home soused, usually bleeding, and his mother running into the bedroom and locking the door and threatening to hit his father with a skillet if he opened the door, and one night his father holding a used condom in front of his face and yelling at him that his mother was a whore, and yelling at her that she should have sucked a nigger and beating up on young Lew and throwing him outside and breaking that lock on the bedroom and getting the skillet in the head, and the next morning everybody going about business as usual because it was not that unusual. And a couple of kids at North Springs Regional School knowing about that particular night, and one trying to be overly nice because of it, and Lew telling her to get her ass the hell out of his sight.

"Why?" asked James Houghton Laurie and there was no Texas in his voice—the kind of voice Lew had once thought came from clean, safe, better worlds.

" 'Cause I ain't trash," said Lew McCardle.

"Whoever said you were?" said Laurie in winded shock. "My God, whoever said you were?"

"No one," said Lew. And hung up.

CHAPTER XXIX

Dr. Semyon Fyodorovitch Petrovitch,
son of Vasily Ivanovitch Petrovitch, member of
the workers' committee, Magnitogorsk
Factory,
and Mariania Sergeyevna Petrovitch, chairman of
the workers' committee of Magnitogorsk
Factory;
member of the Communist Youth;
the Russian Academy of Sciences;
on loan to Oslo University under
the Scandinavian–Soviet Friendship
Pact,
woke up and saw the rough wood of the cabin near his head and realized it was not all a bad dream, and that the night before he had made a pact to save his patient at the risk of his own future.

In the evening, with beautiful cool Olava and the dynamic Lewus, it made so much sense. It was so good and so right the night before.

As a physician, Semyon stated, he thought any trial of the patient, or even further incarceration, might prove fatal.

While for Eugeni there were times of apparent satisfactory adjustment—a smile, a nod, an explanation with the hands moving rapidly, good active physical movement—there were others of deep dark despair. Semyon Petrovitch was not one of those who took lightly interest in, or attempts at, suicide. It was utter foolishness to dismiss these things, for the very expression of desire for death was the proof of sickness.

"Yes, I agree. More than any of you I know my patient must be active in some way. Being a specimen, to be blunt, is not conducive to mental health, and, with all honesty, Olava, you were hard on him. And I am not laying blame."

"I did not think you were," Sister Olav had said.

"To be blunt, also, he is mine. Little Eugeni is mine. I saved him. I nursed him to consciousness. And, not to take any special credit—you know I am not that sort—I did it. I brought him around. His body made it. His mind—his ego, id, soul, or whatever—did not. I am very proud of Eugeni. I join with you. But, after hearing your plan, is there any way I can do this without defying my embassy?"

"If you think your patient has a chance with all the facts out in the open for every bureaucrat to protect his job with, with every political whim washing around his discovery and resurrection, if you think he will survive, then tell everyone everything," said Lew.

"It is very risky," said Semyon.

Lew shrugged. Sister Olav remained like gracious marble. The big kitchen knife stuck up before the three of them in the wooden floor. The patient had certainly put it in there forcefully. All the motor functions had been brought to normal. Better than normal. While the incident in the kitchen had been horrifying, the skill with which Semyon's little patient had done it now gave him a guilty sense of satisfaction. But when he thought about what Lew had suggested, he shook his head.

"It can't work," said Semyon. "If it could work, I would feel obliged to join. I would join. I would lead. But can it work? Are we guaranteed success? We must ask ourselves why send more ruined lives into a disaster, eh?"

"Why won't it work?" asked Lew.

"You should remember, Lewus," said Sister Olav, "that Semyonus's government feels itself in a state of constant siege and has imposed severe penalties for what might be considered lesser crimes in our countries. You can't expect Semyonus to go riding off like some knight on a horse. You have your reasons for what you do. Perhaps he has reasons why he is afraid. Maybe this is too big for him."

Semyon had leaned forward at this point and steadfastly announced that he was willing to take the risk. The risk was not the problem. All life was risk, he said.

"The problem is, Lew, they already know Eugeni is a gladiator whom I brought to total function from a frozen state. They know that, at my embassy."

"How do they know that?" asked Lew.

"Because I told them."

"How did you know that?"

"Because I know. Because I did it."

"Did you? Who told you he was Roman?"

"I listen. I read the reports. I observe."

"I know you're fluent in several languages, Semyon. Is Latin one of them? Specifically, classical Latin?"

"No," said Semyon, and he was beginning to understand.

"I told you. Sister Olav told you. And by the time you must do what you must do, I will have made everything you say most believable."

"And so will I," said Sister Olava.

"They will think of you as a liability, not a criminal," said Lew. "And I think if we brought Eugeni back into this conversation, he would tell you they would not inflict a severe punishment on you because it would do them no good. Your government has its own self-interest. It's not your parents. It's not in the punishment business to improve your attitude, Semyon."

"I will do it, if you will do it. He is my patient, you know," Semyon had said.

And on that they had another glass of wine, and of course late into the night he and Lew drank and sang, and now Semyon was awake, looking at the grains in the wood near his pillow, his mouth dry, and his body drained. He looked very closely at the wood, noticing even the fibers, without moving his head.

The only thing he thought at that moment was that if Dr. Lewellyn McCardle had not left yet, then that would mean everything was off, and there was no obligation for Semyon to do whatever he had to do. He could phone his embassy and tell the entire truth. He hadn't done anything wrong. Yet.

And with that thought, he was able to move out of his bed quickly.

Lew was not in the main room. The patient in clean clothes, those dark, penetrating eyes so sad, sat silently on a footstool, so still, so stonelike.

"Lewus. Lewus," called out Semyon Petrovitch, but there was no answer.

The patient pointed to the door. Semyon saw through the window that the car was gone. The American was going to do it. Just as he said he would, he was going to do it.

Dr. Semyon Petrovitch sighed. All right, he thought, he is going to do it. And if he does it, then I will do what I promised.

And it was still possible the American would show cowardice.

On that bit of hope, Semyon Petrovitch prepared breakfast. The patient watched the eggs boil and made big circular motions with his hands, apparently indicating big. Dr. Petrovitch put three, then four eggs, into the boiling water, and when the patient shook his head, Dr. Petrovitch realized he referred to the size of the egg and not a desire for more.

The patient was amazed by the cans and recognized pictures on the labels of cans. He also wanted to sniff bottles, and he opened jars.

Thus Semyon found himself mashing sardines, clam broth, a pepper liquid that was red, garlic powder into what had to be a rancid paste.

"Garum. Garum," said the patient. He poured it over his eggs and made exaggerated lip-smacking sounds to show he was pleased. Dr. Petrovitch caught its odor and, nauseated, offered his own breakfast eggs, which the patient ate. Petrovitch ate crackers and fruit.

Sister Olav slept, and for such a beautiful woman, snored like dive bombers racing through flak. Semyon waited for her to awake.

He knew the digestive tract that was receiving the food, knew the kidneys, and how they processed out poisonous elements, knew the liver, and knew the heart, and he had put that blood into that body so that it could manufacture its own blood when it was ready.

He had taken that body out of its almost death, perhaps the

closest to death, element by element. And in that process was the sum total of knowledge of his civilization in medicine.

Even twenty years before, man did not possess this knowledge, and one hundred years before there was not even the suspicion of all that Semyon Petrovitch had accomplished. He had done it. His civilization had done it.

Its scientists had done it. The Russian people had done it. From the storming of the Winter Palace to the defeat of the White armies in Siberia, the Russian people had done it. For Semyon Petrovitch would have shoveled manure, like his grandfather, steaming manure on cold days; he would have shoveled until his life had been shoveled into the ground for the leisure time of the aristocracy, were it not for the Communist party, Semyon was sure.

In that patient eating away to end all famine was the victory of the Russian people combined with the scientific achievements of the West and even the East and possibly some early discoveries in the patient's very own time. Knowledge belonged to everyone.

Semyon heard mumblings from Sister Olav's room and wondered whom she was talking to. When he opened the door a crack, he saw her on her knees, praying. He shut the door and listened to her clean her face and prepare herself for the day. She had been beautiful praying, too.

She said good morning to the patient and to Semyon, both nodding like young boys.

"Well, so. Today is the day," she said.

"Yes," said Semyon. "Very much."

"Should we turn on the television to see if Lewus has done his part?"

"It might be a shock to the patient. Let's wait."

"For what?"

"Wait. Wait to phone. In ten minutes, not now. Who knows when he will appear on television, if everything has worked out?" said Semyon.

"Good," said Sister Olav.

The patient was talking a mile a minute, and Semyon was glad to hear him and Sister Olav talk. They could talk all day. He would wait. He would wait happily.

The probabilities were not that bad, Semyon knew. They were

not going to waste his talent, and all that would probably happen would be going home to his wife, who was more dead to him living than a Hebrew slave was in the mind of the patient, the living mind carrying a love nineteen hundred years, undiminished. The body of that woman had been totally recycled into this earth's system, yet she was individual and alive, while Semyon's wife's organs functioned perfectly, and all Semyon remembered clearly was how the sweat collected on a mole adjacent to her left ear when she fornicated in the summer.

But most of all, Semyon remembered his wife whining. She was a symphony of whines. Aggressive whines, wheedling whines, whining whines, demanding whines, crying whines.

The woman whined when she asked for salt at breakfast!

So why was he afraid? Tedium and annoyance, he told himself. And in return for what? For himself, he said. And he knew he was right.

Still, it was frightening.

"Well," said Sister Olav. "Shall I phone the television studio?"

"Why not?" said Semyon, and there was a flare to his answer, a cockiness of bold spirit. And it was entirely fraudulent.

He watched the patient absorbing all the details of Sister Olav dialing a telephone. She talked to him as she did so. He appeared deeply impressed. But these moments of awareness, of healthy appetite, Dr. Petrovitch knew, could be replaced in an instant with the patient seeking his own death.

Sister Olav asked questions of the station, waited, asked more questions, then hung up.

"He did it," she said.

"Oh," said Semyon. "Well. All right. That's it. I will go now into the nearby town. Now. I will do it now."

"Do you know what to say?" Sister Olav asked.

"Yes. Did Lew give you money for everything?"

"Yes."

"Well. That's it," he said.

"That's it," she said.

"I guess I should go now," he said, even now more enamored of her exquisite pale beauty, knowing that if he touched her, he would again be shamed, knowing more that now he was afraid of the future for himself.

"What I am doing is not against the Soviet people or the party, even though they will think that, perhaps. But I want you to know it. This is consonant with building socialism in the best sense. I want you to know that."

"It is a good ideal. As old as the Hippocratic oath," she said. "Eugeni will know, too."

"Yes. Well, I guess the time has come."

"They won't throw you in a prison or concentration camp, will they?"

"No. No. Not at all. Those are the old days. They exaggerate. I am just going home. That's all. I am a doctor. I represent the sweat and the energy of the Soviet people. In their name I do this," and he knew that if he didn't leave that moment, if he stopped for anything, he would not be able to walk out the door, but would break down, phoning his embassy with everything.

He felt her hand on his arm as he reached the door. She pulled him to herself and kissed him on the cheek. And likewise he bent down and kissed her on the cheek also, holding himself back, stiff and gallant.

"You are a beautiful man, Semyon Petrovitch," she said. And she smiled. "God bless you."

"Madame," he said, as though he were some British gentleman out for an afternoon's trot, "it has been my pleasure and my joy. And tell the patient, we will some day regularly achieve suspending animation. What was achieved by accident shall be done on purpose by us."

"He will respect the Soviet Union. I will not defame your system to him."

"No. Us. The Soviet Union. America. Norway. Africa. Asia. We of the twentieth century shall conquer this thing."

He didn't know why he did it, and he felt very foolish, but he had already talked in such a grandiose manner, and to kiss Sister Olav's hand seemed most natural. He saw the Roman smile, and in that recognition of the mind—using the eyesight first—and the reaction of the smile, that smile on that face reminded Dr. Semyon Fyodor Petrovitch that he had done it. He had brought it to life. Yes, life.

He kept his own brave smile on his face long after he could be seen from the house as he walked with brisk stride and purposeful resolution. He waved without looking back at the cabin, and when he was on the neat, paved road, behind a big stand of pine, he vomited up his breakfast and tried to spit the taste of his bile and fear out of his mouth.

It did not go. So he sat a while, on the ground, seeing how neat this countryside was, how naturally manicured it was, and realized that these people were in advance of his own country materially because it took energy and time, which was money, to make roads neat.

But he was not Norwegian. He was Russian. So why did he fear to go home? Home was not what made him frightened. Any possible punishment, which rationally had its limits, did not make him frightened.

What sent weakness through his belly that morning was that Semyon Petrovitch was not a good liar. He had early on in life realized this by being caught so often and had abandoned lying. Especially when the truth seemed always to work out better. It was definitely easier. He had one cigarette left, and he smoked it. A car stopped to offer him a ride. He refused it.

He reminded himself of what Lew, the American, who generally seemed to know what was going on, said. Semyon's authorities would not care that he was lying; it was not in their self-interest to detect him in a lie.

"Now, Semyon," he said to himself, scolding as his father had scolded. "They are simple lies. You will do it well. Don't worry. They are simple and they will work."

He remembered what Lew had said and how clear it was and how rational it was. Very logical.

The American had told him there were only three diversions from the truth. One, that the patient suffered a deep gash across the nose during the killing in the kitchen; two, he was five feet five and a half; and three, Sister Olav had left with Lew.

"But if we are going to misdirect, why not describe the patient as six feet tall? And blond?"

"Because there were enough people who saw him. We could never get away with that. We will get away with this. They will look for a man with a scar, traveling alone, of just about normal size. They will think Sister Olav has left to meet me, stricken with love, my love partner, who of course was in on deceiving you.

It will work because it is just the kind of thing they know. It is what they will believe. You only have to worry as if you were trying to convince them of grace, not sin."

"I am surprised at those words," said Sister Olav. "From you."

"Yes, aren't you?" said Lew angrily.

"I'm sorry," said Sister Olav. "I apologize."

So the lies were simple. And they would work, and there was no reason for Semyon to keep delaying on the side of the road.

So he continued walking, and as he approached town he haunted himself with improbable variations of what could happen and go wrong, and when he phoned his embassy in Oslo from a store in the town, he was told to wait.

By the time the car from the embassy arrived in the town, Semyon was numb with fear and could hardly move, and he wondered if he could even remember the three lies. There would be many times he would have to tell them, he knew. He didn't want them to vary.

An older man, with very thick glasses and a very bookish attitude, was the first from his embassy to reach him. He drove up with two others and quickly asked him what had happened, and Semyon started at the beginning, but the man wanted to know what had happened in the hospital with the killing.

Semyon, smoking continuously even though his throat couldn't take much more, described the killing in the kitchen, answered as to why the match was set up, and was told the story didn't make sense.

"Dr. Petrovitch, that is blatantly stupid," said the man in Russian. And Semyon knew he had been met by a security officer, KGB. Semyon started to fall over his words, but the man insisted on details about what happened after the killing. Where did they find the patient? Was the knife bloody? Why did they let him keep the weapon? They all seemed to get along. And he did not speak the language of the patient, correct?

Semyon nodded, Semyon explained, Semyon tried to follow where the man was leading. He was taken to the embassy compound and not allowed to change or shave.

"You will tell the Norwegian police what you have told me, but leave out what the American and the nun told you about the patient you saved. That is too stupid of you even to mention."

The Norwegian police inspector was somewhat softer and more conciliatory, but got around to basically the same questions. And a few others.

"Five feet five and a half. Wasn't your patient shorter?"

"No," said Petrovitch, feeling as though electricity ripped through his flesh. They know, he thought. They know everything. They'll find out everything. They know. You can't fool them.

"We've heard from people at the hospital that the man we're looking for is five feet two, five feet three or so."

"No," said Petrovitch. He did not breathe.

"Yes. Of course. Standing next to the six feet three and one-half inch American, he would look shorter. That's logical. He would look like a midget by comparison. And the nun, a citizen of our country, was five feet eight, making him look even shorter, because one expects women to be shorter. Yes."

"A point," said Petrovitch, breathing again. "Good point."

"It's important that we know exactly how tall he is. We need a good description. And for that we thank you. He is dangerous."

There were other questions.

Had Semyon noticed any affection between Dr. Lewellyn McCardle and the nun, Sister Olav?

Semyon thought a moment and then remembered what Lew had cautioned. Tell the truth except for the key lies.

"No. I was not aware they were having an affair. Were they?"

The Norwegian inspector looked to the Russian security officer.

"According to my colleague here, you said Sister Olav left with Dr. McCardle."

"I said they were not there when I woke up."

"The patient was there, correct?"

"Yes."

"We found the cabin," said the inspector. "By the description my colleague and member of your embassy gave us, we found the cabin almost immediately. The phone was working. Why didn't you use it, instead of walking away?"

"I didn't think. I didn't know. I just fled."

"Yes. I can see that. Do you know what kind of car the patient fled in?"

"No. I just left him there. You didn't find anyone?"

"Not yet."

"You should ask the American. He knows. Dr. McCardle knows everything."

"We are certain of that. We believe he was involved in some swindle to do with oil exploration. It went awry and he shot himself this afternoon before we could talk to him. Was he despondent?"

"He was drinking heavily."

"That often happens to alcoholics. Were you aware that he had a serious drinking problem?"

"No. I knew he drank heavily."

"His company said he had to be relieved of duty, sort of stricken from the rolls, so to speak, because he had become unreliable. They had hoped he would be able to effect his cure while assigned to a public service project."

"I don't understand politics," said Dr. Petrovitch.

"Not politics. Facts," said the inspector.

"Oh," said Dr. Petrovitch.

"It is a shame you had to be sucked into this, doctor, but on behalf of my government, let me thank you for your wholehearted cooperation."

Semyon offered to shake hands and then realized his were very wet with perspiration. He also realized that he had not been told by Lew how quickly Sister Olav and the little patient would leave after he was gone, or how. Or where they were going in order to help the patient's recovery, to break the depression, and ultimately to enable him to realize what had happened.

They were gone. Both of them. From his life. With just as much finality as Lew was gone. The American had acted much like a poultice, sucking all the evil humors to his own self. With his life. The least Semyon could do was to endure now whatever the bureaucracy would do to what they considered an innocent fool. It came quickly from a minor diplomatic officer.

Dr. Petrovitch was sourly told he had compromised the embassy itself. The embassy did not consider him helpful. There was a time, he was told, that he helped foster the friendly presence of the Union of Soviet Socialist Republics here in Norway by his cooperative work, sharing the advancement of Soviet science with a friendly nation.

Now, this was not the case.

Did Dr. Petrovitch realize the significance of what had happened? This asked by a somber, resolute, young assistant deputy consul for embassy affairs. Did he?

Dr. Petrovitch shrugged, gathering back his dignity.

"No. I do not know," he said.

"Does it help to know the victim was Ferdinand d'Ouelette?"

Dr. Petrovitch shrugged.

"The second best man with foil in the world is Anastas Boreskian," said the assistant deputy consul for embassy affairs.

"Yes?"

"You haven't heard of the name?"

"No. That is not a sport I am interested in."

"Well, one of our citizens has just gotten himself associated with the murder of the best fencer in the world. Now do you understand the significance of what you have allowed yourself to be duped into? Yes?"

"I understand that I have spent forty-two years avoiding the slime of politics, and you, son, reaffirm my basic decision."

"You know we cannot afford to leave you here to go wandering around like a trusted and responsible citizen. You know that, of course," said the young man with his little triumph. "But in case you don't understand the significance of what has happened, let me tell you that the sum total of your work is to add a slight taint to a Soviet athlete when he wins his rightful place at the next Olympics. People will forever wonder if Boreskian would ever have been able to honestly defeat d'Ouelette."

Semyon Petrovitch asked the young man if there was anything else he wanted.

No, he was told, there was nothing else.

"Then take some vitamin C, you're coming down with a cold," said Dr. Petrovitch.

"Now, wait a minute," snorted the assistant deputy consul for embassy affairs.

"Stick out your tongue," said Dr. Petrovitch, and when the young man did so, Semyon Petrovitch, physician, knew everything would be all right. He was still a doctor, and he would be needed.

The KGB officer understood the significance of what had happened. This only went to show the inevitable results of keeping a limited security staff in a country designated "nonstrategic." With a limited staff, citizens like Dr. Semyon Petrovitch could be lured by the wiles of almost any foreigner, and even worse could happen unless the embassy staff at Oslo were brought up to the comparable French or British operation.

Dr. Petrovitch was going home.

At Ringerike, at the Dominican convent, the mother superior heard that Sister Olav might never be coming back, that there was evidence she might have been involved romantically with an alcoholic swindler, now dead. And she was off, pardon the expression, Mother Superior, to God knew where.

When the priest came the next morning to say Mass, the mother superior prayed for Sister Olav, whom she always believed had a vocation elsewhere outside the convent.

When the sad happening was discussed with the office of the metropolitan, she said she believed not that Sister Olav had been involved in some unpleasantness or evil; rather, she felt, Sister Olav had realized possibly some calling that none of them at this time understood. And that everything would some day be clear.

"Considering the facts, Mother Superior," said a brother working at the metropolitan's office, "that seems a bit too much to hope for."

"Nothing on this earth is too much to hope for," said the mother superior.

CHAPTER XXX

Olava watched Semyonus disappear, then looked at the timepiece on her wrist. And counted. She counted to two hundred, and I could tell it was to force herself to slow down. She wanted to make sure she was not rushing.

At two hundred, she told me to put on fresh clothes and take only a few things. I put on a dark shirt and a bright pair of pants, but when Olava saw this she said the color combination would attract attention.

She selected a shirt and a pair of pants, the house being stocked with things to fit me, although most of them were white.

"Do you have shoes for me?" I asked, for I had worn sandals and I had not seen others wear them, only the complicated lacing boots that ended at the ankles. I had been told that every time someone wanted to put on these boots he had to loosen the thongs, and then tighten them and then tie them. Each time a person had to do this, on both feet.

"No. No. Use the sandals you've been using."

"That will not cause notice?"

"No. No. Some people wear them today."

"Why are we running?"

"To go to a better place, Eugeni. Hurry. Get dressed."

"No, woman. There is no place I want to go. I have no place. I have no place. You record everything and hear nothing. Don't you listen?"

"Lewus has sacrificed his career for you and maybe more. Semyonus is giving up his research here for you. For them, Eugeni, come. Get ready."

"If they suffer for me, then I will do the same for them. I will cut my leg. I will bang my head against that wall. I will not eat. Or better yet, in their honor I shall eat things I despise. I shall eat raw meat for them. I will not get ready."

"Eugeni, please."

"No. I have promised only not to take my own life right away."

"I beg."

"Do so."

"If we don't run, we will never see Rome."

"We are going to Rome?"

"Yes."

"I saw those pictures. There has been some damage."

"Eugeni!"

"I will go. But there is no one there I know. Is there? There couldn't be, could there?"

"No, Eugeni. Turn away. I've got to dress," she said. "At least let me close the door."

"You are dressed," I said.

"In other clothes. I want to dress in privacy. Give me privacy."

Her black robe, bunched in handfuls, paused at her ankles that were clothed in white linen. I did not move, nor did I let her close the door.

She turned her back and disrobed anyhow, protecting her breasts and vagina from my sight, as though a gaze could contaminate. Her undergarments, too, were a latticework of webbing and strapping. But they were plain.

She took the binding from her head, showing choppy pale white hair cut short. Over her shoulder she glanced at me.

"I don't have time to ask you why you are doing this," she said.

"I lust for your body, Olava."

"I don't think so, Eugeni."

"You do not think you are desirable?"

"You are working on me as though I were on sand with you."

"I have no sword," I said. But she was right. She dressed hurriedly, in men's leggings, and a man's shirt, although she made no effort to hide her womanness.

We left all the machines, and all the food, and everything that was in that small house without lock or guard, and together we went in the opposite direction from where Semyonus had so stiffly walked.

There was an automobile for us on the side of the soft, black road, not stone at all, even here in the hinterland of the north country where stone would wear better, I assumed. The automobile had probably been sent here or driven here previously by Lewus.

The key, without which the car would not start, was tucked under a simple visor that was used to shield the eyes from the sun. Olava had with her a packet the size of a small shield. She handed me a very small book. Inside was my picture, a machine-made product, called a photograph.

This was a document nation-states issued to their citizens to control their passage. Lewus had this one for me for a while. According to Olava, it was his plan, at one point, to get me to flee with this passport out of the country, if need be. Not a serious plan. It was at a time before the match in the kitchen.

Remembering this and their reaction I said: "Murder. You have just committed murder."

"I didn't hit anyone with this car," she said.

"You must have hit a bug. Is that not murder? If a performance is murder, then hitting a bug might be murder too."

"It's not."

"Oh."

"And you know it's not, Eugeni."

"I do."

Her shirt was a checkered jumble of colored lines in an insane, disorganized pattern, made more disordered by the straightness of the line. It was a design of one of the Briton tribes. I had been matched with Britons, or at least everyone thought they were Britons. The problem with Britons had been making them matter, I told Olava, but she was so intent on steering our automobile that she did not fall on this bone, as she normally did.

"Are those pictures on our papers of passage used to find people?"

"Yes."

"Then we may have troubles."

"Or not. Lewus has performed a deception that should work. Like you for your family. Most of the troubles will fall on him, but they will also look for the wrong people."

"You didn't trust Semyonus; that's why we waited, yes?"

"He's already giving up an awful lot. Why put more of a burden on him than he can bear?"

"I will dedicate my evening meal to Semyonus by eating stones."

"You who caused perhaps the greatest riot in all history, in all history . . ."

"Hail the god History."

"You who caused what might have been the greatest riot in the history of the city, offering up everything you owned for your mother who was not alive."

"Ah, you will talk to me."

"I am explaining why you should at least respect Lewus and Semyonus and live for them and yourself. Your life has been paid for, Eugeni."

"To do what?"

"To learn. To understand this great thing they have done. To . . . I am not sure."

"I most certainly will die for them because they have made my second passing necessary. Two deaths in a lifetime is more than one should die."

"You don't think of it as a second lifetime?"

"I had lived my life with plans for a single one. I would say, looking back on it now . . ." And when I thought of Miriamne and Petronius, and the peristilium, the daily negotiations in my atrium, and even the cautious preparations for the arena, I became woefully sad and watched the road come up beneath us, and come up beneath us, and come up beneath us.

Olava now made arrangements to change automobiles, and with that I asked her if she also did not trust Lewus.

"For a virgin, you have much stealth."

"Lewus told me to do this. He is your friend."

"I like him. I wished he could have stayed, and you would have done what he did, whatever that was."

"I understand, Eugeni. You shared a commonality."

"I liked him."

"Yes. I heard."

"Hear? No. You must live to hear other humans. You don't live. You have taken virginity and made it into a wall."

"I have made vows, Eugeni, that require—"

"I knew virgins," I yelled at her stone-still head. "I knew virgins. They had property. They had concerns. They had families. They had fears. I knew vestals. They were at the games. They were people."

"I am steering, Eugeni," she said.

"At this moment," I said, meaning while she was operating the automobile, now; later she would not be, and her attitude would yet remain the same.

Her jaw muscles twitched now. When she brushed her hands off on her leggings, I saw her hands were perspiring. At the height of this anxiety in her, she did a strange thing. She smiled at me as though this were a simple, joyous day.

At one shop she bought dresses. She put on cosmetics, clumsily. To this she added a perfume, like a sow's afterbirth rotting in the sun. Then she asked if I was hungry, and further asked why I laughed at the question. Apparently, she was attractive to these people, for the men gave her smiling stares.

There was a boat we took, larger than any I had ever seen, that carried us and many other automobiles over to Germany. When we were in Germany, she told me she had greatly feared being captured. But her fear did not leave, rather the real gnawing thing that sapped the marrow from her bone continued through the day. And we stayed at a hostel, Germany having been built up by this age with all manner of roads and the most modern of these inventions. And now, every German one saw, almost, was washed quite clean. They would no more think of covering themselves with grease than a Roman would.

When the door shut behind us, Olava selected a chair to sleep in. I refused. She was bigger, and I did not like beds anyway. She was tired. In her eyes and her body, she was spent.

I had seen this tiredness before. It came after an honest match, and a hard one, where the person has gone farther than they ever suspected they could.

Her blue eyes looked into the nowhere. I found the switch for the light and turned it off by myself. I curled up in the chair and fell asleep.

I awakened in the dark, and suddenly I didn't know where I was, and I was calling for a slave to bring a lamp.

"No slaves, Eugeni. This is the new time." It was Olava, and she was crying. That was what had awakened me.

Grave and stalwart—like the Roman tribune in a woman's body, like the Romans thought all tribunes were, while only the best were—this hard person, when she broke, broke like stone into so many little, helpless pieces, without give or bend in any of them.

I could not find the light, but I found Olava. She was in the clothes and in the spot I had left her when I put out the lights. Her face was wet, her hands were cold. She was trembling as though no warmth could cut this shield of the north pain. I grabbed her massive shoulders and held. I squeezed until she said it hurt, and then my arms eased their hold.

"Woman, we are alone. And we are lost," I said in the blackness, somewhere in Germany, many centuries beyond where I could help anyone.

"I prayed last night. And when I started to pray, Eugeni, I could not. I have sinned, but I did not know what else to do. There was nothing else I could do. I had to go with you. I have to escort you. You have no one else. Lewus is gone, you know. He is dead. We print things in writing of events of the day. I saw that this evening. He is dead."

"Is that what frightens you?"

"No."

"What frightens you?"

"I am not sure anymore. I knew before what the dangers were to my soul, which is my spirit. I love my God, Eugeni. In Him is my future, and I no longer know the way to Him. I am not sure of things anymore."

"You mean, Olava, this is the first time you have been unsure in your life?"

"Yes. As bad as this. Yes. This is the first time. I could always reason things out. I reasoned out God, too."

She said she had joined her cult in a special way, vowing obedience and chastity and poverty, these things being given up now for a greater reward later, gifts to her god and to herself.

This was her Christian sect, an outgrowth of the one that had come to Rome in my time. Today there were many Christian sects.

She had left her order of virgins without permission because she felt an obligation to help me, because this was what she thought her god wanted. But now she was not sure anymore, and she was alone and deeply troubled.

My arms hurt from holding such a large person, but when I released, I felt her gasp.

"Eugeni, hold me. Hold me. Please. Do not let me go. I will give you anything. Do anything. Please hold me. I need you. Please." Her voice was weak and tender.

And I held her, and I felt myself wanting her in a man's way to a woman.

We were quiet there in the dark, and I kissed her shorn hair, like I used to kiss Petronius' when he was very young.

"I don't know what I feel," she said.

"You feel nothing, woman. It will pass. May I let go?"

"Not yet. In a while."

"Let me tell you how Miriamne and I performed the ceremony of marriage," I said.

"Good. But don't let go."

"I can't hold you much longer, woman."

"A while."

"We ate bread and drank wine and promised fidelity to each other."

"Yes?"

"Aren't you interested?"

"Yes. Did anyone touch the bread first?"

"Glad you asked, woman. Yes. It was an important thing that bread. Holy it was, and one of her Jewish priests held the bread and made it holy."

"What did he say?"

"Holy words."

"What words?" said Olava.

"What words?" Olava whispered again, weakly. She was limp. I was not.

"Words."

"Yes. Oh. What was his name?"

"Whose?"

"The priest's name? Anyone's name. Name me anything."

"I don't know. The man didn't have a sesterce to his name. He wore rags. I did it for Miriamne. She wanted this ceremony. I did it as a favor."

"Did he say 'this is my body, this is my blood,' did he say that?"

"I don't know. The man was a beggar. He was not a real priest, Olava, not really. He had been a fisherman in Judea."

Olava stiffened and jumped up, as though new life breathed into her veins. She moved with such force I was knocked backward onto the soft, high bed. The lights came on with such glaring I could not see. My eyes hurt and I covered them, but Olava was on me with questions before I could even see. Naturally, my desire went, like a punctured wineskin.

"What was his name? What did he look like? What did he say? What did he do? Where did he live? Who were his friends?"

"Wait. Wait. My eyes hurt."

"Tell me."

"In a moment, woman. In a moment. My eyes hurt. I hear you are back and healthy, being your same unpleasant self."

"Talk."

"I am Lucius Aurelius Eugenianus, barbarian. You will treat me with respect."

"You didn't even know Juvenal who lived at your time, and you expect me to respect you."

"I may have owned Juvenal."

"You couldn't. He wasn't a slave."

"He was so important, I was not sure who he was."

"You were so ignorant you were not sure who he was."

"I could read. My mother was Greek. That village taught me to read even before I bought scholars. I had many scholars, and historians like yourself, although they knew manners. So did your Peter."

At that she gasped, covering her mouth. Her cosmetics were in colorful disarray across her face, having been spread by tear and hand. Her clothes were rumpled and her hair a mess of white yellow thatching.

People in other rooms yelled at us, and Olava lowered her voice. I did too.

"Peter?" she whispered, leaning forward, her big, pale, bony hands clasped anxiously in front of her chest. Both our passions had gone, and she was a worthy match of wits and will.

"The priest. The Jew."

"Was he one of the original followers of Jesus, this Peter? You see, it is important that I know. Important to me and my faith and history, too. We look to him as our first chief priest."

"All of you?"

"In our sect. We believe God has taken him unto himself as a special person, called a saint."

"Then it must have been another Peter. The Peter who performed the ceremony was nothing unusual. A very common man. But I married Miriamne, nevertheless, in her ceremony. The important official one came later. It didn't matter."

"What do you remember about this Peter?"

"He was nice."

"In what way?"

"He was respectful."

"In what way?"

"In every way. He was in the home of Lucius Aurelius Eugenianus. And he knew it."

"What did he look like?"

"Like a fisherman, although this one had not fished for many years. I gave him a donative of two or three sesterces. He was overjoyed. It was more than he deserved, but I loved Miriamne."

"What did he say?"

"He said I was a fitting tribute in my sword and manhood to his god."

"He didn't say that."

"You're right. A priest of Apollo said that. But so what? If there are so many people who believe, we can say whatever we want. But, woman, the Peter I know of could not have been your chief priest."

"Why?"

"It is better that you don't know in case he was the Peter."

"Eugeni, I want to know." She was firm on this, this formidable woman.

"All right, but I give you one moment to take back the question. You won't like the answer. Do you still want to hear?"

"Yes," she said.

"He was executed like a common criminal. Upside down." At this she let out a shriek of laughter and clapped her hands in joy.

"That was our Peter. He was crucified. Our first father of our church. I think it was. That was how he died. You see, we value giving up things for our God. He gave his life."

"Better the blood of a cow or a pig, woman. I don't like your god who asks those sacrifices."

"What about a legionnaire sacrificing his life for Rome?"

"The legions got paid, and they got paid regularly. Why do you think they worked so well, woman?"

"There was honor, too. You can't tell me there wasn't, Eugeni."

"Oh, yes. Some people cast away their one life for honor, some for drink, but most because they do not think they can die. Yes, there was honor. But it is the most specious of arguments that tries to justify one stupidity with the fact that there is a worse one."

She laughed at this, quite broadly.

"There were even people," I said, "who would die for history. Now what sort of a judge is history when your first priest is remembered, and Lucius Aurelius Eugenianus is not? Despite the decree and everything, I should have been remembered, and that very ordinary man should not have been."

"I will not argue that with you . . . for now. But you have shown honor. There on the bed where you sit. You showed it. You did not take me because you knew of my vows, and for that, Eugeni, thank you."

"I did not take you because of how you felt about your vows. Not because of your vows, which I think are stupid. I think a copulation would do you wonders. Many copulations. And often."

"Perhaps for my body but not me."

"Intelligence is like a sword, but more often people who have it fall on it. Would you most graciously tell me the difference between your body and you? How have you separated yourself from your body?"

On this we argued late into the dawn, with occasional demands from people in adjoining rooms for quiet.

We were both very tired when we heard people awakening near us through the very thin walls. One banged on the door, and I got my blade, the one I had performed with. Olava yelled back in a begging tone, and finally the man left. Olava had been afraid of what might happen to him, if he successfully carried out what obviously were threats to break down the door.

We turned out the lights again, but now shafts of sun came

through the drapery. It was dark, but not completely dark. As I fell asleep, I hoped I would remember to ask why they built the rooms with openings to the street, when it was so obvious to any rational person that they had to cover them again. I longed for a couch in which I would awaken and see the pool of the peristilium again and hear the slaves working easily in the morning trying to be quiet so as not to wake me.

I thought I heard a slave bang a pot—one of those noisy accidents Miriamne arranged when she did not want to be responsible for awakening me. But it was a horn. The kind they used in automobiles. And I went to sleep with those noises coming into the little sealed room lacking the tiniest grace of plants or water and my friend Olava snoring like gravel avalanches through the caves of Dacia.

Germany was now highly civilized, one could tell from the roads. The Germans had recently waged wars against neighbors simultaneously and lost, the country being divided into two parts now, we driving south in the western part.

The noise was so bad from so many cars in one gigantic German city, I had thought I heard Olava say these people had thrown millions of others into ovens. Concentrating on driving, she further confused me by saying it was not some device of war, but rather a national effort to annihilate a people.

"To take their land?"

"No. They had no land. Quiet, this is difficult."

"So are you."

"Must you always contend?"

"Rather than surrender to you?"

"You're worse than my brothers. Quiet," she said.

From the snatches, I gathered they accused a people of all manner of evil, and then systematically, yes, millions, killed them. And this to eliminate them, the purpose being elimination. If I heard correctly.

"They didn't eat them?"

"Cannibalism up here has been gone many centuries. Quiet. I am trying to read the signs."

Two days we crossed the land of the Germans, from north to south. If we had taken the exact route of my march going backwards across it, I would not have recognized a bit of it.

Even the forests were neat. They had built cities here and roads, and all manner of civilized things. They had come a long way. Thus time had shown to be a lie the Roman contention that the German was a happy, brave, but wild person, unable to accept discipline and too emotional for grave matters.

This of course was as much nonsense many centuries ago as it was now. It is not the blood in a man's veins that counts, it is what he does with it.

Those born high like to contend their prominence reflects some natural law like horses running or birds flying, just as those born low often like to think of wealth and fame as something dishonestly gotten; the former establishing the justice of his good fortune, the latter an excuse for his bad.

The Helvetians were now bankers and famous around the world for it. We passed through their land, too, and then into Italy, once again unified under Rome, but no longer with power. But there was another change. We drove through a tunnel into Italy where legions used to guard each pass in these mountains—each pass having its own legion to keep invaders out. An open tunnel. No legionnaire, just normal custodes checking people's automobiles.

"Hannibal had to march over," said Olava. "Do you know of Hannibal?"

"Yes. I am no fool. He was a Carthaginian. He invaded Italy down into Latium, but couldn't get the other cities to join him in enough number. He needed another big battle to get the cities to side with him, but Quintus Fabius, the delayer, wouldn't give him one, and eventually he went back to Carthage and was defeated there."

"Very good, you show great strength in some areas."

"We did Hannibal once. We had gladiators on elephants fight men on foot. It was very nice and no one was charged with murdering an elephant."

"Did you participate?"

"Yes, after. In a single match, against Hannibal's descendant, who had vowed to defeat Rome's Eugeni, whose ancestor had died swearing that, while his meager body might be crushed under Carthaginian elephant hoofs, lo, Roman blood could never be crushed, and challenging with his dying words to a single match, descendant to descendant."

"That is utterly ridiculous, Eugeni."

"You haven't heard it all."

"I don't want to hear it all."

"You ask me about this poet and that poet and this historian and that historian, of whom I have only the scantiest knowledge, but what I really do know about, what I was good at, what I understood, you show no interest in."

"Other things are more important to our civilization."

"Yes. Jewish beggars, historians you could own for less gold than would fill a cup. The garbage of Rome. It is not that Peter was important."

"He was," said Olava stoutly.

"Let me finish. It was not that Peter was so important, but that your cult is today. People do not magnify the significance of their ancestors because the ancestors are important, but because *they* are. Would Peter be important if your cult were not big?"

"Our size is the proof of Peter's importance."

"Well, I liked him."

"Did you? That's nice of you. So did God. The great Lucius Aurelius Eugenianus liked Saint Peter, liked Peter the Fisherman."

"At the time I liked him, he was not as popular as you say he is today," I said. "When I liked him, he needed friends."

"Where were you at his execution?"

"Safely, prudently, and intelligently at home with Miriamne. And if Peter had been as prudent, he would have been lying on a couch instead of nailed upside down to two boards."

"How did his execution happen? What were the facts surrounding it?"

"I don't know. There was political turmoil, and they were giving games out of everyone's treasury. Four times I was matched that year, and they would have forced me into a hundred if they could. One match, I didn't even know my opponent until I was on the sand. And he was good, and people started booing."

"Why was that?"

"You care about the arena?"

"Yes."

"Good. Because a real match, one in which men are feinting and judging and looking for an advantage and trying not to give one, is quite boring. And it is too quick for the eye in a big arena. You can have a real and good match, but you need an audience equal to it, do you understand?"

"Yes. I think I do," she said. Her short hair was now combed in a perky manner, and her cosmetics were more subdued. She still had her hard, nervous drive, but that would remain until, if ever, she decided to release her sexual juices. Still she was beautiful, if the looks she got from men were any gauge.

"Now I have good news for you, Olava. I have been saving it. I did the *Aeneid,* the poem you love so much."

She turned from her driving, even as the automobile went forward.

"You did what?" she asked, shocked, her face confused yet verging on anger.

"I did the *Aeneid.* I was not going to tell you, but since we are establishing something here, I will allow it. Yes. I did the *Aeneid.*"

"I didn't know it was made into some form of play, or that you were an actor."

"An actor? Never. I did the *Aeneid* in the arena."

"Really? And how could that be?" she asked with some contempt and amusement in her voice.

"I am glad you asked," I said. "We were quite inventive. Dido was a prostitute who could fornicate with bulls. I was Aeneas, and—"

"Stop . . ."

"I'm going to tell you about the *Aeneid.*"

"That was not the *Aeneid.* That was using the poem for your own selfish ends. Eugeni, don't you know the poem?"

"I had people who knew it."

"You should know it yourself. It is beautiful. It is such a beautiful poem, such a beautiful language that I could lose myself in it. It was such a danger to my own faith and my service, this love I had. Most look at Greek as the language of arts, but I always loved Latin."

"It was a better performance than the kitchen," I said with some sullenness.

She said she would show me the Flaminian Way. And while we looked for its entrance, I tried to remember things about the priest—the fisherman. But all I could remember was how happy this made Miriamne, and how the other slaves were happy too, and how she said this ceremony was the greatest gift I could have given her.

In her happiness I knew joy like I had never known before, and I wondered if Olava would be interested or if she cared. I wanted to tell her, but I was afraid she might ask a cold question about this, and I did not want coldness in this most precious moment.

"Why are you crying, Eugeni?"

"I remember something beautiful."

"Will you share it?"

"It was beautiful and tender."

"Will you share it?"

"I was remembering how happy I was in Miriamne's happiness. I lived it again. It may have been the happiest, or one of the happiest, moments of my life."

Olava stopped the automobile. She leaned to me and kissed my cheek.

"God bless you, Eugeni."

And I cried some more. "He did that, too. Peter did. And said that," I said.

Olava kissed me twice, loud, smacking kisses with much gusto.

"You know, Eugeni," she said with much joy, "perhaps Saint Peter has been protecting you."

"That sort of protection I will live without, because before his kiss, I was a wealthy man. What do I own now?"

"You own time. Look, the Flaminian."

We had been parked near it. But it was a horror. To describe it as being in disrepair would have been unduly complimentary. Grass grew on its stone. Blocks were worn down. The beautiful, even, smoothed road was gutted beyond belief. Stone had surrendered to time.

But this had been one of the better preserved roads. Some were worse.

"Are we near Vindobonum?" I asked.

"I don't know. But we can get books. That would show us."

It was a moist and warm day. The trees were in leaf and the sky so pale blue, like Olava's eyes, and little puffs of white clouds, like clouds so long ago, hung in the sky waiting for the winds of the gods to blow them away.

"Are you all right, Eugeni?"

"Yes."

"You look so sad."

"I am sad. There was a saying that Jupiter blows all clouds away and by that it meant all things bad pass. You see those clouds," I said, pointing to the sky which this age had conquered, "they have been blown away and come again. But Jupiter is not here. Nor is Mars. Nor is Apollo. They are not here. Just Eugeni. Only Eugeni is here."

There were three contiguous latifundia I had owned near here. I was sure of it. Now the town's name was Vindobonum and I had donated the baths there, to the town.

By law, Vindobonum citizens had to return slaves who escaped, and vigilance rewarded is vigilance pursued. I did not know if we were near Surmius, and Olava took me away from the ruined road, and we took other roads. The buildings were old and yet new. And by the features of the people, it looked as though all the slaves had escaped, leaving only occasional Romans.

On toward Rome, but after two days' ride, we came to a town called Assisi, which I was sure was Asisum. The hills nearby were right. The road was the same. I had not owned property here, but I knew the town.

And amid the new rubbish of buildings was the old, faded temple of Minerva tucked in like a precious old friend between two strangers.

Olava warned me not to go in.

"It has been changed. My cult has taken it over."

"Sacrilege. How dare you?"

"No one worships Minerva today."

"I will."

"You never did before."

"I want to now. She is so forgotten. So alone."

"I cannot let you do that. I cannot let you make a prayer to Minerva in that temple of my God."

"I will do it," I said pushing her aside. She had good speed and bulk, but she was not athletic, and I pushed her away easily. And she fell. The forum was quite reasonable, surrounded by many buildings, a far finer arrangement than in the northern countries. Yet in this square were the leavings of water here and there. Olava fell in one. And people looked out from windows, for nothing entertains like someone else's distress. I marched forward to the little temple, stripped of much of its external marble. I could feel Olava run after me, clumping along with her big body.

I let her grab me and carried her forward. She held on. Men with broad felt hats came, yelling things. Someone threw something at them. I slipped my blade out of my pants leg. This forum was as good as any place to honor the dead.

CHAPTER XXXI

It was, of course, chaos. Sister Olava had to put herself between Eugeni and the carabinieri, who thought their size and authority gave them an advantage.

She had noticed that the respect had disappeared with her black nun's habit, to be replaced by a sexual concern, an almost hovering, hidden agenda for bed with so many passing men. It was tiring at first, and somewhat strange, then complimentary, but more often annoying.

Now the carabinieri were at it, going to impress her, she knew, with the way they handled the little man who had thrown her in the puddle. But Eugeni had that blade and what they could not know was that, with all their size and numbers, they would more than likely be only victims, fast and bloody victims in an ancient game for an ancient reason they did not know.

The carabinieri threatened him with gestures. The townspeople, now looking out of their windows around the square, were yelling down. Eugeni was yelling back. It was drama to him.

One carabiniere started to close on the knife. She got in the way. And obviously he thought she was protecting the little fellow instead of him.

Her right hand stinging from where the heel of it had scraped the stone paving, and the mud tasting bitter in her mouth, Olava kept easily in front of the carabinieri with fast moves, which seemed sluggish for Eugeni, who was around her with ease.

Eugeni, apparently feeling the crowd, became someone else again. A grin came to his hard face, so wide it hardly looked as though a mouth could contain it. He made sweeping hand gestures to the people looking out the windows. Some started to clap. Others yelled. He ran to the central fountain, right through the legs of one of the carabinieri.

He leaped on the fountain, then ran around the rim of its basin, then jumped on the back of one of the carabinieri. Olava knew someone was going to get killed. They did not understand he was only exercising them for the slaughter.

They could only think of him as some agile miscreant they were going to fine or jail when they got their hands on him.

The carabiniere Eugene had mounted tried to spin him off. In desperation he lunged backward, but Eugeni was off his shoulders and dancing around. He offered the blade handle first to another carabiniere, running up for support. The man reached for it, and got air, the blade was at his throat, and then it flashed, and it wasn't there again. The people knew a performance when they saw one. The carabiniere, who could have been killed, wasn't.

Two thousand years and a crowd was a crowd, and this man came alive for it. He pretended to fall. He lay stricken, on the stones of the square, until a carabiniere tried to get a handcuff on him. Then his legs closed around the caribiniere's head, and it appeared as though the man were performing a homosexual act, but Olava noticed that the groin area really pressed against the bridge of the nose. The little gladiator would never risk so sensitive a part of his body to teeth.

While hiding this fact easily, Eugeni undulated his body as though in sexual rapture. Laughter filled the square.

Eugeni was up and running, falling to his knees, supplicating the carabinieri until coins rang out, hitting the stones with sharp little pings. People threw paper lire, also, and the carabinieri, no fools, decided to retrieve their self-respect by pretending to be part of the act. They knew he was too much for them.

Olava told Eugeni to give them the knife, and she would get him another. He asked if there would be one as good elsewhere, and she told him there were many in almost any kitchen.

But he would not give up the knife. He made great comic gestures and the carabinieri, now playing along, did not try to take the knife but treated it as a stage prop. For if it were a stage prop and not a weapon, they would not have to risk embarrassment.

And thus they drove from the town and the once temple of Minerva, and Olava, her nerves shredded by these frightening and strange new duties she had, finally pulled the car to the side of the road and told Eugeni exactly what had happened to Christianity. It was about time.

The old gods of Rome were dead. Gone many, many centuries. In its place was Christianity and its many sects, no longer a Jewish sect, but a far bigger religion than the worship of any god Eugeni ever feigned worshiping. Any cult ever.

It was a desecration to make sacrifices to Minerva in a Christian church, just as much as it would be to smash a statue of Minerva when the temple belonged to Minerva. Did Eugeni understand?

What, he asked, was her god afraid of? It must be a weak god to be so fearful of one small prayer to Minerva, now dead these centuries.

She knew he was jousting with her, but she could not control her rage. She screamed out helplessly that Eugeni was not cooperating, that he could understand if he wanted to understand, and he wasn't trying. It did no good. He answered that he had made his prayer to Minerva by the little games to mark her passing. She was a nice goddess, he said. Nicer than Olava's god.

She knew this was a challenge, but she was too tired to take it. She found a hotel and begged Eugeni for no more games. He practiced shaving with a razor, while she slumped onto the bed and tried to think.

She had no idea what would happen next, other than that it was something she could no more handle than could an emperor with a riot on his hands. Already everything felt beyond her grasp, or even reach, it seemed. She was so unprepared for this sort of test. And in a moment of fury she prayed, not as she had been taught to pray, but as a Roman might pray who had just built a temple to a god and now demanded performance.

God, she said in her mind, you will help me tomorrow because

I won't be able to handle it, and I can't handle things right now. So do it. It is a real effort being chaste. But I'll do it. But you've got to help me tomorrow. There's just no other way. I am not getting through tomorrow without your help. So do it. Because your performance has been minimal until now.

Minimal, she told God, and sleep became easier. She longed for morning prayers and evening prayers, and most of all she longed to go to the altar and open her mouth and receive God on her tongue in the form of the eucharist. She longed for people who prayed as she prayed. She longed for the mass. She longed for the convent. She even longed for the familiar acts of penance. This was so hard, and tomorrow would be the hardest.

She felt a peace come over her, having given the responsibility for that next day to God. And if anything went wrong it was his fault, primarily for choosing her and giving her this test which she felt was beyond her, especially when it was said he never gave a test beyond what a person could do. The score so far was one dead, one in Russia, probably in prison, and she herself being whittled down to the emotions and stability of a child.

One more day, she thought. If she could do one more day. Eugeni finished shaving, and went to sleep in a chair curled around his knife, the pommel near his cheek.

She was so tired. Nerve-drawn tired. Bang-slapped tired, beyond tired. She could go only so long without knowing whether Eugeni would fall on that knife in deep depression or cut up a village. Those carabinieri had been so close to death. Just a flick away, had one done something to launch Eugeni, as he had been launched in the kitchen back in the university hospital.

She could imagine the blood on the stones, and there would be no laughing from surrounding sidewalks then.

It was hard going to sleep this night, despite her weariness, and she lifted her head from the pillow of this hotel room and stared at her charge curled up on the chair.

She had never needed anyone as much as she had needed him the first night alone with him. He could have taken her sexually, she knew, for she would have done anything just to keep someone holding her.

She had been shattered that night; her will had been broken into uselessness. She was sure he did not understand what her chastity meant in relationship to her God. But he did know vows and obviously knew her and what the breaking of that vow would mean, and he gave her, that first night, the same gift she now passed on to her God—her virginity. He could have taken it and, not taking it, forswore it forever.

She knew, as frightened as she was now, she would not be as weak as that first night away without permission from the convent.

She turned in the soft bed, and she could not sleep. She needed sleep, a mind-cleansing rest, more desperately than she could remember.

But one did not force sleep, any more than one tried to force the grace of God.

She had not slept well since that day they left the cabin, and each moment driving she feared, unreasonably, she knew, being stopped by some policeman and asked if Eugeni was the man who had mercilessly butchered the world's finest fencer. Was he that man? Was she the nun from Ringerike?

That would not happen, she knew. Lewus had paid the price of their freedom. So had Semyonus. She thought of herself now as Olava and the dead American as Lewus and the Russian doctor as Semyonus—Eugeni's terms.

Everyone had paid a price, and she had thought, that night back in the cabin, hers might be the easiest. She had thought there would be some apprehension, by staying away from her order for a while. But she had not expected this.

This was nightmare.

The leaving without permission had unhinged something so deep in her that she only now realized she had felt invincible before, never knowing how strong indeed she was, until that strength had left her and she found herself just begging to be held at any price that night, just to have warm human arms around her.

Now at the center of her being was a frightened little girl who had run away from home. She had never needed before, and she needed now. She needed her mind back again with all its security. She needed to know for certain she was doing right. If she knew that, she could be strong again.

Eugeni was speaking in his sleep. Olava listened. A word here or there was recognizable, much like the first tapes of his voice. He slept with that kitchen knife inside his curled arms like a child with a doll. He talked much in his sleep. The only night he hadn't talked in his sleep, perhaps, was that one that lasted centuries.

He had seen her weaker than anyone had ever seen her. And he had given the hand of a friend, when he could have been a lover. Perhaps she was not beautiful enough in his eyes. Whatever it was, she was grateful that on that one night a man could have had her, that man did not. He helped her with her gift to her God. It was so hard to know him. He went from depressed to happy and back again so quickly, she was not sure what triggered these things. Was he insane? Olava wondered. Would any other response be anything but sane?

He wept easily, but perhaps not too easily given the way he was raised. Perhaps those tears, when he saw the Via Flaminia, when he looked for that town that had gone, were a gift of God, like a wound bleeding clean, or like the soul getting rid of pain it could not handle.

Sometimes he wept with his hands over his face, but at the Via Flaminia moisture rimmed his eyes, and he was quiet. The wound was deep.

Olava looked up at the dark ceiling and listened to her charge mutter away. Dreams, too, were where people cleansed their wounds.

And now Olava realized why she was not allowing herself to sleep. Because if she slept, she would have to awaken. And that would be tomorrow.

And she did not want tomorrow.

For tomorrow was Rome. She had promised Lewus and Semyonus that Eugeni would walk the city he had lived in. He would return where he had been. This had been agreed on. She would first take him out of the country, and then, it seemed so natural and wise at the time, take him back to Rome.

"Show him where he has been," Lewus had said.

But what terrified Olava this night, what she had not understood in the cabin in Norway, when nobility and correctness seemed like such a clear duty, was how Eugeni would react to Rome.

If the little temple of Minerva, a goddess he had made no special sacrifice to when she was worshiped back in pagan times, could evoke that display in the square in an instant. . .

What then would he do when he returned to Rome and found home had left him so long ago?

CHAPTER XXXII

Rome?

Did she expect me to believe this was Rome? Did she expect anyone to believe this was Rome?

All right, I could grant a road falling to disrepair. But did time have teeth to eat stone as it ate all flesh?

"Yes, Eugeni," she answered.

She was highly distraught, a condition which at times was hard to discern because Olava's natural way was an inner tautness. But today it was worse, so I went silently from one disaster to another.

I had expected damage, but Olava had said there were preserved things. Nothing was preserved. There were poor, pitiful, worn stones. It could have been anywhere. The lovely temple at Caesar's forum was a mound of rubble and a few worn columns. I tried to remember what the temple had said above it. If I remembered, the temple was beautiful white marble with fine sculpture above inscriptions that the Julian Caesar had donated this temple. It was so grand, one could smell the incense in the entire forum. Now there were bushes and grass, and some wildflowers, as there probably had been before the founding of the city.

"To the left, there were statues, Olava, and the workmanship was so fine you would have sworn they could breathe. Between those little pillars there," I said.

Olava nodded. She understood. She smiled too quickly this day, and darkness had begun to appear under her eyes.

"There was no grass here, of course, there was marble. Are you sure this was Caesar's forum?"

"Yes. It was."

There had been a tomb we had passed that was still left. I forgot the man's name, but I remembered that he had built it so that for eternity people would know who he was.

The marble had been stripped like an apple skin. Olava had said that many of the buildings had been shorn of their fine marble covers to build other buildings in later ages.

But what buildings could they have built to justify these desecrations? There was nothing but tenement garbage. I remembered the stacked cubicles the poor lived in, and now everyone lived like that. The finest hostel Olava pointed to, just inside the remnants of a city gate, stripped to its inner brick, was like a tenement. My slaves outside my house lived like that, and now everyone, even the rich, lived like that.

Olava thought I would mind the vendors, but vendors were one of the few things that reminded me of Rome. Still this was called Rome.

"What a price to pay for so little in return," I said of the new buildings being built from old.

What had been done to the vestals was worse than rape.

I looked at a little field set aside.

"This is the House of the Vestal Virgins, where it had been. See. Some statues are left," said Olava.

"Statues. They look scarcely carved. The features have been melted back into the stone they came from. And worse. If this were . . ."

"Yes?"

"If this were the home of vestals, then those statues would have been on the inside. But there is no outside."

Olava said something about the old style of the House of the Vestals being copied by cults within her religion.

"Olava, I am going to talk to you."

"I don't want to argue with you today, Eugeni. I am very tired."

"Arguing is the nicest part of knowing you. You are good at it.

Don't fear me. You are inconsistent and illogical, but you do not shame either your race or sex."

Olava cocked an eyebrow. There are many who, given so much in ability, rarely have to use it all. So that when they are called upon to strain, it appears to them like some gigantic, insurmountable obstacle. Had Olava come to my Rome, instead of me to hers, in one week she would have been at Domitian's elbow or someone equally important. Olava's tiredness came from knowing the fear and uncertainty that most people dine on as a weekly fare. For her it was the first time. And that was why she was tired. And that was way she was distraught. And while she asked for respite, I knew she didn't need it. Many, while tired, are stronger than those who are fresh.

"I am not going to argue," she said, which, if I gauged correctly, meant she was going to argue, but this time would allow her normally courteous self a bit of vindictiveness.

"Woman, I may have been like the fish or the meat, stone and cold, but to me, looking at this field with some stones in it is difficult. To me, it is but a year since I was marched from the city. Miriamne is dead a year. Petronius is a young boy, and yet, if he had been lucky, he would have been an old man, and gone so many years before. I cannot accept that this was the House of the Vestals."

"That is all right," she said.

"You give me permission?"

She did not answer. But I pursued my line. "So here we have a garbage dump in place of Rome, and you telling me that your cult has taken this or that from my time. And I see all has passed, and not even a game to mark its going. And I am told this is preserved and that is preserved and lives still and nothing lives. Nothing. It is dead. Dead."

"You are angry with me."

"I cannot be angry with time. You will have to do," I said, and I smiled, to let her know that in my anger was also a bit of jest.

On a street where there had once been so many temples it was called the "sacred street," we found only a few bitter pieces of marble that were supposed to have once been the temple of Romulus, according to Olava.

"I don't remember there being a temple to Romulus," I said. "No. That has gone from my memory. There was a temple here. But I don't think it was Romulus."

Now Olava was reading from a little book—the marvel of this age being machines producing things like that in perfect uniformity. Any nation in this day could put an army into the field with the same helmets, helmets still being used although not as necessary as once.

"Romulus, the temple of Romulus," she said.

Now I knew by legend that Romulus was a founder of Rome. Olava read from her little book.

"Ah, yes. Of course," she said. "This Romulus was the son of Maxentius, and it was built in the year 300, our time. Christian era. That's after you." She turned the pages in her little book.

"On the Tiber, Eugeni, is a small circular temple, and a rectangular one in excellent condition."

"Then do you have statues to your executed god in them?"

"No. They are preserved, according to this book, close to what they were at the Forum Boarius."

A fenced-in park marked where the temples were, the round, Mars, and the rectangular, Portunus.

"I made public sacrifices to Mars there," I said, and Olava, who had not written since the night in the cabin, now furiously wrote a short note into the book. The word I could read. It was "Mars."

"They do not say that in the book?"

"No. They didn't know. It's a very old temple, old even in imperial times, what we call your age now."

"No it wasn't."

"No?"

"I donated it. To honor my manumission and love of Rome, I believe. It was an Aurelian temple."

"Then how would they not know this temple?"

"Maiestas, Olava. I offended the gods. I pay this price now."

"Eugeni, you did not believe in the gods then, why now? Do you believe that the senate could vote you two thousand years of time and this return? What do you believe?"

"I believe what I believe," I said. Automobiles on black-topped streets moved where chariots and fine horses had once pranced a graceful gait. Where there had been marble, there was now brick glass and all manner of tedious building. There was no triumph in this city anymore, and the worst of it was that I did not see a Roman face. Not one Roman face. There were Germans, and Gauls, and Jews, and Egyptians, and mostly everyone mixed together with Greek. It was not that I thought less of the people, it was that I remembered what to me was last year. One year, and even my fondest enemies were no more. I even missed the arena.

Given a match, I would gladly die on the sand if given guarantees that it would be a single death I died. But what I missed most was what I had once considered a chore. Those morning dealings with retainers and emissaries in my atrium, judging and gauging men, buying and selling, deceiving and being deceived, passing a comment for the moment, sharing a good thought, learning one. The daily business of my atrium.

One year. Two thousand years. Ten thousand years. Where was my merciful end?

"Do you wish to make an offering to Mars, Eugeni? He was your household god. Here I would not object."

"No. Not in front of you, any of you. Those children over there. The automobiles. No. Not there. Not there at all. In no way do I wish it. No."

The sun set late, it being summer, and another thing I remembered, that was so long gone, was the smell. We had human waste smells and there was none, nothing but the burned fuel of the cars. It was perhaps cleaner, but it was not Rome.

At the Flavian amphitheater, not only had they taken the marble skin and cut out a gigantic wedge, like some monster half the size of the city taking a bite of stone, but someone had taken it upon himself to build another structure inside with little bricks like a tenement. This, Olava explained, was from a later age. They built the structure inside where the tunnels underneath the sand had once been. Even that paltry desecration was tumbling.

In every arch—and there had been beautiful arched portals around the circumference of the entire Flavian—there had been statues. All had been removed without a trace.

There was a plaque from the pontifex in bronze on one of the old stones. Olava said it was not the pontifex who was the dean of all the priests of Rome, but the one who often acted as the chief augur for the games, but their descendant of Peter—the name pontifex having been taken from us.

"Is there nothing you have not taken?" I asked. "What does Peter's heir say about my arena? You take things, you add things, without thought or proportion."

"It is a plaque to commemorate Christians who were martyred here," she said.

"Ridiculous," I said. And then I found myself yelling. "Look around. This was an arena. Up there was an awning. They could fill the base with water and have sea battles. This was a gladiator's arena. If I had been matched with the secutor here instead of the Vatican, I would not have had to witness this lie. This filth. These little runts running around where real men built real buildings. I would have grown old with Miriamne. Publius would still be my friend. This was the largest suitable gladiator arena. Look at the seats."

They were shorn, but anyone could see how everything could focus toward the center where a fight could be concentrated on.

"Look. Look. This was not a place for Christians. This was for gladiators. Christians were executed at the great circle where they raced horses. They were executed in numbers at the Vatican arena. The Flavian was never for Christians. It was too nice for that sort of thing. It was too nice an arena just for executions. It was for animals and gladiators."

"Eugeni," she said sharply. "The plaque acknowledges that. It acknowledges that Christians were killed elsewhere, but it commemorates all those who died."

I read the sounds of the plaque, recognizing a word here or there, the letters being familiar. "I do not see secutor. I do not see tridens. I do not see Samnite. Or bestiarius who fought animals. I do not see even the great animals listed. Elephant or tiger or the African hippopotamus. Show me these things where true merit reigns. Show me."

"They are not commemorated, Eugeni."

"Those who died commemorating others are not themselves commemorated?"

"Yes," she said, and she was firm in this.

"That is life. But I tell you, when so many fine secutors died here, it is an abomination only to commemorate the criminals, Jews, Germans, Britons, and Gauls, those who did not compete here. Abomination. Yes, you called it murder. But you do not understand."

"Likewise, you do not understand, Eugeni."

"This is my arena, woman."

"Mine, now, by time."

We were in a passage that had been public and was public again. A man my size, who looked very much like Plutarch but without the flesh, and of course dressed in modern leggings and speaking a modern debasement of what was spoken here so long ago, a year ago, forever ago, when this was beautiful, this man talked to me and Olava.

The supports for the seats could be seen bare now. If I had lived the normal span, I never would have seen them bare as they were while being built.

Quiet it was, but for the noise of the machines circling outside. The man was insistent and Olava shook her head.

"What does he want?"

"He wants to show you around."

"Me?" I said, and then yelling. "Me? Me? Show me? The Greekling would show me, Lucius Aurelius Eugenianus? Me? He would show me? I'll show him his liver in his hands."

"Please," begged Olava throwing herself in the way.

"Show me? Me? Show me?"

"He doesn't know, Eugeni. He couldn't know, Eugeni. Please, Eugeni."

"Show me?"

"Eugeni."

"Me, he would show me."

"Please."

"He would show me an automobile with fishermen in it, he would show me. Show me."

"He doesn't know."

"My arena."

"Yours," she said quietly, both of us knowing I was wrong. No longer mine it was but, as she had said, hers.

It was not a battle I was equipped for, seeing this again, so far away, this far arena, so far from home. So long ago. A week ago. A year ago. Two thousand years ago.

"Generations after yours, a follower of Peter who followed Jesus ordered this preserved in honor of the martyred Christians. So it is here because of our pontifex, whom we call pontiff, not yours," said Olava, and there was no triumph in her voice. She shared a small part of my great loss.

"Well, this was the smaller arena. There must be more of the larger one at the Vatican."

"No, Eugeni. We will go later."

"I want to go now."

"Eugeni, the big arena is not there. Something has been built on it."

"All of it?"

"All of it," she said.

"Completely," she said.

"What?" I said.

"Tomorrow. We will see tomorrow."

"No," I said, in rage so helpless I felt like a child. My hand was on the blade but I would not use it, not really, here, not on that thin Plutarch-looking stranger. Enough had been disgraced without adding the blade of Lucius Aurelius Eugenianus to murder.

Already I had used the word "Greekling" for the first time, so helpless I was. It was not an insult to him, nor a relief for me. It was as though I swam now in an open sewer and, to be a part of it, I would add the defecation of my spirit. Perhaps it was that there were no Romans to hate anymore. Perhaps it was all these people who went mindlessly about their business not realizing they walked on the graves of the people and structures I knew but last year. One year to me.

I had seen one of Olava's pictures of the remains of the Flavian, but the picture did not capture the emptiness of it, the silence of it. It did not capture who was not there.

Of course the great statue with Vespasian's head on it was gone. But the people still called it "Colosseum," Olava said.

There were automobiles with drivers who charged a fee to take you anywhere. We got to one nearby, and Olava told the driver: "Vatican. Vatican."

He obviously didn't understand we wanted to go to the Vatican, because he left us off at a great new palace of refreshingly Roman grandeur. The first really Roman feeling I had in this place called Rome.

The columns were clean and massed in a great circle around an open space. Atop the enclosure was a profusion of statues, one after the other so that, while they stood atop the columns, they still had that old feeling of my Flavian.

Sretching backwards were banks of marble steps leading to another great edifice atop which was a dome. Adjoining at an angle was another palace. Somehow, Rome had lived through the onslaught of the ages.

"Whose castle is this? Magnificent."

"The fisherman, Eugeni. We are at the Vatican. The big arena near here is no more. That is Peter's tomb and his church. Look you at the little fisherman's monument. Behold."

"Peter's?"

"Yes," she said, and there was triumph in her voice. The great arena was gone. I looked around for the other hills to be certain that indeed this was the Vatican. Olava said it was, her chalk-white face shining pride, her hair wildly yellow, standing here on the Vatican hill, free and uncomplicated.

I looked again at the vast courtyard with magnificent columns surrounding it, and great statues in profusion upon the circle of columns. They were not gods but saints, which, Olava said, should not be confused with gods, even though they had special powers and were now immortal. I asked if people believed these nongods could provide various kinds of good fortune, and she said yes. I asked if there were saints for one thing and saints for other things. She said yes, but I should not confuse this with the pantheon of gods, since these saints were real people.

"Yours are real and ours weren't," I said. "Are you sure this is Peter's?"

"Again, yes. Saint Peter's."

"He couldn't afford this, Olava. I might, at the peak of my wealth, be able to, if I cared to suffer some. But I don't think Domitian could. The Flavians couldn't. The Julians I don't think could. No. They squandered and they never had really that much. I am trying to think. The Aurelians, never. Quintus Fabius Cornelius might have, but wouldn't."

"Where does Domitian rest? Or Augustus? Mark me, Eugeni, the monument for the Julian, called Caesar, gone they are. Behold poor Peter, crucified upside down with real nails in his body and real blood and real pain, and behold. Who lies and who dies? Look at what the heart of man says, and the hand of God inspires. Even while he died, this was coming. Love, Eugeni, is the most powerful thing. It is the great thing, Eugeni. The one great thing. God."

She presented her contention almost in an oratorical stance.

The summer sun, setting red around us so the sky was aflame, her yellow hair peaked like a bristled helmet, strength in her now. A formidable woman and possibly even beautiful. We rushed in, for I wanted to see where the fisherman was buried. Inside was the true, spacious magnificence of Rome, the public building of Rome.

In the center were modern twisting pillars of black stone, which, Olava said, surrounded an altar, altars today not being covered with blood, but the sacrifice of her God being so pre-eminent, blood sacrifices of animals became useless, a desecration of sorts.

So overwhelmed by the beauty and perfection, finer even than the mosaics of my peristilium, I hardly paid attention to Olava's explanation of sacrifice. Beneath this magnificent altar was another altar. And the one beneath was of pure gold, with gold doors, and giant, hanging gold lamps and two small columns of pink marble. It was splendid.

"I like it, Olava. You are to be commended. My compliments to all of you. This is truly rich."

"Richer still is the Word," she said, which I did not understand. What I had not understood until now was how such a fine and disciplined person could be part of Miriamne's Jewish sect, a follower of a cult that had fishermen as priests. But here in the familiar magnificence, finally it came, as a fog lifting over a strange noise and revealing that it was a waterfall all along.

"I see, Olava. I could not understand before."

Happiness came to her so suddenly she almost cried.

"Eugeni, what? What do you understand?" she asked.

"I did not understand before about you and your discipline and your education and your cleanliness, for you wash as much as any Roman. I did not connect you and the poor little fisherman. I did not know where Rome had gone either. And now I see. I see it all."

"Yes? Yes?" she said, her hands clasping in front of her, her body tense with joy, expectant of the giant revelation I would now share.

"You are not some little Jewish sect following someone executed in a shameful manner. You are Rome living. Here is Rome. Peter would never have been allowed in such a fine building."

The joy left like a hammer smashing a stone smile.

"No. You're totally wrong."

"Look about you. To the backward Jew a beautiful statue is blasphemy. They prohibit graven images. I remember Peter. I remember him. He spoke of no graven images. And Miriamne hated my bust of Mars, where Petronius burned his first hair. I like this place, Olava."

"The form may be Roman. It is the Word that is different. You don't understand."

"I feel at home."

"The Word is everything."

"Hail Rome. Hail Rome," and I cried out the words, and people who had hushed smiled politely, for they too had caught my enthusiasm.

And like Rome, there were all manner of foreign people visiting here, black Aetheops, blond, brown hair, black hair, tall, short. "Most Roman of them all," I said.

"Peter is buried here, not Julius Caesar. Peter who believed in eternal life through love and its sacrifice, who believed the poor were blessed, not the legions. Peter, not Caesar, Eugeni. Christian, not Roman."

"I know only by the fruits that are born, and it is a tasty Roman blossom I feel now. No one else could have built this but the Roman. Not the Christian. Christians don't care for big buildings. Christians worry about how they do things, not how they build things. I knew many Christians. They weren't all Jews, you know. They had Romans and Germans. I knew Christians as well as anyone. And better than you. And this has not the slightest taint of Christian."

"I am a Christian."

"Not at all," I assured Olava.

And we left that place and went to a hotel called the Atlas, which was small like a tenement. But I liked the narrow street. And we ate at a place like a tavern of which there were many.

We were in Rome that night, and not a drop of garum or alum to be had. The food, Italian, which meant many cities, all up and down the Italian peninsula, Sicily and Sardinia being included, was a strange thing, which, Olava said, had come in later years.

"This is spaghetti. The design comes from China and was so well adopted by later Italians that people today think of spaghetti as Italian."

It was not bad, nor was it good, rather a base for a sauce made from tomatoes, which were not eaten regularly and commonly. They made a red sauce, also a later thing. There were meats stuffed into casings called sausages, and Olava did not know if they had been frozen.

She ate very well, with more enthusiasm than she had ever shown. She finished her plate, she finished my plate. I had some cheese. She attracted more looks. She could be beautiful, I thought. The skin was smooth.

Before dessert, she said she knew what she was going to do. She was going to teach me about her God and other things. She was very interested, she said, that I felt at home in Saint Peter's.

"I find out how Roman I am," I said.

That night, she made copious notes, and fell asleep in the chair. I used the bed.

The room was small, with a meager tile on the floor and heavy bars on the window. Why they continued to build windows on the outside and then bar them and drape them and shade them, I would never know.

So short a time ago, I would have owned this building and many like it. I would not have even known I owned it. Which of course struck me funny, because here I was missing something I would not have known I had.

Yet I did miss my peristilium, and I thought that knowing where the Flavian arena was, and gauging by the rising or setting of the sun, I might pace off the distances to where my house was. Olava had said they found houses all the time when they dug for new projects. They might find my peristilium.

But, I thought, if it were like the rest of Rome, better to be gone and gone, instead of gone leaving only a trace.

It was a peaceful moment, and I still had my blade, and perhaps, I thought, if the right time were to present itself, I might then be able, in a sudden move, to take my life. Not now, but some day. After all, I had only failed on the first try. It would be fitting to say good-bye. Both right and just.

I fell asleep missing my Rome, and in the morning Olava was up and humming and praying and washing and asking me why I slept so late. She said if I continued to sleep she would eat my liver which she always wanted, and everyone had lied to me about the eating of human flesh. They all ate human flesh nowadays, Norwegians, which she was, most of all, and if I continued to sleep she could not control herself, especially since I also had a thigh that looked so tasty, a piece already having been taken out.

I was on the bed, my head in a soft pillow, my blade handy, and I gave it to her, telling her to cut whatever part she wanted.

"I am going to throw it away, Eugeni. Thank you," she said, and I was up and at it and got the blade after a very short wrestle, but I was up. And I could not go back to sleep.

"You're happy," I said.

"Yes," she said.

"I liked you better melancholy," I said.

"I liked you better frozen," she said.

"Frozen, I did not have to converse with barbarians as equals."

"That is because we are better, therefore we cannot be equals. Dress," she said, the logic satisfactory only to her.

She was skilled now in her cosmetics, knowing enough to make them be there, and alter her face slightly, but not gross anymore. The colors belonged on her. She wore a light, common white blouse, the understrapping somewhat visible, a short skirt, and flat black shoes. She had everything neat and packed, which she did herself. We had three small trunks now. She carried two. I carried one.

As we left, a slave of the hotel, who of course was not a slave, merely at everyone's call and service, offered me a very big and lascivious wink, looking at Olava pay the bill. She drew attention here, also.

In the desecration of the language now common here, someone almost managed to finish the word beautiful. I gathered from the bowing and light concern that she was indeed most beautiful, yellow white hair being treasured now.

"Today, Eugeni, we go to Pompeii . . ."

"Pompeii, woman, was obliterated even in my time by Vesuvius flowing lava."

"Which is why we have it today. It was kept from the hands of vandals by the burial. The little city of Pompeii has been dug out. It is your Rome. And I think it will help you see some things. Their dark night is your daylight."

And on that, Olava was happy.

"Woman, so often you have said that even in the darkest night there still exists a sunlight so bright we cannot look at it. Now if this is so, somewhere in this bright day is a night so dark the terrors know no bounds. So let us not be so happy."

At that she laughed.

"I wish you could have seen the real Rome, you would not have taken me to this one, Olava," I said.

"We go to the real Rome," she said. "In Pompeii is the spirit."

We drove in Olava's automobile, and she sang and orated all morning.

We entered Pompeii by a sailor's gate and had to pay to enter.

The advantage of Pompeii was not that it had withstood time unscathed, for it had not. It was as though an army of slaves had gone through it with clubs and scrapers, leaving only the stones of the streets, shells of houses, and some interior. Almost all the external marble and wall paintings were gone. And, of course, the people—the living people—were not to return again, whether felled by lava or not. Whether felled by volcano or not, all were dead now.

There were no lights without fire, nor automobiles, nor glass grinning from every structure. What they had done was keep ensuing centuries out more than my time in, which was enough. It was almost home again, if I forgot the nearby towns, and ignored the new volcano Vesuvius. Olava told me I was crying. I did not know it.

Groups of people walked together, pausing every once in a while to hear a man tell them things in a foreign tongue. It was a guide, who was paid to show people poor Pompeii. Everyone was interested in common things. We followed one group to Jupiter's temple. His head was still there on a metal statue, although the temple was removed. It was open to the seasons.

I told Olava where people sat, what the sacrifices were, how there had been contention for who would be priest of this temple, and how a bribe of but a few sesterces decided the will of the gods. I knew the name of the priest and how he worked at making Jupiter the most revered god of all by making a triad of Juno, Minerva, and Jupiter. I said hello to Jupiter and informed him I had outlived him. Olava smiled.

"Do you know, Olava, this triad once spoke?"

"I find that hard to believe, Eugeni."

"It is so. They said, 'We are three, but we are but stones. There are three that do rule, but they are one, and in one they are here but not here.' "

"What?" said Olava, her large, pale hands seizing my shoulders.

"Oh, it was quite an incident. The priests suppressed what the three stones said, but I remember most of it."

"What was it?"

"How much would you pay for exactly what came from the mouths of stones?"

"You could get much money."

"Then I will tell you for nothing what they said. They said it is not lies that people dislike, but specific lies. If they look down upon the Roman games, it is not that they look down on games, but Roman games. If I, Eugenianus, should mount a woman for profit, that is disgraceful and Greek. But should I tell you the lie that three stones suddenly spoke with human voice to vindicate the fancy stories of your cult, then it is most valuable and not disgraceful at all."

"You've told me a lot already, even in your lie. You've told me about early Christian belief concerning the trinity. You know more of Christians than you allow."

"I knew the respected cults better. But if Christians are respected now, I will know so many things you will be stunned, Olava."

"You would know for profit."

"There are worse motives."

"Profit doesn't last, Eugeni. Even stones don't last. I had hoped you would see what was obvious to me, that the Word lasts. The Word, Eugeni. Even the misnaming of the Colosseum has lasted longer than its marble. And the good things last longer still. The two cults that lived on the Word, Jewish worship and the Christian flowering from it, both relied on the Word, not the stone. In the beginning and the end, Eugeni, is the Word."

The group went by us and another group came up the good and regular stone walks. I thought a moment. I remembered the food shops of this city.

"Do you know if they discovered garum or alum when they dug Pompeii out?"

"I talk to you of eternity and you think of your stomach."

"Not only can eternity wait, woman, it does not growl."

There was little left of the forum, and I showed Olava which temples were where, and which shops were where, and I told her which were assumed to be profitable, and which were not, and where some of my investments were, and the politics of the times. The games had been banned here by a decree of the senate, for there had been a battle between Pompeians and Nucerians over the games. Many were injured, although not one fraction of the damage done by a good riot in Rome had occurred. However, morality is a garment watched more closely on others.

We went to the baths, the caldarium, the frigidarium, and it was strange—the first time I had entered the women's baths. Somehow I felt I was stealing something. This was Olava's first time in Pompeii, she said, and my twentieth. I had always liked Pompeii, although Herculaneum nearby was considered a better place. Pompeii was once a Greek-controlled city, before Rome took over the entire peninsula, which was now one country again and unified as Italy.

Under a glass case was a slave's bones encased in concrete. The volcano had come down upon everyone, covering all with dust. The flesh decomposed, but the form was recreated by injecting mortar into the spaces left by the disappeared flesh. It was a rough likeness. The slave—I could tell he was one by his belt—was about my size. I did not recognize him.

Looking down with me at this slave was Domitian. I could not believe it! That fat face, the handsome nose, the strong eyes, the weak mouth. Except of course it was not Domitian. For this man, while his face was pure Domitian, had a body as gigantic as Olava's. And then I knew it was very possible that Domitian's seed—not a hoarded commodity—had like other seeds gone on and on. Like the apple I had eaten in the car when my friend Lewus found me. Seeds in the apple. From all came seeds. Whoever was here now had ancestors who had lived once in my time. Each seed dying, yet it survived by being born again. Better than rock did it survive.

The man became upset at my staring and Olava explained. I could tell he was threatening even as he left, and I smiled most politely, even though, if he should assault us, I could decorate these remnants of baths with his insides.

We went into a house said to be owned by the Vetti. I told Olava I honestly didn't remember. One room here had wall paintings of sexual acts, and most people walked out of it with grins. The house, although smaller, reminded me of my own peristilium and it was good to stand for a moment at the central garden and remember, although the smells were gone, and no longer did one smell human waste about.

I tried to find the house of Messalus. He had had a daughter who was promiscuous, and there was a race to get her with husband before she was with child. They married her to a drooling boy barely eleven.

"How did it end?" asked Olava, as we passed the cold ovens of the baker's, large cones and tables and the grinding stone for once living wheat, now cold and useless. It was a good oven.

"How did it end?" she asked again.

"What end?"

"The daughter of Messalus and the drooling boy?"

"Like they all end, Olava. They end. The hot passion and the drowning avalanche of love, the daily caress and the screaming hate, the quiet boredom and the sufferance of another body. They end. Emperor's throne and slave's belt. They end. Like the legions and the flowers. Like even the stone some day. It ended. That is the end of all things. Words, too."

And as we walked I talked of this house that had ended and that house, and this merchant and that one whom I had never known, and he had ended without my knowledge as he had begun. No, I did not know the poets and the historians, but they ended the same. The slave merchants and the lanistae, whom I did know, ended. Like Peter ended and Domitian ended, and Petronius ended and Miriamne, and like Olava would, untouched by hand of man, as the very same prostitutes down the street ended, and the vestal virgins ended, and I would end.

We walked all day through the little city. Finally, we passed the gladiators' school; now we entered the arena. I took her to the very best seat at the closest edge, although all the seats were good here, most now covered well with the grass and the sand of centuries and centuries, just the bare stone unadorned by marble.

Still the form of this arena, old when I was here last, had held the original tight design. A gladiator's arena if ever there was one. It had lasted.

For me.

It was both right and fitting, in a world most unfitting. My age and city gone without a game or song to mark its passing, now I was here to give it its farewell.

With my hand, made great by them, known by them, and now forgotten partly through maiestas and the senate's decree, but most of all by their leaving with their memories and respect for me, I, Lucius Aurelius Eugenianus, took blade in hand and, saluting the shades of their passing, raised blade to the sun-filled sky.

"For the eternal glory of the senate and the people of Rome, I now commit my flesh. Father and mother both, I honor you, I honor all of us."

With blade in front of me, high and obvious to every seat, although only one was filled, I leaped from the little wall above the cinder and grass and gravel that had once held sand. As I dove down, the blade went handle forward to hit the ground first, the point directed at my chest.

I had always wanted to enter an arena like this but never found the situation quite right, because in later years when I controlled things I never worked in a small arena, and this entrance required a closeness of the audience.

I caught the upcoming point between my left arm and left side, and rolled over it. The beauty here being that the crowd could have seen the blade appear to come up through my back. Obviously it worked perfectly.

Olava screamed.

CHAPTER XXXIII

Sister Olav,

born Marit Vik;
daughter of Per Vik, physician,
and Kirsten Rud Vik, teacher;
member of the order of Saint Dominic;
graduate of Norwegian schools;
scholar at Oxford;
legal owner of no property on earth;
lover of the Creator of all things and
professed daughter of same,

shrieked as she saw her friend dive into the arena from the little retaining wall. The knife point came out of his back, and he rolled forward, and there was no blood. It was a theatrical trick, and it had worked.

In this empty stone arena, she had witnessed a perfect entrance. She called down to him that he should not have frightened her this way, and he did not answer her. Eugeni was performing for this little arena of ghosts. He slowly ran around the edge, his arms above his head as though giving himself to the games, as a witness they had begun.

And Olava knew these were the last games to mark the passing of the civilization he knew, not that it had disappeared without its strong echoes living still. Rather his friends and his enemies were gone, and most of what they believed was gone. And the great structures were but worn markers of what had been, like tombstones in a world they had once ruled.

Eugeni hopped easily from arena floor to wall. He was a tumbler, also. His feet made crunching sounds on the Vesuvian cinder that had replaced the white sand.

He stopped and saluted her, as though she were the emperor or local magistrate, whoever was the honored personage at the games. He announced whom he would fight, this to be a succession of foes. And he paused and walked over close to her, the blade at his side. He explained, as he would to a friend, how the arena could be cut off, and where he wanted to be all the time during the match, and how this really was the best size for a long match, because here everyone could see everything and appreciate it. And then he told her something that put tears suddenly into the rims of her eyes, and she was glad they were so sudden he did not see them, because he was walking back to face an imagined retiarius with tridens and net.

He had said he was the best ever and that Olava should not worry. And then he told her what had made her cry, suddenly. He was glad he had a friend to see his last performance, and by that he meant that he had a friend. The tears were wiped away by the time he gracefully turned to salute her again, and then commanded that she should pay attention, because this was what was important in Rome, the likes of Vergil or Peter probably not even being able to fill this arena and certainly not to cause as much passion.

In the midst of defeating the imagined retiarius, with moves that seemed either overdrawn or very jerky, but which Olava knew too well were deadly, Eugeni stopped, tripped, and lost the blade. But the blade stuck upright, which showed he had not lost it at all. He got it back immediately.

From inside this arena where she sat, she could not see the surrounding modern town. The air was clean, and the seat was hard stone, and Eugeni's moves made a rhythmic shuffling sound coming to her from the arena floor so close.

She understood now what made a language dead and what

made it live. It was not great thoughts, but the little things that made languages live, asking for directions or to pass the salt or how one felt that morning. That was what made a language live, and all the Vergil and Church edicts and precision of its structure could not add one breath of life as meaningful as when a person said: "Not that door, use another. . . . No, I don't want salt. . . . Where did you put the shirt? . . . What did you say? . . . How many of these do you want? . . . I don't understand."

Words lasted with great ideas, but languages did not. And in that, Olava had known she had done the right thing, and she was at peace with her God. This was the journey He wanted for her. It was her way of going home to Him, and she hoped she could bring her friend Eugeni with her. She would teach him about a living God as friend. She would also teach him of his poets whom he ignored when they were fresh. She would teach him living languages.

And she would take copious notes, releasing them at a better time. She would protect him from the world as much as the world from him, for being that great showman of Rome, he could do more damage to historical study, once sensing a profit, than all the revisionist historians who ever rewrote an old fact to fit a new trend.

She shuddered to think what he would do with some village priest. Probably sell the poor old thing pieces of the True Cross. Olava could, without stretching the imagination much, see Eugeni setting up a very profitable factory manufacturing pieces of the True Cross or medals blessed by Saint Peter himself.

Or in Moscow, Eugeni would have personally told of little communes or sworn before audience after audience that while slavery was bad, freedmen working for wages was even worse, and in socialism he personally had discovered what all men yearned for.

She was made and trained for this match with her friend Eugeni, this journey. This knowledge was what had brought peace to her back in Rome.

"Olava!" Eugeni called from the arena floor. "Olava!" He wanted her to pay attention.

This was a perfect gladiator's arena, he said again. Did she notice how everything could be seen?

She did, she said, and it was so. She felt right on top of him, at the first row of seats ringing the arena floor that crunched with ashes left from the disaster that had preserved it.

She saw how the arena could be cut into four parts, and how one could dominate by controlling the center, how a match could take a long time, and how it could be short. She could see the quarters now, as Eugeni explained how he had the center and would not let the imaginary retiarius with net and tridens move out of the quarter, but would keep him in that wedge. It meant something now.

She understood now why a giant arena like the one at the Vatican was so bad for a single gladiator. Who could see the moves? Even the Flavian arena would not let you see how important each move was.

She wanted to yell out to him that she understood now, but there were so many Latin words for "understand," each with a precise different meaning, from acceptance to comprehension in one manner or another.

He stumbled, but it was a practiced stumble. He showed how letting an arm dangle made him look wounded and explained that if he rubbed blood on it, she would swear he was damaged in that arm. She saw how blood could be used.

She now fully understood how, while he wanted to keep all this out of his private home, he could still take pride in his skill.

And she knew now, too, why he would not surrender the knife. It was not to kill anyone. It was the one thing he knew, had trained to know since he was eight. That was why he slept with it.

He would not kill randomly in the society with it any more than she would start a fire with a great manuscript. To use his blade against a person because he didn't like him would be murder. Yes, he would save his life. He would save the lives of others. But would not desecrate his sword.

His lanista was the first man to give Eugeni love and care, as brutal as it was. In return, Eugeni had given him *the* Eugeni, both dead and alive.

Dead because his audience was dead. Alive because he was alive.

He told her she was now a vestal, although the vestals did not come to Pompeii, if he remembered correctly. He finally trampled over the retiarius and waited for her.

But she would not signal for death, that thrust of the hand into the chest calling for dispatch.

And in that tongue that was now so natural to her, she said:

"I want him to live."

"He lost. He dies."

"Not if he's valiant."

"He's wounded anyhow. It's kinder."

"No."

"Do it."

"I am the virgin, not you, Eugeni. Not you."

He started to explain how she was supposed to follow the will of the crowd.

"Look out," she screamed. And she had never seen anyone move so quickly. The knife snapped in a slash behind him, as his body turned simultaneously around it. He had turned around a blade! There he was explaining something, and then he was ready to fight instantly. How many practiced years had gone into that perfect move?

She dared not count.

But she smiled. She was now even for her fright.

His thrust, blade very straight, downward as though killing someone, was clear. It was like a very fast poke. The ideal stroke was the straightest. He probably didn't even remember when he had learned it.

And she realized from athletics in her own youth that this man had perfected delivering that simple stroke so that there was no grand preparation; rather the blade was just there where he wanted it in an instant. When he did do something grand, it was only deception for the crowds—the bigger the crowd, the bigger the deception. His real power was subtle beyond her amateur perception, she thought.

"Roman," Olava screamed, orating to the little empty stone arena in this beautiful language, "I want your liver, puny weakling. In my right hand, a whole tree ripped from a northern forest and seasoned rich in Roman blood. In my left, a shield seized from a legionnaire whose eyes I sucked like grapes. First you I devour, then these ugly little Romans now in the stands waiting like the slaves they really are."

And with that she swung an imaginary club above her head and lowered herself into the arena.

"Only your body is giant," yelled back Eugeni. "The spirit of Rome and the virtue of the sons and fathers and husbands of these good people of Pompeii shall give me the strength I need, though

I am wounded and small. For their virtue is now coursing through my body."

"They have no virtue. They are cowards. Black-haired cowards."

"I will show you their cowardice," he yelled back, the conversation loud for the imaginary audience.

And so they did mock battle, Olava claiming that she had scored several victories with her club, knowing of course that if there were a real club she would not have touched him. Eugeni would not play that he had been struck fatally.

"I cannot do that, Olava, just as you could not playfully signal for another's death."

She was panting heavily from the running, and Eugeni told her this was but a fraction of the tiredness she would feel if she were in a real arena, fear draining the body like a wound.

It was quiet, and from the arena floor they could see only the clouds and reddish evening sky above them without an intruding airplane in it.

They were in Pompeii on this fine spring evening, and the land was good, and the air and sky comforting, as it was in this part of the world at this time of the year—today as it was two thousand years before.

"I understand," he said.

"What do you understand?" she asked.

"That I have been here, really here. So long ago. Once so long ago, now here, and now here."

"Yes," said Olava, and the term he had used for "understand" was the one a person used to accept "what was."

She had completed her pact with Lewus and Semyonus. It was done.

They heard something in one of the stone tunnels coming into the arena from outside. A guard in a blue uniform, one of the many assigned by the tourist agency to this site, came to the edge of the retaining wall. He signaled they should follow.

They had to go, he said. The city was closing for the night, and everyone else had left.